MW00938790

The Tree of Everlasting Knowledge

Christine Nolfi

Copyright © 2012 by Christine Nolfi

All rights reserved. Created in paperback format in the United States of America. No part of this book may be used or reproduced in any manner whatsoever without written permission from the author except in the case of brief quotations embodied in articles and reviews. The scanning, uploading, and distribution of this book via the Internet or any other means without permission of the author is illegal and punishable by law.

This is a work of fiction. Names, characters, places and incidents either are the product of the author's imagination or are used fictitiously, and any resemblance to actual persons, living or dead, business establishments, events or locales is entirely coincidental. The publisher and author do not have any control and do not assume responsibility for author or third-party websites or their content.

Author website: www.christinenolfi.com

ISBN 978-1468199277

To Christian, Jameson, Marlie and Marguerite,
the children of my heart.

Chapter 1

Staring at the tables wouldn't put Rennie at one of them.

Nursing a cup of coffee, Troy Fagan wondered if she'd decided to decline the work. Bow out with embarrassment, or beg forgiveness—if Rennie didn't come to her senses, he'd fire her.

How didn't matter. He'd find a way.

Resigned to his decision, Troy returned his attention to the crowd of men converging on the lawn. The air sizzled with excitement as carpenters, masons and specialty trades greeted each other before taking their seats. For men accustomed to meager paychecks and unpredictable stints between jobs, Fagan wealth promised to make the pay generous even if the schedule was tight.

Troy didn't share the men's early morning cheer. Remodeling his parents' mansion filled him with anxiety. Thankfully they'd left early this morning, driving through the crisp April sunshine to the other end of the thousand-acre estate, to the factory, where Fagan's Orchard shipped produce and condiments across the Midwest. He prayed the demands of managing the company would keep them occupied as construction began on the mansion.

This would be the first time the stately rooms and antique furnishings were disturbed since his brother's murder fifteen years ago. He worried about sending his parents back into grief. As saws roared and plaster sifted down, would Jason's ghost whisper across the ruins?

One hundred men would contribute sweat and labor to build the mansion's new south wing. The thirteen-course foundation was already in place. The best Amish carpenters in the county had erected the exterior walls and laid five thousand square feet of base flooring. Now the real work would begin, as the other trades jostled for space inside the two-story structure.

Troy was always tense at the beginning of a new project. Today he was worse than usual—a typical construction schedule would increase to warp speed to beat the arrival of his younger sister's baby. Luckily, the very pregnant Dianne Fagan-Zagorski had left the site at daybreak. Given his own anxiety, he couldn't handle hers this morning.

Striding before the tables, he brought the chatter to a halt. He was about to launch into his speech when Rennie Perini skirted across the lawn and slipped into a chair in back.

Seeing a woman in the midst of the stubble-faced trades was jarring. What made the situation worse? Rennie looked beautiful today.

Troy grimaced. She always looked beautiful.

Her simple blue work shirt and faded jeans were a mockery. With her classic Italian beauty, she caused a stir on any job site. Troy's throat convulsed with sorrow and longing as she took a seat at the table in back, her whiskey-hued eyes dark with worry.

Returning to the day's business, he launched into an explanation of the construction timeline. Given the size of the mansion's new wing, there wasn't room for scheduling errors. As he emphasized the demand for strict compliance, several of the men shifted uneasily in their chairs.

Finishing, he added, "The schedule is set in stone. Forget about taking side jobs. From now until the finish date, I own you."

At the table in front the lead plumber said, "You don't own my crew. After the 'meet and greet' today, we won't return until next week. I'm taking my men to another job in town."

"Not a problem, Gar. However, once you start here you'll stay put."

"Understood."

Troy looked out over the sea of faces. "We're building the

new wing in record time and I expect the best from each of you. If you aren't confident your work will be of the highest caliber, leave now."

Crash, the Amish carpenter in charge of the main crew, tugged his salt and pepper beard. "My men are ready. What assurance can you give that the others won't hold us up?"

"Any man falling behind will be fired. I have a list of subs waiting to come on board. If you can't cut it, you're out."

"The woman won't get special treatment?" Crash swiveled around to glare at Rennie. "My crew can handle tight schedules. I have twenty men. How will she keep up with only one employee?"

The question provided the opportunity Troy needed. Getting rid of Rennie might be easier than he'd imagined. While the trades enjoyed lusting after her on sites across Liberty, this time was different. They were being paid top dollar to complete the new wing quickly. They didn't want a woman standing in the way.

Troy drilled her with a hard stare. "Crash has an understandable concern. Perini Electric never handles jobs this large. How will you manage?"

Rennie's eyes rounded with fear but only for a moment. "I've gone over the details with my assistant," she said. "We'll keep pace with the carpenters."

"With only one employee, is that realistic?" Troy asked.

"We'll work overtime if needed." She came to her feet. "We can handle the schedule."

"Naturally my sister likes the idea of awarding the electrical contract to a company run by a woman. But this is a big job. You're out of your depth."

Every man in attendance zeroed in on the woman standing in their midst. Several murmured in agreement. Despite Troy's desire to be rid of her, he felt pity. And respect—damn if Rennie wasn't holding her ground.

To sweeten the deal, he added, "The retainer isn't a problem. Keep it."

"I want the job." She layered steel on her voice. "Your sister hired me. We're building her new home. Doesn't she have the final say?"

He set his jaw.

Evidently she sensed triumph in his silence. "Then it's settled." She sat. "I'm staying."

Frustrated, he turned back to the others. She'd won—for now. "I want to meet with each trade this afternoon," he said, getting back on track. "Have your timeline ready. I'll need to coordinate schedules. Spend the morning getting acquainted with each other."

Crash sent Rennie a chilly look before regarding Troy. "Where should we have supplies delivered?" he asked.

"Unload them on the south side of the mansion by noon today. My parents and sister will continue living here as we proceed. Keep the front entrance free of materials so we don't disrupt them more than necessary." Troy rocked back on his heels. "That's it for now."

The men dispersed. He was about to do the same when Rennie cornered him.

"Where do you get off telling me to leave?" She appeared ready to take a swing at him. "Your sister accepted my bid."

Her anger came as a surprise. A world of hurt brimmed in her almond-shaped eyes, the kind of pain that brought most women to tears. Yet she'd managed to bring on the fire instead. Did she really want to stay? Her company must be strapped for cash if she'd risk working for him.

"Why did you take so long in supplying the bid?" he countered, and her eyes again rounded. She looked vulnerable and irrepressibly feminine despite the tool belt slung low on her hips. "My sister contacted Perini Electric six weeks ago. You waited until the last minute to provide a quote."

"I was rechecking my bid. For accuracy."

"You weren't stalling? Afraid you were getting in over your head?"

"No!"

Her cheeks flamed and he knew she was lying. "I spoke to three of your competitors and got bids within days. The way you held off has me wondering if you were thinking about turning us down."

She rubbed her lips together. From the looks of it, she was having trouble reining in her notable temper. The sharp ring of her smartphone spared her from replying. She yanked it from her pocket and swiveled away.

Troy simmered while she whispered tightly into the phone. Keeping the GC waiting sure as hell wasn't a way to earn Brownie Points. Tapping his foot, he felt his own anger rising.

She snapped the cell shut. "Sorry." The flush spread engagingly across her face. "I have a problem."

"What, exactly?"

She greeted the question with a wavering smile. "Where am I on your afternoon schedule? I have to run a few errands."

The threads of his temper frayed. "Weren't you listening? No one leaves. Have your supplies delivered. Do so this morning."

"It's not about the supplies. They're here."

She pursed her lips and the memory of kissing her struck him like a blow. Rennie, arching into the heat of his ardor with the same bold disregard she displayed today. He wasn't prepared for the raw bolt of pleasure catapulting through his veins.

He fled from the memory as she added, "I won't be gone long. I'll meet with Crash before I leave in case he has any questions."

"What about my sister? Dianne plans to meet with each trade this morning."

"And I'm looking forward to meeting her. I'll return before she arrives."

"You aren't going anywhere." Troy nodded at the men merging into small groups on the lawn. "Get up to speed with the carpenters and the guys on heating and cooling."

"It won't take long—"

"You're staying put." He pointed to the men. "Get to know them. As it is, you've already made a few enemies."

Her eyes blazed. The air gelled between them for ten seconds. Then she stalked away.

The bruises were an angry purple beneath the girl's toffee colored skin. They marked a passage from her jawbone to her cheek, a distressing series of welts inflicted with brutal force. Sorrow for the child welled in Rennie's chest.

Pushing the emotion down, Rennie glanced at her watch.

There wasn't time to feel pity for yet another helpless child dumped into the mire of Jobs & Family Services. There were always children, dozens of them, forced into the system by neglect and abuse. Usually she cared about them deeply. Today would've been the same if her blood pressure weren't approaching dangerous limits after she'd disobeyed Troy's command and quietly left the Fagan job site for an hour.

Shuffling down the corridor toward the approaching child, she wondered at her reckless behavior. She was out of her mind. If Troy discovered her missing, the new job would be over before it began.

With a mix of resignation and worry, she let her gaze drift back to the girl. The child skipped forward with fierce concentration, her expression at odds with her carefree movements. The folds of her dress billowed out like a sail. A Barbie doll dangled in her grip. Rennie stepped aside to allow her to pass. Reaching the juncture where the corridors met in a T, the girl paused.

The ceiling's fluorescent lights gave off a nearly imperceptible hum. Footsteps echoed further off. The girl turned toward the sound.

Rennie paused, unsure of what to do. Where was the kid's social worker? "Sweetie, are you lost?"

Out of habit she dug into the pocket of her jacket and rooted around for her antacids. She'd just popped one into her mouth when a woman's voice, soft as rain, called out. The child dashed away.

It took a moment for Rennie to regain her composure. The fleeting exchange was unsettling, an added stress she didn't need this morning.

Grimly, she continued down the corridor. Irritation dogged every step. Not only was she putting the Fagan job at risk. She was doing so because, once again, she couldn't find the courage to stand up to her mother.

In bustling Liberty, Ohio, Lianna Perini was something of a titan. She managed Jobs & Family Services for all of Jeffordsville County, championing children's causes before state judges and local media. In a state with more than its share of poverty and drug abuse, the caseload never diminished. In fact, the sheer number of children rescued by the agency increased with depressing predictability.

Which was probably why she'd demanded to see Rennie.

Pausing at the door to her mother's office, Rennie balled her fists. "No. Can't," she practiced under her breath. "Sorry, big job, maybe some other time."

Inside, her mother bobbed between the file cabinet and the paperwork on her desk.

"Pick one," Rennie said by way of greeting. "If I were you, I'd start with the crap on your desk."

Lianna slammed the cabinet drawer shut. "I'm running a marathon. It seems everyone else has crossed the finish line."

"You have a staff. Delegate more."

"My staff puts in the same hours I do." Sitting, her mother unearthed a manila folder. "Ah. The Korchek case," she added, and the heart-shaped curve of her face relaxed. Time left her features like a private beach washed away by the tide.

The transformation never failed to surprise. In repose, her mother's stern expression gave way to beauty. No wonder children in her care were drawn to her. Kids living in the tumult of abuse and neglect were skittish creatures. They rarely trusted adults, even those sent to rescue them. Yet most trusted the elegant woman who ran the social agency.

Surely Lianna had such a child fixed in her mind's eye now.

No, not a child. Rennie was better with teenagers. Would her mother ask her to provide a foster home for a kid in junior high? It was probably a juvie case. Or a teenager whose delinquency made his parents seek foster care as a last resort.

The particulars didn't matter. Rennie's thoughts veered to the Fagan job and the demands of wiring the new wing of the mansion. There wasn't room for anything else in her life.

Her stomach coiled into a painful knot when her mother said, "I'm sure you understand why I wanted to see you."

"Actually I'm hoping I don't."

"The Korchek case just came in. Wife deceased, husband clearly grieving—and abusive. I need a short-term foster home while I sort this out."

Rennie studied her work boots. "The Fagan job started this morning. I shouldn't have left the site."

11

"Well, you're here and I'm glad."

"Mother, I shouldn't have come. I could lose the job." Her comment met with silence. She resisted the urge to glance at her watch. "I can't help now. Ask some other time."

"Don't you think I checked everywhere before calling you? No other foster homes are available."

"Keep trying."

"There isn't a rock I haven't looked under. If your father's health were better, we'd take this on." Lianna released a labored sigh. "You're it, Rennie. At least until Mr. Korchek completes anger management therapy."

"Mother, *no.*"

Disappointment cascaded through her mother's expression, stirring the guilt that had always held Rennie hostage. She'd never measured up—in her mother's eyes or her own. The realization beat against the insulation she'd spent years packing around her heart.

When the silence grew daunting, she said, "You shouldn't have asked me to get the foster-adopt certification." She stopped, despising the contrition in her voice. It shouldn't matter if she let her mother down, but it did. "I'm not parent material."

The small confession eased the burden on her heart. She was surprised by the unexpected void of emotion the words left behind. Disconnecting from the guilt left her momentarily grounded and safe from mishap.

"Nick and Anna have helped in the past."

"Anthony hasn't." Or, she mused, her younger sister Frannie.

"He will, after he and Mary settle into marriage." Disapproval filtered through Lianna's stern gaze. "You aren't suggesting he should've volunteered in the past, are you? When Blossom was ill?"

She wasn't, and she said, "Try to understand. The Fagan job is crucial." It was still hard to believe Dianne Fagan had accepted a bid that arrived weeks behind the competition. If the final decision had been Troy's, he would've picked anyone else. "If I do a good job, Dianne will invite me to bid on the electrical subcontract for the new processing plant."

She neglected to add that Perini Electric was bleeding greenbacks. Rent, the cost of supplies, hiring Squeak Grantham, her lumbering if sweet employee—the expenses added up. Somehow she'd found the courage to take on the residential job for the mansion's new wing even though she'd never planned to visit the estate again. After Jason Fagan's death, she was glad to stay away.

"Fagan's Orchard is building a new plant?" Lianna asked.

"Next year. They'll double the size of the processing facilities." If she persuaded her mother the work was important Lianna might badger someone else into providing emergency foster care. A neighbor or a friend—anyone else. "Residential work's all right. A commercial job will turn Perini Electric into a real company."

"If you hire a whole crew you'll spend most of your time managing the books. You enjoy the work."

Rennie silently agreed. She loved working with her hands, loved electricity. The heat and the spark—and the danger. She also craved the isolation her job provided, the long hours working alone. The bullet that took Jason from the world had taken something from her, too. In all the intervening years, she'd never repaired what was broken inside her.

Pulling from the depressing reverie, she said, "I agreed to the foster-adopt classes because I knew you'd expect me to help in the future. But not now. Troy is a tough contractor. His parents' mansion was built in 1842. I have no idea what I'll find in those walls, how I'll tie it all together."

Lianna flipped open the folder in her grasp. "Walt and Emma will go directly from school to afternoon programs."

Two kids? Providing emergency care for one unruly teenager was hellish enough.

"I can't handle two teenagers." She gripped the chair's armrests. "One, maybe. For a week. All right—two weeks."

"They aren't teenagers. Walt is eight years old. Emma is seven."

My God. How could she refuse to help children? They couldn't bunk at a juvenile correction facility until a foster home was located. They should be placed with a couple. She was an unmarried electrician with the most important job of her career looming.

"No one would describe me as remotely maternal." Voicing

the truth hurt. She'd lost so much after they'd buried Jason. Her confidence, surely, and her belief in anything but the grind of work. "The next time you need short-term care for a teenager I'll do my bit. Just don't ask me to provide shelter and three square meals for a couple of kids. I wouldn't know where to start."

"I'll help you."

"I'll fail."

Her mother rocked in her chair with an irritating sheen of patience fanning across her features. "For the record, you have maternal instincts even if you hide them behind a tool belt and jeans."

Rennie pushed to her feet before the words caused further damage to her heart. "I have to go."

"Why don't you meet Walt and Emma before you decide?"

She started for the door. "I'll see you later."

"Wait! They're here. Jenalyn brought them to meet you."

She swung into the corridor. "I *had* an appointment with Troy and Dianne. I've probably missed it."

She marched down the corridor with the guilt sending a wave of acid through her stomach. No problem—she kept a jumbo bottle of antacids in the truck.

A secretary approached with a sheaf of papers hugged to her breasts. Rennie skirted around her. If she didn't hurry, Troy would read her the riot act the moment she arrived. Or worse, fire her.

He wasn't the type to forgive a subcontractor who cut out on him, and certainly not after he'd demanded she stay on site. The guilt needling her gave way to the anxiety that jolted her whenever he invaded her thoughts. But she'd learned: they were both good at dropping a backhoe's worth of work on top of their emotionally charged past.

This time would prove harder. Seeing Troy on his home turf would make the past impossible to avoid. Jason's ghost would haunt their conversations.

Somehow she managed to bury her thoughts as she quickened her stride. At the reception desk the neglected phone blinked with calls. She'd escaped into the waiting room when a voice brought her to a standstill.

"There you are! I thought we were meeting in your mother's

office."

With misgiving she spotted Jenalyn Hampton in the corridor. Yet the lovely Filipino social worker didn't hold her attention. Rennie locked gazes with the girl she'd seen earlier. A step behind, a boy with similar honeyed features gave an appraising look as bitter as winter frost.

Her heart lurched. The children were a stunning blend of black and white with large, expressive eyes as green as emeralds. Glossy curls danced around their faces in a wild chorus of lengths.

"I'd like you to meet Walt and Emma," Jenalyn was saying.

Rennie couldn't hear past the buzzing in her ears. These were the children her mother expected her to foster? Walt was skin and bones and he dwarfed his sister. At best, Emma Korchek weighed fifty pounds. The little wisp of a girl met Rennie's eyes with a stare void of emotion. That too was no surprise—abuse had the potential to cause the death of a soul. A child left in such an environment too long became something less than human. Sociopaths weren't born into the world; they were beaten into existence.

She abruptly withdrew from her thoughts when Emma said, "Why do you wear boy clothes?"

Rennie blinked. "I don't wear boy clothes. These are *work* clothes."

Jenalyn patted the curious girl's head. "Miss Perini is an electrician," she said.

The explanation glanced off Emma. "Boy clothes are ugly on a girl." She took an abrupt step forward. "Do you like being ugly?"

"Of course not. I'm just not into frilly chick stuff—" Rennie clamped her mouth shut. The dress Emma Korchek wore was a ruffled mess, circa 1995. No doubt Jenalyn had bought the old frock at the local Goodwill. "Some girls like feminine things but others don't."

"You aren't a girl." Emma held Rennie's gaze hostage. "Girls are small. You're big. How come you aon't know that?"

"I do, I just—"

Walt came forward. The gash on his cheek gleamed in the corridor's fluorescent glow. "You don't smell good, either." He regarded Jenalyn. "Get someone who smells nice."

Emma bounced her thumb toward the social worker. "*She smells nice.*"

Jenalyn blushed. "It's *White Shoulders,*" she confided. "Not a trendy perfume but I adore it."

"It's nice," Rennie said from behind a manufactured smile. The perfume wafting past was sweet enough to glaze the entire town of Liberty.

"Worms smell bad," Walt put in reasonably. "Especially after it rains. That's when I squish 'em."

Wincing, Rennie suspected delinquency lurked behind his angelic face. "It's disgusting to squish worms." She imagined the boy trooping through her house with the slimy corpses on his shoes.

He smiled, revealing a chipped front tooth. "That's why I like stompin' on 'em."

"Have any other hobbies? Anything that won't land you on the wrong side of the law?"

He gave the query shallow consideration. "I throw rocks at squirrels. Chipmunks, too. The squirrels are easier to hit."

Great. Just great. She recalled the case studies she'd read during the coursework for foster-adopt certification. By the time they reached Walt's age, many of the children shuttled through foster care began acting out. Causing harm to animals often led to more serious misbehavior. If someone didn't teach the boy healthier activities, in a few years he'd move on to breaking and entering. She wasn't the right candidate to keep him toeing the straight and narrow but she *did* possess talents to encourage him toward more constructive forms of play.

"I'm good at baseball," she told him. "I can show you how to play."

Emma snorted. "You *are* a boy."

"No, I'm sporty."

"Boys play baseball. Girls don't."

"Sexism lives," she replied irritably. "Lots of women play sports. They also wear work shirts and boots. There's nothing wrong with it."

Jenalyn nodded in agreement. "Of course there isn't." She drew Walt forward. "Why don't you tell Miss Perini about yourself?"

The boy crossed his arms, mimicking Rennie's stance. "You first."

She peered at her watch then rattled off a quick personal history. The growing unrest on the children's faces merely added to her discomfort. At this rate, she'd never leave. Troy would be livid when she *did* arrive. Forcing a patient smile, she wondered if she should follow up with her Social Security number and her savings account balance. This was worse than taking out a bank loan.

When she finished, Walt said, "Just so you know, Pa wants us back. You can't keep us."

Rennie drew in a steadying breath. She couldn't help but feel sympathy. Walt and Emma were so young. Clearly they'd been through too much. Was it surprising if they weren't delighted to meet her? They'd settle down. Or they wouldn't. Either way, she only needed to provide safe harbor for a short time.

Still, it seemed prudent to take a firm stance. From what she'd learned in the foster-adopt classes, coddling rarely worked. Traumatized children responded more appropriately to firm, consistent parenting.

"I have some rules," she said. "You'll have to follow them."

"I don't eat liver," Walt replied before she got on a roll. "I don't care how many onions you put on top—I won't eat it."

"I don't make liver. In fact, I rarely cook."

"So you'll starve us?"

"I can make the basics. Hamburgers. Spaghetti. Stuff like that."

Emma nudged past her brother. "I have rules, too. No washing floors. It hurts my knees."

The announcement lifted Rennie's brows. Some idiot had made the kid wash floors? "I don't make kids clean my house," she explained, crouching before them like she'd seen her mother do with children unlucky enough to be dumped into a foster care system as unpredictable as the world they'd arrived from. "My house is nice. It's on South Street near Liberty Square."

Emma's eyes grew wide. "Do I get a bed?"

"Don't you usually sleep in a bed?"

Jenalyn caught her attention. "Uh, Rennie—"

Emma cut in to ask, "Can we *always* sleep in the house?"

A sense of foreboding guided Rennie to her feet. Clearly the social worker preferred to discuss the case privately but she needed to hear this firsthand.

Running her fingers through her hair, Rennie softened her tone. "Where else would you sleep?" she asked Emma.

The child's bravado slipped. A tremble went across her shoulders as she lowered her head. Rennie's breath caught. Was Emma too frightened to discuss the matter?

She stepped back, distraught by the possibilities. "At my house you'll always sleep in your bedroom," she said, and her heart overturned. "That's the rule. Kids always sleep in a bed."

"There's no barn?" Walt asked.

She was assaulted by a sudden wave of anger. Northeast Ohio was experiencing a particularly chilly April. Buck Korchek had forced his children to sleep in a barn? A miracle they hadn't caught pneumonia.

She placed her hand on his shoulder. "I have three bedrooms. You'll each have your own room. Okay?"

The children merely shrugged.

At the end of the corridor her mother approached with an annoying spark of pleasure brightening her gaze. Rennie looked from Lianna back to the kids, sizing them up like she'd done with her truck before driving it home from the dealership.

Why consider this? She didn't have the skills to parent one child, let alone two. They deserved better. And they'd already made her late for her meeting at the mansion.

The future of Perini Electric hinged on her ability to make a good impression on Dianne Fagan while steering clear of Troy. Walt and Emma Korchek didn't factor into the equation. They'd be a hindrance during the most important stage of her career.

All of which swirled through her head as her mother neared. When Lianna came to a halt, Rennie said, "I'll take them."

Chapter 2

"I should've picked the electrical contractor," Troy said as the *rhtt rhtt* of a pneumatic nail gun knifed the air. "Rennie has gone AWOL."

Two-by-fours spiked the air with the scent of wood. Twenty paces off, Crash and the framing crew stood deep in conversation. The mason was gone. So was the plumber, after leaving catalogs of kitchen fixtures and brochures on hot tub designs. All of which delighted the abundantly pregnant Dianne Fagan-Zagorski.

At twenty-four, Diane was always upbeat. Today her ebullient mood was a sheer annoyance for Troy, who'd given up on checking for the return of the Perini Electric truck. Never in memory had a subcontractor on one of his jobs ignored a command to stay put.

Beside him, Dianne stroked her blossoming belly and swung her briefcase in a careless arc. From the pocket of her blazer her smartphone emitted a barely detectable hum—no doubt their father was calling from the factory on the other side of the estate to inquire when she'd return. Not that Dennis Fagan wouldn't prefer for his daughter to take a sabbatical until after the birth of his first grandchild. Predictably, Dianne had refused. Six months pregnant and sporting puffy circles beneath her eyes, she appeared giddy with pleasure amidst the construction mayhem.

She set her briefcase down in the sawdust covering the sub flooring. "Troy, relax. So Rennie left for an hour. Not the end of the world."

"I gave her a direct order."

"You're always giving orders, but she's a woman." Dianne nodded toward the carpenters. "She won't obey like the men."

"Why are you defending her?"

"Because she *is* a woman." Dianne smiled impishly. "They induct us into a secret society when we reach maturity. That's why we stick together. Didn't you know?"

Troy glowered at the mischief sparking in her green eyes. Of course, Dianne was unaware of his history with Rennie. Nor did she recall Rennie chumming around the mansion with their late brother. The painful events that had propelled Troy into adulthood couldn't mean anything to his younger sister—she'd been in elementary school when Jason died. Sorrow leaked into his thoughts, and regret. He rose above them.

"Dianne, I'm firing her." He let the pronouncement sink in before adding, "She isn't right for the job. I need a firm with a big crew to keep pace with the other trades."

"You'll do nothing of the sort. Troy, *please.*" She regarded the men hauling lumber and setting in windows. "I can't talk to the men. What do they know about decorating or paint chips?"

"Rennie is just like them. She's no decorator, if that's what you're looking for."

"We'll become great friends. I'm sure of it." She gave him a playful nudge. "So it's settled. Rennie stays."

He raked his hand across his scalp. "Don't you have a meeting at the factory?"

"It'll wait. Now, wipe that scowl off your face." She rose on tiptoes to pat his cheek with unflappable cheer, a petite redhead with the luck of the Irish and the good sense to know it.

Fagan's Orchard shipped produce and condiments throughout the U.S. The company had made them all millionaires, Troy included, even though he'd left the family business years ago to pursue a love of construction. Unlike him, Dianne wore her wealth easily while remaining earthy and warm. The diminutive marketing genius gladly sorted Granny Smiths and Macintoshes on the plant's assembly line, smiling whenever one of the workers told a bawdy joke. She wrapped holiday presents for everyone on staff and never missed a birthday.

Troy's parents were the same. They never allowed wealth to build walls around their lives. They remained on a first-name basis with everyone in their employ, from the pickers in the orchards to the executives working beside them on the factory's second floor. Like a couple of cheery elves, their physical size was of inverse proportion to their generous hearts.

Compared to his family, Troy was a giant. During childhood his parents had joked that he'd inherited his height from Scandinavia in a distant past when a Viking ship strayed onto Gaelic shores. Jason, when he'd been alive, enjoyed bragging that his brooding, older brother was Black Irish—and tall enough to prune the apple trees without a ladder. It wasn't true, of course, and before his death Jason reached five foot six, an acceptable height for a man. Troy didn't stop growing until he towered at six foot two. In a family of petite redheads, his physical contrast was another seed of discontent in his increasingly barren soul.

Drawing him from his thoughts, Dianne said, "There she is." Outside in the curving driveway, Rennie dashed across the estate's sloping lawn. "You see? She's just a few minutes late."

"I don't need a delay." Troy hooked his fingers through the soft leather of his tool belt. "I'm building your new home at record speed. I can't allow anyone to hold up progress."

"I've heard Rennie is a dream to work with. She never tracks mud or breaks anything. She'll hang my lighting fixtures the same week the carpeting is installed—and the carpet's white. Well, oyster." Dianne patted his forearm, her hand a pale butterfly on the span of muscle. "It's a relief to have a woman here, especially someone with her experience."

Despite his reservations, Troy couldn't fault the assessment. The average electrician left debris in his wake. Once he'd foolishly hired a novice for the electrical on upscale Robin's Gate Drive. The rookie dropped a socket wrench on the master bath's marble steps, chipping them badly. Then he broke the Jacuzzi's sprayer head when he lost his footing.

Troy nearly lost the contract.

He dismissed the thought as Rennie approached with her long, curly hair bobbing in a ponytail. Beneath his anger, desire stirred. It was galling how her beauty affected him. Or perhaps the allure came from the way she ignored the physical attributes she possessed in abundance.

He didn't believe in soul mates but he did believe in fate. Something had always drawn them into a combustible mix. When she'd been little more than a child and he an adolescent, they'd forged a relationship based on hatred. By the time he completed his senior year of high school and she entered ninth grade, Troy worried there was more to it. By then she was gifted with beauty and a body built for sex. Half of the young men in Liberty had pursued her. Not that Rennie had noticed. Mouthy, with tunnel vision, she'd trod her own path.

She captured his sister's attention, two young women predisposed to hit it off. Dianne offered her hand in greeting.

Clasping it, Rennie made a quick introduction then said, "You've probably received lots of catalogs from the other trades. I work differently. Whenever you're ready, I'll go with you to choose the lighting. It helps to get a second opinion right in the showroom."

"I'd like lighting similar to my parents' side of the mansion," Dianne said.

"You wouldn't want a jarring change."

"I'm not sure how to accomplish it. The mansion's fixtures were installed during the Roaring Twenties."

Rennie trailed her thumb beneath the heart-shaped curve of her chin. "A company outside New York City does wonderful reproductions," she said.

Troy crossed his arms, waiting. Even as she enthralled his sister, her gaze strayed to his. Tired of the unspoken questions— he was livid and she knew it—he finally growled, "Where have you been?"

She shrugged. "I had an emergency."

"We've been waiting."

"It won't happen again."

"Get your priorities straight or work somewhere else. Got it?"

The heat in his voice drew a gasp from Dianne.

Rennie looked like she'd been slapped. In a flash, she dusted off her pride.

He sensed danger when she asked, "How's the tooth?"

He flinched at the audacity of the question. Then he

remembered. Rennie didn't have the sense to walk away from a battle. She never had.

He swiped his tongue across the false tooth, caught himself, and stopped. "It's fine."

The irritation in his voice increased the mirth on her face. Which wasn't the worst of it. Dianne caught on fast. He sent a few silent curses heavenward when her expression altered from curiosity to delight.

"Oh, I don't believe this." She thwacked him on the chest. "Is Rennie the girl you hated in school? It's been so many years . . . it's her, right? The picture. The darts."

He grappled for control. "Drop it."

She chortled and he glimpsed doom. "She's the pitcher who threw the curveball when you were watching the younger kids play. I'm right, aren't I?" When he set his jaw, she laughed. "Big brother, you've made my day."

"Let's move on." He refused to reminisce about the fastball Rennie nailed him with when she'd been in elementary school. Stiffly, he tapped his meddling sister on the shoulder. "Have any other questions? I need to check on the other crews."

Dianne wasn't listening. She remained focused on Rennie, whose Mediterranean features went obligingly pink in a way that made her breathtaking. The mellow gold of her skin deepened, accenting the rich brown of her eyes and bringing her rosy lips into high relief. She'd done a hasty job of putting up her hair and a long curl hung loose against the curve of her cheek. She swiped at it, brushing away the barest hint of moisture from her brow. Troy forced his attention away.

To Rennie, Dianne said, "Even if you did knock out my brother's tooth, I can't imagine why the dolt threw darts at your yearbook picture. You're stunning."

The unexpected compliment darted pleasure across Rennie's mouth. "Thank you."

Troy seared his sister with a look. "That's enough strolling down memory lane."

"We've just started!"

He grabbed her by the arm. "Time for work."

"Okay—I'm going." She elbowed him in the ribs before beaming at Rennie. "It's been a pleasure. I have to hurry now to the factory."

"It was nice to finally meet you," Rennie said.

Dianne waggled her fingers in Troy's face before dashing off, her heels pecking on the sub flooring. No doubt she'd regale everyone at the factory with the story of the girl whose curveball knocked out Troy's tooth.

Rennie wavered. "I shouldn't have brought it up. It was unprofessional."

He studied her features for an under note to the apology. Mockery, something. Concluding she was sincere, he said, "Your assistant left a dog tied up outside." Why, was beyond imagining. The mutt looked like a burn victim with its missing ear and scar tissue running down its snout. "Mind explaining why Squeak thinks this is a kennel?"

She swallowed. "He brought Princess with him?"

"Princess?" It was the ugliest dog in North America. Troy was about to tell her to get the mongrel off the site when she began wringing her hands. Her sudden vulnerability made him back off. "Just keep the dog outside. All right?"

"Sure," she said, clearly relieved. "I'll tell Squeak."

She walked away, and he meant to get back to work. Instead he watched her move past the carpenters and hurry up the stairwell. He didn't relish having her on the site even if she *was* the best electrician in the county. He didn't relish having her stir up emotions he'd spent years suppressing, the sad and the sweet.

Day by day, her presence would prove an excruciating reminder of his late brother. If Jason hadn't been murdered, if he hadn't been on Cleveland's mean streets at precisely the wrong moment, his relationship with Rennie might have evolved into something deeper.

And Troy? He knew he bore responsibility for every misstep he'd ever made with her. He'd bullied her until he'd left for college. It would've been far more courageous to admit that, like Jason, he'd harbored complex emotions for the wild-hearted girl.

His emotions were a tangle, still.

After Jason's murder, Troy had roamed the orchard with his ungovernable remorse. Absolution had never arrived but he'd found a way to go on.

If he walked the orchard now, his self-loathing left a fading taste, like ash, in his mouth as the moon's cold light led him ever higher, to the Great Oak. He'd spend long minutes seated beneath the tree wondering if he'd forged an uneasy truce with his guilt.

Now, lost in his musings, he visualized the Great Oak that spanned the summit above the orchard's rolling acres. Reputed to be the oldest tree in Ohio, it was a sentry of immeasurable power. To this day, couples visited the summit above the tumultuous waters of the Chagrin River and stood in the tree's encircling shade. They came onto Fagan property uninvited because they understood the tree's magic. Beneath the sheltering leaves they voiced their love and let the far-flung branches cradle them in enchantment and dreams.

Yet an agony grew along the tree's roots. Nourished by a thousand tears, it was Troy's alone. Though the Great Oak was a shelter for love, he'd used it for hate when he'd been too young to understand its power.

He'd transmuted good into evil when he'd made love to Rennie beneath the oak's wide-swept arms, not because he'd loved her but because she'd belonged to Jason.

Chapter 3

A cacophony of electric saws and pneumatic nail guns punctuated the air. More than a dozen men, setting in stud walls and framing in bedrooms, filled the expanse like diligent bees.

A construction job of this magnitude usually took nearly a year to complete. Fagan wealth promised to accelerate the timeline. She was determined to keep pace on a job slated to finish by summer.

Standing in the center of the commotion, Rennie allowed a sense of wonder eat through her irritation at her assistant, who'd been crazy enough to bring a dog to work. The construction plans called for five bedrooms on the second floor. Dianne's private study was also upstairs. Located a few steps from the master bedroom, it would require enough electricity to run computers, printers, a photocopy machine—Rennie planned to load the room with as much power as possible.

Dianne was the key to more work for Perini Electric. If she put in a good word, the elder Fagans would invite Rennie to bid on the orchard's new processing plant, slated for construction next year. A stellar job on the mansion's new wing guaranteed the lucrative industrial contract would follow.

"Rennie!" Despite his girth, Squeak Grantham easily dodged two carpenters struggling with a sheet of plywood. "Where've you been? I've been looking everywhere for you."

She was assaulted by the distressing image of Walt and Emma Korchek grilling her on her vital statistics. Next came the memory of the dartboard that had hung in Troy's bedroom during his youth. Why had she brought up his tooth? Poking fun as if they were still embroiled in an adolescent battle was foolhardy.

"I was delayed," she said.

Her young assistant's head bobbed like a buoy on the ocean. "Is everything okay?"

"Listen, if I'm ever delayed for more than an hour, I'll call. I won't leave you wandering around a job site without direction." She steered him to the wall for privacy. "Why did you bring your dog without my go-ahead?"

His doughy face went through several contortions, all of which were shadings of hurt. "There are so many trades here. No one will notice Princess tagging along."

"Hard to miss a dog on a construction site."

"Are the Fagans mad?"

In truth, the Fagans were a family of Lilliputians enamored with all things canine. Except Troy—he certainly wasn't petite, and Rennie had no idea whether he liked dogs or not. When she'd been in high school and Jason Fagan's close friend, he'd been devoted to his Great Dane, Duke. The beast slept on his bed as if they were an old married couple. Three Cocker Spaniels followed the elder Fagans around the mansion as if tied by heartstrings to their heels. Even Dianne, a child enrolled in so many activities Rennie barely glimpsed her, had owned a white Cockapoo. Animal lovers like the Fagans wouldn't care if Princess stayed.

"Troy isn't happy but he let it pass," she said. Squeak muttered an apology and she waved him into silence. "Did you fill a bowl with water when you tied her up outside?"

"Of course I did. I gave her a cheeseburger, too. We stopped at Buddy Burger."

"Start packing dog food. Fast food isn't healthy."

"So it's okay if I bring Princess?" When she glared, he hastily added, "Don't worry, boss. I'll pack dog chow tomorrow."

She regarded him with faint impatience. Even though she was tall, she only came up midway on Squeak's chest. He was huge, forgetful—people often mistook him for an oversized idiot—but when it came to electrical work, the kid knew his stuff.

Which probably explained why she harbored a soft spot for

28

Squeak. He was like a bumbling yet brilliant kid brother. Which also explained why she felt compelled to say, "I'll call tomorrow morning to remind you to bag some kibble for the pooch. I can't stand to watch you poison her with fatty garbage."

"She likes burgers and fries. They make her smile."

"Dogs don't smile. Take better care of her."

"Geez, you're touchy this morning."

Again she pictured Walt and Emma, and nearly groaned. Explaining that she'd been hauled onto the mommy track wasn't a conversation she'd comfortably have with Squeak.

She strolled across the room sizing up the electrical needs. "Princess has had enough bad luck for one lifetime, you know."

Squeak followed. "I didn't think you liked my dog." He paused before a cutout that would become a doorway to one of the bedrooms. "I'm glad you do."

"Princess. What a ridiculous name." She opted to ignore his comment about liking the dog since she adored the mutt. "Who names an ugly dog Princess? It's silly."

"I think she's pretty." He ran his fingers across the studs where they'd run the electrical.

They looked around for a moment then she started for the stairwell. "We should check out the fuse boxes and see what shape they're in. Troy said they're in the basement near the wine cellar."

Squeak lumbered down the steps behind her. "Wow. I've never been inside a wine cellar."

"And you won't be in one today." Squinting, she stepped out into the April sunshine. She could only imagine Troy's reaction if he found her assistant checking out the Merlots and the Chardonnays in his parents' wine cellar. "After we take a look, we'll head back here."

The fuse boxes were surprisingly easy to find in a basement large enough to hold a bowling alley. Sure enough, they were located in a utility room past the wine cellar. Speckled with rust, they looked decades old. She decided to suggest to Troy that she replace them all. She'd also install a fifth box to supply power to the mansion's new wing.

"The electrical plans are in my truck. So is my toolbox." She'd been so worried about arriving late that she'd simply parked and leapt out. "I have to get them."

Squeak angled his head to study the cables spiraling across the ceiling. "The heating and cooling guys just got here. They parked behind you. There's stuff all over the lawn."

She followed him out. "I hate it when the other trades leave crap everywhere." Reaching the top of the stairwell and the mansion's first floor, she added, "You run the gauntlet. I'll check on Princess."

"You've got it, boss."

After he left she wandered into the foyer. Overhead the chandelier dripped crystal tears in an arresting, pyramidal design. In the dining room to her left, a maid placed an arrangement of lilies on the impossibly long table. She wore a grey dress and a white apron like a domestic in an old movie. The mansion, too, was from a more genteel era with its well-appointed rooms and Aubusson carpets. Regret sifted through her. She'd loved coming here during high school. When Jason was alive.

Something of his murder still clung to the air, a palpable sadness layered over the elegant furnishings like an invisible coating of dust.

Steadying herself, she entered the gleaming kitchen with its black granite countertops and subdued mint green cabinetry. Beyond the bank of windows a maple tree danced. A thousand leaves rustled in a waterfall of sound. At the sink, a maid polished a candelabrum. Careful not to disturb her, Rennie tiptoed out to the patio in search of Squeak's dog.

Where was Princess? Twenty paces away a groundsman pruned a hedge of boxwood that formed a wall of deep emerald. The rose beds were beginning to bud and a stand of rhododendron trimmed the blue sky with splashes of lavender. The grass undulated in a green band, with grey shadows forming a demarcation line into the forest. Nestled in such privacy, it was difficult to imagine the countless workers tending the acres of fruit trees on the other side of the estate. The forest shielded the grand house from the commotion of the commercial enterprise that was Fagan's Orchard.

No dog in sight. Saws buzzed and hammers cracked the air. She paused beside a bed of blood red azaleas with an odd sense of unease seeping into her bones.

It's Jason. During all the years since his murder she'd never returned until now. Doing so brought the images rushing back: Jason regaling her with his plans for Fagan's Orchard once he finished college. Jason admitting to a crush on a cheerleader, a girl Rennie thought of as dimwitted even though he was crazy about her. Gillie—Gillie with the laugh of a hyena. Or had her name been Molly? So many memories. Being here, walking on the grass where they'd once strolled, sharing laughter and dreams . . . why wouldn't the memories prove upsetting?

Shrugging off her unease, she wheeled her attention across the lawn. At the forest's edge Princess stood tied to a tree.

Relieved, Rennie slowed her gait. Approach too quickly and the dog would pee. All things considered, it was no wonder Princess suffered from nerves.

On the side of the dog's head and torso the black fur was seared away, exposing mottled flesh. The flap of her left ear was a ghoulish lump. Last year a few Liberty punks had caught the starving pup near the railroad tracks outside town. They tied Princess to the tracks, doused her haunches with gasoline and set her on fire. If a passing motorist hadn't acted quickly, she would've died.

Afterward schoolchildren in Liberty took up a collection to pay for her care. Rennie's niece Blossom had led the drive with her friends Tyler and Snoops. A local vet offered free hospitalization at his clinic. Three months later Princess went up for adoption.

Which was another reason why Rennie harbored a soft spot for Squeak. Most twenty-something males were out chasing women, not bottle-feeding a maimed animal.

Nearing, she made a soft, cooing sound. She chuckled at the dog's glittery pink collar, an incongruous form of decoration for an animal with beady, coal-black eyes and a skittish, less-than-regal temperament.

"Hey, Princess," she whispered. "It's me. We should be friends by now."

The dog's withers shuddered. She crouched before the animal and reached out her hand. The moment she did, ice slid through her veins.

The reaction was visceral and deep, urging her to flee. She might have obeyed the adrenaline surging through her blood if not for Princess, panting now, her muzzle lifting. The dog shuffled her rump forward on a whimper of fear. The snap of twigs shot Rennie's attention forward.

Inside the forest, a man leaned against a tree. Shadows concealed his face. Sunlight caught his tool belt, and his hammer glinted.

Rising swiftly, she stepped back.

He approached, his brown hair fluttering in the breeze. A few wiry strands of steel grey were mixed into the mess. Was he one of the carpenters? Something in his gait struck her as predatory. There were men in the world who were dangerous. Some were lethal.

The shadows pooling on his shoulders were flung away as he stepped into the sunlight. His eyes were void of emotion, the eyes of a shark—cold and killing.

"This your mutt?" he asked before she found her voice.

She came forward to shield Princess. "She belongs to my assistant."

"Mutt been in a fire?"

"Yes."

"What happened?"

She was loath to explain. Everything about the man sent warning bells clanging through her. "Last summer she was set on fire by a couple of boys," she finally said. "On Clement Avenue. It was in the newspaper."

"Don't think I read about it."

"It wasn't front page news."

While they made conversation, she studied Princess. The dog appeared fine. Surely the man hadn't harmed her. He was merely one of the workers taking a break to enjoy the forest's cool shade.

Haphazard lines knit across his cheeks like the scrawl marks from a child's pencil. His age was a mystery, anywhere from forty to sixty years old. On his barrel chest, his plaid shirt fit tightly. The tattoo on his right forearm was impossible to make out as he crossed his arms.

She was about to ask his name when he said, "You working

here, too?"

"Electrical."

"Pretty thing like you does electrical?" Rolling his tongue, he worked the wad of chewing tobacco in his cheek. "Girl like you shouldn't be alone on a site with so many men. Might not be safe."

The words, a challenge, competed with the fear chilling her blood. "I'm not a girl," she snapped, the anger trumping fear. "I can take care of myself."

He studied her appraisingly. His eyes were a foreign language, his expression impossible to read. He was like an image at the edge of a dream that melted away as you rose to consciousness, unsure if you'd welcomed his appearance during the night or had thrashed in your sheets.

"Not many women like construction," he said while she tried to get a fix on him. "Never thought I'd see one as pretty as you in this line of work."

Ignoring the compliment, she gave Princess a pat. Remarkably the dog stopped trembling. By the trunk of the tree lay a fast food wrapper. Looking past it she spotted the water bowl Squeak had faithfully placed nearby.

The nerves she'd put at bay scuttled back through her. Anger followed.

Brown flecks of tobacco floated in the water. Someone had spit chew into the bowl—the man. An unnerving smile formed on his mouth. It sent another wave of anger whipping through her.

She snatched up the bowl. "Why did you do this?" Water sloshed over the rim. "What's wrong with you?"

He chuckled as she dumped the water on the grass. "The mutt doesn't mind."

"You're an asshole." She tried to back the insult with heat but his smile grew dangerous. "Shouldn't you get back to work?"

The smile sank from his lips like the moon dipping beneath dark waters. "Yeah, I should." He gave Princess a passing glance. "Dog should be put down. She's got no business being alive."

"She's perfectly healthy. It's just scarring."

The man settled his gaze long enough to stab some indefinable emotion into her heart. She was still trying to grasp its meaning when he walked away.

There wasn't time to consider the chilling exchange with the man. Rennie returned to the site to find Squeak arguing with Crash, the lead carpenter.

At this morning's meeting, Crash had called into question her ability to handle a job as large as the new wing. She was humiliated, especially after Troy chimed in. All of the men looked on with amusement, and, in some cases, hostility. She'd defended herself, but barely.

Evidently Crash was still trying to drive her off. On the lawn, he stood nose-to-nose with Squeak.

Gently, she pushed her assistant aside and faced him. "What's going on?"

Crash closed in on her. "Your sidekick is in our way. He can't stockpile supplies on the first floor. My men are still framing in rooms."

Silently, Rennie chastised herself. She'd been in such a hurry she'd forgotten to give Squeak the carpenters' schedule.

She offered a conciliatory smile. "We'll move our gear out of the way."

"Don't bother. My men are taking care of it."

He jerked his chin toward the new wing. A man strode through the door and flung an armload of supplies on the lawn. Insulating wire, tools, conduit piping—her supplies tumbled across the grass.

"What the hell? You're damaging my stuff!"

Squeak stepped in front of her. "Why don't I do some damage to him?" He flexed his fingers. "Rennie, I tried to move our stuff. Honest, I did. Crash told his guys to throw me out."

"They *threw* you out?"

"Threw me out on my—" Squeak caught himself. "It wasn't right."

She rounded on Crash. "Tell your men to stop. If they don't, you're paying for everything they break."

"It's not my problem if you can't follow directions. My crew has the first floor until tomorrow. Find somewhere else to work."

From behind, Troy growled, "What's going on?"

Rennie closed her eyes. Now she'd managed to get on Troy's

bad side twice in one day. What were the odds? She found the courage to face him as Crash stormed off.

Troy dealt with Squeak first. "Back off, son. Find something to do while I talk to your boss."

Amazingly, the kid held his ground. "If you're going to yell, I'm sticking around. She didn't do anything wrong."

Squeak's ready defense was sweet, if poorly timed. "I'll handle this," she said, nudging him toward the new wing. "Grab the rest of our stuff before Crash destroys everything."

"Sure you're okay?"

"Go on, Squeak."

After he left, she said to Troy, "This was just a misunderstanding. Crash will cool down."

From the advantage of height Troy appraised her with a mix of frustration and rising temper. His eyes, as deep as the ocean and just as unpredictable, darkened to an unsettling midnight blue.

"This won't work out." He stepped closer, undoubtedly to rattle her. An unnecessary ploy—she was already nervous. "I'm sure you need this job. Rennie, I do understand. But facts don't change. We do better to steer clear of each other. Most of the time we don't work the same sites. All things considered, it's a good strategy."

"We both worked the Smithfield addition two years ago," she said, frantic for a way out of the impasse.

"On different days. We never ran into each other."

True, and she'd been relieved. Seeing Troy always brought up memories best forgotten and stirred emotions best ignored. "We'll work this out."

"I'm the general contractor. You can't avoid me."

"I'll stay out of your way."

"It's not just me. You're already on Crash's bad side. I'm cutting you loose."

"You're firing me over an argument with Crash?" Desperation rolled through her. "I've already used part of the advance. And what about Squeak? He's a great kid who deserves a steady paycheck."

"Rennie, you'll have to work overtime just to keep pace with the other crews. Dianne never should've asked for your bid."

"But she did. You saw her this morning—she's excited to have me here."

"None of the men like it."

"But your sister does." It was a small triumph when he sighed. "You know she likes me. Admit it. She likes me a lot."

"Unfortunately she does."

The admission seemed to soften him. Troy had lost his brother in a shocking murder. Dianne was all he had left. Reason enough for him to dote on her.

Relenting, he said, "Consider this probation. Don't fight with Crash and don't even think about going AWOL if I tell you to stay put. Give me enough reason, and it won't matter what Dianne thinks. I *will* fire you."

His threat haunted her for the rest of the day. He left in the afternoon to pick up supplies and she was relieved to see him go. More workers arrived. She stayed clear of Crash and his men by ordering Squeak to the second floor to begin wiring the bedrooms. Worry over losing the job kept her moving at a brisk pace. By day's end they'd finished work in three rooms.

Oddly, the confrontation with the man in the forest posed the greater worry. Something about him made her skin crawl. It was impossible to spot the man in the general chaos—not that she dared to seek him out. You found all types on a construction site from courteous architects to trades who'd done a stint in prison. One carpenter packed egg salad sandwiches lovingly prepared by his wife. The next guy smelled of despair and drank on the sly. You never knew what you'd find. The man in the forest was probably a drifter staying in Liberty for a few months because he'd heard about the Fagan job in a bar. Troy was paying good money to get the addition built quickly. Trades from as far away as Columbus were bidding on work. There was no telling where the man had come from.

The man's comment about putting down a young dog like Princess was disturbing. Better to avoid him. Tomorrow she'd tell Squeak to leave his dog within eyeshot of the addition.

By the time she drove home she'd managed to dismiss the unnerving exchange.

Rennie found her mother's tan Camry parked before her brick bungalow. An inconvenience since she'd only planned to stop home for a few minutes before heading back out. Some of the electrical supplies hadn't arrived today at Fagan's. She needed to drive to the supply store in Mentor to pick them up.

Her mother wasn't the only one in the house. Her niece, Marcy, sang off-key as she dusted the end table beside the couch. Leggy, with a tumble of chocolate brown curls, she wore a soccer tee-shirt and had rimmed her eyes with heavy silver shadow.

In the center of the living room Lianna ran the vacuum. Most of the mud was gone from the carpeting. A miracle, really. Rennie tried to remember the last time she'd picked up the place. Definitely not in the last few weeks.

Her mother flicked off the vacuum. "This is shameful," she said when Rennie sauntered into the living room. "You make decent money. Hire a cleaning service."

Rennie picked up several chocolates strewn across the couch. "Why didn't you tell me you were cleaning my house? Not that you should. I would've appreciated a heads up."

Marcy stopped polishing long enough to chortle. "Yeah. Right. We should've told you we were coming. You would've changed the locks."

Given the intrusion, it wasn't a bad idea. "You haven't been in my bedroom, have you?" She popped a chocolate into her mouth.

Her mother sighed. "We haven't stepped foot inside the sacred space. We have, however, scoured the other bedrooms and purchased a few items to make them presentable. I was wondering why you keep power tools in your guest bedrooms. I'm not sure I can stomach the truth."

"Because it makes them easy to find?" This was her house. She'd keep power tools wherever she liked. It wasn't as if she'd entertain guests anytime soon—

Choking down the chocolate, she glared at her mother. "Wait a minute. Those kids aren't coming today are they? I just agreed to take them this morning. I'm not ready."

Lianna steered the vacuum into the corner. "Better get ready. Jenalyn is bringing Walt and Emma any minute now. Did you leave your antacids in the truck? Go get them."

"This is too fast! You aren't giving me time to adjust."

There wasn't a scrap of food in the house. A trip to the

grocery store wasn't on the agenda. She had to pick up supplies then review the plans for Dianne Fagan's new digs. No way was she handling Walt and Emma Korchek tonight. Not even under the threat of electrocution.

"This is emergency foster care," Lianna said. "That means there's been an *emergency*. I understand how difficult change is for you. In an *emergency* you have to flex."

"I hate it when you talk to me like I'm an idiot."

Marcy angled her hip. "Only an idiot leaves a chain saw in a guest bedroom. Creepy."

"I use the extra rooms for storage. What's the big deal?"

"Can't you tell the difference between a bedroom and a garage?" Marcy wrinkled her nose. "There's also a jar full of nails in the bathroom. You leave more crap around than anyone."

"I was working on the roof last weekend." Rennie tore off her tool belt and flung it on the couch. She took a deep breath. Was there any sense in becoming more upset? "Okay. Walt and Emma will be here soon. Which is cool. I'll survive. Tell me the schedule."

Marcy grinned wickedly. "It's complicated. Taking on two shrimps is labor intensive. Trust me. I was a kid once."

"You're fifteen. You're still a kid." Which, now that she thought about it, was a redeeming trait. "Hey, kiddo—why don't you spend the night and help out with Walt and Emma? You can bunk with me."

"How much will you pay me?"

"Will a twenty cover it?"

Her mother scowled. "Marcy, you shouldn't demand payment every time you contribute. It's bad enough you play sports twelve months of the year. Your parents spend good money for soccer camp, uniforms—"

"It's no problem," Rennie cut in. Would Anna let Marcy stay a few days? Maybe she'd let her stay all week.

Rennie dug into her pocket and handed over the cash. "I'm happy to pay." Perhaps Marcy would take care of bath time. Homework too. "Let's start by scaring up dinner. There might be something in the freezer that isn't past its expiration date. If you'll feed Walt and Emma, I can run errands."

Marcy held up her cell phone. "One sec." She flopped onto

the couch. "I have to text my friends."

"But I just gave you twenty bucks!"

"Will you two argue later?" Lianna took Rennie by the elbow and dragged her to the kitchen. "Liza sent over several dishes. So did Anna. How they found time to cook with their schedules I can't imagine."

"Liza wasn't in court today." She recalled her sister-in-law mentioning the postponement of one of her cases. "As for Anna . . . maybe she skipped a shopping spree in lieu of cooking for me. It would be strange but given the day I've had, I'd believe anything."

She opened the refrigerator and gasped. The shelves were packed with neatly wrapped casseroles and side dishes. Liza had even baked a sweet potato pie.

Her pleasure was short lived. Outside a car door slammed shut. Children's voices rang out. They were followed by a muffled command from the social worker, Jenalyn. Retracing her steps to the living room, Rennie let her sense of misgiving compete in hand-to-hand combat with her nerves. On the other side of the door a scuffle burst forth.

Walt and Emma had arrived.

Muttering an oath, she flung open the door. On the front stoop, the pretty Filipino social worker tried to corral the children fleeing her clutches. At the sight of Rennie glowering in the doorway, Walt stopped thrashing. Emma clutched a ratty Barbie doll to her waist and rubbed her damp cheeks.

Emma's despair needled Rennie with shame. With effort, she put sugar in her voice. "Hello, kids. Won't you come in?" She stepped aside. "Make yourselves at home."

Walt scowled. Emma sniffled.

Neither moved.

Rennie bit down on her lower lip. Dear God, what had she gotten herself into?

Chapter 4

She didn't like it here.

The smell of peppermint mixed with lemons. The shiny floors that scuffed when she ran across them. The tidy kitchen and the living room couch with the pillows lined up so nice she couldn't imagine sitting there. The rooms were so big she felt lost in them. When Jenalyn had shown her and Walt around she'd kept her hands pressed to her sides for fear of knocking something over.

She was afraid of this big house, of the woman who dressed like a boy, of everything unfamiliar. But then the only thing in her life that *was* familiar was Walt. And her dad.

At the front door Rennie was saying goodbye to her mama and Jenalyn. They'd forgotten to close the living room drapes. Night crept down the street, drawing a sheet of black across the houses. Emma shivered.

Hush little baby, don't say a word—

She pressed her nose to the glass. Shadows bled across front lawns and driveways. Her blood *whooshed* in her ears as she scanned the street for the familiar grey truck.

Mama's gonna buy you a mockingbird.

The truck wasn't parked in front of the house next door. It wasn't parked in front of any of the houses. Across the street a red car rolled to a stop before a yellow house. A lady got out and walked through the shadows to her mailbox. She didn't notice night coming, or hurry to get out of the dark.

Emma held her breath against the tremor in her blood. No other cars came down the street—no truck. He wasn't here. Pressing her Barbie doll close, she patted her doll on the back until the *whooshing* melted from her ears. When it had, she tiptoed down the hallway toward the bedroom that was now Walt's room.

She paused outside. Clutching her Barbie doll until her fists knotted, she made a wish. She wished Mama were still alive.

She missed Tennessee. The tastes, the smells, the bacon crackling on the stove, the bite of turnip greens when she put them in her mouth followed by the sweet when she began to chew. She missed the bitter smell that clung to Mama's uniform when she came home covered in black oil from the factory in a hurry to see her babies. Mama barely got her arms around Walt before he squirmed away. But Emma was Mama's bitty-baby. She'd stay in a rocking embrace. Hugging Mama was warm and good and she smelled just a bit funny from all the machine oil on her clothes.

There were other smells, too, better smells—like the flowers rising off Mama's skin when, giggling, she took Emma by the hand and shut them in the bathroom. They always waited until Pa left for work. He didn't approve of Mama having fun. Once they were curled together beside the rusty old tub, Mama would say, *Girls need nice things, don't they?* On a sigh, she'd remove the treasure hidden in the pocket of her jeans.

The perfume bottle was pencil thin. Mama dabbed the spicy scent on her wrists, and Emma's. Then she reached into the hole in the wall behind the tub. The hole was dark, scary. It smelled like nighttime when the rain poured down and the mud crawled up the sides of the house. Mama said it was a place where someone meant to put in plumbing so people could do their business indoors.

But people rarely found money for indoor plumbing, and the hole stayed dark and musty. It *was* a good hiding place. Mama pulled out the magazines the women at the factory gave to her once they'd finished reading. She showed Emma pictures of pretty ladies in sparkly clothes with their hair curled nice and the smiles on their faces as bright as July. Most of the photos were marred by coffee stains and Mama would say, *Now isn't that a shame? No one dressed so fine should have coffee on them.* She moved her finger in slow circles around a lady wearing a necklace of stars. *Isn't that fine jewelry, Emma? Think your pa will get me something that nice when I turn twenty-seven?*

But Mama didn't turn twenty-seven.

One day at the factory, she turned the wrong way. A machine lever caught her from behind. The factory called, and sunlight fled across the kitchen floor. Pa gripped the phone.

Hanging up, he put a quiet in the house so tight Emma couldn't draw in air. Walt shuffled from the kitchen and she knew to leave him alone. She tiptoed to the bathroom. She wasn't brave enough to remove Mama's pretty magazines from their hiding place, not with Pa nearby. Instead, she curled up on the floor as the shivery dread settled into her bones.

Pa was gone for most of the next day or the next two days. Four ladies from the factory arrived in their uniforms clucking like hens. The smell of machine oil trailing them made Emma's heart ache. They kept a good distance from Pa. He towered over them with his arms crossed and shadows growing thick on his face.

Walt nodded at the women. "They smell just like Mama." He led Emma away from the stark reminder of everything they'd lost.

In the yard, the Dixie Mart girl strolled in a circle around one of Pa's trucks. Pa never drove any of his trucks for long. Something in the engine would break, and Emma would tear out of the yard the moment he began cussing at the old carcass. He'd leave the truck wherever it had died on the yellow grass by the other wrecks. On stormy days the rain bounced off hoods and gathered in rusty holes like blood on a ravaged beast. On sunny days every last carcass blazed with light. Emma didn't dare go near. Even if Pa couldn't drive the trucks, he'd raise Cain if she laid so much as a finger on any of them.

The Dixie Mart girl didn't know the rules. She stood before the hood of a Ford with her belly jiggling beneath her white blouse. She stared at a hole so large, the greasy hills and valleys of the engine were in plain sight.

"This vehicle is a mess." She bounced her gaze off one wreck after another. "Why doesn't your father call the junkyard to haul them away?"

"Pa keeps things," Walt said. The Dixie Mart girl ran her hand across the hood and he added, "Don't do that. He'll get mad."

"Why?"

"No one's allowed to touch his stuff."

She shook her head. "Silliest thing I ever heard." Rummaging around the pocket of her roomy jeans, she withdrew a pack of gum. "Want some?"

Walt opened his palm. "Thanks."

Emma stepped back, hurt that he'd enjoy sweets. Mama still wasn't home. She always came eventually, even if she worked a double shift because Toyota needed cars built fast as lightning. Was it true what the ladies were whispering inside the house? Was Mama gone *forever*? Emma couldn't hold onto the idea—it was slippery and awful. She watched the road with her throat tight as leather.

But the road was silent.

Finally Pa ushered the factory ladies from the house. He gave the Dixie Mart girl five dollars for babysitting. Popping the gum in her cheek, she wandered into the sinking sun.

In the house, the factory ladies had left a molasses cake on the kitchen counter. Staring at the thick frosting, Emma flinched against the sharp rumbling in her stomach. Pa got the bottle down from the cupboard, the one that smelled like fire. He drank at the table, even after the moon came out and sat on the windowsill.

Drinking down fire, he emptied the bottle. And he kept whispering things. Scary things.

With effort, Emma struggled from the memory's grip.

A film of sweat covered her arms. Blinking in the soft light of Rennie's hallway, she tried to clear away the memory of that day. *Don't think about Pa.* But his voice still rattled in her head.

"Emma?"

She spun around.

Walt came out of the bedroom and joined her in the hallway. He poked her in the chest. "What's wrong with you?"

The words refused to leave her throat. Shrugging, he returned to the bedroom. She hurried in behind him, her stomach tumbling, and paused beside the Matchbox cars lined up on the green carpet. Her toe bumped a yellow Corvette, rolling it forward.

"Watch what you're doing!"

She groaned as the Matchbox car rolled under the bed. Walt flung himself after it. She gripped her Barbie doll close as he thrashed beneath the bed.

Suddenly he stopped squirming. "This is weird. Come look."

"I don't want to."

"Don't be chicken. Come see."

Against her better judgment she knelt beside him.

He didn't have to explain. She spotted the boxes for herself and the smelly old rug. There were other surprises under the bed—old towels, three books, and a bicycle wheel.

"Why is all this here?" she asked. Walt waved at her to *be quiet.* She shaped her voice into a whisper. "Maybe there are bugs in those boxes."

"Ohio isn't like Tennessee. The bugs are smaller here."

"Even the spiders?"

"I think so." Walt slid a box out.

"Put it back. We'll get in trouble."

She tried to stop him but he slapped her hand away. Ice filled her belly. Rennie was saying goodbye to her mama and Jenalyn. What if she'd finished? What would she do if she caught them going through her stuff?

Walt tossed the lid aside. "I want to look."

She squeezed her eyes shut. Pa leapt into her thoughts, his anger rolling toward her like thunder. There was no accounting for his rage, no way to prepare. It just *came.*

Was Rennie's anger the same? She wore men's clothes. She talked hard like a man. Would she beat them?

"Look here," Walt said, and she dared to peel her eyes open. He laid a baseball on the floor. "You ever seen anything so fine? I want to keep it."

When she refused to touch the ball, he rolled it into the closet. Next he withdrew a brown envelope and Emma couldn't help but stare.

"Is that a report card?" she asked, breathless.

"Rennie Perini, grade five." He danced his fingers across the writing. "Math, D. Science, D. Gym, A." He chortled. "English, F."

"Show me!" Pa would beat Walt for grades like that. "Walt, do you think she's—"

From the doorway, Rennie said, "I wasn't stupid. I just didn't learn fast like other kids."

Emma stumbled to her feet. Walt tossed the report card down and stepped in front of her like he did whenever he took on Pa.

"Didn't you do your homework?" he asked.

The question crashed through the room's dangerous silence. Fear wicked the dampness from Emma's mouth.

"I did homework all the time." Pain shot through Rennie's voice. "Not everyone gets good grades. That doesn't mean they're stupid. Some people have trouble with book-learning."

"Pa says lazy bastards get bad grades."

Walt, be quiet. Drawing up her flimsy courage, Emma made herself look at Rennie. What she saw didn't make sense. Shivers ran across Rennie's lips. The hurt in her eyes was like Walt's whenever Pa laid into him. Walt would try to hold still, like Rennie did now. But he couldn't stop the fear from showing through.

Rennie's niece, Marcy, appeared in the doorway. "Can we all go to bed now?" she asked. "I'm tired."

Walt swung his arms in an arc. "Me, too." Miraculously he'd taken on Rennie and escaped without bruises or a black eye. Emma was still trying to absorb his good luck when he added, "I already brushed my teeth."

"Emma, your room is across the hall." Rennie stepped inside. "Should I tuck you into bed?"

The question sent shivers down Emma's back. She always slept curled against Walt's ribs. Even before Mama died, they'd shared the same bed.

Walt said, "She can find the room by herself."

She swallowed, grateful her brother had stood up for her. Why couldn't they share a bed? Nothing bad would happen if he were nearby.

She was still trying to find her voice when Rennie said, "I'll tuck you in, sweetie."

Walt climbed into his bed. "Whatever."

In the doorway, Marcy rolled her eyes. Then she stalked down the hallway to Rennie's room.

"Well, if there isn't anything else," Rennie said, "let's get you tucked in."

In the room across the hall, the rug was shaped like a big strawberry. The bed wore a pink and yellow bedspread. The dresser shined like new. Everything looked store bought but she couldn't enjoy the pretty colors. Not without Walt here with her.

Slipping past Rennie, she leapt into the bed and threw the covers over her head. Tears came quickly. She couldn't stop them. Finally the door closed and the house fell into silence.

Rain tapped on the window. Holding her Barbie doll tight, she tried to escape thoughts of her dad's nighttime visits, Pa stumbling near with the smell of firewater on his breath, ordering Walt to sleep in the barn so he'd be alone with her—

Go away, go away.

Rain *tap, tap, tapped* on the window. The wind, rising, howled like a wild dog. Her heart rolled as the door opened with a groan. She peered out from beneath the covers with her heartbeat ringing in her ears.

The creak of the door, and Walt tiptoed through the dark. "Are you awake?"

"Yes! I don't like it here."

"Don't worry." He put on a smile but she knew he was scared. He was just better at hiding it. "I know how to make Rennie let us go."

Fresh tears came fast. "What will you do?"

He led her to the door. "You'll see."

Chapter 5

For a seasoned social worker, Lianna was more unnerved than was sensible. Somehow she kept her voice level and her questions direct. Across the desk, Buck Korchek wound and unwound the jewel-encrusted chain on his fist with intimidating focus.

Translucent gems captured the morning light streaming through the office windows. The flash of rubies and sapphires, the glint of diamonds and emeralds—surely they were faux gems. The possibility they might be real was stunning.

Even more upsetting? The thread of jewels composed a rosary.

The rosary was one of the most revered devotions of the Catholic faith. Lianna's own rosary remained tucked in her purse for quiet moments of prayer. She couldn't fathom why a man as ill natured as Buck owned such a precious object. He wound the rosary around the fleshy portion of his hand like a weapon meant to add power to the damage caused by his fist.

Was he a parishioner at St. Mary's? She'd never seen him in the pews with his children. If Walt and Emma received solace in their difficult lives it wasn't through Father John's good graces.

She dragged her attention from the rosary to Buck's guarded eyes. "How are you getting on with therapy?" she asked.

He drew the fragile thread of jewels taut, nearly breaking it. "I'm going, aren't I?"

"Are you learning to manage your anger?"

"You tell me."

She regarded him with thinning patience, this virtual stranger who'd recently moved to Liberty from Tennessee with his two neglected children and a history of sorrow. Not a stranger, actually—Buck had grown up in Liberty. Three decades had passed, enough time to shape him into the hard, angry man seated before her.

Twenty minutes into the interview it was clear he didn't recognize her. She felt relief and an odd twinge of shame.

The years, a labyrinth, brought her full circle back to her youth. How to measure the man before her against the memory of the sullen teenager she'd once known? In high school, Buck had slept through class in his soiled clothes. She'd pitied him, especially when the athletes on the Liberty Eagles taunted him as he shuffled by.

The simple act of remembering splintered pain through her chest. Those days were settled deep beneath the ocean of her life. She'd spent years on the busy work of forgetting the one, brutal event that had affected every student at the high school. The town had never experienced a crime so vicious. For months afterward, every young woman in Liberty, including Lianna, was escorted to summer jobs and nights out at the movies. They were grateful for the protection.

With misgiving she recalled the sea swell of grief that carried her through those final weeks of school. She nearly drowned in it, and Buck—a boy ridiculed for his bad teeth and pockmarked face—Buck had dropped out before graduation. Did a diminished life follow? No one bothered to ask what became of him. No one cared.

Now, appraising him, she noted how time had winnowed away the glow in his cheeks. She wondered if he'd known happiness. It was difficult imagining him starting a family when she'd already become a grandmother. What had his late wife, La Vonda, found so attractive in a man twice her age? Buck certainly hadn't aged well. His ropy build was somehow threatening. He sat perfectly still yet she sensed movement, a skimming threat beneath the surface calm.

Getting back on track, she said, "Counseling only works if

you form a bond of trust with your therapist. Do you understand?"

The web-work of lines on his face deepened. "I get it."

"The court has ordered therapy. Even if you're uncomfortable with the sessions, I'd like assurance you're making an effort."

"I'm doing my part." He let his hand fall to his lap. "What else you want to know?"

She corralled her nerves behind a placid smile. "Have you found work?" She reminded herself that he was a client of Jobs & Family Services, not someone to fear.

"I found something part-time."

"A letter from your employer will help your case when you go before the judge."

He leaned across the desk and apprehension rippled up her spine. "When do I get Walt and Emma back?" he asked.

"We need to see progress before making a decision."

"Who decides?"

"I do." When his mouth dipped into a frown, she added, "My goal is to reunite the family whenever possible."

"Whenever possible," he mimicked, unwinding the rosary from his fist. "Sometimes it's not possible? You take kids away for good?"

She nodded, her mouth dry. "Only in extreme circumstances."

A strange emotion pierced his gaze and Lianna stilled beneath the awful thought taking shape. Involving her daughter in the case had been reckless. Buck was a wild card, a dangerous man. Choosing Rennie to provide emergency care for his children was a mistake. It would've been far wiser to send the children to another county for foster care.

Her worry went unnoticed. "You got no right taking Walt and Emma," he said. "I want this mess straightened out and my kids back."

The smile she offered was a thin film on her frantic thoughts. "Continue working with the psychologist. I strongly suggest you look into Alcoholics Anonymous. The meetings are held in the town hall." She wrote down the address and slid the note across the desk. "Show progress and you will be reunited with Walt and Emma."

He held her gaze like a vice. "They aren't yours." He stuffed the note in his pocket, the muscles in his forearms bulging in violent hills. "You can't keep my kids forever."

In the truck's passenger seat, Marcy rose from a simmering silence. "Turn the truck around."

Rennie drummed on the steering wheel. "The bell rings in ten minutes. You have to go to school, kiddo."

"No way." The teen dumped her book bag, which reeked of spoilt milk, on the floor at her feet. "Will you at least say something to him? Don't let him get away with this."

"Calm down. Everything is fine."

"Are you kidding? Look at my forehead!"

From the back seat, Walt shot forward. "Is your bump still growing?"

Marcy whirled on him. "It's your fault I look like this."

Rennie sighed. "Walt, put your seatbelt back on."

Liberty Square came into view, the red brick buildings and leafy maple trees oddly serene in the chilly morning air. Her mood grim, Rennie drove past The Second Chance Grill. Why had she fallen asleep last night? A savvier woman would've patrolled the halls to ensure her foster kids were in bed.

There wasn't time this morning to repair the damage wreaked on the house. Repairing the damage to her niece took high priority.

At first light, Marcy had found her book bag's contents dumped on the kitchen table. Spiral notebooks and other gear were smeared with food. Hurtling toward her World Studies report, *Athens versus Sparta,* she careened through a puddle of milk. She lost her balance and banged her head on the table's edge. The ancient Greeks were spared. Marcy was rewarded with an angry goose egg on her brow.

The morning went downhill from there.

While applying an ice pack, Rennie discovered a nasty surprise on the back of her niece's head. Someone had lopped off a few of her curls. It was a toss-up what upset Marcy more—the blossoming egg due north of her temple or the hack job done on her hair.

Recalling the girl's howling tears, Rennie palmed her own face. Why had she escaped unmolested? It was like winning at craps while Marcy was taken for her last dime.

The house also lost out badly. Walt managed to dodge the confessional but Emma, contrite, admitted they'd crept into the kitchen past midnight and plowed through the fridge. Spaghetti dripped from the counters and gobs of sweet potato pie formed spatter art on the walls.

Cleaning up the mess would have to wait.

In the back seat, Walt, evidently still upset by his sister's treachery, poked her in the stomach. She squealed like a siren.

"Stop hassling your sister." Rennie dared a glance at her wristwatch. *Don't even think about Troy.* Pondering the dressing down she'd receive for arriving late wasn't a morning pick-me-up.

Marcy toed her book bag. "I'm serious. If you don't take me home, I'm hitchhiking."

"I'll make it up to you."

"Yeah? How?"

Rennie wriggled her wallet from her jeans. Marcy grabbed it and snatched forty dollars.

Emma piped up. "We want to go home, too."

Rennie suffered a pang of sympathy. No doubt the kids were just as scared of being here as she was of parenting them. Sadly, they preferred their abusive father. He was a familiar part of their lives, especially now that they'd lost their mother.

"Emma, you can't go home until Jenalyn says you can," she said, clinging to the remnants of her patience.

Walt butted his head against the window. "Pa wants us back. Take us home."

Marcy glared at him. "Listen, buster—you're going to school." Narrowing her regard, she brought his thrashing to a halt. "When we get back to Rennie's place tonight, you're helping me clean up the mess. The floors, the walls—everything."

"You can't make me!"

"We're doing the Mighty Maids routine together. Understand?"

At the light by the courthouse, Rennie brought the truck to a jerky halt. Marcy would stay another night? Given her purpling goose egg and new 'do, it was a miracle she'd consider it.

"You're coming back?" The school compound came into view and Rennie eased off the accelerator. "That's great. I appreciate it."

"Yeah, if you take me home *now*. Damn it, no one walks around school looking like this."

Walt threw off his seatbelt and hurtled forward. "You said a bad word! I heard you!"

Marcy hung across the seat and buckled him in. She came back up with a look of desperation. "My friends can't see me like this. Have you looked at the back of my head, Aunt Rennie? The kid gave me a hack job."

Rummaging under the seat, Rennie found a Perini Electric cap. "Wear this. It'll hide the damage. Well, some of it." Reconsidering, she dug into her jeans. "Here's another twenty. Don't spend it all in one place."

Marcy snatched the bill. "Consider this a down payment for pain and suffering."

Emma rubbed her stomach. "My tummy hurts."

"You're fine," Rennie said. "Midnight noshing upset your stomach. Not a big surprise."

Walt offered, "She gets sick when people fight."

The disclosure gave Rennie pause. Had Buck Korchek and his wife fought in front of their children? The case study she'd read had provided only a cursory background on the family. Worry flitted through her as she parked before the junior high building. Had the children witnessed something worse?

The line of busses emptied a crowd of teenagers before the low brick building. Joining the queue, Marcy slunk inside with the cap hiding most of her face. With luck, the other students wouldn't make a fuss about her forehead or notice the curls missing from her scalp.

And the moon is made of green cheese.

Wincing, Rennie pulled back into traffic and veered toward the next building, which housed the elementary school. She was now officially one hour late for work. Assuming, of course, she still had a job.

She unbuckled Walt. "Let's go." He shot into the school and

she regarded Emma, glued to the seat with her green eyes snapping. "C'mon, sweetie. Time for school."

"My tummy hurts. Make it go away."

A belch popped from Emma's lips. When it became obvious she'd never exit the truck without prodding, Rennie scooted across the seat.

She unbuckled the seatbelt. On a groan, Emma vomited . . . all over Rennie.

She was late again.

Plastering on a cordial expression, Troy clamped down on his irritation before it evolved into fury.

Deke Nelson, the building inspector, was less inclined to hide his displeasure. Climbing into his truck, he sent an unintelligible curse Troy's way. No doubt the oath was intended for the MIA subcontractor who'd had the gall to skip the meeting.

Rennie.

Now they'd have to reschedule, a waste of precious time. The notion bubbled through Troy as he ruminated over the fifty ways he'd shoot Rennie when she did arrive.

Beside him, her assistant shook like an epileptic in mid-seizure. At least the big oaf had the sense to smell danger.

Troy swung around. They stood nose-to-nose while he got his game on. "Where the hell is she?"

Squeak tried to shield his face with his cell phone. "I'll try her again. I'm not sure why she isn't picking up."

Troy jabbed a finger at the cell. "Dial." Delayed fury worked through his bloodstream as the kid made the call. How she had the balls to be late for work two days in a row was beyond comprehension.

The thought rose unbidden. *She doesn't have balls.* What Rennie did have was a tight feminine package and a remarkable face. He'd never known her to screw up on a job but when she did, he bet her looks stopped the average contractor from chewing her out. What man wanted to read the riot act to a beautiful woman?

Given their sexual history, doing so should've been infinitely harder for Troy. There certainly wasn't any enjoyment in playing hardball with her. But if she was counting on their complicated past for job security, she'd miscalculated.

Squeak gulped down air. "Still no answer. There must be an emergency. She always picks up."

A string of curses threatened to burst forth. "How long have you worked for her, sport?"

"Five weeks." The kid paled. "Why?"

"Start reading the Want Ads. She won't be in business much longer."

The threat froze Squeak. He stopped trembling so quickly Troy wondered if he'd stopped breathing. If the timid giant went into a swoon, stepping back was a good idea.

The kid surprised him by rising from the dead. "Don't fire us." He grabbed Troy by the arm in a startling display of desperation. "Give us a chance—please. You've worked with Rennie on other jobs, right? She's always reliable, isn't she?"

"Like hell. She's an hour late."

"There's a good reason. She takes her job seriously."

Rubbing his jaw, he considered the possibilities. A death in the family? That would be unfortunate and forgivable. She was climbing out of a ten-car pileup on Route 44? He'd give her that one.

Maybe.

"Keep dialing." Troy started across the lawn. From over his shoulder, he added, "Tell her to get to work now or don't come in at all."

Chapter 6

The tires spit gravel. Slamming on the brakes, Rennie swerved into a lonely stretch of the orchard compound. Rows of apple trees spiraled in all directions, the white blossoms sending out a perfume to compete with spring's first hyacinth.

Thankfully no workers were in sight. She leapt from the truck and scanned the grassy aisles between the neat rows of trees. Find the nearest spigot, and she could wash up.

There hadn't been time to return home after carrying Emma into the school office. Several teachers had immediately taken charge. They were familiar with the Korchek case and pleased to meet the girl's new foster mother. Which might have been a delightful experience if Rennie's shirt wasn't spattered with vomit. After the school nurse cleaned Emma up, the child took a snowy-haired teacher by the hand and skipped off to her classroom. She'd left without so much as a backward glance.

Now, as precious minutes ticked by, Rennie wondered how to make herself presentable before appearing at the mansion.

Returning to the truck, she unearthed an extra work shirt from beneath the driver's seat. Ten paces away a water spigot jutted out of the earth, the thin pipe collecting droplets of moisture. Turning the water on full blast, she thrust her arms beneath the icy flow. Shivering, she splashed water on her face and doused her hair, which, naturally, she'd forgotten to pull into a ponytail this morning.

Shutting off the spigot, she took a deep breath. If she didn't calm down, she'd never make it past Troy. The last thing she needed was another argument.

Leaves rustled, and a chickadee twittered on a nearby branch. Two Cardinals as bright as fire appeared on the branch above her head. She'd forgotten how beautiful the orchard appeared in spring, how much she'd enjoyed strolling the acres when Troy's late brother, Jason, had been alive.

Her attention glided across the treetops. In the distance, the summit rose to a startling height. The perch was an oasis of green above the orchard's white carpet of blossoms. At the center of the summit the Great Oak stood bleakly against the sky.

From here it was impossible to see the gorge that plunged on the summit's opposite side, or hear the churning thunder of the Chagrin River. If she hiked all the way to the Great Oak she could stand at the precipice and listen to the river's song, a ballad with no beginning and no end. Clinging to the tree's craggy bark, she'd peer at the waters raging below—as she'd done fifteen years ago, on the night she'd found Troy there.

Regret and longing wove through her heart. She'd been braver then, or more foolish, a teenager hurtling through life with her arms opened wide. Troy had leaned against the oak's massive trunk in moody silence as she flung an arm over the precipice, daring fate, daring him to reach for her.

Was she standing on a similar cliff now? Managing a new job, grasping for purchase despite the appearance of Walt and Emma in her life—would she lose her balance? Juggling both the Fagan job and the children might prove impossible.

Searching for courage, Rennie studied the Great Oak's silhouette. Even from a distance, it was possible to glimpse tender leaves sprouting on thick branches. The sight of spring's promise was an irresistible lure even though she was inexcusably late and needed to hurry to the other side of the estate.

It was impossible not to admire an oak. In autumn the majestic tree remained clothed in leaves as the wind blew cold and the sky dulled ashen in preparation for winter. The leaves turned brittle yet held to sturdy branches even as the Canadian snow drove south, past Lake Erie, and took Ohio in its fearsome grip. Death layered over the autumn colors and the last of the

Black-eyed Susans but the oak stood fast against winter's threat. It clung to life even as the wind cut down the last corn stalk and drove wildlife into burrows. The oak refused to release the bounty of its leaves, the hard-earned flesh of spring and summer, until every other tree, from the maples to the birches, was driven by the cold into silence. Only then did it release its bounty. Rennie would find papery leaves pressed against the screens in her kitchen as she shut the windows and listened for the teakettle to sing.

Turning from the sight, she returned to the truck. The road wound through the orchard in a haphazard fashion. By the time she reached the mansion, she'd managed to work herself up into a queasy panic.

The moment she parked in the line of trucks, Troy stalked across the lawn. "Where the hell have you been?" he demanded. "The building inspector was here. You were supposed to do a walk-through."

She hadn't expected to be cornered so quickly. "I'm having personal issues at home." She reached for her toolbox. "Please don't ask for the specifics."

He scowled. "Personal issues."

"As in private." *As in none of your business.* "If it'll help, I'll call the inspector to explain this wasn't your fault."

"I don't give a damn if you send roses. He's not used to being stood up by a sub." Troy motioned at the curls cascading around her face. "Mind explaining that?"

"My hair?" She dug her fingers into the mop of curls. "I forgot to put it up."

"Get it done. You can't go vamping around like that."

"Hey! I never vamp."

He leaned in, effectively backing her against the truck. "What the hell." He stepped back. "You smell like shit."

"Thanks for the news flash. And here I thought I smelled as fresh as a daisy."

"*Why* do you smell? Do you have a drinking problem?"

She didn't like the way he folded his arms across his chest as if preparing to hear a whopper of a story. "A little girl threw up on me, okay?"

His brows lifted. "You have a daughter?"

"She's not my daughter. But her stomach *was* upset this morning."

The ire furrowing his brow disappeared. "We'd get along better if you'd play the honesty card." When she remained silent, he added, "I'm your boss. We need open lines of communication."

"You keep threatening to fire me. No offense, but your attitude doesn't fill me with confidence."

"Maybe I went too far."

"You think?"

He rubbed his chin. "If there's a problem, I can help."

Frustration brought laughter gurgling from her throat. This morning a pair of tot-sized terrorists had laid waste to her house. Thanks to Troy, she was on permanent probation at work. Crash, the lead carpenter, wanted her fired. And a strange man on one of the crews had it out for Squeak's dog, Princess.

"My problems aren't work-related," she said. "Not unless you count Crash, and I doubt you can make us best friends. If there was a problem with the job I'd tell you."

"No, you wouldn't. You don't trust me." His mouth settled into a grim line. "I don't mind telling you how much it bothers me."

The admission took her off-guard. Troy wanted her trust? Sure, he prided himself on managing his crews well. He wasn't a GC who withheld pay and ignored safety precautions on a site. But Rennie knew this was different. She shared a history with Troy littered with anger and lust. They'd only managed to overcome the past in the most tentative way.

"Why should I trust you?" she countered, hurt sifting through her voice. "You've been threatening me since I started here. Given half a chance, you'll send me packing."

His concern vanished behind a defensive posture. "I'm taking my sister's wishes into consideration. Dianne likes having you on board."

"So you'll play nice one minute then threaten me the next?" She squared off before him. "I'm not afraid of you, Troy. I need this job. You won't drive me off."

The outburst lifted his brows clear to his hairline. Satisfaction spread through her. Sure, her clothing stank and her stomach roiled with agitation, but she was all right. So what if she was exhausted from twenty-four hours of foster parenting and her job was in jeopardy because she shared a past with the boss they'd both like to forget. No problem. She'd stick it out, with the kids and with Troy. She wasn't a quitter. She'd withstand the pressure. She was steel.

Without warning, Troy flicked her nose. The gesture was so sweet and unexpected that she stumbled back. Pleasure sparked in his eyes.

"Rennie, you're a hard ass," he said, his features suddenly open. "And my offer stands. If you have a problem, consider allowing me to help. It's in my best interest, seeing that you're in my employ."

She thought of Walt's hostility and Emma's silence. "I wouldn't know where to begin."

"An evasion."

"So sue me."

"You used to be different." The faintest hint of regret settled on his face. "You laughed easily. You knew how to let people in."

She imagined Jason striding through the orchard the week before his murder. Heartache followed.

"Life forced me to grow up," she said. Life, and death too. "You've also changed, Troy. Oh, you were always moody. Now you're also demanding."

"Fair enough." For a long moment he studied his work boots. Then he surveyed the stretch of lawn sweeping away from the mansion as if searching for answers. "My sister . . . Dianne isn't like us. She's lighthearted."

"You mean she isn't jaded." Dianne was too young to remember much about Jason or recall the horror of his murder.

The comment pulled Troy's gaze back to hers. "Is that what we are?" he asked softly. "Are we jaded?"

The truth was unbearably sad. Losing Jason had worn something down in both of them. They'd both lost the brightest part of their youth.

When she remained silent, Troy said, "I never wanted to be this way. I expected my life to be different. Better." He looked away. "It isn't."

The sorrow building in her chest brought with it her voice. "Maybe it will be someday," she replied.

"Do you believe that?"

Emotion tightened her throat. They were talking about forgiveness, and an absolution that would never come. Weren't they both responsible for Jason's death? Surely Rennie bore the most guilt. But if she had the courage to ask, she was sure Troy would insist on shouldering equal blame.

The conversation had become uncomfortable. Needing to end it, she nodded toward the mansion. "Where are the maids' quarters? Someone will take pity and let me jump in a shower."

Troy muttered under his breath. Then he led her up the mansion's steps. "They're behind the kitchen. You'll see a hallway." He threw open the door and stood back to allow her to pass. "If you can't find the way, have Bitsy show you. She's the cook."

Rennie stepped inside. "Thanks."

Even though Rennie and her sidekick worked hard all day, Troy was in a sour mood at quitting time. Only a few shots of Jack Daniels and the mindless chaos of Bongo's Tavern could pull him out of his funk.

He'd always liked Bongo's. They didn't serve liquor in Baccarat tumblers. No one discussed the financial health of his portfolio. The food was lousy but the bar featured a live band, which was good. It was easy to lose yourself in the throng of blue-collar types bemoaning dead-end jobs and DOA relationships.

Troy wasn't sure how his parents or his sister would react if they learned he frequented a dive rigged up to look like a ship marooned in the cornfields outside Liberty. The bar represented the antithesis of a life of privilege, the cultivated world where he towered over his family like an awkward relation. *Different.* He was an aberration in the Fagan gene pool.

Jeffrey, the corpulent bartender, grinned. "Speak of the devil." In the background, the band burst into an oldie, the Stones' *Brown Sugar.* "Troy, I was just talking about your trick with the darts."

"He was," a man said. The guy smiled, revealing yellow teeth. "Is it true you can hit a bulls-eye without looking?"

Troy slid onto a barstool. "Jeffrey, get me a drink." After a double shot of Jack Daniel's appeared, he regarded the man. "Yeah, it's true."

"Prove it."

"Some other time, pal."

He threw back the drink. Closing his eyes, he concentrated on the sensation of heat gliding down his throat. He felt edgy, and not simply because Rennie was tardy for work. He'd been edgy his whole life.

Jeffrey eased his forearms onto the bar. "C'mon, Troy—one time. I'll buy your next drink."

"The next two drinks."

"Deal."

Farther down the bar, a biker with stringy blond hair pulled out his wallet. He was nearly as big as Jeffrey, with a beer belly and SUCK ME written on his black shirt. Troy was afraid to analyze why he found the statement amusing. Probably because it was dark and offensive, like the part of his soul he kept hidden from his family—kept hidden from himself most of the time.

The biker held up a ten-note. "Prove you can hit the bull's-eye and it's yours."

Troy leaned back on his barstool, his dusty jeans and air of discontent putting him on par with the biker. Maybe that was why he liked Bongo's. No one looking at him would guess he'd been a millionaire since birth, the money tucked away in accounts his parents tended like a garden of possibility. He'd never touched a cent of his inheritance and they'd never asked why. If they had, he wouldn't have been able to offer a suitable explanation.

He nearly laughed as the biker wagged the bill through the air. The cash was probably the last of his paycheck. No doubt the rest had been squandered on beer and women.

Troy stood. "Anybody else think I can't do it?" He waited as tradesmen and bikers seated all the way down the counter pulled out wallets and slapped down bills. He regarded Jeffrey. "Okay. What do I hit this time?"

The bartender flushed crimson. "Revenge is mine." Reaching under the bar, he produced a folder stuffed with tax documents. "How 'bout sales tax?" He yanked a letter from the mess.

"Columbus says I'm late with my payments. Kill it, Troy. Kill it dead."

The biker pushed through the throng. Taking the document, he jabbed at the State of Ohio seal. "Think you can hit that?"

The seal was larger than a half dollar, an easy shot. Pleased, Troy nodded at the bulletin board on the back wall. "Tack it up and get everyone out of the way. I don't need a lawsuit if I miss the mark and nail someone who's standing too close. I've already had a bitch of a day."

The biker cleared a path from the bar to the bulletin board, twenty paces off. On the beer-soaked dais, the band stopped playing. They did whenever Jeffrey talked Troy into doing his monkey act. *They ought to pay me for entertainment.* Troy chuckled to himself, reconsidered. *No, I ought to pay Jeffrey for getting me out of this crappy mood.*

He took the dart.

Oblivious to the silence descending upon the bar, he counted off the steps to the bulletin board. With care he studied the tax notice. The State seal was dead even with his chin, which pleased him. Low shots were more difficult.

He returned to the bar. With his back to the dartboard—which drew a delighted murmur from the crowd—he poised the dart between the thumb and forefinger of his left hand. He settled his attention on Jeffrey, smiling with anticipation, but he visualized the seal. He had a near photographic memory and the honing instincts of a wolf tracking a kill. Two other strange traits bequeathed to him alone from the Fagan gene pool.

"Now," Jeffrey said.

Troy sent the dart sailing over his right shoulder. The *thud* of impact, and the tavern roared with approval.

Sitting, he tapped the side of his glass. Jeffrey poured another drink. The biker, slack-jawed, gathered winnings from disenchanted patrons all the way down the bar.

Taking the cash, Troy swiveled around to examine his handiwork. Sure enough, he'd hit the center of the seal.

The self-congratulatory high was short-lived.

A man strode to the board and yanked the dart free. He was taller than average with hair as deep a chestnut as Troy's but with strands of grey mixed in. When he turned around, Troy blinked. The guy was working at the mansion. With the masons or the carpenters? It was impossible to recall every man hired by his subs.

With a start, he recalled seeing the man yesterday. The bastard had been talking to Rennie near the forest. She'd appeared angry. From the second story of the addition, it was too far away to hear their voices. Troy was about to go out and protect Rennie if the guy made a pass. She'd stalked off before intervention was necessary.

Clearly, she hadn't liked the guy.

It was easy to understand why. There was something vaguely combative about the man, something off-center. He approached the bar, and instinct pulled Troy to his feet. They stood gauging each other like two combatants called into a battle neither understood. Troy connected with the man's vacant eyes and sensed something missing, a spark of compassion. He knew instantly that the man didn't land a punch quickly or often. But when he did, he aimed to kill.

Evidently he wasn't looking for a brawl. Turning the dart between his fingers, he unleashed a voice bleached of emotion. "You're pretty good," he said. "But you aren't great."

On impulse, Troy curled his hand into a fist.

Catching the movement, the man smiled. The laughter didn't reach his eyes. "Cool down, boy. I'm not here to fight." He nodded at the cash heaped on the bar. "I want your winnings."

"What?" Troy couldn't recall the last time he'd felt so unnerved. Then his features hardened. "I'm not giving you my winnings, pal."

"I'm not asking for a handout. I'll get them fair and square." The stranger drew his gaze to Jeffrey. Sweat glossed the bartender's brow. "What else you got in that folder?"

Speechless, Jeffrey slid the folder across. "Ah. Here we go." The man chose a tax form with a State seal no bigger than a dime. He regarded Troy. "I'll hit this without looking. When I do, you'll hand over the cash."

Troy would've laughed if his gut hadn't warned against it. Hitting something the size of a dime from twenty paces off was impossible unless you were staring straight at it. Even then the odds weren't good.

"Go for it," he said.

He suffered a growing unease as the stranger went through the same paces he'd executed a moment ago. The man instructed the biker to put the tax form on the bulletin board. He walked up to the board slowly, measuring his steps. When he returned, he faced Jeffrey with the dart poised in his left hand exactly as Troy had done.

Jesus. Troy stiffened, his blood running cold.

But the man didn't wait for Jeffrey's signal. He threw the dart over his shoulder with the precision of a robot.

And hit the center of the seal, dead on.

Chapter 7

Rennie picked up the children from daycare with the simple goal of getting them into bed early and spending the evening scraping food off the walls.

Was Marcy at the house? After the number the kids had done on her, who could blame the teen if she reneged? No one sensible volunteered for torture by tots two days in a row. Rennie faced the intimidating possibility that she might be on her own tonight.

Or maybe not. Spirits lifting, she pulled into the driveway and spotted her older brother, Nick. He strolled over to the truck with a wrench in his hand and a loopy grin on his face.

Nearing forty, Nick's olive-toned features wore an expression of perpetual mirth. According to their parents, he'd arrived in the world beaming good cheer, his arms twitching to pull someone into a bear hug. A sales rep for an insurance company in Cleveland, he'd inherited their parents' drive to succeed.

"Rumor has it you're having trouble keeping your wheels on the mommy track," he said as she climbed out of the truck.

"I've totally derailed." She tried to help Walt and Emma out. Dodging her, they bounded down the driveway. "Is Marcy here?"

"Yeah, and none too happy about it." Nick grabbed her by the shoulders. "You look like shit. Taking vitamins?"

"I need something stronger." She tried to wriggle free. "Do you mind? I'd like to go inside. Relax, scrape food off the walls.

Check Walt and Emma's pillowcases for weapons." She regarded them, standing by the mailbox in an angelic silence. "No scissors tonight," she shouted. "Touch one hair on my head and you're in trouble."

Emma flapped her arms. "Okey-dokey." She returned to Rennie's side.

Following, Walt gave the thumbs-up.

Nick grabbed Walt and gave him a gentle shake. "You're Walt, right?" He released the boy and yanked Emma forward. A squeak popped from her mouth. "And you're Emma? Cute name."

Rennie batted the affectionate oaf on the arm. "Ease off. You're crushing her."

"Naw, she likes me." He ruffled Emma's curls, drawing another squeak of protest. "Guess what, kids? I've got a surprise."

Walt, sensibly out of reach, crossed his arms. "What kind of surprise?"

"Check the backyard. You'll love it." They dashed off, and he poked Rennie in the ribs. "Thank me later for performing this rescue operation. Golf clubs are always nice."

She found Marcy pacing around the maple tree in the back yard with her book bag slung over her shoulder. She'd pulled the Perini Electric cap down nearly to her nose. Had she hitched a ride over with Uncle Nick, who was—miracle of miracles—assembling a spanking new swing set?

"This is great. A real lifesaver." Rennie smoothed her hand across the set's orange bars. "Where did it come from?"

"I bought it for you, goofball." Her brother knelt to tighten a screw on one of the bars. Emma sat on a swing and he poked her in the back. "Hey. Don't you have something to say?"

"No," Emma said.

Walt sauntered up. "He's wants you to thank him."

Emma's curls bounced as she pushed off, sending the swing toward the sun. "This is nice." She arced past Nick's shoulder with a look of puzzlement. "Who are you?"

"Uncle Nick. Think of me as manna from heaven."

Walt snickered. "There is no heaven. It's pretend, like Santa Claus."

"Heaven is real, son. So is Santa Claus. How old are you, anyway?"

"Eight." Walt settled on a swing next to his sister, his feet stubbornly planted on the ground. "Everyone knows Santa Claus is fake. My dad says so. He says heaven is pretend, too."

The explanation stole the cheer from Nick's face. He made the sign of the cross. To Rennie, he whispered, "Dose these kids with religion. *ASAP.*"

She tugged him toward Marcy, standing out of earshot of the kids. "I'll take them to Mass on Sunday if I can haul myself out of bed."

"Not good enough. Put them in religion class. Ask Father John to sprinkle their heads with holy water. If Walt doesn't believe in heaven, what's he got?"

"Be sensible. I can't educate them. They're only bunking here for a few weeks."

"Says who?"

"Says Mom. I only have them until they're reunited with their father."

Marcy put an arm around Rennie's waist and patted softly. Nick shook his head.

She looked from one to the other. "What? They're not my kids. Damn it, we met twenty four hours ago!"

Nick palmed his forehead. "Don't swear. Kids are mimics. They'll pick up your trash mouth."

Doubtful her trash mouth would influence Walt or Emma. Given what they'd done to Marcy they were skilled in the Dark Arts. Even so, she suffered a twinge of shame over the negligible possibility she might prove a bad influence.

"I'll try not to swear, all right?" She glowered as Nick held off laughter. "I'm not used to watching my tongue. I'm never around kids. Give me a break."

"You give me a break, little sister. Three of your siblings have kids. Besides you, Frannie is the only holdout. You're around the young and impressionable all the time." He grabbed her chin and squeezed until she yelped. "If Walt and Emma are nearby, ditch the gutter mouth. Got it, dip-shit?"

"Don't call me a dip-shit!"

"You *do* have a bad mouth," Marcy said, apparently deaf to Uncle Nick's language. "I learned my first swear word from you. I said 'oh, hell' in front of Dad when I was about Walt's age and got in big trouble."

"You did?" Rennie was astonished that her niece listened closely enough to pick up her language in all its tainted glory.

"You were my hero," Marcy said, deepening the blow. "You were cool, dressing like a guy and holding a manly job. You never baked brownies like Mom or sewed curtains like Grandma. When you rewired my parents' dining room, you did this cool fireworks thing with the chandelier."

Nick snorted. "She nearly electrocuted your old man. Joe almost fried."

"I was still learning my trade." So what if she wasn't book-smart like everyone else in the family? She'd always been able to work with her hands. "It wasn't a big deal. Joe only had first-degree burns."

Nick rolled his eyes. "It looked like he'd dipped his hands in boiling water. Anna had visions of killing you."

"You're exaggerating."

"Sure I am. We were all scared shitless whenever you were carrying a tool box." He nodded at the starburst scar on her hand. "Look what you did in high school. Landed in the hospital, remember?"

"I survived." She drew her hand behind her back.

Marcy smiled brightly. "But you were cool. A real stand-up guy."

When had she become *Uncle* Rennie in Marcy's eyes? Sure, she didn't dress with the panache of Nick's wife, Liza. She never was beautifully turned out like her mother or her fashion-hog sister, Anna. That didn't make her less of a woman.

She straightened her spine. "For the record, I'm in touch with my feminine side."

Nick poked her ribcage. "Give us a break. You weren't girly even when you were a girl. When we were kids, your sports Zen embarrassed the crap out of me."

An old complaint. Wounded, Rennie tried to stop the pain from seeping into her expression. She'd been the best athlete in the family—not the sort of accomplishment her brother lauded. On any given weekend Lianna took Anna and Frannie shopping in a show of classic mother-daughter bonding. Rennie camped out in the backyard practicing her killer pitch with the neighbor boys.

Unwilling to let it go, her brother said, "You know what it's like to have a kid sister who's a better ball player? After you knocked out Troy Fagan's tooth, I went through school wondering when he'd beat the crap out of me." Nick shivered for effect. "What's it like working for him? A stint in purgatory?"

"It's great." A lie, but Troy *had* asked for her trust this morning. Not that she had any intention of giving it. Their past kept her perpetually on guard. "After I finish the job at the mansion, I'll bid on the processing plant Fagan's Orchard is building next year."

Doubt filtered across her brother's face. "Your specialty is residential. You don't have the expertise to swing an industrial job."

"I'll learn."

"On the job? Sure you will."

"I will, all right?"

She'd prove him wrong. This wasn't simply a foray into commercial work. Putting Perini Electric in the black would establish her place in a family of high achievers. She reminded herself that her brother Anthony hadn't attended college either. He'd turned out all right. The Gas & Go he owned was turning a healthy profit, and his wife Mary had recently opened the first family medical practice in Liberty.

"Just wait. I'll win the bid," she said with enough confidence to make Nick back off. Pity she couldn't dispel her private doubts as easily.

"Good luck. Impress the Fagans with your macho ways and maybe they'll grant your wish."

Stung, she gave him a playful shove. "I'm not macho."

"Guess again. You'll never get on Troy's good side because he doesn't have one. Your manly ways might put you in Aces with his kid sister. Not that Dianne is macho. She's frilly like my wife."

Rennie's brows rose. Nick's wife, *frilly?* No way. Liza was the finest family law attorney in Jeffordsville County, a willowy black woman with a brilliant mind. Her only mistake was marrying an idiot. In one of life's great mysteries, she still loved him after years of marriage.

"Liza isn't frilly," Rennie said. "She'd belt you if she heard you say that."

Marcy shook her head. "Aunt Liza is *very* feminine. She gave me some makeup tips. She felt bad about what Walt and Emma did to me."

For proof, the teen batted her lashes. The pink hue on her lids was subtle, a real improvement over the silvery gunk she usually slathered on. Evidently Liza *was* trying to make her feel better. A good plan since Marcy roamed school today looking like a victim in a horror flick.

Rennie suffered a pang of guilt. Why hadn't she thought to help her niece?

"I wear makeup," she said, wondering if Marcy would've turned down an offer of a makeup lesson. "Look. Mascara. I use eyeliner, too."

Nick leaned in to inspect. "Not enough. Ask my wife to help you out."

She considered smacking him but her attention strayed to Emma, leaping off the swing. The child miscalculated the landing and tumbled across the grass. She rolled to a stop with a startled expression. Sobs burst from her throat.

Rennie dashed across the yard. "Are you all right?" She reached out, the urge to help bringing on Emma's waterworks full blast. "Hey, it's okay. Let's go inside and eat dinner. You'll feel better."

The suggestion died beneath the child's howling sobs. Walt got off his swing and sauntered over. His blank expression sent a chill down Rennie's spine. He appeared unaffected by his sister's suffering.

"Stop crying," he said, his voice low and strangely adult. "You know the rule."

"She can cry if she wants to." Rennie yearned to bundle Emma into her arms. "There's nothing wrong with tears. Children cry when they're hurt. Adults do, too."

"I don't."

"Ever?"

His expression hardened so quickly the air froze in her lungs. He dropped down beside her with a jackal's speed. "*No crying.* It's the rule."

Rennie was accosted by an image of Buck Korchek towering

over his son with the threat of the devil in his eyes. *No crying.* She'd never seen so much as a photograph of the man, but she glimpsed his shadow in Walt's face. What cruelty had Walt endured? What punishments had he suffered?

Unexpectedly, Emma's bawling cut off. Her watery gaze lifted to the house. The screen door slammed shut. Liza hurried over.

Disbelief flooded Rennie as Emma stumbled to her feet. With an awkward gait, the child staggered into Liza's arms. The similarity in their coloring was striking, the rich brown hair and golden skin. Longing gripped Rennie's heart—they looked like they belonged together.

Emma's mother had been black. Jobs & Family Service's report on the Korchek family gave few specifics about her life. La Vonda had married Buck at the tender age of seventeen. Imagining her loving such a cruel man was difficult. It probably hadn't been love, Rennie mused. From what she'd gathered in the report, La Vonda had been uneducated and poor. Perhaps marriage was a desperate solution to a life of poverty. Some women were attracted to older men and the financial stability they mistook for an easier life. Rennie feared that before La Vonda died, she'd learned that life with a man like Buck was anything but stable.

A sudden kinship with the woman surged through Rennie. She was sheltering La Vonda's children.

The implications struck hard as she came to a standstill midway across the grass. Liza molded Emma's legs around her hips as if she were a strong tree and Emma was the vine. The child lowered her head to Liza's shoulder. Contentment softened her lips. She closed her eyes, the tears forgotten.

There was an instinct to mothering, a mysterious code as unintelligible as a foreign dialect. Rennie doubted she possessed such gifts. Her sister-in-law murmured softly to the child cradled in her arms and Rennie felt the deficiency so strongly, her heart emptied. She tried to swallow down the lump in her throat.

"Dinner's ready," Liza said. They went into the kitchen with Walt following behind. "I can't say I cleaned up the entire mess in your house but I gave it the old college try."

Something bubbled on the stove, filling the air with the

savory aroma of garlic. "Most of what you and Anna sent over landed on the walls," Rennie said.

"I noticed."

"What is this?" Rennie lifted the pot's lid. "Stew?"

"Made with a tomato base." Liza settled Emma into a chair at the table. "What vegetables do you eat, sweetie?"

"Do you have carrots?" Emma rubbed her nose. "Walt likes them."

"Coming right up."

Rennie found a bag of carrots in the refrigerator. She handed them over.

Liza frowned. "For heaven's sake, how old are these?"

Rennie shrugged. "I'm not sure."

Her sister-in-law bent a carrot in half. "In future, buy fresh produce every few days." She dropped the carrots into a bowl. "In a pinch you can firm up most vegetables by soaking them in water. Don't try this with fruits. It won't work."

Frilly. Rennie stepped aside as Liza poured milk and set the table with single-minded efficiency. She felt inadequate by comparison—clearly, Liza did the mothering bit as well as the lawyer gig. Nick and Marcy came in and sat at the table.

Marcy tossed her book bag under her chair. The scent of spoilt milk was gone from the fabric. Had Liza run the bag through the wash?

"I hope you're going to bed early," Marcy said to Emma. "You don't look perky. It's a good thing."

Emma yawned. "I'm sleepy."

Liza set a bowl of stew and a plate of carrot sticks before her. "You'll take a bath before we tuck you in."

Emma gazed at her with wide-eyed wonder. "Okay."

Was it wrong to feel pain—to feel jealousy, actually—over the child's affection for Liza? In less than twenty minutes they'd formed a tight bond.

By the stove Rennie cornered her sister-in-law. "How do you *do* that? I can't get either of them to obey me."

Dropping her voice to a whisper, Liza thrust a bowl of stew into her hands. "You make everything difficult. They'd listen if you gave the slightest indication you like them. You're angry Lianna forced you into this. Don't take it out on Emma and Walt."

"I'm not angry."

"Nonsense. The kids see it. They've been through hell, by the way. I'm disappointed in you."

Rennie lowered her eyes. Having her less-than-admirable behavior spelled out was as enjoyable as walking through fire. She returned to the table cradling soup and her tattered emotions.

"Here you go, Walt," she said with enough sugar to give him cavities. The bowl was barely placed before him when he slipped out of his chair. "Hey! Where are you going?"

He disappeared into the living room. At the stove, Liza shrugged.

Nick scooted Emma's glass of milk beneath her nose. "You like milk, don't you?"

She rubbed her eyes. "Yep."

Marcy flung her elbows onto the table. "Are we saying grace, or what?"

They'd just started into prayer when Walt returned with something cupped in his hands. He made a beeline toward Marcy. She pushed her chair from the table—evidently to bolt if there was something alive, and squirming, in his grasp.

A handful of curls floated into her lap.

"I shouldn't have taken them." He toed the floor. "You can have them back."

"Thanks." Marcy patted the Perini Electric cap on her head. "I think I'll keep this on for the time being. I don't have any glue with me."

He considered this. "Want me to find some?"

"Naw. I've been here before. Déjà vu all over again." When he looked at her with confusion, she added, "In sixth grade the whole class got lice. I freaked because my mom cut my hair short. I looked like a Marine."

Walt tried to make sense of the explanation. The sweet confusion on his face squeezed Rennie's heart. "Did it hurt?" he asked.

Marcy sighed. "The boys in class laughed at me. I thought I'd die."

"How come you didn't?"

She flicked his nose. "Someone upstairs was looking out for

me."

Walt stared at the ceiling. "There's an attic?" He turned to Rennie. "Can I play up there?"

She patted his chair. "Sit down, please. Eat your stew."

Plopping down, he dug in. They ate in companionable silence. After dinner the children bathed without incident. No protest, no crying—they padded to their bedrooms without complaint. Together, Rennie and Liza tucked them in.

The women returned to the kitchen to find Nick drying the last pot. He announced he was heading out. Liza promised to follow soon.

Marcy yawned. "I'll finish my homework in your bedroom," she said to Rennie as Liza pulled a bottle of Chablis from the refrigerator.

Rennie gave her a quick hug. "Sure thing."

"Will you need me tomorrow night?"

"No, I'll be okay."

"You're sure?"

"Positive." Rennie took the glass of wine Liza offered. "Go on, Marcy. You've been a real help."

After the girl trudged off, Rennie followed her sister-in-law into the backyard. They sat in wicker chairs listening to the crickets bringing in the night. On the opposite side of the hedge, Denny Farnsworth was soaping up his parents' Buick in a springtime ritual. The moon rose, painting splashes of silver on the daffodils bordering the patio. Sipping their wine, the women sank into silence.

After long minutes, Liza said, "Working full-time and handling kids is possible. The trick is staying organized."

"Think I'm in this for the long haul?"

"Your mother and her team at Social Services may not see improvement in Buck Korchek's behavior for several months, if at all. Lianna will try but her efforts may come to naught. He was beating the kids, Rennie. They won't admit to the abuse but I've seen the medical report. Job & Family Services may find it necessary to terminate his parental rights."

The explanation was upsetting. "What will happen to Walt and Emma?"

"They'll remain in foster care. Finding an adoptive home for a sibling group takes time, sometimes years. Sadly, most prospective parents choose to adopt an infant."

She drew a startled breath. "I'll have them for several years?"

Liza smiled. "No one expects you to go the distance. You'll have them for a few months, tops. Eventually the kids will be placed in a foster home better suited for long-term care."

"Meaning Walt and Emma might live in a lot of homes before they find something permanent?"

When Liza remained silent, Rennie took a long sip from her glass. Her worried gaze roamed the shadows pooling on the lawn.

"Liza, I don't want them shuffled from place to place." A new school and new foster parents every few months, the loss of any real permanency—how would they survive? "There must be a better solution."

"This isn't merely a problem of locating an adoptive home. Your mother's team has to find parents willing and able to take in *two* troubled kids."

"Yeah, but they're great kids. Wonderful kids. Have you seen Emma's drawings?"

Liza swirled the wine in her glass. "Your mother mentioned her artistic streak."

"Hell, she's got real talent. And she's got a thing about hair— you should see the hairstyles she does for her Barbie doll. And Walt? Sure, he's mischievous. But he's a great athlete. He's got a star athlete's pitching arm."

Liza grinned. "Sounds like you're starting to like them."

"Of course I like them. Who said I didn't?"

The idea, crazy and bold, took shape. Provide a foster home for the long haul? She'd have to make real changes to her lifestyle and find time for children's activities, doctor visits and the rest. Doing a stellar job was out of the question—she wasn't anyone's notion of a great parent. Not that a lack of skill was the only problem. This morning she'd arrived late for work, the second day in a row. If she lost the Fagan contract, what would become of Walt and Emma? She couldn't provide for them from the unemployment line.

"I almost lost my job today," she said. "Troy was furious

because I was late again. But there's more to it." She brought the glass to her lips, swallowed quickly. "We have a history. It's never been a problem."

"Until now?"

Rennie closed her eyes—a mistake. An image of Troy's late brother, Jason, spilled through her mind. "It's the mansion," she remarked suddenly. "In high school I was close to Troy's younger brother. I hadn't been to the mansion since Jason's death. I don't know . . . maybe Troy feels it, too. All those memories. Working together has stirred everything up." She tried to smile. It hurt too much and besides, she felt like crying. "Forget it. Ancient history. I'm too exhausted to go digging."

Liza's eyes grew dark with concern. Knitting her fingers together, she said, "I now invoke the attorney-client privilege. Your secrets are safe." She patted Rennie's knee. "Now, why don't you tell me everything?"

Chapter 8

Darkness crept across the patio, stealing the last color from the daffodils. Liza smiled with encouragement.

Taking a deep breath, Rennie plunged in. "You aren't from Liberty so you don't know much about the Fagans. They've always been influential."

"I can understand why. They employ several hundred people."

"It's hard to find a family in Liberty without a tie to the company." People referred to the Fagans as the Heinz family of Ohio. Successful across the Midwest, it was only a matter of time before they took Fagan's Orchard national. "Once the new processing plant is built, they'll hire more people. Even Liberty's mayor worked at the orchard when she was young."

"From what Nick tells me, your grandmother did too. She found work as a cook in the mansion a few weeks after she emigrated from Italy." Liza lifted her shoulders in a careless shrug. "So the Fagans have influence. So what?"

How to make someone as self-assured as Liza understand? Rennie didn't have much in the way of self-confidence. She hid the lack behind cocky language and posture masculine enough to allow her to hold her own in a roomful of men. But the bravado was a ruse.

"I'm not just talking about their wealth." She came to her feet. "If you cross a Fagan, you regret it."

"And you crossed Troy?"

"When we were kids. In retrospect, our feud seems ridiculous. I was pitching on the fifth grade team and my curveball went wide."

"You didn't hit him on purpose, did you?"

"No—purely by accident." She'd been terrified of Troy. By eighth grade he'd reached six feet in height and possessed a man's hard, handsome features. "Not that Troy was convinced. He thought some bratty kid had aimed for him. The curveball started our feud."

"And you became the enemy of an older and influential kid." Liza set her wineglass on the cement and rose. She hugged Rennie. "How difficult for you."

Rennie blew out a stream of air. "He hounded me year after year. Making cracks if I ran into him in the school cafeteria, shouting taunts on the ball field. Finally I got sick of running away. I learned how to retaliate by embarrassing him right back."

Now, from an adult's perspective, she wondered if they'd both felt disenfranchised. She'd struggled with academics while Troy had cloaked himself with sullen indifference. Even surrounded by his boisterous friends, he gave off an air of isolation and discontent. The wealthy Fagans could've sent their children to Avery Richards Academy or Good Shepherd Catholic. People assumed they chose public school to instill a down-to-earth attitude in their privileged children. The strategy worked for Jason and later, Dianne. Troy never fit in.

She withdrew from her thoughts as Liza said, "How did you resolve your differences?"

"We didn't." She smiled with false cheer. "We would've killed each other if not for his younger brother, Jason." Rennie swiped her hand across her eyes. My God, she wasn't going to cry, was she? "Jason was a year older than me—good looking, if you like redheads. Whenever Troy cornered me in school or on the ball field, Jason miraculously appeared. By the time Troy left for college, Jason and I were midway through high school. We'd become close."

Dredging up the memories was excruciating. She'd tried to bury them with the first shovelful of dirt hurtled onto Jason's casket. At the back of the crowd at All Souls cemetery, she'd been blinded by tears and wrapped in dread. The other mourners murmured and sobbed in small groups. They were unaware the girl in their midst was to blame for the death of a young prince, a wealthy Fagan.

Afterward the guilt shut down her heart. She simply went on, a faded version of the girl she'd been. Work became an obsession. Even today, if she ran into friends from high school, she listened with silent remorse as they reminisced. It hurt too much to discuss Jason.

Adrift in her awful thoughts, Rennie studied the night sky. Stars glittered in the heavens. They were airy, light. By comparison she felt heavy, held fast by the gravity of a thousand regrets.

Absently she traced the starburst scar that spiraled from her wrist to her knuckles. "I never told anyone *why* I got this."

Liza tipped her head to the side. "In high school, right? I recall Nick mentioning the scar."

She nodded. "Jason and I took an electronics class together. He wanted to dodge the pre-Calc class needed for college. I went along for the ride."

Liza traced the scar's starburst pattern. "And this?"

She forced herself on. "I'd hidden Troy's photo in my shirt pocket," she confided. "It fell out as Jason was connecting a circuit. I grabbed for the photo and crossed the wires. The burn hurt like hell." At Liza's questioning look, she added, "If you're looking for logic, give up. There isn't any. Yes, Troy and I were enemies. In high school, something changed between us. By then I was spending a lot of time at the mansion. I'd catch Troy chatting with his mother or caring for Dianne. On home turf he was different. Kind. Almost sweet. Sometimes . . ."

Liza's brows lifted, prodding her on.

Heat rose in Rennie's cheeks. "If I bumped into Troy when he was home, on his own turf, he'd look at me like I was the sun. Like I was . . ." Her voice trailed off in confusion.

Her sister-in-law chuckled softly. "Ah. I see. You weren't the only one with a crush."

Adrift, Rennie wandered to the edge of the patio. "He left for college and I didn't see him again until Jason's grad party. There was a band set up in the orchard and hundreds of kids—the works. Most of us were throwing back shots. Mr. and Mrs. Fagan didn't have a clue how much booze we sneaked in. Then Jason and I began arguing. I don't know why he was so upset."

If you know a secret that will destroy someone's life should you reveal it?

Posing the question, he'd topped off her glass with Seagram's. Above them, the apple trees were strung with lights. Music pounded through the orchard and their friends danced like frenzied dervishes. Rennie wasn't drunk but she felt woozy, free. She'd replied, *"Yes, Jason. You should always be honest."*

The comment made him agitated. They'd argued—

"Around midnight I took off across the orchard and headed for high ground," she told Liza. "I headed for the Great Oak. I was hurt and angry—I wanted to get away from Jason before the argument ruined our friendship."

"You were wandering around drunk?" Liza returned to her seat with a look of faint disapproval. "The Fagan property is hundreds of acres. You might've been lost until sunup."

"I was boozy, sure. It would've been easier to forgive myself if I had been drunk." The memory was an agony. At last she added, "I found Troy at the Great Oak, looking down over the acres like the king of the mountain. He was drinking Jack Daniels in a typically pissed-off mood. You could hear the music and see the lights strung across the orchard below. The place looked like Christmas except it was July and hot as hell. I think Troy was up there stewing because he was jealous of Jason's big night."

"Not uncommon, sibling rivalry being what it is." Liza folded her arms. "So you found Troy alone at a tree."

"A very special tree." Liza hadn't grown up on town lore. She couldn't possibly understand. "The Great Oak is hundreds of years old. People think it's magic."

"Oh! *That* tree. Nick's mentioned something about people getting engaged there."

"They've been doing so since the 1840s."

"He also said a number of townspeople have become pregnant beneath the tree." Liza arched a brow. "I thought he was joking."

"He wasn't. People believe the Great Oak is a shelter for love—not that Troy or I were capable of understanding. We began flinging insults, like we'd done when we were kids. I got cocky and leaned off the precipice, as if I'd hurl myself down into the Chagrin River rather than listen to him toss another insult my way. Troy pulled me back. I thought he'd push me away once he knew I was safe. But he didn't." Her heart became a dull ache in her chest. "He kissed me."

The memories disgorged like a logjam breaking free in angry waters. The remarkable heat of Troy's mouth. The sharp taste of whiskey on his lips. The arousal turning his blue eyes to jet. In the slice of a second, he transmuted anger into passion. She cried out as he pulled her tight against his hips, his erection pulsating against her belly. Desire surged through her blood, an unwanted opiate. She opened her mouth beneath his and drank him in like a poison she was eager to ingest.

With wild, reckless passion Troy took her beneath the leafy refuge of the Great Oak and drove himself deep into her emotions, carrying her into womanhood before she was ready.

"What we did . . . we didn't make love." She never should've let him kiss her. She should've stopped him before they went too far. "We were like a couple of animals tearing off each other's clothes—we didn't make love. He hated me. A few weeks later I told Jason."

"Oh, sweetie. Was that wise?"

Shame coursed through her but she'd begun to unburden herself. She'd finish. "I didn't stop to consider what my confession would do to Jason. I wanted to believe that if I hadn't argued with him, I never would've run into his older brother. Maybe I wanted Jason to feel as bad as I did."

"You were a girl in a confusing situation."

Snatching up her glass, Rennie downed the last of the wine. "I was a coward." She began to cry. The tears made her angry.

"Let it go," Liza whispered. "This *is* ancient history. Don't let the past tear you up."

Her compassion sent a groundswell of emotion through Rennie's heart. She couldn't let it go, not when some mistakes marked a life. Some mistakes were unforgivable.

"I never should've told Jason." She swiped her hand across her runny nose, adding, "We were standing in my driveway and I simply blurted it out. He went dead white. Then he said he needed to get drunk or he'd find Troy and bloody his face." Her voice broke but she struggled on. "The next morning I learned Jason had been murdered in Cleveland, a block from the bar where he'd been drinking. He walked into a convenience store during a robbery."

Speechless, Liza stared at her. She drained her glass.

"One night with Troy destroyed his brother—destroyed my best friend." She was raw with grief. "Since then, Troy and I have done everything in our power to avoid each other. We've never discussed our night together or Jason's death."

"Oh, honey." Liza steered her back into the chair. "Working together at the mansion will be difficult."

Taking the job *was* a reckless decision. Her desire to win the industrial contract had blinded her to the difficulties of working with Troy. "I dread the day we break through from the new wing to the mansion," she admitted. "The Fagans keep Jason's bedroom like a shrine. Everything exactly as it was on the day he died. I've heard the maids don't even like to go inside, it upsets them as much as the Fagans. So his bedroom has become this holy, unwelcome space but we'll tear the room down. We'll tear down the last tangible evidence of his life, as if he never lived."

In gloomy silence, they sat watching the night. They'd just decided to go in when the patio lights blinked on. Lianna stepped outside. Though her beige blazer and black skirt were spotless, she looked exhausted.

Rennie lifted the wine bottle. "We'll fetch another glass." She sent her mother a half-hearted smile. "Looks like you need one."

Surveying the cozy scene, Lianna sensed something amiss. Rennie's eyes were puffy. Had she been crying?

"I would like a glass of wine." She regarded her daughter as Liza went to fetch a wineglass. "I never thought I'd escape the office. I hope your father found something in the fridge. I'd promised to make clam linguine."

"Dad will survive." Rennie eyed her closely. "What held you up at work?"

"Everything. The home study I swore I'd finish. The meeting with several social workers." Liza returned and Lianna took the offered wine. "A teenager in foster care—he's become aggressive.

I may have to place him in an institutional setting."

Rennie slouched low in her chair. "I hate the way the system works. Amazing you don't have an ulcer."

"Like you, I'm working on one."

"Take comfort in what you've done for Walt and Emma," Rennie said, the sincerity in her voice a surprise. "Thanks to Liza and Nick, we had an easier night."

Motioning into the dark, Liza offered, "My valiant husband built a swing set. The children were delighted."

Lianna peered through the shadows then gave up on glimpsing her son's handiwork. "You're settling into a routine with Walt and Emma?" she asked Rennie.

Her daughter pulled her lush hair from the constraining rubber band. "I think so." She ran her fingers through the glossy curls tumbling across her shoulders. "We'll see if they sneak out of bed tonight. Let's hope they don't."

"You're expecting late night prowling?"

"Hopefully not. Those two cowboys are tuckered out."

"They need a proper schedule, something I doubt they received with their father." Lianna hesitated, unsure of how to proceed. Steeling herself, she added, "Honey, I met with Buck today. I haven't told you all the specifics of the case. It's been a hectic week."

Rennie stopped playing with her hair. "What did you forget?"

"Buck isn't privy to the name of the foster family."

"He doesn't know I'm watching his kids?" Rennie crossed her arms, her combative pose oddly reassuring. "Should I care?"

Liza waved a hand, silencing her. Naturally Liza, a family law attorney, understood the ramifications. "Lianna, did Mr. Korchek voluntarily release his children to Job & Family Services?" she asked.

"We received custody after his OVI citation. The children were in the back seat when Buck was pulled over."

Liza shook her head with disgust. "He was driving drunk with his kids in the car?"

"That wasn't the worst of it. Once we examined Walt and Emma, it was clear they'd suffered abuse."

Rennie leaned forward. "So the drunk driving citation

allowed you to get the kids away from him?"

"Only while he's in therapy."

Liza asked, "What about the elementary school?"

Rennie frowned. "What about the school?"

Lianna chose her words with exquisite care. "Buck doesn't know which school his children attend," she said, hoping the disclosure wouldn't frighten her daughter. "He's resisting therapy and he's angry. For now, he'll visit the children under the social worker's supervision at Job & Family Services."

"You're doing this to ensure Walt and Emma's safety?" Rennie asked, clearly alarmed. "In case he . . . I don't know, tries to grab them?"

"I'm sorry to report such problems have occurred with other abusive fathers. The school is also sadly familiar with cases like this one. Even if Buck were to locate the school, they wouldn't reveal your name or address."

"I don't care if they do." Rennie's temper came gloriously to the fore. "If he hassles me, I'll show him a few kickboxing moves."

Liza grinned. "The tomboy lives." She held up her glass. "I've had too much. Should I make coffee?"

"Don't bother on my account," Lianna said. "It's time I went home."

She came to her feet with a feeling of reassurance. Her daughter was a strong woman. Rennie would keep the children safe. There was nothing to fear.

Rennie followed her around the side of the house, her movements amusingly fluid. "You didn't drink your wine!"

"And you don't need another sip. Tell Liza to go home. You're both tired."

Opening the driver's side door of her car, Lianna paused to appreciate the balmy night air. The moon was out, fat and golden. The street rested in a tranquil quiet.

An engine's roar broke the silence. Headlights sliced across the lawn. Startled, she spun around. A truck hurtled toward the streetlamp's pool of light. The blurred image of a man's chiseled features, the scowl on his lips and the thick hair thrown across his forehead—

Panic spilled through her. *Buck*.

Every fear she'd suppressed broke loose. He'd found the

foster home—her daughter's home. His children were in danger.

Her child was in danger.

Fumbling with her purse, she searched for her cell phone to alert the police.

She'd just gained purchase on the smartphone when the truck sped into the streetlamp's harsh glare. Lianna blinked. The man at the wheel wasn't Buck.

Rennie shoved past. "What the hell." She stormed into the street, and the truck's greyish exhaust. "Why is Troy driving by my house?"

Chapter 9

Spotting Rennie in the rearview mirror, Troy muttered a curse. Her long hair caught the turbulence from his truck and fanned out, curling like dark ribbons around her shoulders. She planted her hands on her hips with unmistakable irritation.

He muffled a second curse. She'd seen him all right.

The decision to take South Street out of town wasn't deliberate. Not that it mattered now. The way she'd stalked into the street certainly indicated displeasure, as if he were a stalker driving by for a glimpse of her home. For a glimpse of her.

Streets shrouded in grey flashed by. The road widened, the acreage between houses increasing. Rolling down the window, Troy reached the countryside with the freshly tilled farmlands readied for spring planting and the scent of damp earth spiking the air. The surroundings barely registered as he tried to calm his breathing. Too much liquor at Bongo's, too strange a night.

For reasons beyond comprehension, seeing Rennie made the competition with the darts more disturbing.

The man at Bongo's had made the shot with a flair Troy assumed was his singular gift. A second Southpaw executing a blind throw, a second man with dead accurate aim—the odds were beyond belief. The silence that descended on the tavern was a curtain dropped, obliterating the world Troy knew. The intimidating way he towered over his family, the discomfort he nursed working in manual labor despite the options available to a privileged Fagan—he nearly relished the self-imposed isolation of his chosen life. And he prided himself on his uncommon dexterity, the razor-sharp precision of his eyesight and his aim.

But he wasn't alone. Another man shared his gifts.

The tavern's silence had given way to a roar of giddy disbelief. In the deafening chorus, he felt jealousy surge through him. Fear galloped on its heels. There'd always been something wolflike in his temperament, an instinct he wasn't proud of yet trusted. Immediately Troy sensed the danger ushered into his world. The hard intelligence in the man's eyes was uncomfortably familiar. As was the fierce musculature girdling his shoulders and the cold precision of his movements.

They were predators from the same pack.

Soon after Troy handed over his winnings and left the tavern. It wasn't until he'd pulled out of the parking lot that he made the connection: the man worked on the masons' crew. This morning he'd sauntered past Troy with the stink of tobacco on his clothes and a canvas bag of tools under his arm. Tomorrow would he brag to the other trades about besting the boss at darts? Troy didn't give a damn. Losing didn't bother him.

What bothered him was something darker. The man's appearance in his life was a warning Troy couldn't decipher.

Up ahead, County Road rose from the night in a dusty ribbon of gravel. A mile off, the orchard's boundless acres rose from the evening mist. The factory's security lights washed the acres a bluish white. Higher up, the mansion stood ablaze.

On a frown, he idled the engine. Dust curled around the truck like snakes. Why was his family still awake?

He considered bunking at the apartment in Liberty, rarely visited since beginning construction at the mansion. Gunning the engine, he steered onto the road leading into the estate. There was no sense delaying the inevitable.

Branches smacked the truck's windshield, sending a shower of apple blossoms across the hood. Their beauty went unappreciated as he worked out what to say. His mother never handled any conversation well that mentioned Jason.

At the mansion, conversation drifted into the foyer. Tossing down his keys, Troy strode into the living room. A crystal bowl of shrimp swam in ice on an end table. In the chaise lounge his mother Jackie appeared a bit sleepy. On the tapestry couch, his very pregnant sister and his father chatted in animated voices. Their heads bobbed in time with their conversation.

"Troy!" Dianne eased her distended body from the couch and met him midway across the carpet. "You'll never guess what Simon Allenden did for my husband. They were wrapping up a meeting and Frank—you know how confident he is—he told Simon he hoped it wouldn't create problems if Blue Organic carries our brands."

"We don't sell to Blue Organic. They compete with Allenden's. They're off-limits."

"Not anymore." Dianne rubbed her blossoming stomach. "Your daddy has *chutzpah*, little girl," she said to her belly. "He'll do anything to win another account."

Troy arched a brow. "Girl?"

She grinned. "Or boy. I haven't peeked at the ultrasounds. But the baby feels like a girl." She patted her tummy. "You *are* a girl, aren't you?"

Troy steered her to the couch. He regarded his father. "She's babbling."

His father rested his hands on his paunch, which would soon hold its own against Dianne's pregnancy if he didn't cut out the toffee he favored. "The last months of pregnancy," Dennis remarked, his green eyes sparkling. "Your sister is worse at the plant. Babbling all the time."

She tweaked his upturned nose, which was a carbon copy of her own. "I'm not ditzy. I'm happy." To Troy, she said, "My brilliant husband landed the Blue Organic account. Can you believe it?"

"Not really." Troy stifled his peevish tone. "Sorry, sis. Ignore me."

"You're always in a bad mood. I don't mind." She shifted on the couch, her pink dress drawing taut across her bulging midsection. "As for Frank, he mentioned the Blue Organic chain to Simon. And guess what? Simon's wife does charity work with the Osteens."

"The Osteens?"

"They own Blue Organic. Frank was worried about losing the Allenden account if we sold to a competitor. But Simon's wife has made them all friends. The deal is locked up."

A maid tiptoed in and handed Troy a glass of iced water. After she left, he said, "Might be time to give Frank another raise."

"Oh definitely." Dianne winked at their mother. "We have our new home to decorate. Our own wing in this lovely mansion. We'll need money."

Jackie popped a shrimp into her mouth. "You have more money than Midas. Decorate whenever you like."

Dianne began chattering about her plans for the décor. Troy sank into silence. He'd never shared his family's animated personalities or their penchant for spending money. For people grown rich on the fruits of the land they were more apt to vacation in Paris or Milan. They'd jet off with their countless bags of luggage and he'd rent a cabin in upstate New York where the isolation mirrored the loneliness in his soul.

Halting in midstream, Dianne patted his cheek as if he were an ill-tempered mutt she'd come to enjoy. "Swear that my new home isn't the source of your bad mood. Did the plumbing fixtures arrive? The marble sconces?"

"Ease off, will you?" Pregnancy, he mused, kept a woman at full throttle.

She stared at him with maddening curiosity. Then she mouthed the despised words, *How is she?*

Rennie.

Refusing to fall for the bait, he stretched out his legs. Carefully he appraised his mother, twirling a honey-red curl nestled by her ear. Petite like Dianne and slightly rounded with age, she appeared relaxed on the chaise lounge, serene. A state of affairs he dreaded altering.

He closed his eyes long enough to steady himself. "My crews are nearing break-through. The bedrooms in the south wing have to be cleared." The announcement urged his mother from her reclined position. "Ask your staff to pack away the antiques next week."

"You're breaking through to the mansion?" Jackie's hand fluttered across her heart. "So quickly?"

"Mother, you knew this was coming. The construction schedule is tight."

Her expression remained placid as she ran nervous fingers

across her cheek. Despite the late hour, her lips were polished and her eyes made up. The care she took with her appearance lured him back to the memory of a happy childhood. He'd been fascinated by the scents of bergamot and ylang-ylang kept in jewel-toned bottles in her master bath. The tube of lipstick she produced was a particular fascination. Spreading on the color, she chuckled softly at his mimicry as he puckered his lips. The mirror blended their images. He'd savored the moments when she'd let him hold the gold tube, the color as rich as her smile.

Troy loved his sister and his father. He adored his mother. In a family known for light, she never questioned his dark nature. And because they remained close, he sensed rather than glimpsed her distress at the prospect of packing up Jason's bedroom.

Her voice, when she spoke, was whisper-thin. "I thought we'd leave the packing until May."

"It's time."

Oblivious to the grief bearing down on them, Dianne said, "We should get started with the antiques and the Waterford. There are six bedrooms in the south wing. It is a big job. A dreadful amount of work."

"I can't involve the maids." Though the room was stifling hot, Jackie rubbed her arms with fierce little strokes. "All those valuables? I can't leave the chore to the help. I'll do it myself."

"What? Am I incapable of handling crystal?" Dianne said, eager to keep the crews on schedule. "I'll be on extended leave soon and bored out of my mind."

"You can't help, pumpkin."

"You don't trust me with the crystal?"

"I *do* trust you but you're so pregnant, you're about to pop. Perhaps Bitsy will lend a hand. She's older, careful—I'll speak with her tomorrow."

Dennis sent his wife a worried glance. "Who'll cook if Bitsy packs?"

"Good heavens, dear. We can eat out."

Dianne sighed heavily. "Pregnancy is not a handicap. Why can't I pitch in?"

"You're not helping your mother." Dennis palmed the blazing hair receding from his forehead. "If Frank were here, he'd back me up."

"This is ridiculous! I'm having a perfectly normal pregnancy. I'm happy to pack the Waterford."

"Not while I'm head of the household, you won't."

"Daddy, we can all agree Bitsy is the head of the household. We're lucky she puts up with us. She's not even Irish."

Jackie swung her legs over the side of the chaise lounge. She began pacing before the fireplace. Dianne and his father, engaged in a cheery squabble, didn't see the tightening of skin between her eyes. Her shoulders lifted to her ears, as if the sky rained shards of glass and she stood beneath the peril.

Rising swiftly, Troy took her by the wrist. "I'll help." She barely reached midway up his chest and the familiar worry dogged him: he'd been a strapping baby, nearly twelve pounds. How had such a delicate woman brought him into the world? "Pick the times when we'll work. I'll rearrange my schedule," he added, and the tenderness warming his heart carried into his words, gentling them.

She hesitated and his attention glided to her feet. They were encased in stylish sandals, strings of gold.

She tottered on the thin heels. "I can't impose. You have the addition to build."

"My crews will manage." He took her arm to steady her. "You can't do this alone."

"I've scheduled movers for the second week of May. I'll ask them to send over a few men early to crate the valuables."

"You'll let the movers pack your antiques?" More than a few were museum quality. "Be reasonable."

Gently she placed her palm flat on his chest, startling him. She made a slow circle around his heart as if her touch had the power to repair the broken mass. "You can't stand this either, dear," she whispered, her eyes dull with a private agony. "I can't bear to see you upset."

"I won't be."

The lie came easily. It lifted his mother's gaze. He cursed the fear blooming on her face, which went undetected by Dianne and his father. They didn't see the ghost she'd glimpsed or how frightened she was of setting foot in Jason's bedroom.

Her hand fell to her side. "It would be a terrible hardship.

You were so close to your brother."

Without thinking, he drew back the curtain on her grief. "One foot in front of the other," he said.

Tears pricked her eyes. "One step," she agreed.

She returned to her seat. Troy knew he'd won.

We mustn't cry forever.

After Jason's funeral, she'd whispered the words to buoy his spirits. Troy had stood in the foyer with Dianne pressed to his hip as his father stepped outside to escort the last guests to their cars. His mother shut the door. And Dianne, too young to comprehend the break in their lives or that Jason was gone forever—she pulled at the hem of her lacy dress because she wanted to change into play clothes. His throat bleached, Troy swallowed down tears. His mother retreated from the door with the finality of a woman walking through ashes. She'd been as ravaged as he when she'd said, *we mustn't cry forever. Always walk forward, Troy. Never look back.*

No matter how many years passed, the words remained nested in his heart. *Always walk forward.* He wanted to believe he'd built a new life despite the wreckage of Jason's murder.

In the following days as the pace of construction accelerated he began to wonder if, in fact, he remained shackled to the past. Working with the carpenters to frame in a room, he'd stop abruptly to nurse his doubts. After the crews left for the day, he'd emerge from the turbid depths of his thoughts to find himself alone with the sawdust drifting down and the silence crashing around him. Assessing his life was torture. He'd never married. Work anchored his days. At thirty-five, the path to middle age was clear. He'd achieved success yet carried the same self-doubts he'd always known, even before Jason's murder.

He refused to examine the emotion burdening him whenever he invited Rennie into his thoughts. He avoided recalling the night long ago when he'd bedded her beneath the Great Oak. He didn't dare. It was less painful—though more troubling—to ponder instead the night at Bongo's and the mason's eerie performance with the darts.

During the following week the man was absent from the site. His departure was a relief. The masons weren't scheduled to return until May to brick in the fireplace and lay the slate for the patio. As the carpenters toiled with finish work, Troy prepared the site for break-through.

Day by day, he rarely glimpsed Rennie. His threat to fire her was a galvanizing force. She cut the electrical in every section of the south wall and rewired the mansion at record speed. If Crash and the carpenters roughed in a room ahead of schedule, she followed within hours with bundles of wiring slung over her shoulder and her lumbering assistant tight on her heels. Troy came to admire her finesse.

On a Monday near the end of April, Troy drove down to the factory. After twenty minutes of cajoling, he secured a promise from his mother to begin packing the bedrooms in the south wing the following morning. It would be just the two of them.

Returning to the mansion, he allowed his heart to carry him away from the construction site and up the front steps of the grand house. He wavered in the foyer. The low hum of a vacuum cleaner barely nicked the silence. Before his nerve might vanish he ascended the wide staircase and strode into the south wing.

The darkened hallway was thickly carpeted. From the new wing, the muffled thump of hammers vibrated up the walls. Above, the row of chandeliers swayed. Squinting, he padded his fingers across the wall in search of the light switch. Before he located it, he glimpsed movement in the shadows.

Far down the hall, Rennie crept from a bedroom. She couldn't see him in the dim light. He meant to approach to ask for an update on her progress with the fuse boxes. The finality with which she closed the door rooted him to the spot.

She placed her palms flat against the wood. Slowly she made small circles on the walnut plank. The gesture carried the same affection as his mother's when she'd circled her palm on his chest in a fruitless attempt at healing. Was Rennie attempting a similar rescue? She couldn't save the girl she'd been, wild and careless. She couldn't erase the past. That she'd try to make peace was a heartrending display of stoicism.

The diminished light hid her face. Yet her whispered prayer drifted through the shadows. When she straightened to stare blankly at the door, a crushing agony filled Troy.

And he understood: she'd come to the south wing for the same reason as he, to say goodbye to Jason.

Chapter 10

Trapped in the dentist's waiting room, Rennie glued her nose to the brochure.

Walt slumped in his chair. "Nobody *ever* makes us go to the dentist," he said for the tenth time in as many minutes.

"This is just a checkup." Revealing Dr. Norris's decision to cap his chipped tooth and perform a thorough cleaning wasn't wise.

"This place smells funny."

"Walt, please. Would you stop talking?" She rubbed her temples in a vain attempt to make her headache retreat. No dice.

She returned to the brochure. Yesterday she'd shot digitals of the lighting throughout the mansion, gorgeous brass chandeliers of burnished gold and pewter sconces so beautiful they might have been forged centuries ago in Williamsburg. After transmitting the photographs to Home Lighting Emporium in New York City for an estimate on reproductions, she'd downloaded the company's brochure. Next week she'd give Dianne a detailed estimate. It was yet another way to impress the vivacious young woman she'd come to think of as a Keebler elf.

"I *hate* this," Walt said, upping the ante.

He swung his legs wildly. In the chair opposite, a slender woman sent a warning glance. The woman's daughter, a debutante in plaid, wrinkled her nose.

"Calm down," Rennie hissed. "Try to be like your sister." Who, she noticed, had crawled inside the playhouse in the corner of the waiting room. Catching Emma's gaze, she added, "Look. She's not frightened. Right, sweetie?"

Emma closed the playhouse's plastic shutters, sealing herself in.

Rennie got to her feet. "Fine. You're both scared."

She stalked past the debutante and tapped on the receptionist's window. The frosted glass slid open. Merideth Tyler, who'd worked at Liberty Dental since Rennie's childhood, smiled brightly.

Grateful for the familiar face, Rennie whispered, "Is there any way to hurry this up? My kids—I mean, my foster kids—they're nervous."

"Oh, heavens." Merideth waddled to the door separating them. "Why don't you come right in? I'll tell Dr. Norris it's an emergency."

Rennie scooted inside. "It's not an emergency. Not really." What was the protocol? Was she allowed to shout "fire" and the entire dental team would come running?

"Don't worry. Your mother called. She asked us to take good care of your kids."

"*Foster* kids."

"Of course." Merideth took her wrist with surprising force for a woman past sixty. "Lianna said it's doubtful your cherubs ever received dental care, the poor dears. Go and fetch them. I'll tell the doctor."

It took five minutes to pry Walt from his chair. Emma was hellishly worse. When she refused to vacate the playhouse, Rennie suffered the embarrassment of dragging her out by her ankles. The child's howling terror sent the debutante fleeing into the corner.

Flailing arms and legs, and Rennie's patience snapped. She flung Emma over her shoulder like a sack of old wiring and stumbled into the examination room.

"No! No! No!" Emma hollered. "Walt, save me! Pleeeease!"

Rennie planted her feet to stop from toppling over.

Walt charged. On a growl, he landed a punch on Rennie's hip.

She careened into the wall. Thankfully she made impact with her left hip, sparing Emma. At her waist, Walt landed a series of jabs with the ferocity of a gnat. The kid didn't have much in the way of strength but he was asking for it.

"Buster, sit down in that chair," she said through gritted teeth. "Go."

"No."

"Right now."

"I hate you." Walt sat.

In a fluid movement, she slid Emma from her shoulder and set her feet on terra firma. When she tried to bolt, Rennie scooped her back up. She'd managed to clamp Emma's arms beneath her own when Dr. Norris rushed in.

"Rennie, how are you?" Like Merideth, the chubby dentist was a fixture from childhood. "Ah, who do we have here?"

Emma stopped thrashing, her eyes wide. "I'm Emma," she whispered. "Don't hurt me."

"Heavens, child, I would never hurt you."

"*She* hurts me," Emma pinioned Rennie with a nasty look. "She's mean."

"I am not." For proof, Rennie brushed her mouth across Emma's cheek. Her skin was impossibly soft and reminiscent of apricots. Rennie's heart shifted. Lifting her head, she caught a dart of pleasure skimming through Emma's gaze.

They were stuck for a moment, staring. Dr. Norris cleared her throat.

Walt scrambled out of the examination chair. "I want to go home," he announced.

Rennie let Emma go. She stood back, astonished, as the child crawled onto the examination chair vacated by her brother and sat daintily with her hands folded in her lap. Dr. Norris, wasting no time, chatted her way through a quick survey of the child's mouth. The obstinate Walt was next. Mouth open, he glared at the dentist throughout the ordeal. A young male assistant came in. Dr. Norris asked Rennie to wait outside while they took X-rays.

When she'd finished she ushered Rennie into her cramped office.

From her jacket Rennie withdrew the lighting brochure and thumbed the pages. It wasn't a good crutch and her anxiety swelled. The concern on Dr. Norris's face didn't bode well.

"Emma has three cavities," she said. "All are in baby teeth. We'll let it go for now. If they present a problem later, we'll pull them."

"And Walt?"

"I'll cap his front tooth as planned." Dr. Norris hesitated. "His sinus infection is the bigger problem. I suspect he's had it for a long time. With so many cavities, it's doubtful he used a toothbrush much."

Worry for the boy surged through Rennie. She recalled the sinus infection she'd suffered while studying for her electrician's accreditation. The days had been a miserable blur of ice packs and headaches.

"How is Walt's appetite?" Dr. Norris asked, nudging her from her thoughts.

"Doesn't eat much. Seems to prefer applesauce and oatmeal."

"Soft foods."

"What?"

"He's in pain when he chews." Dr. Norris tapped her chin. "This can't wait. I've already asked Merideth to clear my afternoon schedule. After I cap his tooth I'll fill several of his cavities and pack the others with antibiotic swabs. We'll also get him started on an oral antibiotic." She turned to her keyboard and began typing. "Bring him back next Thursday for a check-up. Let's say one o'clock."

"I can't bring him in on a Thursday." If she walked off the site again Troy would fire her. She was certain. "How about next Saturday?"

"I need assurance the antibiotic is working. I'll see the boy on Thursday, dear."

"What about Thursday evening?"

"My schedule is booked. One o'clock it is." Dr. Norris finished typing. "Now, Merideth and I will need your help. My other assistant is busy with a cleaning."

Rennie followed her out. "What exactly should I do?"

The dentist's smile grew soft. "You'll help Merideth hold Walt still. I'll numb his gums but I can't risk putting him under. Not with all the infection."

The next forty minutes were sheer terror. Rennie spent

harrowing minutes with Walt pinned beneath her. Merideth held his legs. When he gave out an ear-splitting scream, Rennie murmured soothing nonsense into his ear. When he gave into raw, tortured crying, she rained kisses on his temple.

Dr. Norris worked at miraculous speed. Finishing up, she handed Rennie a box of tissues and left with Merideth padding close behind. Walt blinked slowly, woozy with pain.

Rennie helped him into a sitting position. "It's all right—I'm here," she assured him. From behind the gauze packed in his cheeks relief bloomed on his face. She yanked a tissue from the box to dab at the saliva dribbling from his mouth. The metallic scent in the air made her queasy but she ignored her unease. "What do you say? Think we should head back to the ranch, cowpoke? I'll tuck you in on the couch. You can watch TV for the rest of the day."

"I can?" he garbled.

"Once the bleeding stops you can have all the ice cream you want." She'd call Nick and ask him to pick up several cartons. "Any flavors you'd like. You name it."

"Chocolate."

"What else?"

He worked the gauze, his eyes fluid with pain and the slightest hint of wonderment. "There's more? Like what?"

For the love of God, he'd never tasted a banana split with several flavors of ice cream and all the trimmings? A smile broke across her face. She'd buy him three flavors to sample. No. Five.

"There's cherry, strawberry, Rocky Road—" she cut off when his head lolled. Carefully, she helped him up.

In the waiting room, Emma offered to carry the lighting brochure. She held it in front of her like a totem meant to ward off evil spirits.

At home, she continued to banish the evil she associated with the dentist. Walt rested on the couch beneath the comforter Rennie dragged from her bed. While she tended to him, Emma found a roll of gauze in the bathroom and wound filmy strips around her Barbie doll's head. She perched a stuffed bear on Walt's shoulder and littered his lap with tokens of love—her favorite barrette, a plastic seashell and a picture she hastily drew of a boy surrounded by hearts.

After Nick dropped off the ice cream, Emma took her doll and went out to play on the swing set. It was nearly dinnertime. The brochure lay forgotten. Rennie would never get to it tonight, not with a sick boy camped out on her couch. With luck, she'd eke out a few hours at her computer tomorrow. The hard work might spare her the indignity of losing the Fagan job.

She'd started the day pumped up, the savvy president of Perini Electric. Now she was Nurse Nightingale. Wearily, she pulled a carton of eggs from the fridge. A fruitless effort since Walt couldn't chew and Emma was too wound up to eat. And there was Troy to consider. How would she ever find the nerve to announce she was leaving early on Thursday?

In a lousy coincidence, the carpenters had chosen the upcoming week to begin breaking through the outer wall of the mansion to connect the new wing. Every trade was scheduled to work, from the heating guys to the masons. The structural integrity of the mansion, a century home, was questionable. Troy wasn't taking chances.

Would he fire her for clocking out early?

It was a necessary gamble. She couldn't let Walt down.

Resigned to her decision, she glanced out the kitchen window. On the swing set Emma rode a beam of sunlight, hurtling toward heaven.

After the scrambled eggs were prepared, Rennie went to check on Walt. His long lashes fluttered as he dozed. Lowering herself to the floor, she leaned against the couch. His eyes drifted open.

She grabbed a tissue to make a pass across his mouth. "How are you feeling, champ?"

He rolled his tongue around a tube of gauze. "Can I take this out? I'm not bleeding anymore."

"Spit." She held a tissue at his chin. "Wait a few more minutes to eat, all right? I don't want you to start bleeding again."

"Sure."

From beneath the comforter he withdrew his hand. The bear toppled from his shoulder but he didn't seem to mind. Impulsively, she placed her fingers on his. Walt's other hand appeared from beneath the nest she'd tucked him in. He grazed her knuckles with the lightest touch. A test, and her heart welled with emotion. Startled by the affection, she glanced at his face. Tears rimmed his eyes.

His lips quivered but his gaze remained steady. "My mom was brown," he said. "She was darker than me."

Rennie nodded. "Your father is white. When you mix white with dark brown, you get a yummy golden color. Like this," she added, caressing his wrist.

"You're white, like my dad. But you aren't mean." Walt hesitated. "Not all the time."

She nearly laughed at his logic. Why wouldn't he equate brown people with good, and white people with bad? A child measured the world through the yardstick of his parents' love, miscalculated through a parent's hatred.

"I'm sorry your father is mean," she said, her voice husky with emotion. "He should be nicer."

"My mom was nice."

"I'm glad."

"Rennie?"

"Hmm?"

Walt slipped his hand from beneath hers and gave her fingers a pat. "It's okay you're not brown," he said. "I forgive you."

The engine's familiar rattle propelled Emma from the swing. Gears shifted on a growl. The brakes groaned, and her heart *boom, boom, boomed* in her chest. Fear jumped on her so fast she didn't feel it coming. It just *came*, running down to her bones.

Trembling, she glanced at the kitchen window. Rennie was gone. The urge to sprint to the house tingled through Emma's feet. But running away never worked.

Shadows marked the grass with pencil lines of black. In the driveway Rennie's truck blocked the view of the street. Hugging her Barbie doll close, Emma poked her head around the back of the flatbed. One, two, three houses away, Pa's truck rolled to a stop.

The bushes near the driveway were thick with spring growth. She dashed to them. Underneath, dried leaves covered the ground in a papery mat. Quickly she layered them over her Barbie doll.

Satisfied that her doll was safe, she trudged toward Pa's truck. The song mama taught her long ago whispered through her head. The lullaby made her feel safe.

Hush little baby, don't say a word. Mama's gonna buy you a mockingbird...

There was no sense hiding from Pa. Emma knew the rules. Disobey and there'd be a whooping. Fear slithered through her muscles as she stumbled down the sidewalk. She knew to hide it or Pa's punishment would be worse. She shut the door to her heart, shut it tight and painted a smile on her face.

Next door, a woman called her kids in for supper. A boy with a scraped knee ran past, followed by a girl with yellow hair. They left the street drifting in shadows.

Pa rolled down the truck's window.

Hush little baby.

"Get over here, girl." He leaned out the window. She crept to the side of the truck with her legs cold and her palms wet. "I don't want anyone seeing us."

Don't say a word. Mama's gonna buy you a mocking bird.

"We're safe, sir."

He grinned like the Cheshire cat in the story, only she was the one falling down the rabbit hole. Darkness closed in so fast, she saw Pa through a pinhole. She hoped he wouldn't notice her hands, dancing like bumble bees at her sides.

"What's the family like?" he asked.

And if that mocking bird don't sing,

"There's no family, sir. Only the lady."

"You like her?"

Mama's gonna buy you a diamond ring.

"No."

"Good." He stuck a cigarette in his mouth. "When the bitch from Social Services brought you here, did you say you'd seen me around?"

"No, sir."

"You tell Walt?"

"No."

"Keep it that way." He struck a match. "I'm watching you every minute. Open your trap and I'll know. You got that?"

The fire in his voice sent a trickle of urine down Emma's leg.

"I'll be good." She squeezed her thighs together.

"We're getting the hell out of Ohio soon. You, me and Walt."

He smiled and her heart nearly flew from her chest. Then he ground the gears of his truck and drove away. The engine spit out puffs of smoke. Coughing, she trotted past the houses—one, two, three.

Rennie bolted down the driveway. "Emma, why did you leave the yard without telling me?" Her eyes grew wide. "It's getting dark. You could've wandered into the street, a motorist might not have seen you—it isn't safe. Do you understand, sweetie?"

Emma swallowed.

On a sigh, Rennie peered down the empty street. "What were you doing out here?"

Emma made a smile, a pretty one. "I was singing."

Chapter 11

The day Troy dreaded had arrived.

Silence bore down on the south wing's hallway. The scent of his mother's perfume wafted past, something elusive and feminine and painfully fragile. The ripple of lace peeking out from beneath her ivory blazer brushed the mottled skin of her neck. Thankfully the hives bleeding across her skin hadn't breached the flawless terrain of her face.

He wouldn't let her stay here long.

The threshold into Jason's bedroom was a demarcation line fraught with danger. Troy suffered a stab of pity as his mother reached into the pocket of her blazer. She withdrew an exquisite thread of gems.

Rosarium, Latin for 'rose garden,' perfectly described the jewels of scintillating color. The rosary boasted five decades of gems—rubies, emeralds, aquamarine and a decade each of blue and pink sapphires. Between each decade a diamond hung suspended like a droplet of rain. Following his mother's instructions, a jeweler in Dublin had wrought the traditional Roman cross from the finest platinum, edging his creation in eighteen-carat gold. In Ireland the design was affectionately known as a Fagan Rosary.

Pressing the cross to her breast, Jackie mouthed a prayer. Troy left her where she stood and strode inside.

One of the maids had drawn back the bay window's hunter green drapes. Morning light slashed across the bed. The scent of oranges clung to the air; it was something Dianne used when tidying up a bedroom that was, more than anything else, a time capsule from a happier past.

Troy's heart twisted. They'd dispense with Jason's belongings at record speed, pack away the football trophies lined up on the shelves and the dated music CDs strewn across the dresser exactly as he'd left them. They'd box up his clothing with unspeakable grief.

Troy winced as his mother gripped her rosary, her cheeks sallow. "Mother, are you sure you wouldn't rather go back to the factory?" He surveyed the packing tissue and the boxes on the floor. "I'll do this alone."

The suggestion brought her into the bedroom. "We'll do this together." She trailed her finger across Jason's desk, hesitated. "No dust."

"There wouldn't be."

She looked up with surprise. "I asked the maids to stop cleaning in here ages ago. It upset them so. Who's been dusting?"

"Dianne. She vacuums, too."

"I never hear the vacuum running."

"She waits until you and Dad leave for the factory."

Pain rippled across his mother's face. "She cleans Jason's bedroom? Your brother was terribly private but I'm sure he would've approved. Or laughed at her devotion. He was such a tease."

Retreating from the sorrow etched in her face, Troy dragged a box to the desk. The memories grew thick: Jason dropping athletic gear in a sloppy trail when he arrived home from high school. Jason climbing an apple tree with the frenetic speed of a squirrel. His buoyant personality had been as predictable as the seasons and as bright as a morning in May.

His mother smoothed a crease from the bed's comforter. "How long has Dianne been cleaning his room?"

"Five, six years." Troy reached for the wrapping paper. "Dianne saw it as a duty of sorts."

With good reason. The bedroom became off limits soon after Jason's murder. Troy and his parents couldn't bear to enter. The decision wasn't conscious. It was more an evolution of their grief, a survival strategy. Not so for Dianne.

Before Jason's death, she'd danced around the periphery of her brothers' lives in her pink tutu and ballet slippers. She became pen pals with the tooth fairy the same year they took turns dating Becky Fowler, a vivacious cheerleader at Liberty High. While they competed for the highest academic marks, Dianne made crayon portraits of Sleeping Beauty and Cinderella. They discussed college, John Carroll for Troy and Xavier for Jason, as she danced in a children's troupe at The Cleveland Playhouse. Troy enrolled at JCU and Jason entered his junior year at Liberty High the same year she won a statewide art contest for third graders.

For Dianne, Jason's murder was distant thunder. Troy and their parents were thrust into a maelstrom of emotions—shock, anger and grief. She weathered the news with a child's shallow anguish. She wept, to be sure. But she was more deeply affected by the absence of two devoted parents. The busywork of managing Fagan's Orchard became their only refuge, the only comfort in their shattered world.

Their emotional absence spurred Troy to break from college studies to make time for his sister. They spent hours together in the sun-washed music room as Dianne poured tea for her stuffed animals and for him. Outside the snow fell softly in anticipation of a silent Christmas. He sat gingerly on a pint-sized chair with his long legs warming in the sun. The delicate ritual had precluded any discussion of loss.

He dismissed the memory as his mother approached the bed. "The linens look fresh," she said, pressing a pillow to her face. "Dianne washes the linens, too?"

"And dusts the trophies." He removed one from the shelf and snapped open a sheet of packing paper. "She knows how hard this is for the rest of us."

His mother rested a palm on the inflamed skin of her neck. "We should have undergone therapy, the three of us." She took down a trophy and handed it over. "I never considered if we needed help. Later on, dredging up everything in front of a psychologist seemed foolish. You'd begun work at Devlin Builders. Your father had won the Allenden contract. You were both happy."

Troy recalled how he'd nearly turned down the Devlin

offer. Leaving the family business seemed heartless after Jason's murder. But he'd needed to follow his own interests.

"I owe a lot to Devlin Builders," he said, glad that sorrow hadn't driven him to try to mold himself in his brother's image. Jason had talked incessantly of expanding Fagan's Orchard. "I learned so much working there."

"The owner died a few years ago, didn't he?"

"Heart attack."

"I was upset when you left Fagan's." Jackie opened a dresser drawer and removed an orange jersey. "Your father said you were serious about construction. I refused to believe it. Of my three children, you were the only one with a green thumb. Dianne sees the orchard as a way to fulfill her dreams. Jason was the same. You'd rise at dawn to help prune or plant new stock."

"I needed to strike out on my own."

"Yes, your independent streak." She shook her head with false amusement. "Jason couldn't wait to claim his place in the company and Dianne still follows me around the offices. Not you."

"I'm sorry."

"Oh, sweetheart—don't be!" She released a laugh as fragile as her expression. "I'm proud of you. Starting your own company, all your success—you're better off on your own."

She gave him the questioning look that always pierced him deeply, as if she'd trespassed on his emotions and worried the insult would make him withhold affection. Which was ridiculous—his love was unconditional. Yet her unspoken, undecipherable questions left him wondering if he understood his own heart. Why did she view his love as provisional? Her doubt left him struggling with a question so familiar it seemed organic: What had he done to make her question his devotion?

The riddle was indecipherable. "I do like running my own company," he said, finding it easier to agree in a global way. Tethering himself to surface emotions was easier than delving too deeply—he feared what he might discover in the farthest reaches of his soul. "If I'd stayed at the orchard I would've forced you and Dad into retirement."

"Your sister and her bright young husband will do nothing of the sort. They'll have to divide their affections between work and the baby."

Was mention of Dianne's pregnancy a subtle criticism of his single status? Brushing it off, Troy returned to the shelves. He paused over a photograph taken after he'd earned his driver's license. In the shot, he was a sullen teenager looming over four smiling redheads. He tossed the photo into the box.

"I did like the growing bit." He glanced over his shoulder, relieved to find the stress diminished in his mother's expression. "Working outdoors, tending the saplings—the talk of expanding Fagan's Orchard was boring. Hashing out contracts and moving earnings through investments, the minutiae of wealth creation. If I'd been around when Grandpa worked the orchard I might've stuck with it."

"He wasn't simply good with the plant stock. He was also as skilled a carpenter as you." She removed the remaining clothing from the drawer. "The talents go together, don't you think? Carpentry, horticulture—he never liked the business end. The orchard would've gone bankrupt if your father wasn't so good with numbers."

"You'll be pleased to know Fagan Builders relies on a very competent accountant. She's great."

"A woman accountant. Good for you."

His mother opened the next drawer and withdrew the emerald green sweater that had been Jason's favorite. She hugged it close, her expression collapsing. Then she muffled her despair behind a smile. "Speaking of accomplished women, Dianne mentioned Rennie. I had no idea she became an electrician."

"She has her own company, Perini Electric."

"Just like you. Of course, you're both quite similar. Temperamental, solitary even in a crowd—I used to joke with Jason that he'd fallen for a girl better suited for his older brother."

The observation hurt more than reasonable. "I don't know about that."

"My obtuse son. You and Rennie are two peas in a pod." When he regarded her with hooded eyes, she added, "I haven't seen her since she was in high school. I don't think I could've managed. She was such a bright reminder of Jason."

"She still is."

"Dianne doesn't know her from Adam."

"She doesn't know any of Jason's old friends."

"Is Rennie still beautiful?"

"More so than in high school."

"No wonder Jason had such a crush on her." She shook her shoulders, a subtle movement used to shake off a welling of emotion. "He thought the world of her."

"Rennie thought they were just friends," he said in a casual voice that belied his shame. Suddenly he imagined her, bold with the beauty of early womanhood, embracing him beneath the Great Oak. Self-loathing followed the memory. "She didn't understand Jason's feelings."

"Good heavens, she was always encouraging your brother to chase other girls."

"He tried to make her jealous. Not the best strategy. She never saw behind the ploy."

Sick-hearted, he recalled the strange argument between brothers. They'd argued in this very room on the day of Jason's graduation party. How did a heated exchange about their parents veer into a battle over Rennie? *Troy, what Mom and Dad have done is crazy. You wouldn't believe me if I told you. Trust me, they're bastards. They're wrong to hide the truth. They've lied to you. They've lied to Dianne and me too—*

The cryptic accusations had stung deeply. Their parents had just returned from a vacation in Europe. What they'd done to make Jason furious was impossible to discern. Troy meant to merely defend them and diffuse the situation. Jason refused to listen. With each insult they traded, Troy's temper rose. He began mocking Jason for his slavish devotion to Rennie.

You want to talk crazy, asshole? It's humiliating to watch my kid brother drool over a girl who thinks of him as buddy material. You'll never be hot enough for Rennie. She's out of your league.

Why had he gone on the attack? He'd been older than Jason and Rennie, old enough to let maturity guide him. He certainly shouldn't have taken advantage of her when she found him stewing beneath the Great Oak—

Troy nailed the memory shut.

He brought his mother into focus. "I'm sorry. Did you say

something?"

"I asked if you'd found it yet." She opened one dresser drawer after another with growing agitation.

He yanked the sheets off the bed. "What should I find?"

"Check the drawer in the nightstand."

He gritted his teeth, despising the prospect of sifting through more of Jason's belongings. Wordlessly, he stalked around the bed.

Jackie feathered her hands down her blazer. "It doesn't seem right to pack it away." She straightened, her lips pursed. "I should keep it. Don't you think?"

He paused before the nightstand. "Mother, tell me what I'm looking for."

"Why, the ring. The one your brother bought for Rennie." Pity washed through her gaze. "There never was any talking to him once he'd settled on a plan. And a diamond, for heaven's sake. A promise ring, or so he said. Thank goodness he didn't have the courage to give it to her."

"Jason bought Rennie a ring?" he asked, and his heart shut down.

"Didn't he tell you? Good grief, he never told your father either. Flying off half-cocked without considering his actions— we had an awful row. You can't present a diamond to a girl and pretend you're gearing up for anything less than a proposal. Can you imagine? An eighteen-year-old boy proposing to a girl a year younger?"

Sorrow held Troy in a clammy embrace.

His mother laughed, high and false. "The ring must be there," she said, placing several pairs of jeans in a box. "Find it, please."

With dread he wrenched open the top drawer. The detritus of Jason's life tumbled forward. The acceptance letter to Xavier. A pack of gum. The paycheck he would've cashed on Saturday morning. He would've spent half of his earnings within the day but he was murdered Friday night. He never got to the bank.

A ring box of black velvet.

"Any luck?" his mother asked.

"It's here."

Troy lifted the ring from the box. A tremor ran down his

thighs. He sat heavily on the bed.

In the center of his palm, the diamond spit fire.

Blinking rapidly, his mother approached. She was too immersed in her own grief to recognize his.

She nodded toward the ring. "Lovely, don't you think?"

In the second floor hallway, Troy checked the plastic sheeting tacked from floor to ceiling. Reaching up, he traced his fingers across the barrier meant to save the south wing, and by extension the rest of the mansion, from the worst of the dust and debris. Boxed in by his parents, he nailed a pleasant smile in place.

His pleasure wasn't bone deep. Yesterday the wounds on his grief were torn open. Which he'd expected. What he couldn't assimilate was the fact of the diamond ring. Learning of the depths of his brother's love for Rennie was a torment.

He'd slept with the girl Jason had intended to marry. He'd broken a sacred trust between brothers even though thoughts of Rennie had consumed him long before they became intimate. But his own needs, his own secret, silent dreams, were immaterial. He'd betrayed Jason.

There wasn't time presently for a bout of self-recrimination. His mother's hives had bled up her neck. His father was perspiring. He didn't dare allow them to witness the destruction soon to rain down in their home.

He edged out from between them. "Folks, shouldn't you go to the office?"

His father fiddled with his bow tie. "Oh, we thought we'd stay."

"There won't be anything to see. Plaster falling and wood dust."

From the other side of the wall a loud *thunk* erupted. His father jumped. "Goodness. Have they begun?" he asked.

"Not until I give the order, which I'll do in a minute."

Gib, a carpenter as wide as a Mac truck, lumbered past with a sawhorse clamped under his arm. One glimpse of the approaching giant, and Troy's mother flung herself to the wall. The pearls around her neck bounced as she cowered in his retreating shadow. She was already whiter than the jagged chunks of drywall that would soon litter her pristine home. *Get her out of here.*

Troy's mood headed toward acid but he tried to sweeten his tone. "I insist that you leave." He steered her from the wall. "The noise will make your ears ring. Frankly, I don't have a dust mask small enough to fit you."

"I don't need a mask. I have this."

She wagged a lace handkerchief beneath his nose. He resisted the urge to bellow his frustration at the heavens or at Gib, who'd tossed down the sawhorse and sauntered up.

"What?" Troy glowered at him.

"You're in the way." Gib scratched his belly. He noticed Jackie and stopped. "Oh, and Crash wants you."

"Tell him to hold on." The lead carpenter never called for assistance unless it was urgent. "Has he decided which end of the hallway to start demolition?"

"Nice big bedroom at the other end. Crash says we'll dump crap there and keep moving."

Which meant they'd use Jason's bedroom for a dumping ground. Thankfully his parents didn't understand the explanation.

The news gutted Troy. There wasn't time now to grieve and he buried his sorrow. On the other side of the wall, Crash had lined up a team of carpenters in preparation for breakthrough.

He led his mother to the stairwell. "Once we're underway I'll call down to the factory and give you an update. In an hour. Two, tops."

"You're certain we can't stay?" Ridiculously, she clung to the doorknob of the linen closet in a childish display of resistance.

"Too dangerous." He pried her hands free. From over his shoulder, he shot a look of exasperation at his father. "If you don't help we'll have to feed her a Bloody Mary. A strong one."

"We've already seen that port of call."

"What?"

"We were in a celebratory mood this morning. Five Bloody Marys between us."

Troy squinted. His father did appear tipsy. Not that his features evoked a sense of celebration. His eyes were haunted and his mouth grim. *Jason.*

"You've had *five* drinks?" Troy steered his parents down the stairwell. "Find Bitsy. Get her to scare up some coffee."

"We needed to celebrate," his father said. "Out with the old, in with the new. Dianne's new home connecting to ours."

Troy began firing up a retort about imbibing at daybreak. The words died in his throat. At the bottom of the stairwell, Dianne and Rennie stood together.

Dianne held up a catalog. "Troy, look. Rennie found all the right lighting fixtures for my house. They're wonderful!"

He hurried his parents across the foyer. "Show me later."

Rennie bit down on her lower lip. "Uh, Troy."

"Not now." He paused, started, and glared at her. Something was up. Her light gold skin was unusually pale, her eyes puffy. "Don't you sleep?"

She lifted her chin. "Everyone sleeps. We need to talk."

"Later." He herded them all toward the door.

Dianne held the catalog before his face. "Won't you at least look? The fixtures are gorgeous. Tearing things down, building things up—what fun is this if we can't have a few moments to play?"

"Let's play the interior decorating game some other time. Right now I'm tearing out ninety feet of exterior wall. Go away."

She leaned close. "Happy pills. Get some." Brightening, she grabbed their father by the arm. "Dad, meet Rennie. She's an absolutely gifted electrician. Look what she's found. I can have reproductions made of all my favorite lighting in the mansion."

Escaping Troy's grasp, Dennis approached his daughter.

Troy glowered at Rennie, as if she were at fault for the delay. She opened her mouth, reconsidered, and pressed her lips together.

His father thumbed the catalog's pages. "Dianne, these are marvelous reproductions. I'm particularly fond of the pewter we used in the library but you might consider pewter *and* brass. As we've done in several rooms."

"Mix it up—a wonderful idea!"

Troy started toward his sister. Rennie blocked his path.

"This is urgent." She shifted from foot to foot. "I need a favor."

"Find me later. We'll talk then."

"When?"

"Damn it, I'm not skipping town. Find me at lunchtime."

Intervening in their verbal tussle, Dianne took Rennie by the shoulders and spun her toward Dennis. "Dad, she should install the electrical for the processing plant," Dianne said. "Let's give her the contract."

His father nodded like a benevolent king. Then he placed a hand on Rennie's shoulder. "Would you like to bid?"

Rennie's cheeks flushed a fetching shade of pink. Given their sexual history, Troy knew better than to appreciate how the color brought out the dusky notes in her eyes.

He nudged his father toward the door. "She would like to bid," he said, "at a later date. This morning she's busy with the new fuse boxes she convinced us to install. Which means she called the illuminating company to cut the power at the street. Rennie?"

"Already done."

"And the fuse boxes will be . . ?"

"Up and running by noon. All of them, including the one we've routed to Dianne's wing."

"Great." She appeared ready to salute him. Troy smiled despite himself. A shadow crossed her face, ruining the moment. "Now what?" he demanded.

"I need two minutes. It's about tomorrow."

"The feed to the north wing? You have all day to work on it."

"I'm taking tomorrow afternoon off," she blurted. "I'm not *asking* for permission. I'm *telling* you that I won't be here."

The announcement threw the foyer into silence.

Troy bit back a curse. "You're *telling* me?" He pointed toward the stairwell that led to the basement. "Get back to work. I'll be down in five minutes."

After she stalked off, he glowered at his family. "Now, what do I have to do to get the rest of you the hell out?"

Chapter 12

The sound of Troy thundering down the basement stairwell rattled her already frazzled nerves. Rennie hadn't meant to instigate a confrontation. Yes, she needed to take Walt to the dentist tomorrow. But drawing swords with the boss wasn't a smart move especially since she'd sparked the confrontation in front of his family.

Chastising herself, she yanked the fuse box housing from Squeak's grip.

He stumbled into the wall. "Be careful! That bugger's heavy." He tried to tug the fuse box from her grasp. "Let me set it in."

"I've got it." She stumbled forward, glad for something to take her mind off the impending battle. "Listen, I need to talk to Troy. Why don't you go upstairs and help Crash and the others?"

"Help them tear down walls? It's mayhem up there."

"You can handle a sledgehammer, right?"

He edged past the boxes scattered across the floor of the cramped utility room. "If Troy rips your head off because of Walt's appointment, let's quit this place. I can go without pay for a few days. We'll find something. The boss shouldn't give a woman a hard time if her kid is sick."

"Walt isn't my kid."

"You sure act like he is."

"What's that supposed to mean?"

Squeak colored.

Shouldering the housing in place, she was aware of the tiniest bit of longing warming. There was no question she'd grown fond of Walt and Emma. Not that the affection was reciprocal. Well, perhaps Walt was coming around. Not Emma. Most days she kept to herself, a green-eyed ghost with ultra-feminine ways and a Barbie doll for a sidekick. On the positive side, there were ways to capture her interest—with hair stuff. Barrettes, colorful rubber bands and ribbons—Emma loved anything she could put in her mop of curls. Purchasing the stuff might constitute bribery but Rennie didn't care.

Wiping her hands on her jeans, she sighed. Next week, the kids would spend spring break at First Presbyterian's Bible Camp. God help her, she'd miss them until they returned.

Dismissing the thought, she nudged Squeak. "By the way, Troy doesn't know I have foster kids. Not exactly something to bring up with the boss. Don't mention Walt and Emma."

Squeak ducked his head through the doorway, presumably to peer at Troy stalking through the basement. "Tell him. He'll understand why you're leaving early tomorrow."

"You're joking, right?" Walt and Emma were personal business, not something she'd comfortably discuss. "Go on. Help with breakthrough. Or see if Princess wants a biscuit."

The suggestion stamped worry in Squeak's eyes. "I should check my dog. Remember the guy in the forest? He keeps hanging around Princess like he can't find anywhere else to smoke."

A chill darted through her. "Tell him to stay away from Princess." There was something off-center about the man. "On second thought, ask him nicely to smoke somewhere else. Don't antagonize him."

"He's with the masons, you know. I thought they weren't coming back until May."

"Dianne called them back early. She changed the patio design."

The conversation halted. Troy loomed in the doorway.

An angry sort of electricity accompanied him into the room. Squeak, apparently at a loss, shoved his fists into his pockets and darted out. Rennie gave the fuse box a nudge even though she was sure it was in place. Not that stalling ever worked with Troy.

Perspiration slicked her brow. Towering over her with

intimidating calm, he appeared ready to blow a fuse. She had to give him credit—he was waiting to hear her out. Arms crossed, he leaned against the doorjamb as his midnight blue gaze settled on her . . . forehead. Was he mentally counting to ten before reading her the riot act?

"It's a medical emergency," she said. "I'll be here tomorrow morning. I have to leave at noon for a few hours."

"You're sick?" He pulled his gaze off her forehead and connected with her eyes. Her pulse jumped, sending patches of black through her vision. "By sick, I mean at death's door."

"No, it's nothing like that."

"Reschedule the appointment."

"Not possible."

His brows lowered and she steeled herself for an ultimatum. "No one leaves during the week of breakthrough," he said with a deadly calm that brought the hairs on the back of her neck to attention. "I made that clear weeks ago. Leave the site tomorrow, and you're fired."

Her heart sank. Just minutes ago Dianne and her generous father had practically handed over the plant's electrical contract. Put in a decent bid and the job belonged to Perini Electric. Success was close, but Troy was snatching it away.

"How about if I return later in the day? Say, five p.m., six at the latest." She'd find a babysitter. Maybe Liza would watch the kids if she wasn't mired in legal briefs.

He grunted. "Should I ask the crews to wait until you return? They use pneumatic tools. What if there's a problem with the feed while you're gone?"

"There won't be a problem." She'd tied the south wing to a monster set of generators. "The generators will handle any tools Crash uses. They won't blink out."

"This is construction. There's always an unforeseen event. You aren't leaving in the middle of hell week."

Why was he being so unreasonable? With dismay, she sensed her desperation switching off and her anger switching on. "If anything comes up—and it won't—Squeak will handle it."

"You're leaving Dopey and his ugly dog in charge? That's reassuring."

The insult frayed the last of her patience. Squeak was like a kid brother. She adored him and Princess.

"It's not like you to take a cheap shot," she said, her anger throttling up. "It's really not."

He stepped so close his chin bumped her nose. Common sense should've pulled her back a safe distance. But another, unexpected emotion bolted through her, something unnervingly sweet, almost tender. It mixed with her irritation in a confusing blend.

"For once, can't you treat me fairly?" she demanded, grappling with her emotions. "I'm not trying to set up camp on your bad side. What's wrong with you?"

"I'm tired, Rennie. I've got my hands full without dealing with your bullshit." He glanced at the ceiling. "Thirty men are ripping through my parents' house. My sister offered you a chance at the contract for the plant. You think I'm the one who doesn't play fair? Start acting like a professional."

"I am a professional!"

"Great. Your employer is telling you to be at work tomorrow. All day. No exceptions."

She considered knocking him to the floor. The urge rushed through her, illogical and potent. Given the feelings pouring through her, it wasn't an impossible feat.

His features were thunderous. Unable to quell the emotion, he clawed at his scalp.

Instantly she recalled Walt's much smaller hand, the rich toffee colored skin, the tapered beauty of his fingers as he placed them on hers and forgave her for all the hurts he'd endured in his young life. The moment they shared forged a bond. She'd fight for him. If forced to choose, she'd take Walt over her job.

The notion sent the feelings barricaded in her heart flooding out.

She despised strong emotion. It was like feeding power through a line too fragile for the surge. Instantly she was back at the Great Oak on the night of Jason's graduation party. She'd found Troy stewing there with the same expression on his face, the distressing mix of desire and hatred. Desire had overridden his loathing, and they'd made love with a desperation ground deep in her memories.

The reason for Troy's obstinacy struck suddenly. *Jason.*

"Don't you know how much I miss him?" she blurted. Giving into anger, she pushed against his chest. "You aren't the only one who hurts. They're upstairs tearing down his bedroom and I'm heartbroken. But I'm not being a bastard. I'm not taking my grief out on anyone else. What gives you the right?"

She surged forward, to push him again. Troy clamped onto her wrist. He held her still and their eyes dueled. "This isn't about Jason," he replied, but his voice broke.

The thick emotion startled him. His gaze churned, his suffering transparent.

He'd ringed her wrist in a painful grip. She maneuvered her hand, twining their fingers, forcing him to let her take on a small portion of his suffering. Compassion flowed from the gesture, and regret.

For an excruciating moment he stood frozen with the color peeking beneath his cheeks and his attention scuttling. Then he lost whatever personal battle he waged. Letting her go, he scrubbed his palms across his face. She tried to speak, to offer a consoling phrase. His crumbling expression rendered her mute.

"I miss him too," he said, the admission ripped from deep inside him. "My kid sister is on top of the world because she'll get what she wants. We'll tear down every memory of Jason to build her new home and make her happy. She can't see what's happening to the rest of us."

"Be fair. She was young when Jason died. She hardly remembers him."

"Which is what I tell myself to keep from feeling like shit," he snapped, his expression fluid. "When I was her age I couldn't wait to move out. Now my parents are getting older and Dianne loves it here. So I'll tear down Jason's room, tear it down to make her happy—"

"It's not your fault," she whispered, but the words went unheard.

"And my parents? They'll let me destroy every memory of my brother because they're thrilled about becoming grandparents. Why shouldn't they be? If the baby is a boy, Dianne will name him Jason. I'm sure she will and it'll tear me up. But it shouldn't. I'll be glad my brother lives on in some small way."

She scrambled to read his ravaged face. His image blurred

beneath the heaviness weighing down on her. A sob burst from her throat. Her face was wet and her nose runny. She couldn't tend to the mess or move away, not while he looked so haunted.

"Rennie, don't cry."

She clung to his gaze. "I'm not crying."

"You are."

Troy hesitated for a beat. Then he swept his thumb beneath her eyes. Riveted by the task, he collected the tears with the care one used in handling precious gems. His expression flashed with emotion but she couldn't decipher the message, couldn't clear her mind of the hurt. They'd each carried the sorrow alone. Their private grief had marked the years between Jason's death and the diminished life that followed.

Finishing the task, Troy rested his palm against her cheek. His touch lured her closer.

How to measure his sudden tenderness against the youth who'd once loved her feverishly? The frenzied coupling of shallow attraction; they'd stripped off their clothes as if time were hunting them down. No conversation, no sweet endearments—Troy had steered her willingly onto the grass. The world pivoted off its axis, revealing the uncertain gravity of her true emotions. As he moved on top of her, she'd understood. She didn't hate him. The emotion he stirred in her had nothing to do with hate.

Now that melancholy youth lay hidden beneath his skin. The man before her was stable, reliable. Crow's feet framed his eyes. A speckling of white frosted the five o'clock shadow on his jaw and wove through the chestnut locks framing his brow. Why hadn't she noticed the signs of maturity? The man he'd become was infinitely more appealing than the sullen youth residing in her memories.

Impetuously Rennie went up on tiptoes to brush her lips across his. A simple act of healing, and Troy's breath stuttered. He pinioned her with a look of confusion, regret—then need. He settled his hands on her hips and her heart tumbled.

Dipping his head he mimicked her affection, brushing his lips across hers, testing the softness of her mouth. The sensation was deeply satisfying. A whimper of need floated from her throat, the audible proof of her longing, and he took her mouth fully.

All the pent-up yearning they'd suppressed was carried in their kiss. She wound her arms around his waist, increasing the fury of his mouth. Desire surged through her.

Suddenly it wasn't enough. She began touching him everywhere, sliding her hands up his chest, stroking his neck, raking her fingers through his hair. Her frenzied caresses slipped the latch on his self-control. Groaning, Troy slid his hands lower to cup her bottom. Dizzy, she leaned into him.

The moment ended without warning. He let her go. Panting, he stepped back.

They were both breathing hard. Rennie tried to clear her head. Given the heat roiling through her blood, the task wasn't easy.

Pain sifted across his face. "I'm sorry." He tried to add something but failed.

"No need to apologize."

"I shouldn't have kissed you."

Longing thrummed beneath her ribcage but she managed to smile. "I kissed you," she pointed out.

She let her gaze linger on him. She couldn't stop. Evidently the close inspection made him uncomfortable. He looked away.

"I'm sorry," he repeated, and she knew he was grappling for composure. "It should've dawned how hard this is for you too."

A watery laugh escaped her. "I mapped out my schedule so I wouldn't be upstairs when they broke through to Jason's bedroom," she admitted.

Troy gave a sympathetic nod. "Tomorrow will be easier. Crash will have the entire section torn down. They'll work at the other end of the wing."

Apparently they wouldn't discuss what had just happened. Why had she kissed him? More importantly, why had Troy returned her ardor? The embarrassment that was her due refused to materialize. Despite the tears, she felt good. And Troy: beneath the troubling lights in his eyes a hint of pleasure lurked.

"I told myself that Jason would like the renovations," she said, steering the conversation to neutral ground. "He would've been happy for Dianne."

"He was always generous."

The urge to protect Troy's heart made her ask, "Can you work in the new wing until they're done tearing everything up? Leave Crash in charge of breakthrough?"

Her sincerity put amusement on his lips. "I can't dump the responsibility on Crash's shoulders. But don't follow my lead. Stay down here if it's easier for you." He hesitated, the amusement fading. Then he surprised her when he asked, "How long will you be gone tomorrow?"

His reversal was stunning. "Two hours. Three, tops," she said.

"Keep your cell phone close. If there's a problem return immediately."

Grateful, she began to thank him. He was already gone.

The next morning Rennie drove to work in an exceptionally good mood.

Yesterday's conversation with Troy was a heartwarming surprise. The kiss they'd shared was a blunder, but they'd both felt awful about Jason's bedroom coming down. The affection was nothing more than an unexpected byproduct of grief. She refused to read more into it.

That Troy had treated her kindly was reason enough to celebrate her good fortune. He'd backpedaled, allowing her to take Walt to the dentist this afternoon. By acknowledging their mutual grief over Jason, they were forging a tentative friendship. The emotions that drove them apart after the murder were now revealed as a common bond of loss. By voicing the pain, they'd begun to heal wounds left festering for years.

On County Line Road, a mile from Fagan's Orchard, she placed her attention on the day's tasks. The children's social worker, Jenalyn, had called. She'd scheduled a visit for Walt and Emma with their father tonight at Jobs & Family Services. The call handily solved the problem of finding a babysitter. Rennie would return to work by late afternoon.

Relieved with the turn of events, she parked in the row of trucks before the mansion. On the second floor of the new wing, saws roared and hammers pounded. The tang of burning metal soured her mouth and she glanced skyward, at the rectangular gash in the roofline where the new wing abutted the mansion. Men scrambled across open beams with buckets of roofing cement.

With growing unease she walked into the section where Jason's bedroom had stood one short day ago.

A portion of the room was still intact though the exterior wall was gone. The destruction was disorienting. Plastic sheeting separated the new wing from the much older mansion. Overhead, chunks of plaster hung in a jagged line. Ragged sheets of drywall and lengths of lumber were scattered across the floor. Nearing, she muttered a curse. The carpenters had left a section of the wall undisturbed.

The reason was obvious. A bundle of wires and several outlets dangled from the wall's gutted remains.

Crash appeared, his overalls streaming dust. "This is why we don't want a woman on a construction site." He nodded at the wires. "You're holding us up."

She brushed off his combative tone. "Give me a few minutes to take care of it."

"I'll have to send someone back down here when you're done. I don't like splitting up my crews."

"I didn't miss the feed on purpose. Give me a break."

"Just hurry." Crash left.

Chastising herself for missing the electrical feed, she dragged a ladder close. Removing a section of the wall was a fairly straightforward task. Climbing the ladder, she pulled on her leather gloves. Shards of drywall broke off easily. With a start, she realized she'd uncovered the back of an L-shaped closet.

Dust spun through the air like planets in a lonely universe. A layer of velvet grit covered the floor, and she spotted an old pair of tennis shoes. Obviously the closet had been part of the original mansion. She suspected it had connected to Jason's walk-in closet, which was already torn out.

A shelf papered with yellowing forget-me-nots ran into the darkness. The edges of the paper curled away from the simple pine board underneath. Who had so lovingly papered an area as inconspicuous as a bedroom closet? One of the maids perhaps, or the impeccable Jackie Fagan.

Using a saws-all, Rennie cut out a slice of drywall wide enough to allow her to slip inside the closet. A sea of dust rippled across the floor. Stretching, she felt along the shelf's chalky surface. Puffs of grime drifted upward like the smoke signals of a lost nation.

Reaching deep into the shelf proved impossible. Slipping back out, she grabbed a sledgehammer. She'd have to make a larger cut and drag the ladder inside.

"Rennie? Where are you?" Squeak paused inside the bedroom's makeshift remains. The floor began to quake, and he leaned against a shuddering wall. "Crash said we missed something."

"I'm taking care of it now." She'd just dragged the ladder inside the closet when the floor's quaking increased. "Why doesn't Crash move his crews to the other end of the wing?"

"We aren't the only ones who screwed up. Some of his carpenters did a bad job."

"Step away from the wall, Squeak. If they break through, they'll knock you out cold."

He pulled himself upright. "Oh. Sure." He started off, turned around. "I'll work downstairs. Think I'll grab some pizza on the way out. Troy had thirty pies delivered."

"Who eats pizza first thing in the morning?"

"Every guy you know. Think Troy will spare a slice for Princess?"

She laughed. "Stop feeding the pooch junk food." Straining, she reached across the shelf in another failed attempt to reach the stud wall and the wiring. Her thoughts turned to the unnerving man on the masons' crew. "Where did you leave Princess this morning?"

"I didn't tie her up by the woods where the mason smokes," he replied, mirroring her concern. "She's near the new wing."

Rennie cut out another section of drywall and moved the ladder to the end of the shelf. "If you left her on the Fagans' patio, I'll never hear the end of it." Embarking on friendship with Troy wasn't reason to press her luck. "Dianne is giving me a chance to bid on the processing plant. She'll be put off if your pooch does her business in the wrong place."

The wall went quiet and Squeak drew up his massive girth.

He frowned into the unexpected silence. "I told Princess not to pee near the mansion," he replied soberly. "We worked it out."

"You had a conversation with your dog?"

"Princess likes conversation. Why do you make fun of us?"

She tossed out a shard of drywall. "Kid, you're one of a kind. Having a heart to heart with your dog is as silly as—" Her fingers bumped against a cool surface far into the shelf's dark recesses. "Grab some pizza and get going," she added, wondering what she'd found.

Nodding, he lumbered from the room.

Something was stashed far in the corner. She felt a tinge of sadness. Troy and his mother had missed one of Jason's belongings. Curious, she reached across the shelf with both hands.

And withdrew a grey metal box.

No lock, just a simple clasp with a lacy imprint of rust around the edges. Climbing down the ladder, she cradled the box between her palms. Were Jason's high school love letters tucked inside? Childhood mementos? Tears pricked her eyes.

Should she find Troy? The contents had belonged to his brother. Of course, she'd been Jason's closest friend. The distinction didn't matter, and she battled the temptation to look. Waffling, she ran her thumb beneath the lock. The clasp obligingly flipped open.

No. It was wrong to look.

What if the contents were embarrassing? During high school, Jason's closet had brimmed with sports gear and the general mess accumulated by any teenage boy. Lord only knew what else was kept out of sight.

Drugs? It was the sort of revelation sure to upset the Fagans. Not pills—Jason had been too responsible for such behavior. What about pot? Many of the teenagers at Liberty High smoked at least one joint before graduation. Jason hadn't been immune to the pressures of youth.

What if she'd stumbled on a private stash of joints? Better to throw them out and spare the Fagans the embarrassment.

Inside, the contents made an irresistible thump. She crouched down to place the box on the floor. At the other end of the wing, the rumbling of sledgehammers resumed. Her skull vibrated with the racket. Then the memory of Jason's laughter slipped into her thoughts, the way his merriment had bubbled like champagne until she'd found herself laughing along at whatever inane joke he'd made. The carpenter's pounding came to a halt but she hardly noticed.

Hello, Jason. She patted the lid.

Sunlight tiptoed near, a golden arc. Outside the window, several Amish voices drifted toward the clouds in lilting, Germanic tones. Breezy April birdsong punctuated the conversation.

A fleeting moment's hesitation, and a shadow darkened the floor. Rennie floundered, unsure. Was the maiden, Pandora, seated at her elbow?

Taking the risk, she opened the box.

Chapter 13

Dear Mrs. Fagan,

The Sisters are very kind. Since my arrival they have needlessly pampered me. Sister Anne says our Holy Mother brought them a timid child to care for because their vows preclude the joys of motherhood. My health has improved greatly.

You'll be delighted to hear that I have dispensed with the crutches. My eyesight is much improved although my vision blurs when I'm tired. Sister Anne brings books on horticulture to ease my melancholy. On those days when I'm strong enough, she urges me to work beside her in the gardens. I love her dearly.

Has baby Troy's colic improved? In my prayers I thank God for the blessing of bringing you into our lives.

Very truly yours,
Mae Sullivan

Dear Mrs. Fagan (Jackie),

Are you sure I may use your first name? As you mentioned, I too feel bound by our mutual love for Troy. Yet it seems disrespectful to refer to you like an equal. Doing so makes me feel grown up, more grown up than I'm prepared to be.

How is Troy on this, his first birthday? The photographs you sent are a joy. Sr. Anne has asked me not to look at them too long. She continues to fret over my melancholy, which she believes is best cured by long walks and vigorous work tending the parish gardens.

I work daily in the greenhouse in a terribly absentminded fashion. Yesterday after leaving the greenhouse, I forgot the "shoe rule" and tracked a glorious sea of mud through the rectory. Father Cyprian looked like thunder when he escorted me back out.

Give my best to your husband, and my love to your blessed baby boy.

Very truly yours,
Mae Sullivan

Dearest Jackie,

How is Troy on this, his seventh birthday? I so enjoyed the photograph with little Jason standing nearby. Did Troy learn to ride the new bicycle? No doubt he now speeds through the orchards like a young god circling his merry kingdom. Perhaps he'll soon teach his little brother to ride.

All is well at St. Justin Martyr. I have started the impatiens in the greenhouse. Father Cyprian continues to help whenever his arthritis allows. The begonias are next; the shipment of summer bulbs arrives tomorrow. Pittsburgh slumbers in deep snow and Mass attendance is down. Many of our elderly parishioners fear the icy streets. At Sister Anne's urging, I've organized some of the younger members to bring their older brethren to Sunday services.

Sr. Anne complains of a head cold she believes won't abate until she can warm herself in the springtime sun. She'll have to stay content with the imaginings of a spring thaw for a few more weeks.

I pray all is well with you and your precious family.

Sincerely yours in Christ,
Mae

Chapter 14

Wordlessly Rennie opened the back door to the house. Rushing past, Emma flung her book bag to the floor.

Walt shuffled in last. Woozy from an hour beneath Dr. Norris's drill, he dabbed saliva from his mouth. "Can we have hamburgers for dinner?" He opened the refrigerator and withdrew the milk carton. "I want a salad too."

Emma snatched the glass of milk he'd poured. "Make it with lots of carrots," she chimed in. She sat at the table and sipped her milk. "Can you put snowflakes on top of the green stuff?" They're pretty."

"Salad with Parmesan cheese. Check." Rennie palmed the tight curls on Walt's head. "How can you think about food after visiting the dentist?"

"It wasn't as bad this time." Cradling milk and cookies, he wandered out of the room.

She sank into a chair. The question that had plagued her all afternoon returned: why had she opened the box found in Jason's closet? Why hadn't she located Troy instead and handed over the letters?

Dearest Jackie, How is Troy on this, his seventh birthday?

There hadn't been an opportunity at the dentist's office to read most of the letters. She'd only skimmed a few. The possibility of what the letters meant—what they meant to Troy—was impossible to deduce. Trying to work out the meaning, she unbuckled her tool belt and laid it on the table.

In a surprising show of affection, Emma squeezed in between her legs. "Why are you sad?" she demanded with laser-like curiosity. "You won't be pretty if you're sad. Don't you want to be pretty?"

"Emma, honey—not now."

The child took a dainty sip of her milk then sat the glass down. "I'll help you." She reached for her book bag.

"Please don't, kiddo."

She unzipped the bag. "I'll make you pretty."

Now? At any other moment her attention would be welcome. Usually she was standoffish. But a dozen questions whizzed through Rennie's mind like bees startled from the hive. The letters, yellowed and old, were written by a woman named Mae Sullivan. Who was she?

Slouching low in the chair, Rennie regarded the insistent child. "Can I be pretty later? Please?"

Fashion lust glowed on Emma's face. "The barrettes are sparkly. You'll like them."

"Why don't you do your Barbie doll's hair? She loves to get jazzed up."

Returning, Walt grabbed a yogurt from the fridge. "Rennie, you're silly. A doll doesn't have feelings. It's a doll. Get it?"

Emma stuck her tongue out at her brother. "Barbie has more feelings than you." The insult sent her rummaging through her book bag in earnest. A purple ladybug hairbrush and four floral barrettes landed on the table. "Hold still," she instructed, plunging her delicate hands into Rennie's hair. Clipping barrettes in place, she growled, "Why won't your rubber band come out?"

"Emma, stop! Here's an idea. Leave me alone, and I'll buy anything you like."

Walt honed in on her desperation. "Can we watch cartoons? We don't have much homework."

"By all means. Take glamour girl with you."

The children bolted from the kitchen. Her heart racing, Rennie slipped outside to her truck. On a wave of nerves she withdrew the metal box from beneath the driver's seat and sprinted back to the house.

There were nine letters in all. Pressed for time, she grabbed an envelope at random and studied the return address.

Miss Mae Sullivan, St. Justin Martyr Church, Pittsburgh.

Why would a woman residing in Pittsburgh correspond with Jackie Fagan during Troy's childhood? Predictably the letters arrived on Troy's birthday. Was Mae a distant relative?

Music from the cartoon the kids had chosen blared through the house, a silly blend of crashing cymbals and wailing violins. Tuning it out, Rennie withdrew two more letters. All of the missives bore the same return address.

Another thought intruded. The box was hidden in Jason's closet. Which meant he'd been familiar with the contents. Absently she opened a cupboard and took down a glass. How did he come into possession of letters written to his mother to celebrate his older brother's birthdays? The letters were about Troy, not Jason.

At the kitchen sink, she drew a startled breath. Her thoughts spun back to the week before Jason's graduation party.

His parents had been vacationing in Europe with Dianne. In anticipation of the party, Jason had announced he'd locate the key to their well-stocked liquor cabinet. While Rennie waited nervously in the mansion's library, he raced up the staircase to rummage through the master suite. The search proved successful. Later that evening he dodged the maids with glee and plundered his parents' bar. They added the stolen liquor to the stockpile already hidden in the mansion's basement for the grad party.

Did Jason find the box of letters in the master suite?

During the following days he'd behaved oddly, skipping school twice—something out-of-character for the college-bound student. On the night of the party, he was agitated despite the crowd in attendance for his big night. His parents had gone to considerable expense with the decorations and the dance floor that sat cradled by apple trees in full bloom. Couples swayed beneath the starlit heavens. Behind the rows of picnic tables the orchard glowed with lights twinkling from a thousand branches.

Glum and short-tempered, Jason hung on the sidelines. When Rennie confronted him, he topped off her glass then dragged her into the shadows to ask a bizarre question—the question now filling her ears as clearly as if he were standing here beside her.

If you know a secret that will destroy someone's life, should you reveal it?

Pondering the memory, she went into autopilot preparing dinner. She fetched hamburger from the refrigerator with Jason's question dogging her. If you know a secret. Her mind whirling, she placed a frying pan on the stove. Was Jason's odd question about the letters, and Troy?

Walt startled her from her thoughts. "We're hungry," he said pointedly.

Flinching, she yanked the pan from the flames. "Oh, shoot!" The tang of charred beef spiked the air.

He grinned. "You didn't swear. I'm proud of you." He patted her hip. Clouds of dust rose from her jeans. "Want me to get the lettuce for the salad?"

"Would you also chop up a carrot?" Lately he enjoyed practicing his culinary skills with a suitably blunt knife.

"Not today." He wiggled his fingers. "I'm protecting these so I can pitch. It's your turn to bat."

"Thanks for the reminder." She'd promised to teach him a few more moves tonight. Walt's newfound love of baseball kept him from throwing rocks at the squirrels. "Can we reschedule? After dinner I have to return to the Fagans. Besides, Jenalyn will be here soon."

"Why's she coming over?"

Rennie cupped his cheek. "She's set up a visit tonight with your father at Jobs & Family Services."

"We have to go?"

"Just for a short visit."

Emma drifted into the kitchen. "We saw Pa last week. Can't we stay here?"

Walt tore lettuce leaves into small shreds. He carefully placed equal amounts in three bowls. "We'll go to bed early, honest."

She gave him a quick hug. "This isn't my decision. Don't worry. Jenalyn will stay with you. Before you know it, you'll be back home."

The comment brought Emma's head up. "Is this our home?"

"Uh . . . yeah. I guess it is."

She held Rennie's gaze hostage. "For how long?"

"I'm not sure."

Walt flashed a winning smile. "Can we vote on how long to stay?"

Emma slowly raised her hand. "I vote to stay here for a long time." She held up her doll. "So does Barbie."

The entreaty on their faces squeezed Rennie's heart. She wasn't an expert at mothering, but she was doing well enough to have them clamoring to stay. Maybe Emma wasn't completely sold on life in foster care but Rennie was making strides. A small victory.

Warmed by their acceptance, she said, "You can stay for as long as Jenalyn allows. She's your social worker. It's her call. For the record I think you're both Aces even if you do leave toys in the bathtub."

They finished dinner in a comfortable silence. The kids were clearing the dishes when Jenalyn rapped on the back door.

"I'm early." The caseworker surveyed the table. "Wow, no takeout. You made dinner." She waved at Emma, dashing from the kitchen, before returning her attention to the table. "And a salad. Bravo."

The praise lifted Rennie's spirits. "They like balsamic vinegar and Parmesan cheese on top." After Walt darted out, she jokingly added, "I'm remaking them in my image. They're Italian now."

Jenalyn chuckled. "Consider getting some books on black culture." She arched a brow. "What's with the hair? Did Emma give you a 'do?"

Rennie scrambled for the barrettes stuck all over her head. "The kid will manage a spa one day. Some place with great hairdressers and decadent services like hot stone massages and herbal wraps." Tossing the barrettes aside, she switched topics. "Jenalyn, will you give me your take on a hypothetical situation?"

The social worker flipped her ebony hair over her shoulders. "Sure." She pulled out a chair. "Feed me coffee in trade. No decaf. I need high octane fuel."

"Coming right up."

"Dump in sugar. The buzz will keep me going while I handle Buck."

A trill of fear darted through Rennie. "Is Buck hard to deal with?" When the social worker glanced toward the living room, she added, "They aren't listening. Frankly, they dread seeing him tonight. They'll stay holed up in their bedrooms until we drag them out."

Jenalyn pushed Walt's empty milk glass to the center of the table. "Buck seems all right when he's with the kids. He does puzzles with them, chats. The kids are perfect angels. Too perfect, like they're afraid that one false move will..."

Rennie returned with the coffee. "Will what?"

"I'm not sure. Walt and Emma fit the pattern of children taught to playact around a volatile parent. And Buck looks at me like he'd happily put me six feet under." Jenalyn rubbed her arms as if banishing a chill. "In seven years of social work I've never met a parent who scares me like this."

"Then he shouldn't get the kids back." The thought of anything happening to them was unbearable.

"Unfortunately the State of Ohio isn't moved by my gut instinct." Jenalyn shrugged. Clearly she wasn't comfortable discussing Buck in much detail. "What's this hypothetical question you want to ask?"

Rennie suffered a moment's misgiving. Was a discussion of the mysterious Mae Sullivan inappropriate? The letters belonged to the Fagans. They were private. Naturally she'd hand them off to Troy, but it seemed sensible to first discover who Mae was—and why Jason had kept the letters hidden.

She settled on a direct approach. "Say a woman has a child. Every year on the child's birthday, she receives a letter from a second woman. Why would two women only correspond on the child's birthday?"

Jenalyn drummed her fingers on the table. "Is the second woman the grandmother?"

"No idea. For argument's sake, let's assume she isn't." Just a guess, but it felt right.

"She's not an aunt or a distant cousin? Nothing like that?"

"I don't think so."

"Is she the birth mother?" Jenalyn asked. She read the shock on Rennie's face with clear amusement. "Oh, come on. Your mother is a social worker. Do you need this spelled out? Two women only correspond on a child's birthday. They aren't related. Wouldn't it make sense the second woman is the child's biological mother?"

Rennie sunk into silence. Wasn't this the possibility she'd dodged since opening the box? If Troy was adopted and Jason had discovered truth, no wonder he'd acted strangely at the party. A family secret of such magnitude would destroy every assumption Troy held about himself.

On the night of the party, Jason had come to her for counsel. She'd given such foolish, flippant advice.

Jason, you should always be honest.

"When did the birth mother stop writing?" Jenalyn asked, pulling her from her thoughts.

"When the boy was seven years old, I think."

"That's about right. Most birth mothers break off by then. They've received photos and have assurance the child is loved. They begin to feel intrusive." Jenalyn toyed with her coffee spoon. "Even if the adoptive mother is happy to continue sending notes and photos, most birth mothers find it painful to watch their child grow beneath another woman's love. After awhile they simply stop writing."

The explanation was irrepressibly sad. "And the adoptive family? Why wouldn't they tell the child he's adopted?"

"They would."

"What if they didn't?"

Jenalyn's eyes flashed. "Rennie, the stigma against adoption has died. When children reach the appropriate age, their adoptive parents do tell them."

"All adoptions are now open?"

"If your mother ever mentioned cases that are sealed, she was talking about decades ago. We've stripped away laws forbidding adopted children from learning of their heritage. Today the courts ensure that if they choose, they can and do locate their birth families."

Frustration surged through Rennie. "You don't understand. This is a wonderful family. There must've been a reason why they never told their son. Can you think of a reason why they remained silent?"

The social worker lowered her cup in the kitchen's uneasy silence. Goosebumps rose on Rennie's arms. She sensed a looming truth entering her life.

It arrived with perilous calm.

The light went out of Jenalyn's eyes. "There are two reasons why adoptive parents may keep a child's history a secret," she said. "The first, which is rare, is if the child is the product of incest."

"And the second?" Rennie asked, her mouth dry.

Jenalyn paused for a shattering moment. "The second is rape."

Above the front stoop water gushed over the gutter's rim like a waterfall unleashed. Rennie sat with her work boots thrust into the torrent and the metal box safely tucked behind her. Thunder cracked overhead. Sitting outside while Mother Nature raged was foolish, she mused, lifting the glass of wine to her lips. Dangerous admittedly, but she was too upset to care.

In the hour since the children had returned from visiting Buck and eagerly gone to bed, she'd finished half a bottle of wine. It wasn't the most courageous act. Still, she needed the fortitude of a heady Merlot.

Intuition warned that Jenalyn's assessment was correct. Troy *was* adopted.

All the pieces fit. He bore no physical resemblance to his family. He towered over his parents and his bubbly younger sister. His deep chestnut hair was nearly as dark as Rennie's. The Fagans were redheads—Dianne and Dennis were true carrot tops, and Jackie's hair was a lush, honey red. All three of the Fagans were endowed with delicate, elfin features. Troy's infinitely more handsome face might have been chiseled from stone. His features came from somewhere—someone—else.

Mae Sullivan.

Was Mae his biological mother? She lived at a church in Pittsburgh. She grew flowers.

A church.

Rennie took a long sip from the wineglass. Did Mae belong to a religious order? It was shocking to consider a nun having a baby. The scandal would rock any parish.

Swiveling on the rain-soaked step, she withdrew the box

from behind her back. She scooted out of the downpour. With the deliberative movements of a woman handling a toxic substance, she placed the box in her lap. Organize the letters by postmark date? Deciphering their secrets would be easier if the missives were read in order. Once she had a full understanding of the contents she'd decide on a proper course of action. Handing the box off to Troy no longer seemed sensible, not until she understood the contents. If he was the product of rape, for all she knew his father was incarcerated in the State pen. The man may have committed other crimes, a horrifying list. Conjecture brought the awful possibilities raining down like the storm raging around her.

If she gave Troy the letters she'd unravel the life of a presumably happy, thirty-five-year old man. And what about the elder Fagans? If they'd adopted him, they'd kept the truth hidden for a reason. Was revealing their unhappy secret even wise?

Rennie stared, unseeing, into her glass. She took another long sip. Finally she reflected on Jason, the last person to carry these secrets. During his life, he'd never kept his mouth shut. He'd been honest to a fault. She was sure that, if Jason had lived, he would've spilled everything to his brother. Eventually the facts of Troy's complicated history would've come out.

A bullet silenced the truth.

Would revealing the truth now honor Jason's memory in some small way?

She couldn't bring him back. The confession she'd made about sleeping with Troy on the night of Jason's murder, the revelation that placed Jason on Cleveland's mean streets on the wrong night—the past was beyond reach. She'd sent him to his death. The guilt remained a stain on her life.

Rain fell in spattering waves. Deaf to it, she opened the box. She was determined to do right by Jason as she withdrew the letters, one by one. She'd read them all and learn every possible detail about Mae Sullivan. Afterward she'd broach the subject with Troy.

A blue envelope lay at the bottom of the stack. Smaller than the rest, it had escaped notice until now.

The letter inside was unlike the others. It didn't carry a birthday greeting. She glanced at the postmark, by far the earliest. Rennie read quickly.

As she did, her world tumbled apart.

Dear Mrs. Fagan,

Were you able to reach Lianna? I miss her greatly, and have written without success. Is she unwilling to reply? If it's not an inconvenience, please tell her that I'm safe in my new life in Pittsburgh.

Tell her there is nothing to forgive. We are children still, even as we walk through altered lives.

Very truly yours,
Mae Sullivan

Chapter 15

Mae Sullivan never dreamt of Sweeper.

She never hid from his madness behind the imprecision of dreams. When she slept she remembered his rage precisely. His sins, as if caught on film, seared her mind. She tasted the blood in her mouth. Above her battered face the Great Oak's leafy canopy shielded the world from her horror.

On most nights she was blessedly safe from his torture. Tonight too, she would've barred him entry into her dreams if not for Father Cyprian's unthinking generosity.

By offering the drink, Father unleashed the demon.

Late in the afternoon at Sister Anne's bidding, Mae had hurried to the basement of the rectory. Parish women bustled in the rectory kitchen while others rushed through the meeting room snapping linen and clattering china. St. Justin Martyr boasted the largest congregation on Pittsburgh's north side and Sister Anne was preparing for the annual dinner honoring the church's steering committee.

At the bottom of the stairwell Mae paused with a wry smile. Remembering the rule, she pocketed her gardening gloves and removed her dirt-caked shoes.

In a parish managed by an elderly priest and two aging nuns, the five-foot-ten groundskeeper stood out. The flawless complexion Mae possessed in her youth was now leathered from decades toiling beneath the sun. Her hands, large for a woman and well shaped, were callused and cracked. A river of hair spilled down the back of her canvas shirt, the pale blonde tide now washed through with tendrils of white.

Her conversation with Sister Anne was brief. Most of the spring annuals were planted, as promised. Sweeping waves of color now flanked the entryway of the massive brick church. She assured Sister that the last of the impatiens would be in the ground before the second grade class received the sacrament of First Communion next Saturday. Finishing the conversation, Mae wove through the crowd of churchwomen in search of Father Cyprian. Their evening stroll through the gardens was a ritual long established. Materializing in the throng, he steadied his cane and sent a grateful wave in greeting. They met at the stairwell.

Taking note of the perspiration glossing her brow, Father stopped a woman hurrying past. On the tray she carried, glasses filled with tantalizing colors drew Mae's attention. She licked her lips.

Smiling, Father handed her a glass.

She assumed the drink was orange juice, her favorite. Downing the glass, she guided him up the stairwell and into the gardens.

Father wheezed as they walked, his black robes fluttering. Birds twittered on the branches of the dogwoods and the flowering plums, searching for food before night descended. Mae was especially fond of the Cardinals, how they dared to burn crimson in a world rendered monochrome by the threat of predators. Their fiery wings beat wildly in defiance of the sinking sun. A tremulous chirping burst forth as a pair of Cardinals crested toward heaven. She followed their ascent with longing.

Father's shoe caught on the stone walkway. His shoulders jerked. Quickly she caught him. As she did, she licked the drink's sweet residue from her lips.

Revulsion lifted her head with a snap. The taste in her mouth wasn't of oranges.

She tasted apples.

"You will obey me, child. Stay away from the men and the factory." Mother stormed across the Fagans' intimidatingly large kitchen. "It isn't proper for a sixteen-year-old girl to run wild like a vagrant. What if Father John begins to question your worthiness to enter the convent? Don't you wish to serve God? Hasn't it been our

dream since your father died?"

In the center of the garden Father Cyprian paused before the statue of Our Lady. The mossy brick walls of the church sank into shadow. The bell tower, lucky in its stature, basked in the sun's dying rays. On the garden's wrought iron railing a variety of birds waited in queue—Mae's beloved Cardinals, nervous finches, demanding sparrows and the fat, overfed pigeons that eyed the elderly priest with anticipation.

Father stopped to admire the railing's growing brood. "Lovely." His face, etched so deeply it was a map of the world, eased into a posture of intense pleasure.

"They *are* lovely. Even so, I'd appreciate it if you'd stop throwing birdseed near my flowerbeds."

"Do you want the birds to starve?"

"They're fat as geese! Do you have any idea how much weeding I undertake to keep the beds groomed?" Mae gave his arm an affection squeeze. "Please watch where you toss seed. It isn't allowed near my beds."

It wasn't allowed, but Mae found ways to spy on the men who lorded over the acres of apple trees. Rich scents rose off the carts as the pickers brought in the Granny Smiths and the Macintoshes, the spice and the sweet. Slipping into the factory's back door to witness the jarring noise of machines at full throttle and the ever-moving carpet of the conveyer belt was a particular joy. The men worked with impressive speed, sorting top grade fruits into crates with Fagan's Orchard written in dark green lettering on the side. Lesser grade fruit landed in metal bins destined for the factory kitchen, where jams and jellies were made.

A hundred callused hands danced over the conveyer belt. Stubbled jaws worked the tobacco the men stuffed into their cheeks. Behind his father and the other men, Sweeper dragged his broom across the floor.

Young Mr. Fagan strolled behind the line of bent heads. Not yet thirty years old, he was confidently in charge. Nattily dressed in a tweed blazer and a green vest, he thumbed his gold pocket watch and made small talk with the men hunched over the bounty of fruit. Furtive glances and grunted responses didn't alter his good cheer.

Mae darted behind a wall of crates stacked higher than her head.

Pride welled up in her heart. She loved Mr. Fagan—loved his pretty wife even more. Rulers of a productive kingdom, they bestowed largess on many in their realm. Gratitude shimmered through her as she slipped her hand into the pocket of her dress and fondled the rosary. The string of jewels was shockingly beautiful. It was still hard to believe the Fagans had given her such a rare gift after learning of her decision to serve God.

"When you go to the convent, take this with you," Mrs. Fagan had told Mae when she arrived at the mansion after school.

Mae had gasped in wonderment at the thread of jewels pressed into her palm. Rubies spit fire. Emeralds and sapphires gleamed like scintillating versions of field and sky. Diamonds burst with the light of heaven.

Mrs. Fagan had patted Mae's cheek, adding, "You'll take a vow of poverty but Mother Superior will let you keep our gift. Our Divine Father created these jewels, just as he created you. You're a jewel chosen by God."

A gust of wind snapped Mae out of the memory. Father Cyprian shuddered. "Spring tests and tempts us," he said, leaning heavily on his cane. "The garden is in splendid bloom but the temperature is dropping."

"Should I fetch your sweater?"

"I would miss your company."

"I'll only be gone for a moment. It *is* getting cold."

Beneath a web work of skin, his lips thinned. "I'm merely stating fact. Let's walk."

He shuffled forward at a slow pace that allowed her to survey the April daffodils and the magnolia tree's cloud of pink blooms. The rhododendron, which she'd foolishly planted beneath the magnolia before learning the gardening trade, bore leathery leaves tinged with yellow. She'd tend to the plant tomorrow. It would flourish if transplanted to the south end of the garden where the sunshine was abundant. As it was, the pitiful thing was being strangled by the magnolia's roots and starved of light.

The moment Mr. Fagan returned to his office on the factory's second floor, the men began to ridicule Sweeper. The cruel pastime lightened the long hours of toil. Hidden behind the crates, Mae pressed her rosary to her bosom and whispered a prayer for the young man. He was a wall of muscle and unusually tall, but he looked beat down in his threadbare pants and fruit-splattered shirt. His shoulders were perpetually bowed, his eyes fixed on the floor.

Sweeper's father was the most seasoned in cruelty. "Hey, Sweeper, you missed a spot," he barked from the conveyor belt. He spit a foul stream of tobacco juice an inch from his son's shoes. "Get moving, boy. Clean it up."

Sweeper jerked the broom in a circle. "I'm not a boy."

"Think you're a man?"

"I am."

One of the workers, a man with the gold tooth, sneered. "Going to take guff from your boy? Are you, Jim?"

"I never do. Do I?"

The broom's handle quaked but Sweeper lifted his head. "I'm not a boy."

His father spit another foul stream. "One more word and you'll catch hell."

"You don't scare me."

"What did you say?"

Her heartbeat tripping, Mae peered frantically across the factory. Tucked away in his office, Mr. Fagan couldn't hear the argument. He couldn't smell the changed air, or see the men's attention lifting in sickly anticipation.

Sweeper's father realized it too. Swinging out from the conveyer belt, he grabbed his son by the collar. The man with the gold tooth gave out a loathsome hoot of pleasure. Sweeper flailed wildly but he didn't dare make a sound. His feet barely skimmed the floor as his father dragged him off.

Fear pooled in Mae's belly. Stumbling from behind one stack of crates to the next, she followed.

On the factory's back wall, huge exhaust fans whirled with a deafening howl. Sweeper was thrown to the ground. He was still rolling when the boot swung into his face, swung with enough force to explode droplets of blood across the yellow grass. Hidden behind a mountain of crates, Mae shoved her fist into her mouth to stop from screaming. Why would the God of Light allow a man to treat his son with such cruelty? Sweeper scrambled to his knees.

His father's rage was everywhere, tearing at him like locusts.

Whimpering terror followed sickening thuds. Sweeper became an animal driven mad by the power of a fist.

Mae recoiled from the memory. Nausea clogged her throat. Father Cyprian shuffled forward, his head bent in mediation. She clung to his robe.

After witnessing Sweeper's beating, she'd scrambled across the orchard to her favorite retreat, the Great Oak. She'd spent hours alone sobbing. Why hadn't she returned to the mansion, found someone to rescue him? The butler or the chauffeur. Why leave him, beaten and bloodied?

From the vantage point of middle age, a child's imperfect logic was unfathomable. Allowing Sweeper to suffer at his father's hand was a terrible sin. She'd endured years of self-recrimination. None of her regrets absolved her of the guilt.

She squinted into the sun dipping low behind the church. The last of the day's warmth bled from the lengthening shadows as she steered Father through the gate and into the rectory's foyer. Voices rumbled from the basement as she ran her tongue across her teeth. There was no abolishing the offensive aftertaste of cider.

The parish secretary, Tike Meyers, rose from her desk. "Goodness, Mae—let me help you. Father, you're freezing!"

Father Cyprian stomped his feet. "I'm fine."

Though the memory of Sweeper lingered, Mae winked at Tiki. "Don't listen to him," Mae said cheerfully. "He's an ice cube. I suggest putting on the tea kettle."

"Will you both stop fussing?" He threw them off. "I don't want tea. I have work to attend to. How long until the dinner for the steering committee?"

"Less than an hour," Tiki supplied. "Should I hold your calls?"

"Please do."

After he'd gone, Mae said, "You're working awfully late." Tiki usually left by four p.m. "Why are you still here?"

"Next week Bernadette takes First Communion with the other children. I had to pull her baptismal certificate from the parish file and finish the paperwork. I've been helping so many other parents, I forgot my own child."

Mae grinned. "So much for your organizational skills."

"I *did* manage to get to the mall for Bernadette's dress."

Most of the parishioners bought communion dresses well before the sacred event. "Was there much selection left?"

"Actually I found several dresses to choose from. Look." Tiki dove through the clutter on her desk and retrieved her smartphone. "Don't you love it? The dress is satin. Look at the veil! Real Irish lace."

The Fagans brought the rosary from Ireland for the girl chosen.

"Mae? Isn't it perfect?"

Chosen by God.

Anguish preyed on Mae's heart. She hadn't entered a religious order. Yet even though her dreams were shattered, she'd planted herself in a new life. *With joy I follow the path you have chosen for me, Lord.*

She dragged her attention back to Tiki. "Bernadette looks glorious in her dress," she said, marveling at the photo. She hesitated, her attention drawn to the sophisticated shoes. "Aren't the shoes a bit much for a child?"

"The heels? All of the girls wear them now." Tiki chuckled. "Mae, you're terribly old-fashioned."

Mae knew her behavior was scandalous. If spying on the men at the factory was a transgression, her other pursuit was truly a sin. Cheeks burning, she approached the sink in the Fagans' kitchen. Mrs. Fagan's cook and one of the maids followed her hesitant steps with worried glances.

"Mae, I'm ashamed to call you my daughter." Her mother scrubbed a turnip with furious concentration. "Where have you been? Were you up by the road waiting for the boy to drive by in his red car?"

"Of course not, mother." She cringed at the lie. She'd lolled by the road in hopes the Mustang would rise over the hill in a flash of color. She'd hoped the boy would stop to talk to her, as he'd done for several weeks now.

"Were you with him? Did he kiss you?"

"No!"

Her mother thrust the turnip beneath the stream of water, her eyes flashing. "What will Father John think if you sully your reputation? You, a girl chosen?"

"I'd better get home," Tiki was saying, and Mae wheeled her attention back to the present.

The emptiness she'd learned to avoid preyed on her sense of wellbeing. The boy in the red Mustang, her reckless infatuation—the events that followed had destroyed her mother as surely as they'd destroyed Mae's hopes of a life serving God.

With effort, she smiled at Tiki. "Have a nice evening."

They exchanged pleasantries and Mae went out to lock the gate to the gardens. At the far end of the parking lot, the last of the lights in the elementary school blinked off. Pittsburgh settled beneath a misty gloom, a harbinger of rain.

Even though Mae was in her fifties and no more comfortable with computers than Father Thomas or Sister Daniel, she *had* learned to rely on the Internet. Moving briskly down Washington Avenue, she recalled the storm featured on The Weather Channel's website. Moving up from the Gulf States in an easterly pattern, the system promised to drench Northeast Ohio, and Liberty. Hopefully the storm would hold until it reached Pennsylvania. The annuals planted before the church were thirsty for a good soaking.

Her heart swelled. So many years had passed, and Troy was now a man. At this precise moment, was he standing in the rain? Was he laughing, caught in a downpour while pruning a branch in the orchard? She wondered if he still lived at the grand Fagan estate. Or did he own a fine house in Liberty? Did a loving wife and beautiful children await his return each night?

Yes. Yes, of course they did.

Considering the joys of her unknown son's life, her strides grew buoyant. She reached the perimeter of the wrought iron railing at a fast clip. A quick left and she started down the path that led to the small brick smokehouse once used by the parish, in the 1800s. Years ago, when Mae arrived, Fagan money had paid for a hasty remodeling. Back then the nuns took turns sleeping in the house and caring for the battered teen they'd found in their midst. Many of those dedicated women were now gone. These days, the smokehouse resembled a fairy tale cottage with clematis trailing the walls and flowerbeds tucked beneath the dappled shade of maple trees.

She ate dinner and brushed her teeth twice to banish the offensive remnants of apple cider. Her bedroom was a bare bones affair with a crucifix over the bed and a pine dresser in the corner. She slipped beneath the covers and studiously focused on the coming storm. The rain would quench the sweep of flowers before the church. The begonias and zinnias ringing the smokehouse would also flourish after a good soaking. Slowing her breathing, she organized her thoughts on tomorrow's gardening tasks.

Thoughts of Troy were saved for last. She imagined him receiving the Eucharist at St. Mary's in Liberty. The Fagans looked on with pride. Troy's wife and children approached the altar behind him.

Mae used every trick she'd ever learned to hide from Sweeper. Yet as her thoughts scattered he came to her, the demon of her dreams.

The red convertible peeled off in a screech of tires. Her young suitor waved heartily as he sped away. In defiance of gravity Mae raced through the orchard, toward the Great Oak. Her shoes barely skimmed the grass.

Was it wrong to admire the boy and his flashy car? She would never love him—she would love only God. But he was handsome, gloriously so, with a mop of brown curls and soulful eyes. Other girls talked of boys, of holding hands and first kisses. Was it wrong to let her emotions soar?

She'd never experienced the pleasures of a passionate kiss. Meeting the boy by the road, their halting conversation and shy glances—their stolen minutes provided but a hint of the happiness other girls would claim. God had chosen Mae for a life of service in His church, a duty she'd gladly meet. There was only this moment to dream of love and weddings and babies she'd never bring into the world. Tugging off her shoes, she ran through the orchard in record time, climbing the precipice on a wave of joy.

The dinner hour approached. Was Mother looking for her? Mae banished the worrisome thoughts. She craved a few minutes alone to revel in the bright emotion brimming in her heart.

The sun dipped behind the summit. In the valley, the last of the orchard's men returned to the factory. It was dreadfully late. Running faster, she dove beneath the oak's heavy branches.

And ran headlong into Sweeper.

The impact sent her reeling. Arms and legs spinning—she couldn't regain her balance. She rolled to a stop on a gasp.

When she did, Sweeper hauled her up by her shoulders. "What are you doing out so late?" He gave her a shake.

An oily smell clung to his skin. The bruise beneath his right eye bled a ghastly yellow across his cheek. His expression chilled her blood.

She wrenched free. Never before had Sweeper spoken to her. His voice was surprisingly low and unnervingly hard. It occurred to her that he sounded exactly like the men who jeered at him whenever he swept the floor of the factory. In vain she grappled for her voice.

He bent down and picked up a rock. "What are you, a mute? I'm talking to you."

"No, I—"

"Why were you by the road? No good acting like a whore."

The word was unfamiliar. She was still trying to work out the meaning when Sweeper's mouth curled.

"Are you a whore?"

"I'm Mae," she finally got out. In response, he tossed the rock skyward and caught it neatly. Her knees threatened to dissolve as he tossed the rock back into the air. "Sweeper, I didn't mean any harm."

The rock dropped with a smack in his palm. His eyes turned to flint. "What did you call me?"

Everyone called him Sweeper. Why was he angry? "I mean no disrespect."

"I'm not a boy. Stupid whore—I'm a man. How about I prove it?"

He lunged at her. Time came to a perilous halt as she scuttled left then right. With a hellish grin he blocked her escape, backing her against the oak. She gulped down a sob. Instinctively her hand plunged into her pocket for her rosary. Our Father who Art in Heaven . . .

She was still scrambling for her rosary when he swung the rock at her cheek. The impact threw her off her feet. Black fire tore through her skull. Her vision clearing, she glimpsed him standing over her. He held his appendage, red and swollen. He licked his lips.

"I'm a man, you worthless slut." Crouching, he shoved her thighs apart.

She tried to scramble away. The rock crashed into her face with lancing pain. Trapped in a seizure of terror she called out— Mother Mary, save me—but she gagged on the blood pooling in her mouth. A hot torrent ran down her forehead and into her eyes. Blinded, she felt Sweeper grab the collar of her dress and rip the fabric all the way to the hem. For an awful moment her vision cleared. She caught a terrifying glimpse of him lifting the rock high above her head.

Mae's heart fell into a dark place. It fell past terror and pain. The rock slammed into her skull but her mind had mercifully unraveled. The impact was little more than a dull thud. Sweeper shoved her thighs apart to spear his rage into her—

On a shout, Mae jackknifed up in bed.

Blackness rippled across the floor. Outside an owl hooted, the sound lonely and fierce. Throwing off the covers, she staggered to the wall in a frantic search for the light switch. Finding it, she stood heaving in the harsh glow.

Dread ran hot in her veins. Shuddering, she willed her pulse to slow. When she'd sufficiently calmed herself, she walked stiffly back to the bed.

Dropping to her knees, she clapped her hands together. Sweeper stood behind her like Satan with the stink of the orchard on his clothes and fire rimming his eyes.

Mae locked her fingers tight. She bowed her head and sought asylum in her prayers.

Chapter 16

The letters strewn across the couch resembled debris from a shipwreck. Each note celebrated Troy's birthday except the first, by far most shocking missive. The note in the blue envelope mentioned Rennie's mother, Lianna. Which begged the question: what infraction had Lianna committed that required the mysterious Mae Sullivan's forgiveness?

Rennie studied the postmark, dated the year her mother had graduated from high school. She'd already done an Internet search but Mae was a ghost in cyberspace.

There was only one way to get to the bottom of this. But first, she needed a babysitter.

She grabbed the phone and dialed quickly.

Her brother picked up on a growl. "Whaddya want?" Nick garbled.

"Nick, it's me. Put your wife on."

"Huh?"

"Bro, wake up!"

On the other end something crashed to the floor. A lusty string of expletives followed. "Sis, it's five a.m. What the hell are you doing awake?"

"I've been up most of the night."

"That's no way to raise kids. Skip too much shut-eye and they'll run you down."

"I didn't realize parenting was the Indy 500. But thanks, I'll keep it in mind." Every time she'd dozed off, the letters' worrying contents had dragged her back to consciousness. "I need an emergency babysitter."

Muffled conversation ensued on the other end. Then Liza said, "Rennie, is it the children?"

Despite her exhaustion she nearly laughed. Last night Walt and Emma had returned from visiting Buck more than happy to crawl into bed. Time spent with their father was always hard on them.

"Liza, the kids are fine. I know it's early but I have to talk to my mother." She didn't dare mention the letters until she'd discussed them with Lianna. "Are you in court this morning?"

"Today I'm in the office."

"Can you get Walt and Emma off to school? I have to catch my mother before she leaves for work."

A pregnant silence and then, "Give me half an hour."

True to her word Liza arrived promptly. Her thick jet hair was encased in rollers and she had a conservative navy suit flung over her arm. Rennie shook her head at the baggy jogging outfit her sister-in-law wore, undoubtedly a castoff from Nick's closet.

"I appreciate this," she said. "Feel free to doze on the couch. The kids don't wake until seven. The school bus arrives at eight."

Liza placed her suit on the couch and smoothed out the skirt. She frowned as Rennie grabbed her tool belt and the grey metal box. "Rennie, you look like one of my clients when I have to explain she's been left out of the family will. You've had some sort of a shock. Talk to me."

"Not now." Tugging on her work boots, she caught the impatience on her sister-in-law's face. "Honestly, I will explain. I need some answers first."

"Answers to *what*?"

"Don't do the lawyer thing, okay? I can't explain right now." She skirted past. "Thanks for taking care of the kids. Tell them I'll see them this afternoon."

She darted outside and climbed into the truck. It was still dark but last night's rain had left the air sweet smelling. She drove with the windows down, inhaling deeply to clear her head.

Reaching her parents' house, she suffered a moment's misgiving. No lights were visible inside the two-story Colonial. Why hadn't she phoned before dashing across Liberty?

Apprehension nudged past her guilt. Cradling the box of letters, she marched up the steps and rang the doorbell.

"Rennie?"

Her father stepped aside to allow her to enter. His curly silver hair was mussed, framing his wide forehead like a porcupine's quills.

"I'm sorry, Dad. I woke you."

Mario ruffled her hair, still unbound and hanging in a wild mass around her shoulders. "You look upset."

"Can I talk to Mom?"

He climbed the stairwell.

She padded down the hallway and flicked on the lights in the kitchen. Photographs of a growing brood of grandchildren covered the refrigerator's faceplate. The scent of licorice lingered, and she noticed the jar of pizzelle cookies on the counter. She brewed coffee and set three mugs out.

Nervous tension knotted at the base of her neck. Now that she'd arrived, second thoughts intruded. In a distressingly predictable way, she'd barged into her parents' house without considering her actions. Asking about Mae wasn't sensible. How to chart a course into the treacherous conversation?

The private chastisement came to an abrupt end. Her parents shuffled into the kitchen in their bathrobes. Donning a thin smile, Rennie splashed coffee into the mugs.

"Who's Mae Sullivan?" she asked her mother.

The question hung in the air. Finally her father asked, "How did you hear about Mae?"

Lianna stared at the box of letters.

Grief pooled in the lines of her face. Her anguish pierced Rennie. Why force a discussion? Clearly a conversation wasn't welcome. For a split second, she wondered if it would be wiser to discard the letters.

At last Lianna said, "I was friends with Mae when we were teenagers. Our mothers worked together at the Fagan estate. Grandma was a cook. She worked there until she died. Mae's mother was Grandma's assistant."

"And Mae?" Rennie opened the box, revealing the yellowed letters.

Lianna stared at the contents with sickly interest. "She was two years younger than me, an exquisite creature with pale blond hair and the face of an angel." Her voice broke. Quickly, she regained her composure. "How long did Mae write to Jackie Fagan after Troy's adoption? I've always wondered."

Rennie snapped the lid shut, the truth difficult to absorb. Troy *was* adopted. The knowledge sent her plummeting toward the letters' dark secrets.

"Mae wrote to Jackie Fagan until Troy's seventh birthday." She waited for her father to seat himself before adding, "Then the letters stopped."

Her father grunted. "Has Troy seen the letters?"

"I just found them. Yesterday. We're tearing out the wall between the addition and the mansion. They were hidden in a closet."

Lianna's eyes held a plea. "Do you intend to show them to Troy?"

What *was* her intention? Showing Troy the contents seemed the right thing to do. And she felt responsible to carry out the task his brother had surely meant to finish. Yet if Troy found the truth unbearable, his anguish would fall on her shoulders.

Lianna wrapped her hand around her mug of coffee. "Mae didn't attend Liberty High." She looked past Rennie to glimpse the years unfurled in a faded banner. "Her mother was a devout Catholic. Mae took classes at a parochial school in Middlefield. We met during my senior year at Liberty High. Mae was in tenth grade, terribly bashful. I was older, popular."

Rennie's father said, "Your mother was the girl to chase." The lighthearted comment eased the tension settling between them.

Rennie silently agreed. She'd seen the photographs of her mother at the height of her beauty, her long, lush hair and large, expressive eyes. In one photo Rennie particularly enjoyed, a group of athletes from the football team crowded around her, the entire squad, including a handsome cornerback—Rennie's father. She wasn't sure how he pulled it off but by the time her parents entered Kent State University, Lianna was his fiancé.

"How does your popularity tie in with Mae?" she asked, prodding her mother on.

"She loved to hear about my social life. Dating, proms, that sort of thing. We'd walk the orchards while our mothers prepared dinner for the Fagans. Mae asked so many questions."

Her mother's voice melted into an awkward silence and Rennie said, "Mae wanted to share your experiences."

"She was eager to hear about the young men I dated. I wanted her to experience some of the pleasure I took for granted. She was just a few months away from entering the convent."

Rennie set her cup down. "In tenth grade?"

Lianna brushed a tendril from her furrowed brow. "It was a different era. Mae's father had died. Her mother encouraged her to enter a religious order."

"So she's a nun?"

"No. She never married either." A grey pallor spread across her mother's face. "You see, I asked one of the athletes on the Liberty Eagles to talk to her. He was a fine young man, someone I trusted. His red Mustang was the envy of every boy at Liberty High. Whenever he found Mae walking on the road on her way to the Fagans, he'd stop and strike up a conversation. They would talk for a few minutes and Mae—when we met up at the Fagans—she'd be dancing on a cloud because of his attentions."

"You wanted to give her a few nice memories before she entered the convent."

Her father rose. Withdrawing from the conversation, he busied himself removing plates from the dishwasher. Something in his actions put Rennie on alert. Steeling herself, she returned her attention to her mother.

"On the last day the boy spoke with Mae, he was in a hurry." Lianna's expression emptied. "A group of us planned to meet at Rugg's Diner on Route Six. I should've asked Mae to go with us. If I had, she never would've gone to the Great Oak alone."

Apprehension filled Rennie. "Mom, this is upsetting you. I don't need to hear the rest."

Deaf to anything but the memory, her mother plodded on. "I should've gone to the Fagans after school," she said, bowing her head to stare unblinking at her lap. "I would've noticed that Mae was missing. There were so many migrant workers in the orchard. They drifted into Liberty and made a few dollars picking apples. Then they drifted away. One of the men raped Mae beneath the Great Oak . . ."

The dishwasher shut with a bang. "Lianna, she's heard enough."

". . . the man bludgeoned Mae. He broke her jaw and her arms. She tried to fend off the blows. If Mr. Cornell hadn't driven by she would've bled to death. Do you remember him?" she asked, her voice high and desperate. "The African American fellow who owned the five and dime on Liberty Square? Such a nice man. Two days later he suffered a heart attack. Two days after he found Mae."

"Lianna, stop—" Rennie's father went to her but she seemed caught in a trance.

"Mae was hospitalized for six weeks. She'd been beaten so severely she was hardly recognizable. The Fagans paid all the expenses. There wasn't anything they wouldn't do. Shortly after she was released from the hospital it became clear she was pregnant."

Horror washed through Rennie. Mae was an angel beaten beyond recognition. Troy was a product of rape.

Pulling to her feet, she grabbed the box of letters. "I have to get to work." She pressed her lips to the clammy skin of her mother's forehead. "I shouldn't have come. I'm sorry."

The urge to gather her mother into her arms grew strong. The emotion was foreign and frightening. Lianna was a consummate professional who ran Jobs & Family Services with detachment and poise. She steered through life's shoals with confidence. Never before had she appeared weak, vulnerable—as she did now. Hovering above her mother's curving spine, Rennie felt the ground shift. The woman before her was broken by the story she'd shared. She began to cry, the muffled sobs ground from her soul.

"Rennie?" She looked up, haunted. "You were a teenager once. Did you ever do anything so foolish you never forgave yourself?"

Rennie gripped the box as the unwanted memories accosted her: The anguish on Jason's face when she told him about her night with Troy. The clouds blotting out the sun as the mourners converged on the cemetery.

"Yes," she replied, sick to her marrow. "I've made worse mistakes."

Stumbling from the house, Rennie drew ragged breaths. A paperboy bicycling past sent a rolled newspaper through the air with casual precision. Beyond him, Anna's silver Mercedes rolled to a stop behind the Perini Electric truck.

Rennie was in no mood for her older sister. On the best of days Anna was difficult and rude. Despite the early hour, she was flawlessly dressed in a pencil-thin lime skirt and a cream tank top.

Approaching, she fingered the pearls at her throat. "If it isn't the prodigal daughter." She gave Rennie the once-over. "Is there anything in your closet besides denim? If you're taking the day off wear something attractive. Think, Rennie. Do you own dress slacks or, God willing, a skirt? If I had your curves I'd live in knits."

"I'm on my way to work." Rennie tried shoving past. Impatience ticked up her pulse when her sister planted her feet. "Get out of my way, Anna. And move your car. I'm leaving."

"Hold on." Her sister nodded at the metal box. "What is that? Come to think of it, why are you visiting Mom and Dad so early in the morning?"

The barrage of questions was an odd relief. Rennie shot past despair and right into the arms of fury. It was a nice waltz, one she'd mastered with her indomitable sister.

"Anna, *move.*" When she didn't, Rennie pushed her out of the way. "Last warning, sis." She climbed into the truck. "Move your car or I'll drive my badass truck right over it."

On the front stoop Lianna flinched as her older daughter howled with rage. Anna dived into the driver's seat and swerved the Mercedes onto the lawn. Rennie's truck nearly clipped the front bumper before tearing down the street.

Anna loved to stop by in the morning. The morning visits were usually welcome. Lianna patted down her hair, the breath whispering past her lips distressingly shallow. She had exactly ten seconds to pull herself together before her older daughter got out of the Mercedes and sniffed trouble in the air.

Mario rested his hand on her shoulder. He meant to comfort, she knew, but a tremor lanced through her.

"Why didn't you tell Rennie the entire story?" he asked before their daughter came within earshot.

Lianna blinked rapidly. "What, dear?"

"When you told Rennie about Mae." He regarded her soberly. "Why didn't you explain that I was the boy in the red Mustang?"

The lady called Aunt Liza let go of Emma's hand. "Look who's here to put you on the bus," she said in a honey voice.

Stubbornly Emma stayed rooted at the curb. Walt ran over to Rennie's truck, his backpack dancing on his shoulders. She didn't like the way he looked at Rennie or how she rubbed her hands through his hair like she needed to touch him. Hurt settled on Emma's bones.

All the way down the street children clustered like hens waiting for feed. Most had mamas with them, fat ladies and skinny ones, ladies in bathrobes and in dresses. The lady in front of the blue house across the street wore a dress with yellow stripes. She smoothed down her squirming boy's hair.

The hurt Emma felt started a sick feeling in her belly. The lady touched her boy's hair the same way Rennie touched Walt's, the way Mama used to show her loving when Walt did a good job sweeping the front porch or Emma clung to her knees, scared during a storm. Rennie stopped and looked around.

She sprinted to the curb. "Hey, kiddo. Aren't you going to say hello?"

Emma lifted her eyes to the sky. She followed a cloud tickling the tops of the trees. "Hello."

"Where's Barbie?"

"In here." She held up her backpack. Rennie neared and she gave her a look to stop her. "I don't want Barbie getting lost. She's safe inside."

"Oh. Of course."

"I can get on the bus by myself. I know how."

"Sure. You're a big girl."

"She's a big girl," Walt chirped, joining them. He waved at

Aunt Liza. "Say goodbye, Emma. She's leaving."

Emma wrinkled her nose. Something was wrong with Rennie. She ran her hands across her face, her fingers twitching. Lines of dampness tracked down her cheeks. Was she asking the tears to go away? Emma unzipped her book bag and stroked her Barbie's hair. She didn't like seeing Rennie this way.

Behind them, the bright yellow bus rolled to a stop. In the windows kids yelled and laughed and sang. Rennie bent over Walt and hugged him close. The door creaked open.

The memory of Mama's love sent Emma flying up the steps. Was Mama watching the school bus from heaven?

Walt tromped down the aisle and plopped down beside her. "Scoot over." He bumped his shoulder against hers. The bus jerked into gear and pulled out. "Why didn't you say goodbye to Rennie and Aunt Liza?"

Pretending not to hear, Emma counted the houses flashing by.

"You're mean," Walt said.

His words hurt worse than a wasp's sting, and she jumped out of her seat to march down the aisle. He didn't understand. He thought it was good to like Rennie and Liza and even Jenalyn. He was starting to trust them. Emma knew better. Bad things happened if you trusted grownups. They got mean or forgot to give you dinner. Or they made you keep secrets.

Sometimes they ran off to heaven.

The bus lady shouted and Emma dived into the seat in back. Gum wrappers were balled up on the shiny green cushion. A boy with braces sat across the aisle with a tall girl. They smiled, but Emma turned away.

Handprints covered the large back window in dirty streaks. Someone tore open a bag of potato chips. The smell of grease burst in the air. It was nasty like the prints of fingers and thumbs that made it hard to see out of the back of the bus. Emma pinched her nose shut.

With her fist she made clean circles on the glass the way Mama had taught her, taking her time and doing a good job. The bus jumped and bounced. She kept working and tried not to think about how Walt traded love like the boys on the school playground traded video games. Would he give all his love to

163

Rennie? Would he trade off his love for Emma? The greasy prints melted away as she worked and it scared her. They simply *disappeared.* She made circles until she'd worked herself up to angry and the window was clean.

Behind the bus, cars followed like beads on a string. The bus jostled through Liberty Square with the procession of drivers following. Shop doors were open and pots of flowers sat on the sidewalk. The bus shuddered—*red light.* She got up on her knees and counted the cars filled with grumpy faces, *one, two, three—*

And her heart fell down. It fell down to her knees when she got to *four.*

Hush little baby, don't say a word—

The fourth car in line wasn't a car at all. The rusty grey truck belched smoke.

Emma's mouth made an *O.*

From behind the steering wheel, Pa lifted his hand and waved.

Strolling through the morning's blessed silence, Troy jotted down notes. He paused inside the roughed in space of the living room, penned a reminder to check the measurements of the alcove the carpenters were slated to build next week. The recessed area would feature floor-to-ceiling bookcases. Baseboard heating required twelve feet on the same wall. He made a mental note to ensure the alcove didn't cut into the space.

He glanced overhead at sturdy rows of two-by-fours. Penning another note, he recalled that most of the carpenters would work upstairs today tearing out the last of the mansion's exterior wall. They were far enough along to allow a small crew to return downstairs. At this rate, Dianne's house would be finished ahead of schedule. Troy allowed himself a moment of self-congratulation.

Still writing, he meandered into the dining room. A muffled thump came from the kitchen on the other side. None of the workers were due in for another twenty minutes. Curious, he went to investigate.

Rennie skirted around a stepladder. Troy glanced at the

wall, where she'd placed marks for the abundance of electrical outlets Dianne requested to run all her culinary gadgets.

"You're early," he said, impressed. He hadn't seen much of her all week. Moving the stepladder out of her way, he stumbled over a small heap of refuse. "I'll get one of the carpenters to clean up the mess."

When she merely nodded, he drew closer. A twinge of apprehension shot through him. She didn't look right.

For starters, she'd forgotten to tie up her hair. She hadn't fixed up her face either. Not that Rennie wore much in the way of makeup. Given her natural beauty, cosmetics were unnecessary. Today however, her lips were pallid and her eyes red-rimmed.

He asked, "Are you coming down with something?"

"I'm okay." She made another X on the wall.

"I'm available, if there's a problem."

The whisper of a smile crossed her lips. "Are we becoming friends, Troy?" She brushed her hands across her thighs. When he appeared troubled by the accuracy of the statement, she added, "Not that I'm complaining."

"It *is* strange, in a good way." He never expected to progress beyond wary tolerance.

Reading his thoughts, she said, "Yeah, I know. I didn't think we'd ever get along, either. I figured the best we'd do was stay out of each other's hair and try to avoid the inevitable fist fight."

"Right. I'm going to start boxing with a woman." He hoped the lighthearted remark put her at ease. Calmly, he added, "Rennie, we're both adults. Until we discussed Jason's bedroom coming down, I'd never spent much time thinking of you in the context of my brother. How close you were to him. Our crazy war in high school—it was half a lifetime ago. It doesn't factor in."

"But the other thing does."

She meant them, how they'd made love the night of Jason's graduation party. Her candor might have been shocking, but this was Rennie. For a woman, she was uncommonly blunt.

"I think we both put that night down to Jack Daniels and the insanity of youth," he said, sparing her the truth.

He'd never dismissed their night together so easily. Years passed before he viewed their passion with any sort of honesty. Sometime during his late twenties he'd finally stared down the facts—their night of lovemaking was the best sex he'd ever enjoyed, for good reason. Despite the traded insults and the feigned stance of mortal enemies, they'd cared deeply for each other. They'd been in love.

Grateful she'd never understood, Troy leaned against the wall and crossed his arms. "If we took a poll of our combined friends, I'm sure half of them slept together during high school or college. It doesn't mean anything." He hesitated. He was unable to stop himself from adding, "Does it?"

"Of course not," she agreed, but the faint blush seeping into her cheeks was startling. "I'm glad we've become friends. I'd like to think we're mature enough to trust each other."

"I never hire anyone I don't trust," he replied brusquely, wrapping up. The pain in his chest was an inconvenience he didn't relish analyzing.

He was about to excuse himself when his cell phone rang. Turning away he took the call from Dianne, already down at the office. Her husband, Frank, was traveling and she preferred to leave for work early whenever he was out of town. Troy's parents had also left the mansion at sunup—something about a shipment of plant stock arriving today. Hanging up, he returned his attention to Rennie.

"That was Dianne," he said. "She wants you to stop down at the factory for a copy of the processing plant's blueprints. You'll need them to work up a quote. Figure on giving her half an hour."

The information brought Rennie to a standstill. She lifted the marker from the wall. "When would she like to see me?"

"Before noon. My parents will sit in on the meeting. Don't let their excitement scare you. The schedule to build the plant is tight, but not impossible. You'll need to hire more electricians. I'll sit down with you to discuss your bid before it's presented to my family."

She glanced at him sharply. "You act as if I've got the job."

"Assuming your quote is reasonable, you have. Dianne is taken with you. It's a safe bet to say she's excited about awarding you the contract."

Oddly, the news didn't please Rennie. Straight-faced, she made another X on the wall. His apprehension returned. Why was she shrugging off good fortune?

He thought of something else. "If you're having second thoughts, you aren't obligated to take the job. Frankly, I don't want you wiring the plant unless you're confident you can handle the work."

"I can handle it." Irritation colored her voice. She fished around her back pocket and withdrew a rubber band. Tying up her hair, she added, "It's not the plant. I'm glad for the work."

"Then why are you upset?"

She pressed her lips together. Color rose in her cheeks. The confusing reaction had him at a loss.

"I can't stand here all day." He glanced over his shoulder. At the other end of the addition men thundered up the stairwell. "What's bothering you?"

She guided the marker to the wall. Her hand shook, and she lowered it to her side. Hell, something *was* bothering her. Something serious.

"I'm not leaving until you explain," he said, and the comment washed her face of color. Scowling, he backed her to the wall. "Rennie—"

"I need to know something," she said, cutting him off.

"Fire away."

"If someone came into possession of sensitive information about your life, how should they proceed?"

Troy angled his neck back. She'd tossed out the question as if she'd rehearsed a dozen times. Was she in trouble? He didn't need a sub going off the deep end.

"Are you looking for advice?" She wouldn't be the first sub to require a bailout midway through a project. "I assume by 'sensitive information' you mean you're having trouble placing an order with one of your suppliers. Pay one guy late and he'll pass on the bad news."

"I'm not having trouble with payables."

"You run a two-man outfit. Small companies always have trouble making ends meet." Her attention remained stubbornly glued on her work boots and so he added, "Okay, we're not talking about money. It's something else. Frankly, you look like you haven't slept in a week."

The comment brought her head up. Fear cascaded across her face.

Troy didn't stop to analyze the protectiveness surging through him. Impulsively, he brushed his knuckles across her cheek. The gesture dragged her eyes back to his. He stepped back, irritated by his unprofessional behavior. Light gathered in her eyes, the spark, the secrets, and his apprehension grew strong like a wind blowing cold. The anxiety emptied him out as Rennie sucked in a steadying breath.

"I'm not talking about me," she said. "I'm talking about you, about your life. And I'm asking: if I've come into possession of facts that will upset you, do you still want to know?"

Chapter 17

Troy's expression became guarded. The question plaguing Rennie ate through her composure. Why hadn't she thrown the letters away?

She'd already caused her mother great pain. The blow would be far worse for Troy.

"Why don't you run that by me again," he said, crossing his arms. The movement made him appear taller, a sensible man poised for bad news. Yet she caught the fear in his voice.

She never should have opened the first letter. Delving into the past without a thought of the consequences was foolhardy. But the truth quickly became apparent, smoldering in his eyes. *He already knows.* Not consciously surely, but on a deeper level. His expression was an hourglass with the sand run out.

"Look, maybe I shouldn't have said anything." She ignored the tremor in her voice and plunged on. "It's just that the facts—"

"Facts about my life?"

Her chest constricted, making it impossible to breathe. "Yes."

"How can you know anything private about me?"

"Troy, I'm sorry about this. If you'd rather not—"

"Tell me."

"Not here." Once told, there was no telling how he'd handle the information. Impatiently she swiveled toward the clatter erupting in the next room. "Can we meet tonight?"

"What time?"

She'd never talk Liza into babysitting twice in one day. Nor could she ask her mother, not after the shock she'd given her this morning. Which, unfortunately, left her sister.

"Can you come to my house at seven?" she asked, resigned to begging Anna to take Walt and Emma out for an hour. "I'm not trying to be mysterious. It's just that—"

She broke off. Squeak appeared in the doorway. He approached, and Troy murmured a greeting.

"I'll be there at seven," Troy agreed, moving away. From over his shoulder, he added, "Don't forget the meeting with Dianne."

"I won't."

He strode from the room at an even gait. Even so, she was positive she'd rattled him. At least he hadn't demanded an explanation on the spot. No, Troy was a careful man. He wouldn't allow her to drop shocking news on his head with the crews arriving.

A burst of delayed nerves whirled through her. Lightheaded, she leaned again the wall.

Squeak, oblivious to her dismay, set his toolbox on the floor. "Ready to get started?" he asked.

"Yeah. Big day ahead of us." Queasy, she flipped open the cooler she'd stashed in the corner, found a thermos of ice water and a bottle of antacids. With effort she buried the worry fluttering in her stomach beneath a businesslike tone. "Let's finish wiring the kitchen. We have to finish quickly. Crash is putting up the drywall today."

Squeak wound his tool belt around his generous middle. "Remember the mason? He made a crack this morning about Princess. I tied her up right behind the mansion so we can see her. He asked why I was hiding her from her admirers."

"Doesn't the guy ever quit?"

"He's got it in for my dog. Why, do you think?"

"Some people are cruel for reasons we'll never understand," she said, her thoughts turning to Walt and Emma and the mistreatment they'd endured at the hands of their father. Was there any sense to abuse? "If the guy keeps hounding you, stop bringing Princess to work. I'm afraid he'll do something to harm her."

The suggestion stamped worry on Squeak's sweet, rubbery face. "I can't leave her alone in my apartment. She howls so loud my neighbors complain."

"You won't be able to bring her on every job. Why not deal with the issue now?"

"I will—after I've saved some money." He grabbed a roll of wire and looped it onto his forearm. "There's a lady in Liberty who baby-sits pets. She's real nice and Princess likes her. I just don't have the money yet."

"Sounds good," she replied, touched by his concern for his dog's welfare. "If we land the industrial job, I'll give you a raise. The pooch can have the best nanny money will buy."

"Princess will like that." Dropping the subject, he squinted at the marks she'd made on the walls. "I'll grab a few more outlets from the truck. Geez, this place will be incredible when we're done." He pointed at an O she'd placed on a stud. "For the computer?"

"You got it."

"I can't wait to see this place when we're finished." He turned in a slow circle. When he came to a stop, he glanced nervously at her. "You'll really give me a raise if we get the job for the plant?"

"Absolutely." Only now she suffered mixed feelings about taking the job. Revealing Troy's adoption would upset the Fagans, Dianne included. Given the circumstances, was it sensible to continue working for them? "Why don't you grab the rest of our supplies," she added, preferring to remain focused on work and not the guilt eroding her confidence.

After Squeak left, she finished marking the walls. She hadn't mentioned the meeting with Dianne about the processing plant.

The reason was obvious. Feeling anything resembling excitement was wrong, even cruel, now that tonight's meeting with Troy lay ahead.

By the time she drove down to the factory she'd succumbed to an oppressive gloom. She steered the truck slowly down the curving dirt road, the incline dotted with hundreds of apple trees. Workers toiled in the distance with their shears glinting and their voices rising. The hypnotic scent of apple blossoms clung to the air and Rennie breathed deeply, wishing for a surge of optimism that wasn't forthcoming. It was a gorgeous day, too lovely to waste on second thoughts.

Yet she sensed a cloud forming above her life, a storm she'd unwittingly brewed.

Entering the factory, she searched for signs of life. A forklift stood with its huge wheels caked with mud. A long conveyer belt, old enough to be labeled an antique, stood quietly in the center of the cavernous space. Her footsteps echoed as she made her way toward it. No one was in sight. The workers were taking advantage of the sunny weather to plant, prune and feed the orchard's countless fruit trees.

Curiosity got the better of her, and she paused beside the conveyer belt. Pockmarks covered the thick black belt. The tart, acidic perfume of crushed apples spiked the air. Breathing in the heady aroma, she ran her fingers across a small section of the belt. For reasons beyond comprehension a sense of foreboding swamped her, as if a menacing presence stood directly behind.

Rennie spun around. The factory stood empty, with long shadows thrown across the cement floor. Nervous laughter bubbled from her lips. Turning from the conveyer belt, she spied tall stacks of empty crates nested in the shadows. The thin boards were stamped with the Fagan's Orchard logo.

She couldn't resist approaching, the sharp aroma of wood a pleasing contrast to the florid scent of apples. Behind the wall of crates, an ancient table sat against the factory's back wall. Employees now dined in the cafeteria at the other end of the factory, a modern expanse.

Nearing, she studied the wall. A flurry of names was carved into the wooden planks. Some were legible while others had been worn down by time.

Rutherford-1929; 1942-Wilfred. Robert-1939; Bennie-1967.

It was touching to think the grown men who'd once worked at the orchard had left proof of their existence carved into a wall. It was also rather endearing, like the marks a child made on a school desk when the teacher wasn't looking. Bennie surely hadn't been educated and Rutherford, either, not if they'd worked the orchard decades ago. Nor had the other men who'd left their marks—Jim, Gil, Terence. Rennie trailed her fingers across the soft grooves chipped into the wood.

A scrawl larger than the rest cut across the names like a wound slashed through flesh. She snatched her hand back.

SWEEPER

The writing carried rage, like a gash upon the world. Unnerved, she looked around quickly and glimpsed a stairwell at the other end of the building. She hurried toward it.

Unlike the factory below, the second floor was a calming retreat. Pastel walls met the gleaming oak floors. In the reception area, a woman in thick bifocals angled a phone on her shoulder as Rennie approached. "Dianne's is the last office," she whispered before returning to her conversation.

The nerves Rennie had put at bay scuttled through her stomach. She stepped inside the long, narrow room.

Even here, the scent of apples was thick. A large framed poster took up much of the opposite wall, a reproduction of a Fagan's advertisement from the early 1900s. Vivid green and a blinding gold—but the image inside the border was soft, of a woman in a flounced skirt and an apron. Her arms cradled an abundance of apples. The slogan read, *Fagan's Bounty. From Our Garden to Your Table.*

"Rennie!"

Dianne approached at an impressive speed for a woman in the third trimester of pregnancy. To her left, a pitcher of water sweated on the long conference table. Pens, pads and a stack of architectural drawings were stacked on the polished wood.

Catching Rennie's appraisal, Dianne drew her to the table. "Go ahead and look," she said. When Rennie slowly turned the top rendering around, Dianne rocked back on her heels. "Isn't it marvelous? The plant boasts forty thousand square feet. Come see."

Rennie let the younger woman steer her past the desk, to the window overlooking the orchard's undulating hills. "We'll build over there," Dianne explained, pointing toward a sweep of trees in the distance. "An old orchard, no longer productive. We'll have to add another road . . . right there. We'll put in the road this fall."

While she chattered on, Rennie battled her gloom. There were hundreds of apple trees in bloom in the acres below, the white-haloed treetops rising ever higher with the land, to the horizon, where the Great Oak stood like a beacon against the sky. The impetuous girl she'd once been had argued then mated with Troy beneath the tree, had fused hate with passion. Earlier still, Jason had enjoyed dreaming there with his back settled on the oak's rough bark and his legs flung out on the patchy grass. Together they'd sat on the summit smoking Marlboros in the summer heat with the oak's generous shade cooling their backs. She hadn't taken to the habit of smoking but Jason had enjoyed it immensely, dangling a cigarette from his fingertips in a boy's charming attempt at sophistication.

Yet before she sat with Jason, before she met Troy beneath the tree's sheltering embrace, the simple patch of ground witnessed a great sacrifice.

Mae Sullivan was an angel.

Emotion rolled through her, a tide rushing over unsuspecting ground. She reminded herself that good had come from the rape. Troy was a proud, sensitive man born into the world through the gift of Mae's sorrow.

"May I sit down?" She sank into a chair midway down the conference table. "I've been going since five a.m."

Dianne slid into a chair beside her, a dainty princess enjoying herself. "Don't be nervous. I want you to have the job. Women rarely work in construction. I'm glad to have you on board. My husband, Frank? He travels constantly. And my parents are always busy. Naturally, there's Troy but he only feigns interest if I show him furniture catalogs and wallpaper swatches."

"I'm not much of an expert on decor. I didn't think there was much need in a factory."

"There will be in *my* factory." Dianne stabbed a finger at a small rectangle on the blueprint. "My office. I'll most definitely do it up. Creams and greens. Do you like emerald green? I know I'm setting myself up for all those jokes about the Irish but I can't help myself. I adore emerald green. We'll also paper the daycare with something fun—zoo animals, perhaps. Something peppy."

"A peppy daycare." Despite her gloom, Rennie grinned.

If you know something that could destroy a person's life, should you tell him?

Beneath the table, she dug her nails into her jeans. She

looked at Dianne and saw her near carbon copy—Jason. They shared the same irrepressible glee, the same sparkle in green Irish eyes.

With effort, she focused on the blueprint. "You're planning all of this for your employees' kids?" she asked.

"Once the plant is built, we'll increase payroll substantially. Daycare is one of the new benefits. I'm also looking into dental coverage."

Dennis Fagan strode into the room, followed by his wife. "I haven't agreed to dental," he told his daughter. His green eyes dancing, he regarded Rennie. "This must be an exciting day for you."

She stumbled to her feet to shake his outstretched hand. "Most certainly." She tried to suppress a sudden wave of nerves as Jackie neared with her unmistakably regal gait. "Mrs. Fagan. Hello."

They returned to the conference table. Dennis sat at the head. He winked at his daughter before returning his attention to Rennie. "When we met last week, I didn't realize you were the girl who knocked out my son's tooth. It was so many years ago. Troy was in such a belligerent stage of puberty. Your pitching arm settled him down. I should thank you."

She couldn't imagine anything settling Troy down—he'd made her school years hell. "It was an accident," she said. "I owe you an apology."

"Relax, dear. And I do regret the other thing with the darts. We weren't aware our son was using your yearbook photo for target practice." Dennis grinned, his expression making him appear more elfish. "Troy was always a natural at darts. The rest of us never did get the hang of it. If I'd known about your photo, I would have removed it from his dartboard. Fagan men are usually known for more chivalry."

Dianne giggled. "Daddy, stop. You're embarrassing her."

"He's not," Rennie said through dry lips. *They love Troy.* "We were just kids." *Why didn't I throw out the letters?* "Forgiven and forgotten."

Jackie seated herself at the opposite end. "Dennis, really. Don't you remember? Rennie was Jason's friend in high school. She used to come by the house. Honestly, you're not yet sixty-five and you've lost your wits."

"I have?"

Jackie poured a glass of water. She handed it solemnly to Dianne. "Pass this to your new friend. She's absolutely parched."

Rennie murmured her thanks. With dismay she appraised Jackie, still looking at her with the slightest hint of sadness. *Seeing me reminds her of a child lost.* Water sloshed to the edge of the glass. She set it down.

"You were Jason's friend?" Dennis asked, breaking into her thoughts.

"We were close," she offered. "I still miss him."

"We all do." Dennis regarded his daughter, aimlessly running her fingers across her generous belly. "Dianne hardly remembers him. A shame. They're so much alike. Freewheeling. Always up to something."

"You're lucky to be like him," Rennie told Dianne. Steering the conversation from talk of Jason seemed impossible and her skin grew clammy. "Your brother was great. I liked him very much."

"Everyone did," Dianne agreed. She held Rennie's gaze for an uncomfortable moment before adding, "I wonder why Troy never mentioned your friendship with Jason. He's terribly secretive. Nothing like the rest of us." Shrugging it off, she turned to the drawings. "Daddy, will you give Rennie the rundown or should I?"

"Go ahead, sweetheart."

She launched into an explanation of the new plant's design. Rennie tried to quiet her heart, beating so loudly she wondered how the frantic pace went undetected by the others. Sliding a notepad near, she diligently took notes about the electrical demands of the factory floor and the lighting requirements of the lavish executive suites.

After this job she was set. She'd move Perini Electric into Liberty's new industrial park.

I can't take the job, not after I tell Troy.

In turmoil, she was still grasping for the fading possibility of joy as she drove back to the mansion. A semi pulled into the long line of trucks. Workers in back of the rig began offloading boxes and chatting loudly. She paused to watch three carpenters working on the roof with the sun beating on their backs.

Squeak was probably wrapping up in the kitchen, and she decided to check on Princess. A gardener was digging fertilizer in around the azaleas bordering the house. The grass smelled as impossibly fresh as the springtime day. She walked across the plush carpet sorting out her emotions, her feet sinking deep into the turf. In the center of the long sweep of lawn, she was surprised to find Squeak with his dog. The way he crouched protectively beside his beloved pet wicked the scent of grass away.

From over his shoulder, he sent a look of distress. She rushed to his side.

"Oh, God—what happened?" She scudded to a halt beside Princess. The dog gave out a low, piteous wail then licked Squeak's hand with desperate affection.

Squeak took an angry swipe at his damp cheeks. "Look at her leg," he said. "She's hurt."

Gently he stroked the dog's haunches, his fingers sweeping around the small gash in the black fur. Blood clotted like red pearls. The sight made Rennie's legs loose and wobbly. She sat heavily on the grass.

"It's the mason." Squeak's eyes flashed. "I'm sure of it. I'm going to kick his ass for hurting my dog."

Chapter 18

Rennie clamped a hand on Squeak's wrist to stop him from launching to his feet. He looked more than ready to put muscle behind his threat against the mason.

"You can't confront someone because you think he hurt your dog." She dragged him back down to kneel beside his dog. "Where's the proof?"

"Look at the wound, Rennie. He must've kicked Princess or cut her with something."

"Did you see him do it?"

"No, but—"

"Think he'll admit it? He won't."

"This isn't fair! What am I supposed to do?"

Unsure, she yanked a bandanna from her pocket and carefully dabbed at the wound. She drew back and Princess laid her head on the grass, panting.

"Squeak, I haven't seen any of the masons." Aside from Troy and his family, she hadn't spoken to anyone else this morning. "Princess may have nicked herself on a tree trunk. Maybe she cut herself on something lying around the site. Anything's possible."

The comment rang false, even to her own ears.

"Princess didn't hurt herself," Squeak insisted, glowering.

"Have you seen the mason?"

"His crew might have left to grab burgers at a drive-through. We do it all the time."

Brushing off his outburst, she gently urged Princess into a

standing position. "Let's get the pooch in your truck. Do you have any blankets?" Squeak's maternal instincts were impeccable and he always traveled with everything his dog needed. "I'll walk her around the side of the mansion—pull your truck up front. Take her to the vet to check if the wound's deep."

He brooded in churlish silence for ten seconds. Then he marched off.

"Come on, baby," Rennie whispered to the shuddering dog. She wound the leash around her wrist and gently urged Princess forward. "We'll get you fresh water and a nice biscuit."

She acknowledged the carpenters walking past with their sack lunches. A breeze gusted toward the forest's deep shade, sending whispers across the lawn. The gardener dragged a hose toward the side of the house. He tipped his cap over a boyish face, a cheerful greeting. She gave a quick wave.

She'd nearly reached the gardener when his expression changed. "Lady, I think he's trying to get your attention." He squinted toward the forest.

Rennie brought Princess to a halt against her knees. "Who is?" She peered over her shoulder.

Shock lanced through her. At the edge of the forest the mason stepped into the sunlight.

He smiled. The blood drained from Rennie's head.

Like the gardener, he tipped his cap at her. Then he withdrew from the light.

"Rennie, Walt needs you *right now*. It's not pretend. It's *urgent*."

Setting the last plate in the dishwasher, Rennie regarded Emma, whose green eyes were as full of entreaty as her voice.

"Okay, okay—tell him I'm coming. Did you get my mitt?"

"I put it right here."

Emma skipped to the kitchen table with her Barbie doll bouncing on her hip. Her peachy bouffant dress, an ancient yet remarkably pristine number Jenalyn had bought at the local Goodwill, moved in pretty folds around her knees. Not one to be outdone, Rennie had also stopped by the Goodwill this week. She'd tried not to breathe in the faintly mothball-scented air while rummaging through the racks to find several pairs of jeans for the more earthy Walt and half a dozen out-of-date dresses for his ultra feminine sister. Walt was ecstatic when she brought the clothes home. Emma, a silent princess accepting deserved gifts, took the bag of dresses and disappeared into her bedroom to carefully hang each frock in the closet. No doubt she'd wear them all.

Which would be a real kick. The way Rennie saw it, Emma's only real sin was that she'd arrived in a world that wasn't 1962.

"Are you going to watch your brother practice?" Rennie asked, masking her nerves with a pleasant smile. The day had been hellish and it wasn't yet over. Emma danced from foot to foot, swishing her dress back and forth. "I assume that means yes?"

Emma scrunched up her brown-berry face. "Bathroom." She flew across the kitchen. From the living room, she called, "Wait for me and Barbie. We both have to tinkle."

"Will do."

Walt banged in through the back door. "What's taking so long?" He tossed a baseball into the air. "I thought we were practicing my pitch before Anna-gorilla takes us for ice cream."

Rennie sighed. "Walt, that's a private nickname. Don't use it in front of my sister."

"Why not? Anna-gorrrrlllla!"

"It's top secret," she replied, glancing at her watch. Her heart jumped as she read the time. "Only use it when we're alone."

He gave her the thumbs up then tossed the ball toward the ceiling. "Got it."

Where *was* Anna? If her sister didn't hurry, Rennie would have no choice but to introduce the kids to Troy when he arrived. Proving her merit in the world of construction was difficult enough. One look at Walt and Emma, and Troy would conclude she'd never succeed at parenting two foster kids *and* managing Perini Electric.

Burying the thought, she asked Walt, "Do you have your mitt?"

"On the picnic table." His young face eased into an expression of concern. "Are you better yet?"

She'd been a wreck when they'd returned home. Lack of sleep, learning of Mae Sullivan, her concern for the Fagans—and topping it off with the unsavory mason who probably *had* hurt Squeak's dog—she'd seen better days.

Sensing her low spirits, Walt had immediately gone into his new "man of the house" mode. He took out the garbage without being asked. He helped Emma with her homework while Rennie made dinner. He even brought in her toolbox from the truck and cleaned out the garbage in her cooler. At dinner, he'd admonished his younger sister when she tried to sneak from the table without eating her salad.

He'd patiently hovered around the edges of Rennie's frayed emotions. With less than an hour before Troy appeared, she still hadn't pulled herself together.

Impulsively, she palmed the curls spiraling from his scalp. "You need another haircut," she murmured, wishing she could display affection this easily with Emma. Which might never happen she mused, resting her hand on Walt's shoulder. "It's getting long in back. Why does your hair grow so fast?"

"All of me grows fast." He shrugged, and she saw him suddenly for what he was: a boy nearing puberty. A man, soon after. The prospect warmed her.

Emma returned with her doll cradled in her arms. "You waited!"

They went out back. Walt trotted across the grass swinging his left arm in a wide arc to loosen the muscles. He liked showing off the windup she'd taught him. His avid mimicry sent something good through Rennie. The emotion cut right through everything else—the worry, her anxiety over Troy's impending visit, her fear of the mason. She put on the catcher's mitt handed down from her father, the leather old and cracked and loved, and savored the sight of a boy who was nothing like her except in the way he angled his hips and drew back his arm with the ball held tight in his grip. The resolve on his face echoed hers, the way he lifted the corner of his mouth and narrowed his eyes as he set the ball loose with enough savage, exhilarating velocity to hurl it toward Rennie and the mitt she had at the ready.

Joy, she thought as the ball connected with her mitt in a dance of speed and heat. *I'm feeling joy.*

๛

In a growing state of restlessness, Troy pressed the doorbell. The decision to arrive fifteen minutes early wasn't polite, but he was in no mood to prolong the mystery. Whatever secret Rennie felt compelled to share with him, they'd get this over quickly.

In the driveway of the house next door, a teenage boy yanked weeds from the bed in front of his parents' white bungalow. His father, a hawk-nosed clone with a receding hairline, tipped a wheelbarrow, releasing a wave of mulch. He eyed Troy appraisingly.

In this middle-class neighborhood with open windows blaring music onto the street and bicycles flung across lawns, Troy's Mercedes stood out. As did he, standing on Rennie's front stoop with a veneer of affluence and a scowl on his lips.

Which was his intention. Only a fool welcomed troubling news. Rennie's agitation this morning had been palpable. Afterward, Troy spent the day quietly mulling over the strange conversation even though he should've kept his mind on work. At day's end, he'd thrown himself through a shower and donned clothing meant to intimidate—the navy slacks and blazer, the red silk tie knotted expertly at his throat.

There'd be no level playing field tonight. It was one thing to blend in with his employees at work, quite another to find himself standing on Rennie's front stoop with a world of questions knocking around his brain and a sense of foreboding filling his gut.

Again he rang the doorbell.

The man next door nodded toward the back of the house. "She's practicing baseball with Walt," he said. "Check in back."

Walt? Who's Walt? Troy nodded in thanks then went around the side of the house. He came to a standstill as he spotted Rennie, still in work clothes, catching a curveball the young boy had whipped through the air.

They didn't notice him. Safely hidden, he enjoyed the way the boy angled his left arm and wound up the pitch, a southpaw proud of his flawless coordination. His movements were intensely familiar. Or perhaps it was the determination on the

183

boy's face that startled Troy, the uncanny focus so rare in a child, the predatory slant of his eyes as he sent the ball hurtling for Rennie's mitt. Appraising him was like peering deep into Troy's own forgotten childhood and glimpsing the same perfect fit of athleticism and intention. Which seemed illogical. The boy was African American, and they'd never met.

"Troy."

Rennie's voice snapped him from his musings. "I'm early," he said.

There was a girl, too. He hadn't noticed her by the swing set. Both of the children were biracial—Rennie's?

She flicked her wrist, clearly uncomfortable. "This is Walt and Emma. My foster kids." He didn't have time to absorb the information that someone as unlikely as Rennie was a foster parent. She was already calling them over. "Kids, come and meet Mr. Fagan. Emma, don't be shy. He doesn't bite."

The girl, Emma, hovered by the swing set. The more confident Walt strode forward with a smile. Liking a kid so bold was easy. When Troy and his brother had been children, Jason hated meeting new people. Troy had come forward fearlessly.

"I'm Walt." The boy thrust out his hand. "Nice to meet you, Mr. Fagan."

"Call me Troy." He took the boy's hand, held tight. Reeling, it dawned that he didn't want to let go. Troy grappled with his emotions, off balance and desperate to prolong the moment for reasons he couldn't discern. "You throw a mean pitch. How long have you been playing ball?"

"Rennie taught me awhile ago."

"You're good. Keep it up."

Walt slipped his hand from Troy's grasp, an immeasurable loss. "I like baseball."

"You're a natural."

Rennie followed his intense inspection of Walt, her brows puckering. "I'm sorry about this," she said, and Troy yanked his attention to her. "My sister must be running late. Anna is taking the kids out for an hour."

"No problem." He shrugged out of his blazer and pressed it on a flustered Rennie. Then he took the catcher's mitt stuffed beneath her left arm. "I don't mind tossing a few balls." He regarded the boy with ill-concealed affection. "What do you say, Walt? Want to practice your pitch with me?"

The suggestion put pleasure in the boy's eyes. "Sure."

Loosening his tie, Troy got into position. Walt darted across the grass. The boy planted his feet, and it was easy to appreciate the beauty of his left-handed pitch as he released the ball, easier still to tamp down the apprehension Troy had entertained over his upcoming conversation with Rennie. He wasn't acquainted with many children but he liked Walt for reasons as murky as his own unfathomable heart.

Troy caught another fastball, and grinned at Rennie. She appeared shell-shocked by his behavior. "Get Walt private lessons with a pitching coach," he advised, lobbing the ball in a fast return. "Find one through Liberty High. Call their athletic director."

"You're serious?"

"Walt's young. Get him the right instructor now and he'll become the starting pitcher in high school. A sure bet for a college scholarship."

Pleased by the assessment, Rennie hugged his blazer close. The image touched him deeply, her features softening as she rocked on her heels.

She looked away. "I can't afford private lessons," she admitted.

Emma wandered up. Rennie lifted her arm, beckoning the girl close. Emma scampered out of reach. Which provided another unusually poignant sight—the normally gruff Rennie with hurt clouding her eyes.

Steering her attention back to him, Troy said, "Some lefties are ambidextrous. Has Walt tried pitching with his right hand?"

"No one pitches with both hands." Rennie flexed the fingers of her right hand and Troy chuckled at her competitive streak. She pitched a mean game right-handed, not left. "It's impossible."

"Guess again. Watch. Hey, Walt—toss it back."

Troy took the ball. He sent an expert pitch to Walt from his left hand then his right.

Rennie gaped at him. "How did you do that?"

Before he could reply Walt shimmied his shoulders, focused. And tossed a decent pitch from the right side.

The boy leapt into the air. "Hey, I can do it too! Did you see, Rennie?"

"I sure did. And I don't believe it."

Amused, Troy went to her. "Like I said, some lefties are ambidextrous. Walt's one. I am, too."

"I've never noticed you're left-handed."

"Why would you?"

Their gazes caught, and clung. The interchange was pleasurable, her large, expressive eyes growing wider still. His blatant appraisal rendered her speechless. Was she attracted to him? He'd never stopped to consider the possibility. Hell, he'd gladly settle for casual friendship. The notion that she might view him as an attractive man instead of her ill-tempered employer was both an invitation and a warning. A warning mostly. He couldn't become involved with a woman in his employ, and certainly not one he'd always cared for more than was sensible.

Regret sifted through him when she halted the exchange. "Walt, would you like to try pitching a few more with your right hand?" she asked the boy. "Anna isn't here yet so you might as well—"

She cut off to send a sidelong glance to the driveway. A woman in a tight skirt trotted toward them on heels so high they propelled her forward. She was a dim reflection of Rennie with the first hints of crow's feet arcing from heavily made up eyes.

"I was tied up in a meeting. Went on forever." The woman glanced dismissively at Rennie before tacking her attention on Troy. "Well, hello. I'm Anna. Who might you be?"

Rennie stepped between them. "This is my boss, Troy Fagan." She regarded the shopping bags in Anna's hands with clear displeasure. "Troy, Anna is my older sister, the shopaholic. Anna, what is all of this?"

"Goodies for Walt and Emma. Mother said they were going to camp on Monday. You can't afford to clothe them, not on an electrician's salary. I'm bailing you out."

"I've already bought—"

"Oh, please. Did you scour garage sales? The least you can do is thank me."

The shiny gold bags brought Emma from her hiding place by the swing set. But Troy's attention clung to Rennie, standing quietly as her sister rummaged through tissue paper and produced clothing with great flourish—shirts, shorts, and the type of tennis shoes with lights in the heels that kids loved. Walt and Emma jumped up and down. Anna filled their arms with the kind of high-end clothing his own sister would buy but that Rennie couldn't possibly afford.

Rennie's shoulders curved with defeat, prodding him to say to her insensitive sister, "This must have set you back a few hundred."

Anna gave a fluttery laugh. "If I don't help my little sister, who will?" She leapt forward suddenly, to flick Rennie's shirt collar. "Honestly, can't you change into something presentable while entertaining a guest? You look like a common laborer."

Troy grunted. "I'm not sure about the common part. She's the finest electrician in three counties." He'd had enough of the insufferable woman. "Rennie, did I remember to give you the advance for the processing plant?"

She blinked. "What?"

"Forgive me. Slipped my mind." Pulling out his wallet, he produced a blank business check. He turned to Anna, eyeing him curiously with her pink leather purse dangling at her elbow. "Got a pen in that thing?" She handed one over. He strode to the picnic table, wrote swiftly, and returned. "Here you go, Rennie. Pay your sister for the clothing."

"Pay my . . ."

"It won't make a dent in your advance."

"Right." The stupor she'd fallen under began to recede. Then her pretty brows hit her hairline when she examined the check. "Wow."

He liked the way she pursed her lips. "You're welcome."

"I can't take this."

"Sure you can. And you're still welcome."

She flapped the check through the air with endearing, genuine gratitude. "You're being far too generous."

"Nonsense. This is a standard advance for an industrial job." She'd only worked residential and wouldn't know he was lying. "Pay your sister for the shopping spree."

"I'll get my checkbook." She stumbled toward the house.

He regarded Anna with an icy smile. "Take the kids out for

an hour and a half," he ordered. He slapped several bills into her hand.

Speechless, she tottered on her heels.

Troy winked at Walt, who beamed. Which was contagious, because Emma beamed up at him, too. "When do you kids usually go to bed?" he asked them.

"Pretty late," Walt said.

"After cartoons, mostly," Emma put in. "Like around eleven?"

Rennie dashed across the grass, waving the check she'd written. "Don't let them fool you, Troy. Bedtime is nine o'clock sharp."

He nodded. "Great. Anna, it was a pleasure. Good bye." He gently removed his blazer from Rennie's arm. "Now, why don't we go inside and talk?"

Chapter 19

Ushering Troy into the house, Rennie was painfully aware she was about to destroy his known world.

The letters would see to it. Once the contents were revealed, she'd strip him of everything he held familiar and dear.

Queasy at the prospect, she placed the check on top of the microwave. Once he heard her out, he'd surely demand it back. Furtively, she glanced up into his shuttered face.

He surveyed the small kitchen. She suspected he was measuring the space against his knowledge of her—how the cheery lemon-colored paint came as a surprise but the clutter on the countertops did not. His gaze wandered to the valance above the window, patterned in whimsical fruits, lemons and oranges.

"How long have you had the kids?" he asked, his voice strained.

No doubt the question was meant to ward off more serious topics. "Not long," she replied. "My mother is the director of Job & Family Services. She has a rule that we all take foster-adopt classes. It's a long slog, nine months of coursework. Afterward she expects us to provide a foster home if she can't find an alternative placement."

"Us?"

"Me and my sibs."

"Right." Troy knit his brows. "So now you have Walt and Emma. Two children—seems like a handful."

"We're doing all right." She reconsidered. "Emma keeps to

herself."

"But not Walt," Troy said. "He's got quite a pitching arm. He'll go far."

His interest might have seemed unusual if she hadn't witnessed their instant rapport. They'd performed the loving ballet of a father and son sharing a game of ball on a springtime evening. Troy's face had been suffused with longing, as if he'd waited on shore for a lifetime until Walt drifted in from the tumultuous sea of his birth.

She opened a cupboard and removed two glasses. "The kids leave on Monday for a week at camp. I'll miss them. After that, I don't know. They might stay for several months longer."

"Their parents are in trouble?"

"Their mother died in Tennessee—an accident at the factory where she worked. Their father is originally from Liberty. Recently moved back with Walt and Emma. He has . . . issues."

Troy stood back while she rummaged through a second cupboard. "Issues," he repeated, his mouth curving wryly. "Sounds like an evasion."

"When your mother is a social worker, you learn the lingo. It's a diplomatic way of saying Walt and Emma's father is a real bastard. They're better off living here." She pulled a bottle of Jack Daniels from the cupboard. "Like a drink?"

He gave a stiff nod, the tension returning to his face.

She poured the whiskey for him and Merlot for herself then led him into the living room with her heart in her throat and her stomach bathed in acid. She remained silent as he took in the room, the worn couch and the easy chair, the inexpensive drapes and the empty walls. His gaze, quick and assessing, held no censure of the dull surroundings. She encouraged him into the easy chair, the most comfortable seat in the room.

The metal box lay on the coffee table. Her gaze stole to it.

The explanation she'd rehearsed fled her brain. Troy murmured something but she couldn't hear past the pounding in her ears. Sinking onto the couch, she tried to steady herself. The irritation gathering on his face spurred her on.

"Crash and the men didn't demolish all of Jason's closet," she began, flipping the box open. "I went in after them to pull out some outlets."

"I recall seeing the outlet." He took a long swallow of whiskey. "It was near the old section of Jason's walk-in closet."

"There was a shelf inside. I found this box of letters." She withdrew the first missive written by Mae to Troy's mother. "I should've found you immediately. I was in a hurry. Walt had an appointment with the dentist."

"What's the letter about?"

"You."

"Hold on. There were letters about me in my brother's closet?"

"Jason hid the box. I think he found the letters right before his high school graduation party."

"Why would he hide a box of letters?"

Coming to her feet, she erased the distance between them with regret and fear thickening her blood. The truth would shatter his family. She'd lose her job. Walt and Emma would move to a more stable foster home. Troy would lash out at her blindly—

Handing over the letter, she sent them both into free fall. "Why don't you read it?"

He did, swiftly, the strong plane of his face frighteningly impassive. He regarded her with faint annoyance. "It's a birthday greeting from some woman to my mother," he said. "My parents have many friends. I'm not sure why you think this is important. I sure as hell don't know why Jason stashed the letters in his closet."

Nervously she handed over the next two letters written by Mae on Troy's second and third birthdays with such fervent devotion, only a fool would conclude she'd merely been an acquaintance of his mother's.

He read with painstaking care, his face tensing on a chasm of concern. Rennie yearned to fold him into her arms to offer the assurance everything would be all right. The desire was sudden and disorienting, an odd complement for the tension weaving through her limbs. She couldn't dismiss the notion as Troy came to the end of the second letter with his brow lowering in a dangerous furrow.

He looked like a man grappling to stand erect on shifting ground. He clawed at his scalp. Ungovernable emotion washed through his eyes. Surprise, disbelief—

Anger. Rennie steeled herself for the earthquake to come.

"Mae Sullivan wrote until your seventh birthday," she offered in a voice no stronger than her wavering pulse. She produced the most problematic letter, the one Mae wrote to her mother. "This letter isn't a birthday greeting. Mae wrote it about my mother, Lianna, before you were born. Given my mother's involvement, I'm sure you'll understand why I went to her before mentioning any of this to you. She told me the entire story about Mae. She was quiet upset."

Troy regarded her with savage intensity. "You've discussed this with your mother?" Muttering a curse, he drained his glass. "Why was she upset?"

"She was close with Mae. Both of their mothers worked at the mansion."

"When, exactly?"

"Thirty-six years ago. Then something awful happened and Mae got pregnant. She was only sixteen years old. She'd planned to become a nun but she was pregnant—" Aware she was talking too quickly, Rennie took a deep breath. In a steadier voice, she said, "Troy, Mae Sullivan is your biological mother. She wasn't old enough to raise you. Do you understand? The correspondence with your adoptive mother was her way of saying goodbye."

Her voice dissolved beneath the skepticism overtaking his face. Well, what had she expected? She was coming at him with facts he couldn't possibly absorb. The information would take weeks to digest.

"You think I'm adopted?" He tossed the letters on the table.

"It's true."

"Like hell," he growled, pulling to his feet. He began pacing with hostile impatience. "I can't explain the letters but they don't signify what you assume they do. I can't begin to guess why your mother invented a story about Mae Sullivan, whoever the hell she is. The story is wrong. I know who I am."

"I'm sorry. I didn't think you knew. I wish I weren't the one to break this to you."

The color seeped from his face. She fought the urge to flee the room. But she couldn't, not while he stood immobile with trembling emotion working across his jaw. Which she understood. It was easier for him, surely, to hide his understanding behind anger and disbelief. The truth was unraveling with a host of new and awful revelations, not the least of which was that he *should have been told by his parents.* The Fagans had withheld the most basic facts of his life.

Sinking onto the couch beside her, Troy dropped his elbows on his knees. "If any of this were true, my parents would've spelled it out. They wouldn't let me believe—they would've explained, Rennie. They aren't secretive. We've always been close. They don't hide things. You don't know them."

"Of course I don't. Not like you do," she murmured, and the vision of Jason appeared before her, Jason on the night of the graduation party asking for her advice because he'd known what Troy had not. The Fagans *did* keep secrets. They'd buried Mae's letters beneath their otherwise happy lives—

"And you think they'd let me believe I don't belong to them?" Troy was saying. "Rennie, I don't know why Jason hid the letters in his closet. Before his murder, he was acting strangely. He was angry with my parents, angry with me. He died before we got the chance to hash it out. Best guess, he came to the same erroneous conclusion as you. It sure as hell would explain his behavior during his last days."

"Troy, my mother told me about Mae. I heard it from her own lips."

"She got the facts wrong. My parents would never lie to me."

"They didn't lie. They simply didn't know how to tell you." She scooted further away on the couch, needing distance from the disgust sparking in his gaze. She wanted to gather up the letters and discard them, forget the misery contained within their pages. Instead, she rushed on blindly. "I'm sure your parents believed it was in your best interest to keep the facts hidden. You see, your biological mother was raped. Reason enough to make broaching a discussion of your adoption difficult for your parents—"

Horrified by the outburst, she clamped her mouth shut.

Troy looked like he'd been slapped. "What exactly did your mother tell you? Tell me word for word."

She did, quickly. Summing up, she added, "I've never known

her to be anything but truthful."

"Where is Mae Sullivan now?"

"Still in Pittsburgh, I think. I can check with my mother, if you'd like."

"Married?"

"No. She's probably still at the church. St. Justin Martyr. I believe she works the grounds."

"She's a gardener?" Troy hesitated. Then he gave out a hollow laugh. "You have me half believing this."

All things considered, he *was* taking the news exceedingly well. "My mother hasn't spoken to Mae in some time," Rennie said, pressing on before her courage vanished. "Something happened between my mother and Mae—I'm not sure what. My mother was so shaken this morning, I didn't press her."

"Maybe *I* should press her." With disdain Troy regarded the letters, the tangible proof of his altered life. "What am I supposed to do with this? I'm not confronting my parents when I don't believe any of this. They've lost one son—I'll be damned if I'll let them think they'll lose the other. I'm a Fagan, not Mae Sullivan's kid. Maybe she *was* raped. Maybe she did have a baby and gave it up for adoption. But the people who took in her kid weren't my parents. I know who my parents are. They're my flesh and blood."

"Mae was raped at the orchard." Rennie hazarded a glance at his face, rigid with fury. "Under the oak tree."

"Beneath the Great Oak?"

"Yes."

"The Great Oak? Where you and I—" He cut off, flabbergasted.

"I'm sorry."

"That's great, Rennie. You've got one damn apology after another, don't you?"

Sick-hearted, she rose. "If you want to speak with my mother, I'll set up a time."

He stalked to the foyer. "I don't need to speak to her."

"What *do* you want?" He hadn't asked for the letters. She didn't dare suggest he should. "If there's anything I can do, please tell me."

"You've done enough already."

He marched into the lackluster night and hurried to his car.

With a feeling of resignation, she watched him back the Mercedes out of the driveway, cut a tight corner and disappear into the gloom.

Chapter 20

Jenalyn's expression held a mix of curiosity and concern. "Arriving at six a.m. is ambitious, isn't it?" she said.

Lianna bit back a peevish reply. She'd finally escaped Mario after tormenting him all weekend with snappish comments and furtive glances at the telephone, even though they'd agreed Rennie was too upset to put in a call. Leaving for work had felt like an escape. Or perhaps banishment, with Mario, gathering up her purse and keys, steering her out. Lord knew he'd grown sick of her mood.

"Why are *you* here early?" she asked Jenalyn.

"I *am* young and ambitious." Mirth twinkled in the social worker's eyes. "Now, c'mon. There must be a reason why you're at the office before the bluebirds sing."

"I had a difficult conversation with Rennie," she said, hating the weakness that made her want, made her *need* to talk about it. "She came across information about my teenage years. She's upset."

"Rennie's upset about something you did as a teenager? Hard to believe."

"More what I didn't do." Learning of Mae's rape sent Rennie fleeing the kitchen before Lianna pulled herself together. "She left before I had a chance to explain."

"Didn't you try to call her later?"

"She's avoiding calls—avoiding me. I should've stopped by last weekend. It seemed best to let her cool off. Now I wish I had gone over."

"I have a solution." Jenalyn smiled encouragingly. "Come with me to First Presbyterian. Walt and Emma leave for camp today. They insisted Rennie bring them to the church. They hate leaving her, even for a week."

"Aren't six or seven of our foster kids going this year?"

"Seven total. Rennie will drop off her kids early." The social worker paused and the stark emotion crossing her features brought Lianna to attention. "She has no choice. Buck insisted on coming to the church to see the kids off."

The new was unwelcome. "They won't run into each other, will they?"

"Buck won't get a glimpse of her. I asked Rennie not to stay for more than a few minutes. Drop the kids off, leave. She understands my concerns."

Lianna did, too. When Walt and Emma first came to the agency's attention, she'd wisely chosen not to divulge the name of the foster home even though, in most instances, the foster parent's name was readily shared. Though the drunk driving citation was the only blemish on Buck's record and Walt and Emma's physical abuse wasn't substantiated, Lianna hadn't hesitated to order Jenalyn to keep the foster home confidential. Years of working with humanity's most troubled souls had given her finely tuned antennae for working with troubled adults. Most of the men and women were souls desperate for help. They responded to a twelve-step program, or worked out their personal demons in therapy. They were simply good people beset with difficult problems.

Some adults, like Buck, were beyond reach. And she was powerless to do anything except spare the foster parent—her daughter—from the discomfort of a man so potently evil banked on the perimeter of her life.

Nervously she shuffled papers, glad for something to do with her hands. "How is Buck?" she asked.

The question put Jenalyn into deep reflection. "He hasn't missed any sessions with Sid, but therapy isn't going well. Sid is frustrated with him."

"Has Buck begun to deal with his alcoholism?"

"Not a chance."

"At least he's in therapy. I'd be more concerned if he were coming up with excuses to skip the sessions."

Jenalyn sighed. "He goes through the motions but doesn't appear capable of change. Those are Sid's words, by the way," she added, and Lianna worried that if one of the most experienced psychologists in Jeffordsville County couldn't make progress, Buck was truly beyond rehabilitation. "The court mandated counseling for another four weeks. We can ask for a continuation of therapy but we can't drag this out forever. At some point, we'll have to return custody."

"Reunite families whenever possible," Lianna murmured, despising the precise verbiage of State statutes when dealing with human lives. Given a free hand, she'd immediately sever Buck's parental rights. Every instinct honed through years of serving children warned he posed a danger to Walt and Emma. Dismissing the option as unrealistic, she added, "Children can't remain in foster care if the parent complies with our directives. Buck has done so. Have you found any reason why we shouldn't reunite this particular family?"

"No."

"But you have reservations?"

"Absolutely. After Buck sees the kids, I have them visit separately with a child psychologist. I'm using Sarah McKinley. I sent you an email."

"You did?" Lianna made a mental note to clean out her inbox today.

"Sarah is having no more success with the kids than Sid is with Buck."

"Children don't readily discuss physical abuse."

"Or sexual abuse," Jenalyn quietly replied. "I shouldn't assume, but . . . I don't know. Nothing was evident when the kids had physicals. Of course, a pediatrician can't always find proof."

Lianna patted her brow, disturbed by the explanation. It was a sadly familiar pattern. Dysfunctional families were rarely beset with one plague. They suffered a variety of scourges— poverty, illiteracy, physical and sexual abuse.

"We have time before I'll consider returning custody," Lianna said in a soothing voice. She thought of something else. "Have you mentioned any of this to Rennie?"

"Of course not. She's very attached to the kids. Frankly, I didn't think they'd grow on her like this. If they're sent back to their father, she'll take it hard."

Lianna's heart went out to her daughter. Had she made a dangerous miscalculation by asking her daughter to provide foster care?

Don't return the children to Buck. Doing so is a grave mistake.

Lianna resisted the unwarranted thought. Yet it clung tightly, thorny and dense, a poisonous notion she feared examining. During her watch as director of the agency, she'd been fortunate. Still, her staff was as overworked and underfunded as every other social agency in the United States. Last year, a boy in Florida starved to death after being returned to his mother, who'd ostensibly kicked her drug habit. Another child died in Minnesota, from gunfire, one short month after returning to a violent home. In a country the size of the United States, children received minimal aid in overburdened social agencies. In Jeffordsville County, hundreds of children had passed through the halls of J & FS. God forbid, if one day—

"Are you coming with me to First Presbyterian?" Jenalyn asked, breaking into her troubled thoughts. "You can patch things up with Rennie."

Lianna stared at her desk, which was as jumbled as her thoughts. "If you don't mind, I will tag along."

Before the white church with its steepled bell tower and arched portal, a small crowd of parents and children chatted with excitement.

Lianna parked beside the *Precious Cargo* bus commissioned to transport the children to camp and motioned for Jenalyn to go on ahead. It was just after seven a.m. Exasperated, Jenalyn shook her head then crossed the parking lot with her black hair swaying.

A cluster of adults parted. Rennie disengaged from the others to approach Jenalyn. Walt appeared a step behind, dressed nicely in hunter green shorts and a striped top. Next Emma shot forward. Hot pink shorts and a matching shirt—a Barbie doll poked out of the front pocket of her shorts. Despite her worry, Lianna chuckled.

Rennie was dressed for work in a masculine canvas shirt and jeans spattered with motor oil. Lianna sighed. She lingered for a moment on the curve of Rennie's face, the inviting swell of her lips and the large ovals of her eyes, the proud yet delicate nose—attributes that Anna hadn't inherited with quite as much success.

Rennie was the daughter Lianna had gifted with beauty.

She'd grown up in the shadow of her older brothers, sharing tee-shirts with Nick and Anthony. On most days she'd followed on Nick's heels, drawn by his irreverent humor and natural ability at sports. Lianna, exhausted after years of swollen ankles and difficult pregnancies, hardly noticed as her oldest son took charge of the boisterous toddler. Rennie had been nothing like Anna, nine years older, the perfect Italian daughter who enjoyed ironing her father's shirts and learning to make pasta by hand. Even Frannie, the youngest, was far more feminine.

Of Lianna's brood, Rennie was the child she'd failed.

Now she'd failed her again. The letters, Mae Sullivan—Lianna's past was laid out before the child least able to make sense of the pieces.

Hadn't Rennie secretly idolized her and begged for love in a million subtle ways? Lianna had inadvertently given her daughter the impression she'd never measured up. The poor grades in school, the disinterest in higher education—it wasn't fair to nudge a child, to poke and to prod when her dreams were at odds with a mother's expectations. Even now it was difficult to look at her daughter and not wonder what she might have achieved. A college degree. A good marriage, and children. The possibilities for happiness were there. Yet they seemed depressingly beyond imagining for a daughter so headstrong and independent.

Across the parking lot, Jenalyn spoke with clear animation. She gestured at the car. Rennie squinted in the sunlight. She whispered something to Walt and Emma before coming forward.

"You didn't have to come," she said, reaching the car. "I'm not ready to talk."

Lianna climbed out. "I haven't seen you in days. How are you?"

"Feeling lousy if you really want to know. My heart-to-heart with Troy sure didn't go as planned."

"You told him about the letters?" Predictably, her daughter had leapt into the fray without considering the consequences.

"He's having trouble believing any of this. The part about Mae's rape just about did him in. I can't imagine what he'll be like at work today."

"You mentioned the rape?"

"It's his life, Mom. He deserved a full accounting."

"Oh, sweetie. Did you have to tell him everything?"

The question brought Rennie's chin up. Her lower lip trembled but she managed to restrain the churning emotion. Clearly she didn't like hurting Troy.

"He has a right to the truth." Rennie pressed her lips together, considering. "Is Mae Sullivan still in Pittsburgh?"

"She lives at St. Justin's. She's the head gardener for the parish grounds."

"Pittsburgh is only a few hours away, and you were good friends. Why hasn't she ever visited?"

"We don't have much contact. I send a card during the holidays," Lianna said, uncomfortable with the turn of conversation.

"The Christmas card with the photo of all of us and the grandkids?"

"No, no—the one from Social Services. You recall the card. There's a drawing of J & FS on the cover."

Rennie looked at her with amazement. "You send her the cheap office card? That's what you send to a friend from high school? Gosh, Mom—you're full of surprises. Why not send the family card? Don't you want her to know what we're like?"

There was a strange justice in the questions issuing from the lips of a child so loved yet thoroughly tutored into believing she came up lacking in the Perini clan. No, Lianna couldn't bear to send the family photograph, to callously reveal how fully she'd benefited from Mae's tragedy. Lianna had wed Mario, the object of Mae's adolescent crush. She'd enjoyed a successful life filled with children, and now grandchildren. Mae lived in relative isolation—

"Answer me." The demand collapsed Rennie's expression.

She clenched and unclenched her fists, her gaze scuttling. "No. Forget it. I'm in enough trouble because of my big mouth. The less I know, the better."

Lianna struggled against the urge to pull her close. "Oh, sweetie—I wanted to explain when you came over. You left so quickly. I've never resolved my feelings toward Mae or my guilt." She lifted her palms heavenward. "There's so much I should have done, *wished* I had done."

"Why do you keep Mae at arm's length?"

Shame embraced Lianna with efficient speed. She'd spent a lifetime elevated in Rennie's eyes. But there were other threads hidden in the tapestry of her life, and her daughter had discovered the most fragile ones. If she tugged too hard, Lianna would unravel.

"Rugg's Diner," Lianna heard herself say, and it was enough to bring the memories back, the smell of fries sizzling in oil as Mr. Rugg dunked the basket, enough for her to remember the girl she'd once been, laughing whenever Tommy Gleason or Jed McCutcheon commented on some new outfit she wore. How to make Rennie understand? "I thought Mae would be pleased when I asked the boy in the red Mustang to flirt with her. I thought it would end there. Perhaps Mae viewed the flirting as a way to join in with my group of friends. She wanted more, a chance to socialize, to shine—a chance to be a normal teenager and not the girl chosen by God. The way her mother talked, you'd think Mae was destined for sainthood."

"Must've been hard on her."

Briefly Lianna closed her eyes. "The day she was raped, she'd asked to go with us to the diner. First time she'd asked me to take her anywhere. We only saw each other after school, at the Fagans. All week long she'd hinted about coming with me."

Rennie's expression softened. "Some guy was flirting with her. Why wouldn't she want to take it further?"

"You're right, of course. And your father enjoyed driving by and chatting with her when she walked to the Fagans after school. All very innocent, really—"

"Dad was the boy in the red Mustang?" Rennie cut in. She planted her hands on her hips. "*Why* would you fix my father up with your friend?"

"Dear, he wasn't your father at the time."

"Not much of a distinction, Mom. He *is* my father. I mean, really. Why did you do that?"

"I didn't care for him, not then," Lianna sputtered. Her eyes began to burn but she hurried on. "Sweetheart, your father was the last boy in school I would have dated. Our families were old country. They came from the same region outside of Rome. You can imagine how they pressured us to date. We both found their encouragement amusing and terribly awkward. I asked your father to show Mae some attention because he was trustworthy, a good friend. I knew he wouldn't take it too far."

She mopped her eyes, furious with the tears and the quaver in her voice. The emotion welled up quickly, but she needed to remain sensible so her daughter would grasp the story. She felt lightheaded and too upset for such an emotionally charged conversation.

Rennie's hand hovered above Lianna's forearm. It lowered, rested tentatively. "Mom, take a deep breath," she said, moving her fingers slowly up and down Lianna's chilled skin, the child comforting the parent in a ritual imprinted from one generation to the next. "You didn't take Mae to Rugg's Diner. She went back to the orchard alone, and . . . okay, I understand."

"I'm to blame for what happened," Lianna whispered. She paused long enough for her daughter to drape an arm across her shoulder and begin rocking her. "If I'd taken her with us, if I hadn't been so shallow—I thought she'd embarrass me in front of my friends. She'd walk into the diner in her parochial school jumper, and I'd be mortified when forced to introduce her all around. Or maybe I was jealous of Mae's blond hair and blue eyes. Was I afraid of the competition? Whatever my motivation, it was unbecoming."

Rennie drew her fully into an embrace. "You were a kid, not a psychic. How could you have known what would happen?"

"She just wanted to sit with a group of teenagers and sip a milkshake. Flirt with your father. It was so little to ask and I was her friend . . ."

Some of the high school seniors had stayed at the diner until eight p.m. Tired of the noise, Mr. Rugg had thrown them out into the balmy spring night. The group piled into Julie Cafferty's white

Cadillac, an old jalopy the size of a powerboat. Rock and roll blared from the radio. Someone in the backseat leaned forward to talk to Jules, bumping her shoulder as she drove, one of the boys from the basketball team, or Miles Simansky, the boisterous quarterback. Whoever he was, he spilled Coke all the way down Jules' dress. She cackled wildly as Bill Reynolds mopped up the mess from her thighs.

As the years of Lianna's life layered one on top of the next, as she nestled one of her babies to her breast or, later, listened absently to a social worker reciting the details of a home study, she'd return suddenly to Jules' car and the faultless spring night. She'd wonder—what torture was Mae subject to at that exact moment? Was the rapist defiling her? Was he straddled atop her, fists raised? Did she cry out as he shattered her jaw? Did her terror lift onto the wind at the precise moment that the music streamed from Jules' car and Lianna laughed along with the others—one short, merciless mile from the harrowing patch of ground where Mae lay bleeding?

Rennie's voice, thin as dreams, drew Lianna back. "Mom, you're not responsible. I can see how ending up with Dad is awkward. You shouldn't tear yourself up." She tipped her head to the side. "How *did* you end up with Dad?"

"We were both grieving." If not for the shock of Mae's rape, she wouldn't have spent so much time with Mario. "By the time we enrolled at Kent State, Mae was gone. No one in Liberty would talk about her disappearance. I didn't have the courage to ask my mother."

"How did you learn she was living at a church in Pittsburgh?"

"Troy's mother sent a note." Lianna had received the letter with shock and sadness. And relief—she was grateful Mae was safe. "Mrs. Fagan encouraged me to write. I didn't until after Anna was born. I couldn't find the words to tell Mae how awful I felt. As for my relationship with your father, we entered college with this awful secret hanging over us. We both felt complicit in what happened to Mae. Within weeks, we formed the tight bond we still share today. A few months after we enrolled in college, we fell in love."

"I'm glad you did. All things considered."

Lianna was about to steer the conversation back to Troy, to ask if he planned to contact Mae, when Jenalyn waved. Agitation peppered the social worker's impatience. More cars entered the lot to disgorge a stream of children, their backpacks bouncing and their voices lifting.

"You have to go." Lianna nudged her daughter in the direction of Walt and Emma. "Say goodbye to the kids."

Rennie took a few steps then drew to a halt. The racket of shifting gears split the air. The vehicle ground its way down the street bordering the church, sputtering and spewing black smoke. The truck swerved into the parking lot, and Lianna's blood went cold.

Buck

She didn't have time to react. Rennie, more agile, dashed to the children. Buck did the same, leaping from the truck and striding forward with irritation simmering on his face.

In silent fury, they met on either side of the children.

Chapter 21

Buck loomed behind the children. Walt lowered his eyes. Emma gripped her doll tightly, her knuckles white beneath her brown skin.

Rennie's breath thinned. Then her mind wheeled: Buck Korchek was the mason who'd terrorized Squeak and his dog.

The truth emptied her mind, causing an emotional brownout that severed the progress of time. Her thoughts whirled, disjointed and fluid. She heard her mother's footsteps clacking from behind and read the message in Jenalyn's eyes—*leave now*. She couldn't, not with Buck's attention narrowing onto her, his lips curling into the grizzled skin of his cheeks. His eyes glittered with pleasure and, she realized with a start, a taunt.

He asked, "You're the foster mom?"

The string of expletives coiled in her mouth refused to launch. The chilling calm of his voice was a paralyzing force.

"If this isn't something," he said. "Working girl like you doesn't seem the type to watch someone else's kids." He turned to Jenalyn, rooted on the pavement in a glazed shock. "Me and the lady work together. We're doing construction at the orchard outside of town. Small world."

The comment roused Jenalyn from her stupor. "Rennie, you know him?"

"Buck is on the masons' crew." Rennie paused a beat as her mother came to halt, heaving in air. "More to the point, he wasn't

207

supposed to arrive for another half hour."

"I'm early?" He stuck his fingers in the belt loops of his trousers. Frowning, he nodded at Rennie's hand. "No ring. Why isn't a pretty thing like you married?"

"My private life is none of your business."

A predatory smile rose on his lips. "I'll bet a pretty thing like you gets lots of offers. You ought to pick a man and have kids of your own."

The comment was a lancing blow. Injured, Rennie suffered the notion that Buck discerned every self-doubt she wrestled with, every worry that warned she couldn't parent Walt and Emma adequately. She felt raw. Then angry when he ruffled Walt's hair and the boy flinched.

The scent of his son's fear drew Buck's attention. "Boy, you excited about camp?"

"I am, sir."

"Better not cause mischief while you're there."

"Yes, sir."

Jenalyn cleared her throat. "Mr. Korchek, why don't you wait by your truck? I'll bring the children over in a moment."

Lianna sprang forward. "A splendid idea. Buck, if you don't mind?"

He ignored their requests with stark calm. "Emma, you excited?" he asked his daughter, his expression filling with sick pleasure as she clamped her arms tight to her sides. "They'll have games at camp. Think you'll enjoy them?"

"I will, sir."

"Nice doll you got there. Don't recall buying you a doll."

Jenalyn put frost in her gaze. "I bought it for her, Mr. Korchek."

"My other Barbie got broke." Emma darted a look then threw her gaze to the pavement. "Remember?"

"How could I forget? Thought you'd never stop bawling. Gave me a headache." He passed his hand over her hair and her shoulders twitched. "Pretty soon you'll be too old for dolls. I'll have to take it away."

The suggestion stamped fear on Emma's face. Her father smiled as if he'd made a joke and they were all too stupid to catch the punch line.

A numbing sickness poured into Rennie's gut. She immediately recalled how Buck had stepped out of the forest's pooling shadows on the day—she was sure of it now—when he'd injured Squeak's dog. Now his hard, square face was just as unreadable although there was no mistaking that he enjoyed the distress his presence provoked. He towered over them, three blanched women, and the kids—they were frozen with dread.

Something flashed inside Rennie. Pure and fierce, the emotion sent her swiftly to Emma's side.

She opened her arms and Emma leapt. The child wound her legs tightly around Rennie's hips with unmistakable need. It was a small victory, but glorious.

"Buck, if you'll excuse us, we haven't said a proper goodbye." She grabbed for Walt. His cold fingers found hers in an instant. "C'mon, kids. Let's have a moment alone."

From the corner of her eye, she was relieved to find her mother and Jenalyn forming a wall to halt Buck from following. Heart pounding, she hurried toward the crowd near the bus with the detached, abstract sense that there was safety in numbers. At the edge of the crowd she lowered Emma to the ground.

"I want both of you to have fun at camp," she said. Emma began to wriggle out of reach but Rennie snagged her wrist. When she reached for Walt, he eagerly bounded forward. "Do you have my cell number?"

He produced the slip of paper. "Right here. When are we allowed to call?"

"Totally up to you."

"What if you're working?"

"Walt, call ten times a day if you'd like."

Emma leaned into Rennie's hips like a child grappling for safety in a treacherous wind. "Make Pa go away." She wound her arms around Rennie, giving form to the plea. "Won't you put me on the bus?"

"I can't, sweetheart," Rennie said with regret. "Lianna and Jenalyn will stay with you. They won't leave you alone, even for a minute."

Walt's lips thinned. "C'mon, Emma. We have to go," he said bravely, and Rennie was assaulted by the irrational desire to grab the children and flee the parking lot. It would be easy to run

and crazy too—

Her desperation left a scent on the air, like blood. Buck shoved past Lianna before she could stop him and Walt—Walt saw him coming at the precise moment Rennie did.

The boy clamped onto his sister's shoulder. "Right now, Emma. C'mon!"

The urgency in his voice galvanized Emma to release her purchase on Rennie's hips. "I'll call ten times a day," Emma cried. "Answer your phone, okay? Promise?"

"Of course I will," Rennie said, her emotions tattered as Walt dragged his sister forward. "I'll call you too, sweetheart. Ten times a day, more."

She barely got out the last of it. Buck's eyes held a warning she was loath to decipher. He grabbed the children and stalked off. Emma sent a backward glance, her eyes mirroring Rennie's anguish.

With every mile Rennie drove from the church, her despair grew.

When she'd first begun fostering Walt and Emma, she'd dreamt of a quick way out of the obligation. How differently she felt now. They were doing all right together, and the kids accepted her clumsy attempts at parenting. In a million subtle ways, they schooled her on how to keep a sensible schedule. They tutored her in remembering to stock the refrigerator and put dinner on the table by six-thirty. It was hard work, the extra loads of laundry, doctor visits and chatter at day's end. She cherished bedtime, the moments of shy affection and the sleepy conversation. After the kids nodded off, she tooled around the Internet logging onto parenting sites, to learn how to do this right.

Last week, a black nurse at the pediatrician's office took Rennie aside and explained that brown skin wouldn't scar if she rubbed cocoa butter onto Walt's knees. Rennie found the courage to broach the subject of caring for black children with Liza, who gave her a list of hair products best suited for tight curls. At eight years old, Walt was a private guy, but Emma loved bath time. She wouldn't allow Rennie to bathe her but she *would* regale her with the activities of her day, the fat boy in the school cafeteria who picked his nose, the raspy sound old Mrs. Leonardo made when instructing a student to recite proper nouns. Emma's Barbie floated in the bathwater beside her as the steam curled in faint tendrils. Placing her foot on the rim of the tub, she allowed Rennie the privilege of washing her toes. Rennie's heart became a throbbing mass as she gently washed the child.

Inexplicably, the ritual brought Rennie back to her own childhood when her father showed her a colorful map of Italy. The paper was thick as oilskin, the provinces outlined in red. City names were printed in bright greens and blues like gems scattered across a land of dreams. A surge of excitement trilled through her when he planted his finger on Rome. Then he'd tap his finger to the east of the great city and whisper, *Bell'Abruzzo*, his fidelity to the province of his roots a lyrical song on his lips. The melody of his love tied her to him, and to her ancestors.

As Emma wiggled her toes beneath the washcloth, Rennie would recall the map, her thoughts turning to an image of Walt on the windup to hurl a baseball forward. His movements were as graceful as his sister's whenever she danced through the living room, swishing her dress to and fro. And Rennie wondered: what region of Africa laid claim to children so long-boned and beautiful?

Foolishly, she'd begun to think of Walt and Emma as her own. Buck tore through the veil of dreams the moment he'd dragged them away.

Now, maneuvering the truck into the orchard's main road, she approached the facts with sadness. Walt and Emma were Buck's flesh and blood. She might dream of spreading out a map of Africa before Walt or teaching Emma how to weave tight braids in her hair. Would such opportunities arise? Buck was a conquering presence in the children's lives. He'd return to claim them as surely as Rennie's own father claimed a province of Italy.

And it was both galling and frightening to consider she'd known Buck all along as the unnerving man in the forest—and as the mason who'd been deviling Squeak. Was it even wise to mention the discovery to Squeak?

Considering, she gripped the steering wheel. No. For now, leaving Squeak in the dark was the safest option.

Also problematic? Mentioning Buck to Troy. She'd like nothing more than to have Buck thrown off the job site. But she couldn't stomach the thought of sharing this with Troy. If he'd spent the weekend in a state of turmoil, thinking about Mae Sullivan, she had no right to add to his worries.

By the time Rennie reached the new wing, she was so close to tears she'd begun to chastise herself for allowing Buck to rattle her. She'd just set her toolbox down when Troy appeared with his very pregnant sister dogging his heels.

Her spirits plummeting, she waved in greeting. Nervously, she wondered if Troy was still furious. On Friday night he'd left her house in a rage. No doubt she'd put her job in jeopardy by telling him about Mae. Loss of a steady paycheck would mean the loss of Walt and Emma—Job & Family Services would move them to a more stable foster home. The dreadful possibilities accosted her as Troy approached.

"My crazy sister is having the chandeliers delivered today," he told her. "Now, don't ask. I didn't give her the go-ahead."

Dianne flipped a blazing red curl from her damp forehead. "Why do I need your permission? They're my chandeliers. I still don't see why you're upset."

"Dianne, look up! Do you see a ceiling? We're just beginning to drywall."

"And you're bringing this to my attention because . . . ?"

"I have to call in painters after that," Troy replied stubbornly. "I have no intention of rushing them through the job. Unless, of course, you want spatter art on your walls."

"Trivial details." She swatted at her cheeks, noticed Rennie's close inspection, and whispered, "Hormones. The nightmare of the third trimester. I feel like I'm having hot flashes. Not that I'm old enough for hot flashes, but still."

"Should you sit down?" Rennie asked. The abundantly pregnant Dianne looked like she was running a space heater beneath her dress. "I'll find a folding chair."

"Don't bother. I have to get to work."

Troy worked his jaw. "The chandeliers?"

Dianne swatted his chest. "Stop complaining. My

chandeliers are magnificent. Rennie will decide where to store them."

Five hundred pounds of crystal? Rennie gaped at the preternaturally cheerful woman. Dianne had ordered two massive Waterford beauties with dripping pendants. Storing the chandeliers anywhere near the construction site was a sure guarantee of their destruction.

Troy said, "Well? Rennie? If this is a girl thing, I'd sure like to hear your solution." He glared at his sister before landing his stony gaze back on her. "Seeing that men are stupid and all."

"We can't store crystal in the new wing. What about a corner of the basement?"

He grunted. "Oh, sure. I'll fetch a dolly. Are you hauling several hundred pounds down two flights of stairs or should we have the Incredible Hulk do it?"

She blew out a stream of air. "I wish you wouldn't call Squeak names."

Dianne grinned impishly. "Should I help? Seeing that men are too stupid to locate something like a dolly."

"Dianne, forget the spotlights. You'll never make it as a stand up comic." Troy hooked his thumbs through his tool belt. To Rennie, he added, "Okay. This is what we'll do. I'll ask a few of the carpenters to carry the boxes to the basement. If they balk, your kid has to help."

"My assistant is not a kid. Squeak's in his twenties."

"Whatever." He smiled thinly at his sister. "Dianne, what time should we expect the delivery?"

"After lunch."

"Great. You can leave."

"*Why* are you so grumpy?" Sighing, Dianne took hold of Rennie's free arm. "Have you made progress on the industrial bid? I'm available to discuss the terms whenever you're ready."

Turn down the work. How could she accept the job after showing Troy the letters?

I can't afford to decline the job. The contract meant a steady paycheck for Squeak, and extra cash to care for Walt and Emma's needs.

Hedging, she said, "I haven't worked out the numbers yet."

Troy added, "Dianne, I'll give you the bid after I've checked the numbers. Now, please—go."

His sister left, and Rennie gave him a look of impatience. "Is there something else?" she asked, hoping there wasn't. "I need to get to work."

"Tell Squeak to start without you," he replied, motioning her outside. "We're going for a walk."

"We are?"

"Yes. Now. Tell your assistant and meet me out back."

His edgy tone propelled her out of the house and across the lawn to Squeak, lounging beside the truck. She gave him instructions to begin wiring the playroom on the second floor. She didn't relish the thought of her assistant getting underfoot if the carpenters were moving drywall around the first floor. He was safer upstairs.

With growing trepidation, she followed Troy around the side of the mansion. Morning formed a blush above the forest. The cracks of hammers punctuated the air. He remained a step ahead with his head bent into the breeze.

Without breaking stride, he led her into the forest. She was too nervous to question their destination. Here, the air was a good five degrees cooler. Mature trees cast shadows deep as night on the dry, rocky ground. The mossy trunks of maples and oaks thrust toward the sky, the latticework of rustling leaves forming a lacey rim around the blue sky.

Racing to keep pace with the irritated Troy, she was aware of the nerves tumbling through her. They were now deep in the forest, all evidence of the sky blotted out by the canopy of leaves overhead. The brush grew spindly and the trees were magnificent. A stand of birch, glowing white amidst the gloom, lured Troy near. He paused in their center.

"I have a friend in Columbus, an attorney," he said. He waited as she gingerly lowered herself onto a boulder before adding, "He did a little digging for me in State Records."

So he *did* believe the letters were legitimate. "Did your friend come up with anything?"

The question put displeasure on his mouth. "My birth certificate was amended. The original isn't available. I'll have to make a written request to the State to have my records unsealed."

"There's a form you'll have to submit to Columbus. I can get a copy for you, if you'd like." Job & Family Services offered a booklet, which Rennie knew her mother handed out to adults who'd discovered they were adopted.

"I'm still having trouble believing any of this." Troy raked his hand across his scalp. "I won't mention anything to my parents until I have all the facts."

He studied her for a long moment. She sensed he was grappling with a decision.

Rennie swallowed. "What is it?"

"Mae Sullivan still resides at St. Justin's Church. I called over the weekend and talked to a secretary. She was about to ask why I was calling but I cut the conversation short. Afterward, I Googled Mae."

"You checked into her background?"

"Everything I could glean from cyberspace, which wasn't much. I punched in credit card numbers so many times, I have no idea what I spent." Clearly troubled, he added, "She was born here in Liberty, attended a small parish school. I went into a few newspaper archives and found two articles about a brutal rape in Liberty, nine months before my birth. Mae's name isn't mentioned and the orchard isn't, either. Which would be my father's doing."

"Your father?" Rennie said, unsettled by the chilling calm on his face.

"He would've kept the rape out of the papers. Bad publicity for Fagan's Orchard. Plus he'd go to great lengths to protect a young girl, especially if her mother worked in the mansion. Dad cares about the employees. Always has." Troy hesitated. "There's also a police report."

On rubbery legs, she rose from her perch on the boulder. "What's in the report?"

"The assailant was probably a migrant worker at the orchard. Never apprehended. Mae couldn't give a description." A muscle twitched in his jaw. "She was in bad shape, hospitalized for more than a month. She had no memory of the assault."

Mae was an angel meant for a life serving God. "I'm glad she couldn't remember," Rennie whispered.

"As am I." He pulled in a breath. "I'm thinking about

checking our employee files to see who left Fagan's around the time of the assault. Assuming I can muster the patience to do so."

She regarded him with faint confusion. Then she groaned. "Nothing was computerized." No doubt a wall of file cabinets awaited Troy, the contents poorly organized. "Should I help? Walt and Emma are gone for the week. We can spend the evenings reading employee records, work into Sunday night—"

Too fast, he cut her off, saying, "I need to know something. No dancing around, Rennie."

His rapier sharp tone snatched her breath away. "Anything."

"Why did you tell me about the letters? It would've been wiser to get rid of them."

She grappled for a response capable of erasing the condemnation on his face. He'd switched moods with a chameleon's speed, leaving her disoriented.

Impatient, he didn't await a reply. "When we talked at your house, you admitted to taking them home with you."

"Yes."

"You read the letters, discussed them with your mother."

"Troy—"

"You knew they were proof of my adoption. And you knew damn well I had no idea."

"I didn't mean to—"

"*Why*, Rennie. Why show me something you knew would gut me? I've had the bottom pulled out of my life. Have any idea what that's like?"

"You deserved the truth."

Troy balled his fists, but his eyes pooled with grief.

Her actions damned her. And why wouldn't they? A man's theology of his life was a fragile construct. A truth held sacred was a compass used to traverse the road. It was a private narrative, an unexamined religion. What *had* she done?

She'd made Troy an atheist in his own world.

An apology built in her throat but she couldn't issue a sound. She was as silent as the wind dying down in the forest. She began to cry and Troy let her. He stood rigidly as her misery peeled away the years until she no longer saw him. She saw only Jason, white as parchment in his coffin; the fury of his red hair subdued by the embalmer's art, his grey suit, a slick formality he never would've chosen, his features set in a waxy composure that wasn't Jason at all. It was just a shell. The beautiful, fragile soul she'd known was gone and with him, the arrogance of her youth.

If you know something that could destroy a person's life, should you tell him?

"I had to tell you," she blurted, gasping on her tears, "for Jason. I owed it to him. I can't bring him back. I can't. But I have to make peace and let him go. He deserves a better place and I want him to rest."

The outburst snapped Troy's head up. "You're finishing what he started? Is that what you're saying?"

"I don't know how else to make peace for everything I did." She stared defiantly although she couldn't see Troy from behind the film of tears. "I want Jason to rest. He was so sweet."

The last of it loosened Troy's hands. He brought them to his face, his beautiful, proud face. He pressed his palms to his cheeks as if his sense of himself had become vaporous, a substance without proof. His shoulders sagged.

Somehow he halted the tremor running up his back. "Jason tried to tell me." He scrubbed his palms across his face, finally came up for air. "I thought we were fighting about you."

"You fought with Jason?" she asked, blinking.

"Right before he left for Cleveland. Before he was murdered." Doubt filtered through his expression. "Did Jason discuss the letters with you? My God, were you planning to tell me together?"

"No. No—" She rushed to him. "I didn't know you were adopted. Jason tried to tell me. I didn't understand what he'd asked."

"Asked you . . . what was the question?"

She explained and he said, "I'm not surprised Jason had qualms about showing me the letters. He knew I wouldn't take the news well."

"I'm sure that's why he asked for my advice."

"What did you tell him?"

Searching for compassion, she stole a furtive glance at his face. When none was forthcoming, she found the courage to say, "I told him that people shouldn't keep secrets."

"That was your great advice?"

"I told him to be honest." She held his gaze, a sacrifice. "And several days after the party, I told him that I'd slept with you. It didn't feel right to withhold the truth from a good friend. I felt awful and I . . . Troy, I was too young to understand how hard he'd take it."

Her admission snuffed the light from his eyes. "Rennie, why? Why'd you do that?"

Battered, she stepped away. She should've known her honesty would cause so much pain, then as now.

"That's why Jason went to Cleveland to get drunk," she said, sick with self-reproach. "I killed him, Troy. He was devastated when I told him. It's my fault and I killed him."

Troy slumped against a tree.

Condemnation knit into his expression. She bowed her head in shame. She was mired in self-loathing but it was a relief, a sick, scarring relief to learn she wasn't alone in her assessment of herself. She'd ensured Troy despised her, too.

She bit back a sob. "Jason thought the truth would destroy your life. But he would've shown you the letters. After weighing the pros and cons . . . he would've made you understand. He loved you. He wanted you to have the truth."

Ice glittered in Troy's gaze. "What about Mae? Hell, what should I do about her? Or doesn't she factor in?"

He'd switched topics so quickly she couldn't get her bearings. "I don't understand."

"I have to settle this." He searched the forest's dark shadows. "Will she talk to me?"

"I'm sure she will."

"Why are you so damn confident? You know, this will hurt her too. She can't possibility imagine I'll appear out of nowhere."

Surely he was mistaken. Mae Sullivan possessed a sensitive heart. She'd loved him enough to pen heartbreaking missives during his first years of life.

"Pittsburgh is only a few hours' drive," she said. "Easy enough to meet with her. I'm sure she'll be delighted."

"I was thinking more in terms of a phone call. If that goes well, I'll consider taking this further."

"Wouldn't you prefer to meet with her directly?"

"I'm not sure."

"The best way to get answers is to begin with her."

The remark sent his hands deep into the pockets of his jeans. "We *could* get a meeting over with quickly," he mused. "Calling wouldn't give me proof. I need to see her with my own eyes." He removed his hands from their hiding place, folded his arms. In a businesslike tone, he added, "Call Mae. Set it up. I have the number at the mansion. Reach her tonight when you get off work."

Rennie nodded. "All right."

"We're having a bitch of a week with the new wing's construction but I can't have this hanging over my head. Tell her to expect us Friday morning." When she glanced at him, baffled, he added, "That's right. We'll screw up the work schedule. Crash won't be thrilled, but I'm leaving him in charge."

"Sure. Whatever you say."

Troy started out of the forest. He turned back abruptly. "I'll meet with her, Rennie. But Jason was right. It could destroy a life—mine. I hope it was worth it to ease your conscience."

Chapter 22

The sound of footsteps wrenched Rennie's attention from the paperwork she'd glumly organized on the kitchen table.

The wall above the stove read nine-fifteen. Curious, she went outside. Her sister-in-law, Liza, strolled across the patio.

Rennie ushered her inside. "This is a surprise."

"I heard you had an unpleasant meeting with Mr. Korchek this morning." Liza opened the refrigerator and poked her head inside. "How are you?"

"Meeting Buck was awful but I survived." She declined to add the conversation with Troy was equally torturous. "Were you in court today?"

"Court, meetings and stuck on the phone arguing over a divorce settlement I thought was resolved last week." Liza pulled out a Tupperware container. "Call it optimism, but I have a feeling that with kids living here, you've acquired rudimentary cooking skills. What is this? It smells great."

"Homemade chicken and rice."

Liza scooped out a bowl. "Wonder of wonders."

While she heated the plate in the microwave, Rennie gathered up the paperwork. She'd made good headway on the Fagan quote despite her reservations about taking the work. After upending Troy's world, she felt guilty about even preparing a quote. Still, she suspected he'd hire her if only to please his sister.

Troy's generous advance was now deposited in the bank.

She'd worked hard on the quote, seeing it as a way to save Walt and Emma. Wouldn't the increase in pay make it easier for her to keep them permanently? A foolish thought perhaps, but she'd begun to hope for the opportunity to adopt the kids.

Liza shrugged out of her blazer. "What is all of that?" She dug into her dinner. "Working up a job quote?"

"For the new processing plant at Fagan's. I think the job's mine."

"You don't seem happy."

"I'm not." Gauging Liza's reaction, she added, "I should be on top of the world but I'm on the outs with Troy."

"Decline the job."

"Dianne has her heart set on hiring me. Evening out the battle of the sexes and all that. She's very persistent."

"Then congratulations." Liza chewed thoughtfully. "Why haven't I heard about this until now? Have you told your parents?"

"I would have mentioned it to Mom when I saw her this morning but we had something else to hash out."

"Does it have to do with your meeting last Friday? When you dragged me over here at dawn?"

Rennie picked up a pencil and rolled it absently back and forth. "Don't ask," she replied, too sad for a rehashing of the letters or Mae Sullivan.

"Okay, I won't." Liza chuckled, clearly in no mood to press. "And you had Mr. Korchek to deal with today. Your mother is livid. She said you handled the situation well. The part about Mr. Korchek working at Fagan's is an issue, given the foster home was meant to remain confidential. You've probably guessed that Jenalyn has serious concerns about returning the kids to Buck."

"She needs proof he mistreated them. They haven't mentioned anything, to me or the therapist."

Contemplating the extent of their suffering filled her with dread. In subtle ways she'd encouraged Walt and Emma to discuss their previous life. Every attempt failed. Life with their father was a nightmare they wanted to forget. Would they stay here, where they were safe? Or would the court return custody to Buck? A decision wouldn't be handed down for a few more weeks.

Her sister-in-law eyed her with concern. "Don't fall in love with them," Liza said. "I've worked a long time in family law. In a case like this one, there's rarely a predictable outcome. I've seen parents surrender rights without a fight even after receiving a variety of services to help them with their problems. Others fight to keep a child when they neither love their offspring nor possess the capacity to parent. State funding—or, more precisely, the lack of it—sends many at-risk children back to the home of origin."

"Walt and Emma deserve better," Rennie said, with heat. "Buck had them sleeping in a barn, Liza. He's hurt them repeatedly."

"There isn't enough public funding to provide a safe foster home for every at-risk child."

"The State can keep my fostering stipend. I don't want it." Rennie tugged her hair from the rubber band. She gave her head a quick shake, tumbling curls around her shoulders. "I'm adopting Walt and Emma."

"It's one thing to raise kids for a couple of months, something different to raise them to adulthood."

True, and she doubted she'd ever possess the requisite gifts. Hadn't she yelled at Walt this morning after he dumped baseball gear in the living room? She'd stumbled across his stuff on her way to the coffeepot. Emma? She'd need years of therapy.

"You *are* thinking about adopting them, aren't you?" Liza asked, drawing her from her thoughts.

"How can I *not* think about it?"

"Talk about a turnaround. You didn't want to take in the kids, remember? Your mother pushed you into this."

"Don't get me wrong. This hasn't been easy." Rennie shook her head with bemusement. "I love watching Emma play hair stylist with her Barbie doll, and draw pictures. She's so damn serious and she's beautiful. And Walt . . . I'm not sure how I ever lived without him. He has so much heart and he's brave. He's so brave. I'll be forever grateful he came into my life."

"You love them."

Rennie laughed. "Head over heels." She grew serious. "I'll do everything in my power to make them my children."

Liza rested her chin to her fist. She sat quietly for a moment. Then she nodded.

"If it comes to that, I'll take care of the adoption paperwork free of charge," she decided. "My gift to the new family."

"Think I have a shot?" she asked, the hopefulness in her voice balanced with doubt.

"Jenalyn doesn't think of you in terms of a potential adoptive mother. However, it's easy to see how well you get along with the kids. You *are* becoming a family. Have you mentioned adoption to her?"

"Not yet." Should she? Rennie looked up suddenly. "Would my interest make it easier to get Buck out of the picture?"

Liza frowned. "I'm sorry to say it has no bearing at all. The State views Buck's parental rights as sacred unless Social Services can prove his behavior puts the children in danger. Parental rights aren't terminated easily. Nor should they be."

After seeing Liza out, Rennie returned inside.

She looked around the kitchen, the table heaped with paperwork, the bright crayon drawings Emma had proudly placed on the refrigerator. Walt's glove lay on the counter. She missed the children.

Tamping down the longing, she glanced at the phone. One last obligation awaited her.

She'd promised to call Mae Sullivan to make arrangements for a visit on Friday. She couldn't disappoint Troy. In a worse case scenario, Mae would refuse to talk. Best case? She'd express joy at the prospect of meeting the son she'd given up for adoption thirty-six years ago.

Taking a deep breath, Rennie picked up her cell and punched in the number Troy had given her. On the third ring, an older woman answered with a brisk "hello."

"I'm sorry for calling so late," she said hurriedly. "This is Rennie Perini."

A long pause and then, "Did you say Perini? Are you one of Lianna's daughters?"

"I am. Is this Mae?"

"Why, yes. Yes, it is!" Mae paused for a moment. When she spoke again, worry glazed her voice. "Is Lianna ill? Has something happened?"

"No, it's nothing like that."

"Thank goodness. How is she?"

"She's great. She sends her regards. Actually, I'm calling for another reason."

Mae's soft laughter carried through the phone. "Well, what is it? Heavens, this is marvelous! Rennie, you sound so much like your mother when she was young. What can I do for you, dear?"

The excitement in her voice added a much-needed boost. "I work with your son, Troy," Rennie explained in a breezy voice. "He's only recently found out about you. Actually, we'd like to visit. May we stop by St. Justin's on Friday? I'll call when we're close, about half an hour from Pittsburgh."

Her ears filled with a long, lonely silence. She bit down on her lower lip.

Floundering, she was about to ask if another day was more convenient. Then the low, muffled sound pulled her to a standstill.

On the other end, Mae Sullivan was crying.

Chapter 23

The tortured sound of Mae's tears carried through the phone. Worried, Rennie searched for words of comfort.

Why had she launched right in, mentioning Troy before they'd finished with opening pleasantries?

"Mae, please don't cry." She dropped into a chair. "Forgive me. This must be a shock. I didn't mean to upset you."

The words left her lips in a stilted flurry. On the other end, Mae's crying broke off. Silently Rennie chastised herself for injuring a woman who'd known so much suffering in her life.

She'd begun launching into a second wave of apology when Mae said, "No, it's fine. I'm happy you called." A shuffling ensued, followed by a thump—was Mae reaching for a tissue to blow her nose? "You're coming to Pittsburgh on Friday?"

"If you don't mind."

"I don't have any plans other than gardening. I'm feeding the trees around the church and our elementary school. Our gardens are quite beautiful. I can't wait to give you a tour." She cleared her throat. "And Troy . . . he's looking forward to the visit?"

The question issued forth with sweet hesitancy. Rennie scrambled for a reply short of lying. Troy viewed their meeting with trepidation. He certainly wasn't looking forward to meeting the woman who'd endured savage cruelty before bringing him into the world. Pity for Mae swamped her.

"He can't wait to meet you," she said, wincing at the bald lie.

"Oh, I'm so glad! Do you need directions to St. Justin's?"

"We have them." Relief flooded her. The emotion was displaced by curiosity as the house phone rang.

The display panel read Little Bear Campground. She'd already talked to Walt and Emma countless times today, about everything from the general layout of the camp to the nature walk the counselors took the kids on before dinner. Now it was late. Why weren't the kids asleep?

"Mae, I'm sorry to cut this short. I have to take another call."

"Go right ahead. Oh, Rennie?

"Yes?"

"You're certain Troy's looking forward to this?"

"Absolutely."

"Well, then. I can't wait to meet you both."

They shared a few more words and Rennie flipped her cell shut. The moment she did, she launched for the wall phone.

"Rennie?"

It was Emma. "Sweetie, why aren't you in bed? It's almost eleven o'clock."

"I can't sleep."

"Why not?"

Emma's voice was breathy and strange. "The lady will tell you."

A woman came on. "Miss Perini? This is Ginnie Kluznik. I'm staying with the children in cabin three."

The tension in the woman's voice put Rennie on alert. "What's going on? Is Emma hurt?"

"No, no—but she *is* upset. She's convinced she saw something in the woods. We were all seated around the campfire. She's quite agitated."

"She's afraid of the dark," Rennie said. Not uncommon for a seven year old.

"That was my initial impression. When I pressed, she admitted she thought she'd seen her father watching from the woods. You wouldn't believe the things children say on the first night of camp. We came back to the cabin and Emma went right to the window. She's only left long enough to change into pajamas. I think she's planning to stand there all night."

"She's at the window now?"

"She's convinced she has to keep watch or her father will

take her away. Walt too."

Fear coursed through Rennie. "I'm driving out." She snatched up a pen. "Give me the directions."

A pause then Ginnie chuckled softly. "That isn't necessary," she said with motherly assurance. "If you talk to her for a moment, I'm sure she'll settle down."

"I'll be there in twenty minutes. Give me the directions. *Now.*"

The demand contained enough urgency to have Ginnie rattling off the directions to the campground. Less than a minute later, Rennie was in her truck barreling south on Route 44 with her heart fluttering and her fear rising. Mercifully the two-lane highway was void of traffic. Above, the waxing moon painted the corn silos and barns streaming past with an eerie glow.

No doubt Emma's concerns proved accurate. Buck *had* stalked her to Little Bear. He relished the notion of terrifying his children by putting in an appearance that went undetected by the camp counselors. The bruises on the kids' faces and the gash on Walt's cheek were now healed, but Rennie couldn't forget. Buck had hurt the kids repeatedly. Of course Ginnie didn't believe a small child's ramblings. She'd only phoned out of a sense of responsibility.

Pulling into the darkened lot, Rennie spotted a cabin with the lights still on. It stood in the row of rustic buildings draped in shadow. Each cabin boasted a front porch with rocking chairs and pretty walkways of fieldstone that shimmered in the moonlight.

She sprinted up the steps and rapped on the door.

A heavyset woman smiled in greeting. "I'm Ginnie," she said. "You must be Miss Perini."

Despite her worry Rennie liked the woman on sight. Her hazel eyes were surprisingly compassionate, her auburn hair sporting streaks of grey. She wore a ratty pink robe and, ridiculously, neon pink slippers shaped like bunny rabbits.

A small kitchenette filled one end of the cabin. A hand-hooked rug warmed the floor. Five bunk beds stood in a row by the wall. A gaggle of girls dressed in pajamas clustered behind Ginnie. A few were nearly as young as Emma. Others were in their early teens. With regret, Rennie wondered if her late hour appearance had frightened the campers.

"Don't worry about the troops," Ginnie said. "They never hit the sack early the first night at camp. If you hadn't arrived, I'd be pulling out board games. Girls, say hello."

Rennie received whispered hellos and lopsided grins. One girl in her early teens, evidently Ginnie's daughter, possessed a similar stocky build and the same style of bunny slippers.

Quickly she surveyed the room. "Where's Emma?"

"Still by the window."

The row of bunk beds concealed a window near the corner of the cabin. Emma stood with her slender hands pressed to the glass like a sentinel assigned to keep out the night. Rennie's heart shifted—beneath the scalloped hem of Emma's nightgown, her calves shook.

"Hello, sweetheart." Crouching, she reached out impulsively to loop her arm around Emma's waist then reconsidered, unsure if the child welcomed the affection. She peered at the trees outside, painted with shadow and thin brushstrokes of moonlight. "Is he still out there?" she asked.

Emma's eyes grew wide. "I'm not sure. I don't see him."

"Maybe he's gone."

"He'll make us go away," Emma said, confirming Rennie's worst fears. "We'll have to run away with him."

"I won't let that happen."

"You can't stop him. When Momma died, Pa made us run lots of times. I don't want to run away."

Desperate to comfort the child, she trailed her fingers down Emma's neck. Goosebumps rose on the child's soft skin.

"He's bigger than you," Emma said, her voice catching. "He'll hit you if you don't let us go."

Rennie tamped down the fear. "Sweetheart, listen. I'll talk to him tomorrow." Allowing the awful possibilities to take her emotions hostage—as well as her judgment—wouldn't protect the children. "I'll remind him that he's not allowed at the camp site. If he shows up again he'll be in big trouble."

"Will they make him stay in the barn?" Emma's voice grew faint, her terror palpable. "When me and Walt were bad, he made us stay in the barn. It was cold and scary. Will Pa go there?"

"He'll go somewhere much worse, I promise you."

Confusion etched the child's face. "Maybe he shouldn't go someplace bad. I don't want him to get scared."

Her generosity of spirit sent emotion barreling into Rennie's throat. "Don't worry about your father," she said, blinking back tears. "He'll be fine, okay? Now, come here."

She sat on the floor Indian style and coaxed Emma into her lap. Ginnie ushered the other girls into the kitchenette. A shuffling of feet, and someone giggled. Glad for the privacy, Rennie dipped her face into Emma's neck, which smelled of soap, and closed her eyes. Emma relaxed on a sigh, her cheek resting tentatively on Rennie's shoulder.

I'll ask Ginnie to show me to Walt's cabin. Checking on him seemed wise. Naturally Buck had stalked Emma first—he enjoyed frightening a defenseless child. Walt, however, was bunking with other boys and several men. Like all bullies, Buck was less inclined to tangle with other men. He'd think twice before stalking Walt.

Emma asked, "Will you stay here tonight?"

She caressed the side of the child's face, considering. Bunking in a cabin full of girls wasn't conducive to rest. Staying meant a night without sleep and she had a full day of work tomorrow.

"I won't leave until you fall asleep." Emma stiffened in her arms, prodding her to add, "Should we go home together? Won't take long to pack your stuff."

In the kitchenette, Ginnie opened a box brimming with packets of hot chocolate "Emma, don't you want to stay? Tomorrow I'll take you in a canoe to catch a fish. Wouldn't you like to fish on the lake?"

Emma pressed her face to Rennie's breast.

Ginnie handed off the packets of chocolate to a lanky brunette. To Rennie, she said, "I'd hate for her to leave. We have wonderful events planned. An arts and crafts day, horseback riding—all great fun."

The conversation brought Emma into a sitting position. She seemed aware she'd crossed a treacherous boundary by allowing Rennie to cradle her. Rising, she returned to the window.

Rennie asked Ginnie, "Do you mind if we talk outside?" When the older woman nodded her assent, she went to the window and gave Emma a hug. "I'll be right back. Why don't you have hot chocolate with the other girls?"

The suggestion pleased Ginnie. She steered Emma toward the kitchenette. "Go on, child. There's ice cream in the freezer if you'd like some."

Emma brightened. "I can have ice cream *and* hot chocolate?"

"If your mother approves."

Rennie opened her mouth then closed it again. Should she correct Ginnie? *I am Emma's mother.* Something in her heart clicked into place.

After a moment, she said, "It's fine. Go on, sweet pea."

The women walked out to the front porch. Crickets sang from the shadows surrounding the cabins, a cacophony of sound. A raccoon ambled into the forest, its fur silvered by moonlight.

"What do you need to discuss?" Ginnie asked.

Safely out of earshot of the children, Rennie gave a rundown of Buck's past behavior. Oddly, the grim explanation didn't alter Ginnie's placid expression.

"Well?" Rennie asked, wrapping up. The amusement creeping onto Ginnie's face irritated her. To hell with it—she'd take the kids home. She'd call the police in Liberty to ask for a cruiser to drive by Buck's place, wherever he lived. Give him a taste of his own medicine to ensure he left the kids alone—

"I'm a black belt," Ginnie said, jostling Rennie from her thoughts. She grinned suddenly, her eyes blazing. "My son's a freshman at Bowling Green. Weighs two-twenty. He made the mistake of laughing at my karate outfit. I flipped him on his back. He never knew what hit him."

"You're saying Emma is safe?"

"I won't let her out of my sight. If her father returns, I'll have the police here in a jiffy. By the time they arrive, Mr. Korchek will be incapacitated. Trust me."

A burst of nervous laughter escaped Rennie. "I think I do."

"You should." Ginnie opened the door a crack and peeked inside. The girls sat in a circle nursing mugs of chocolate. Softly, she shut the door before continuing. "My ex? He had a love affair with vodka and a short fuse. It took a lot of courage to pack up my kids and leave. When I did, I swore I'd never allow another man to threaten me. It's been years but you never forget. Not something like that."

"I imagine you wouldn't."

She eyed Rennie levelly. "Is Emma right? Is her father crazy enough to snatch her and Walt?"

"A possibility, sure. He's angry, an alcoholic—not stable."

"Men like that don't love. They keep. Women, kids—mostly they keep them in terror. You've met Buck?"

"Just this morning."

"Own a gun?"

Rennie's heart lurched. "No, I don't."

"Get one." Ginnie studied her for a long moment before opening the door. "Emma, Kimmy—come here." The girl in the bunny slippers led Emma to the door. Ginnie regarded her daughter. "Where's your smartphone?"

The girl handed over the phone with the hesitancy of a teenager addicted to electronics.

Ginnie placed the phone in Emma's palm. "Keep my daughter's phone this week," she said. "If you see anything out of the ordinary you dial 911. After you dial, shout for me at the top of your lungs."

Emma's eyes rounded. "Look, Rennie. Now we can talk all the time!"

Rennie approached, to tousle Emma's hair, but the child leapt out of reach. "How 'bout you call me in ten minutes?" she asked, hiding her disappointment behind a bright smile. "I have to check on Walt before heading home. We'll chat while I drive."

Emma gave a jerky nod. "You'll make sure Walt's okay before you go?"

"You bet."

"You won't forget to call me?"

"Of course not, sweetheart."

Ginnie motioned into the darkness. "Walt's in cabin eight. I'll call down, tell the men you're coming."

"Thanks." Rennie tried to move but her feet seemed glued in place. She patted Emma's chin, which quivered, before turning back to Ginnie. "I've got a long day tomorrow at work. It's already late. I really have to go."

Ginnie gave a short nod. "I understand."

"I'd stay if I could."

"Of course."

"I'll go and see Walt now." She tried reaching for Emma, who'd predictably turned to stone.

Letting it go, she trotted swiftly down the steps. An owl hooted from deep in the forest. The crickets' chirping died down as the moon slipped out from behind gray clouds. She peered at the forest, her ears pricked for the sound of movement. Was Buck nearby?

She stopped.

A shuffling on the porch spun her around. Ginnie stood at the railing with her arms folded severely across her bosom.

"No need for embarrassment," she said brusquely. "I wouldn't have left either. I'll tell Emma you're crawling in with her as soon as you look in on Walt."

Feeling foolish, Rennie retraced her steps. Delight filled her as Emma shot out the doorway clutching her Barbie doll and the cell phone. She halted at the top of the steps to waver from foot to foot.

Rapidly she stroked her doll's hair. "You'll have my pillow," she said. "I don't mind."

"We'll share." Rennie glanced down the row of cabins. "Want to come with? Help me check on your brother?"

Emma rushed the steps only to halt abruptly. "We should stay together." Solemnly, she held out her hand.

Rennie knit their fingers together. "Always," she agreed.

Chapter 24

Nothing else could possibly go wrong.

The thought gave little comfort as Troy scrawled his signature across the payables checks for Meyer's Heating and Perini Electric. Given the revelations about his adoption, he'd seen better weeks. He'd nearly lost his center when he'd looked into Mae's hidden and complicated history. But damn it, he'd stay level.

Early morning quiet settled over the mansion. Only Bitsy, in the kitchen preparing breakfast, had risen. Hard at work in his father's library, Troy leaned back in the chair—a richly leathered number he cherished—and noticed Frank ambling toward the library.

He liked Dianne's husband. Frank sported a hooknose worthy of a pirate. His laughter, which rang out frequently, bore a distinct similarity to a crone's cackle. The consummate salesman, Frank held too many meetings in restaurants, adding too many inches to his thickening middle. Today he carried a suitcase in one hand and a briefcase in the other. The tie around his neck hung loose.

Troy guessed he'd just returned on the red-eye.

"How's the war for shelf space going?" he asked. Frank was forever regaling him with the diabolical means necessary to get Fagan's products onto grocery store shelves. "You look like someone beat the crap out of you. Don't tell me the rep from Gleason's Jellies gave you a thumping."

Frank dropped onto the couch. "Last I heard he was in Sacramento trying to push us off the shelves of Fazio's. Actually I was in Virginia shoring up accounts."

"Rough going?"

"No more than usual." Frank dug into the breast pocket of his suit coat and withdrew a cigar. "In the metro areas? It's a snap getting shelf space for our new line of condiments. Try convincing grocers in the mid-market to sell apple ketchup. They look at me like I've grown a tail."

"Forget the outlying regions. Focus on the cities. The new condiments you and Dianne have dreamed up will never play in the smaller 'burbs. Too upscale."

"Since when are you a marketing wiz?"

"It's common sense." Troy scowled as Frank lit the cigar, puffed. "That thing will kill you," he said, waving the dank smoke away from the desk.

His brother-in-law pulled the cigar from his mouth. "Naw. It'll just give me a headache." He nodded toward the ceiling. "Is my wife still asleep?"

"I haven't seen anyone yet this morning."

"Did she tell you about the party?"

"What party?"

Frank slung his legs onto the coffee table and grinned maniacally. "I love it when she pisses you off," he replied, chuckling. "She's already got a caterer picked out, and rides. Like at a carnival. The orchard *will* be a carnival by the time she finishes organizing her fiesta for five hundred. I'll bet she convinces someone to haul in a Ferris wheel. I wouldn't put anything past my spunky vixen."

Simmering, Troy held his tongue. What had Dianne done this time? It wasn't enough that she wanted the addition finished by July. The overtime he'd doled out could finance another job. How a party factored in was a question best left unexplored.

His brother-in-law set his stogie in the crystal ashtray, frowning. "She didn't mention the party? No kidding? I wouldn't be cracking jokes if I'd ... heck, I'm sorry."

"Like hell. You look amused."

"Habit." Frank toyed with the cigar, stuck it back between his teeth. "Dianne is having a baby shower on a grand scale. She's inviting all of our friends and their families, some business associates, even the mayor."

"The mayor of Liberty?"

"Cleveland. Knowing Dianne, she's got television coverage mapped out, too."

"Hold on. Baby showers are for women. Men aren't invited."

"Since when does my Irish elf play by the rules?" Frank blew a smoke ring with casual indifference. "She'll expect your crews to attend—you know how egalitarian she is. Wait 'till you see the invites, some crazy thing on purple metallic paper."

Troy pinched the sides of his nose, searching for patience. "Okay. My sister is having an unconventional baby shower, which is my problem because there are building supplies piled around the property and a fleet of trucks parked out front on any given day. Meaning we should finish the addition before the festivities commence. Unfortunately I don't have a firm completion date. Which, naturally, won't matter to my sister."

"Sure won't."

"And she's having invitations printed, which means she's picked out a date." Gritting his teeth, he rocked slowly in the chair. "So, when's the party?"

"June first." With his cigar Frank saluted. "It's a Saturday."

"We'll never complete work in four weeks." Accelerating the trades' schedules, the hours of finish work ahead—only a lunatic would follow Dianne into construction mayhem. "Send the invites back to the printer. I can't guarantee your date."

"I'll pay double overtime." His brother-in-law gave a quelling look. "Listen, I shouldn't joke about this. Dianne's excited. The baby coming at the end of June, putting together her nutty version of a baby shower—I want to keep her happy."

"Who says she isn't?"

"Troy, wake up. She's frightened of labor, but she's insisting on natural childbirth to protect our baby. Planning the party stops her from thinking about what's ahead. Tell me the cost to finish quickly. I'll write the check."

Troy wavered. Accelerate the construction schedule? They were already working at breakneck speed. Not an ideal situation, but he hadn't stopped to consider his sister's worries. Planning a party for five hundred *would* keep her occupied. No doubt his parents were egging her on, glad for a diversion to stop her from worrying about childbirth. They'd do everything possible to protect her. She'd always been afraid of pain, doctors—needles.

During childhood she'd crawled under her bed if he or Jason foolishly mentioned an upcoming checkup. She'd been terrified of shots.

And she planned to forgo pain medication during labor? Troy admired her courage. For weeks now she'd been carrying packages into the mansion, a mobile with blue elephants for the nursery, a white layette so fragile the cloth appeared spun from cloud vapor. She'd ordered Fagan rosaries from Dublin last month as gifts for the godparents she had yet to select from among her countless friends. Not once did his sister complain about the precipice she'd leap to gain purchase on motherhood.

When Mae gave birth to me, did she experience a terrible ordeal?

The jarring thought caught him off-guard. Mae was little more than a child when her world was cleaved in two. She was an innocent teenage girl pregnant by rape and yanked from her everyday world to live sheltered by nuns. Lost at sea, Troy recalled the letters from St. Justin Martyr filled with her careful script. The delicately looped cursive had reminded him of embroidery. One letter bore a blemish, a splotch of ink beside her carefully written name. Had Mae wept while guiding her pen across the page?

His bone-deep survival instinct rebelled against the notion that she'd once nestled his newborn self, slippery with life, to her breast. Then she found the willpower to hand him off to whomever had ferried him, unknowing, into a world he assumed was his birthright. When Mae lifted him from her breast for the last time was her labor, by comparison, easy?

Finding shore, he looked across the desk. Frank stood on the opposite side with his wallet out. "It's signed." He slid the check beneath Troy's nose. "Fill out the rest."

Troy took the check. "No guarantees."

His brother-in-law went to the window, peered at the trucks parking in a rumbling queue. "When will you be certain? I can't disappoint my wife."

"Let me talk to my subs first."

"Strong-arm them." Frank gestured out the window. "Is that one of your subs? She's gorgeous. I'm betting she's Rennie. Dianne has mentioned her."

Troy reached the window in time to see Rennie stroll across the lawn with her hips swaying and her long hair flying. "Yeah, that's her."

"Good God, man. Why haven't you asked her out?"

Troy lingered on the snug fit of her jeans before lifting his appraisal to her pouting lips. Heat surged in his blood. His male instincts didn't care that she'd cut a nasty groove through his life. She'd always been a temptation.

He dragged his attention away. "Rennie's off limits. I can't get involved."

"Sure you can."

Returning to the desk, he launched a look of irritation. "Don't you need to get some rest? Shower? See your wife?"

"Oh, c'mon. Don't tell me you haven't asked her out because she works for you. Make an exception. She's drop dead gorgeous." Mirth danced in Frank's eyes. "It's not like you get out much."

"Change the subject, pal."

The anxiety Troy hadn't fully put at bay dampened his mood. Though he didn't relish the prospect of meeting alone with Mae, traveling to Pittsburgh with Rennie would test his endurance. He was still upset with her about the letters. Not that his emotions had any bearing on his testosterone. Bringing along the woman who'd been orbiting his heart for most of his life put his emotions in jeopardy.

Frank gave out a low whistle. "Look at that. She's stoked."

An icy premonition brought Troy's head up. "Who's stoked?"

"Rennie. She's got him cornered. I say he's kissing the pavement in ten seconds."

Troy caught the raised voices, a man's and Rennie's. A quick glance out the window at the melee, and he dashed from the library. He sprinted down the front steps precisely as Rennie backed the mason against a truck. Disoriented, Troy did a second take. It was the man who'd bested him at darts.

The mason clenched his fists. Rennie, impervious to the

danger, kept advancing. The blood drained from Troy's head as the mason raised his fist.

Launching forward, Troy shoved her out of the way. "What the hell is going on?" When he was sure she was safe behind his back, he swung around and cornered the mason. "Were you going to hit her? Were you? What the hell's wrong with you, man?"

The mason yanked his regard from Rennie, narrowed on Troy. "She started it. Why don't *you* back off?"

The impulse to bloody the man's face was intense. "What did you say?" Troy growled.

Incredibly, the mason took a step closer. "I was minding my own business. She came at me."

"Were you thinking of landing a punch?"

He couldn't clear his head, couldn't hear past the thunder in his ears. If the man had thrown a punch? With terrible certainty, Troy realized he would've murdered him. He would've pummeled him into dust for harming Rennie.

The mason jerked his chin toward Rennie. "I didn't start this. She's threatening me. Tell her to piss off."

The taunt launched Rennie forward. Troy caught her a split second before she leapt into the man's face. "Rennie, what are you doing? Ease off!"

She tussled in his arms. Turning her head, she nicked him with a glance. He tightened his hold.

"He scared the kids." She tried to break free. "Let me go! Buck went out to the camp last night and scared Emma. Ask him."

He frowned at the mason. "You're Buck?"

"I wasn't out at the camp. She's lying."

"I am not."

"Where's your proof, lady? It's bullshit."

With dismay, Troy noticed three slack-jawed carpenters watching the skirmish from fifteen paces off. Alan Klatka, the lead mason, barreled toward them at a fast clip. In his haste, Alan dropped the Cleveland Indians cap he usually wore to hide his balding scalp. Shock and indignation combined on his face.

He halted before Rennie. "Why are you chewing out one of my guys? If you've got a problem, take it up with me." Without awaiting her reply, he turned on Buck. "Get to work. I'm not paying you to fight. Go near her again and you're fired."

"I'm going," the mason said, but he remained furiously in place. Greasy fear filled Troy's gut as the man stabbed his regard back on Rennie. "They aren't your kids. They're my flesh and blood."

Thrashing in Troy's hold, she said, "I'll never let you near them again."

"Yeah? Well, I got me a lawyer now. A good one. He'll have Walt and Emma back to me faster than you can spit." The mason stormed off with Alan a step behind.

Once they'd disappeared across the lawn, Rennie's knees buckled. She went fluid in Troy's arms. Her knees buckled. He fought to steady her. When he spun her around, he found her gaze unsettled. His heart rolled.

More crewmen lingered fifteen paces off, altering his sense of propriety. Gently, he told her, "I'm going to let you go now. I'd like some assurance you can stand on your own."

"I'm fine."

"You're sure?"

"Yes."

Releasing her, he put his hand on the small of her back to steer her toward the mansion. "Let's go. We aren't hashing this out in front of the crews. We've already drawn a crowd."

Obeying, she climbed the steps at an unsteady gait. He ushered her into the library and shut the door. Frank was gone, the pungent scent of his cigar lingering in the air.

Troy had just settled beside her on the couch when a maid slipped in. Wordlessly, she placed a glass of water on the coffee table, the ice clinking against the sides of the glass. Troy nodded in thanks.

The maid left, and he picked up the glass. "Drink." He handed it over. "And take another deep breath."

Rennie did as he asked, her dark curls tumbling forward as she bent to sip from the glass. She was dressed as she did every day, in jeans and a work shirt, but her unbound hair was a sensual distraction. He was seated close enough to smell something musky and warm rising off her skin. Impulsively, he looped the glossy curtain of hair over her shoulder to lend a fuller view of her face. Her gaze slid to his.

"Explain what's going on," he said calmly despite the wild thunder of his heart.

"Buck is their father." She set the glass down. "Walt and Emma's."

"The kids you're fostering? The mason is their father?" Given Buck's age, the fact seemed beyond the boundaries of logic.

"Don't look surprised. He's old enough to be their grandfather but he *is* their father."

"Outside, what did you mean he'd scared them?"

"Last night, at the campground."

"What happened?"

The question drove her from the couch. She ranged across the carpet like a lioness set loose. It was a relief, the distance she put between them. Though he was worried for her and the children, he was also painfully aware that the rising flush on her cheeks made her look like a Botticelli brushed golden by the Tuscan sun. He lingered on her profile, the curve of her forehead, her lightly feathered brows; how the strength of her nose was given beauty by the gently upturned tip. And her mouth—full and well carved, the edges puckering inward as she paced back and forth eluding demons. She was too agitated, too lost in her own counsel to understand that he couldn't look away.

It was an agony he didn't mind greeting. Hadn't he known all along he'd run up against this once they began working together? Seeing her, talking to her, the scent of what he'd swear was cinnamon lingering in her hair when she leaned too close to show him a schematic or ask his opinion. The way her voice trembled across his skin, low and husky—the way her eyes blazed fire across his heart when she shot out her opinion. And she was in trouble, in deep with the mason in a way that scared Troy because he couldn't get a fix on the danger. Which made her vulnerable—her eyes drawing to him now as she paused beside the desk to regard him, her gaze smoky and troubled, her lashes damp.

Would Rennie cry? He didn't like seeing her upset or need a reminder that she was a woman nearing tears and he was only a few, short strides from taking her into his arms.

Chapter 25

Rennie marshaled her thoughts.

As Troy watched her steadily from the couch, the argument with Buck rattled through her. She couldn't navigate the emotions bubbling up. Steering or suppressing them was impossible.

Pausing beside the desk, she found a way to begin. "Last night I received a call from the campground about Emma." Troy raised his brows slightly, urging her on, and she added, "She saw Buck in the woods. He was watching her and the other kids around a campfire. No one believed her."

"But you did."

"I drove out immediately and stayed the night. I was afraid he'd snatch the kids. Emma believed he'd try."

"Has he done anything like this before?"

"I'm not sure. Buck moved the kids around a lot. Simple enough to evade social workers, the police—anyone who'd notice the shape Walt and Emma were in. They finally landed in Tennessee. Buck's wife died there in an industrial accident. The move back to Ohio is recent."

"They're from Liberty?"

"Not the kids—Buck. He grew up here. Left the area decades ago."

"Why did he return?"

"No idea."

Exhausted, she leaned against the desk and closed her eyes.

When she reopened them, Troy had scooted to the edge of the couch. He clasped his hands, the concern on his face deepening.

He asked, "Are they taking precautions at the campgrounds?"

"The camp counselors had a meeting this morning. They won't let the kids out of their sight. Lunch, walks, even when they go to the bathroom someone will escort them."

Troy rubbed his jaw. "What about Pittsburgh tomorrow? Should we cancel the trip?"

The thought of leaving the kids for even a short trip was upsetting. What if something happened while she was away?

Then she considered Mae, how excited she'd seemed on the phone. For years she'd waited to meet her son. Disappointing her was out of the question. And what about Troy? Learning his life was built on secrets had changed him in distressing ways. Rennie first noticed the change during their heated conversation in the woods, the doubt inking his gaze, the sorrow on his lips. He needed answers. He deserved them.

"I'll ask my brother and sister-in-law to check in at the campground while we're away," she said, certain Nick and Liza would agree. "Pittsburgh is only a two-hour drive. If anything comes up, we'll come back quickly."

"What should I do about Buck?"

The question was difficult. Before they met at First Presbyterian, Rennie had assumed counseling would rehabilitate the volatile father of Walt and Emma. One glimpse into Buck's grey, predatory eyes had made clear he'd never alter his behavior.

"Fire him." She couldn't keep the venom from her voice. "Make him pay for what he's done. He's hurt Walt and Emma. Before they were taken from him . . ." She couldn't finish the thought. After a moment, she added, "They're too frightened to talk about their life with him."

"They will. Give it time."

"Their social worker says children have trouble verbalizing their emotions. Buck knows that. You know what I think? He planned for Emma to see him in the woods. Another way to control her."

The compassion softening Troy's expression brought her

perilously close to tears. "What did he do to the kids, Rennie?"

"Beatings . . . I don't know what else. I can't bear to think of what else."

"You believe there *was* more?"

She rubbed her arms, sick with the possibilities. "Yes, I do. And I want to hurt him. He should lose his job. He should lose a lot more, but the job's a start. He'll think twice before stalking the kids again."

She paused to swipe her forearm across her nose. She couldn't stop shaking. Her vision blurred and she realized she was crying because she was so wrung out and the kids—this morning when she'd said goodbye at the campground, they'd buried their faces at her waist. Walt kissed her a dozen times and Emma wept so hard her face wore a film of misery. Walking away from them was the most difficult task of Rennie's life.

"Rennie, don't be frightened. We'll work this out. We'll work everything out."

She was startled to find Troy before her. He'd risen swiftly from the couch.

"Stop worrying," he said softly. "Buck won't get the kids."

"How can you be sure?"

"I won't allow it."

With careful movements, he dried her face with his fingertips. The gesture was sweet, unexpected. He'd barely finished the task when his affection sent new tears down her cheeks.

"How will you stop him?" she demanded hoarsely. She searched his eyes for an inkling of their conversation yesterday, the accusations he'd leveled. She found only tenderness, a weighty tax on her overburdened heart. "What can you possibly do, Troy? Buck is cunning. Smarter than you think. He's made a hobby of torturing Walt and Emma."

"I don't care what's happened in the past. I won't let Buck hurt the kids again—or you. You have my word."

The resolution in his voice silenced her. He *would* keep them safe. His ready protection was undeniable and utterly male. It left the impression he'd unconsciously waited for the moment to demonstrate his stalwart nature.

Through damp lashes she canvassed his face, the hard set of

his jaw and the flinty resolve in his gaze. He found the close inspection pleasurable, his eyes losing their hard glint; and the warmth his regard spilled through Rennie urged her to rest her palms against the sturdy muscles roping his arms. She gripped him tightly, searching for some small measure of his strength, enough strength to see her past the danger Buck represented. In response, he feathered his hand across her hair, his touch devastatingly intimate, his fingers tangling in the unbound lengths. His breathing hitched. The evidence of his need flooded her heart with desire, the passion rising between them a strange complement to the fear Buck had planted in her blood.

Throwing off the last of his doubts, Troy cradled her face in his palms. He was uncommonly tall, a large, well-built man. Yet his touch was feather light as he tipped her chin up and teased her lips with his mouth, a leisurely exploration that pooled moisture between her thighs. He pulled back for a shattering moment, his gaze aflame. With satisfaction he read her hungering expression, the permission for him to proceed. She couldn't think, couldn't do anything but hang her attention on the rugged color staining his cheekbones as he moved back in and took her lips without reservation.

His ardor was slow and thorough and deep. He dragged his mouth to the sensitive skin beneath her earlobe and she arched into him, a willing participant to the plunder of her senses. His breath ragged, he inhaled her deeply. In some small part of her brain, she understood her vulnerability had unhitched the tight reserve he used to govern his behavior; that the menace of Buck, who might well have thrown a punch at her outside, proved a watershed moment for Troy and his very masculine need to keep her safe.

Burying his face in her hair, he said, "The other day . . . I shouldn't have kissed you. Now it's all I can think about."

"Me too," she murmured, astonished by the disclosure's accuracy. Their moments together had lingered beneath daily thoughts of caring for the children and her job.

"I'm tired of fighting the way I feel about you. Doesn't matter what I do. You always manage to bewitch me."

He molded her close, muscle and bone, and the love she harbored for him became a torment. "I find that hard to believe," she said with false calm. Giving in to the temptation, she flung her arms across his shoulders.

"Rennie, don't you know what you do to me? I've spent the better part of my life thinking about the night I made love to you, wishing I could have you again."

"I'm sorry. I never meant—"

"To capture me, heart and soul?" Nuzzling his face to her temple, he gave out a low chuckle that started her quivering. "Your inability to see what you do to me has always been the greater part of your charm. Do you know you're beautiful? I'll never meet another woman capable of standing in your light."

She was about to protest the unexpected compliment when he took her mouth again. She met his kiss with equal heat, transmitting her unspoken love in the simplest, fullest way. Against her breasts, Troy's pulse beat wildly. Desperate to prolong the embrace, she leaned into him fully. Beneath his feverish caresses the fear stalking her evaporated. He molded her closer, sending a message of his own.

Outside a pneumatic nail gun split the air. He sent a quick glance to the window.

He kissed her forehead then released her. "If Buck goes near the kids again, I'll talk to Chief Calabrese," he said, resuming a businesslike tone with uncanny ease. But he sent a long, meaningful look before moving away. "I've known Doug a long time. He'll take my concerns seriously."

"You'd do that?" With difficulty she mimicked his cool demeanor.

"I'll have patrol cars trail Buck. Not likely he'll try to pull off anything else." Troy hesitated, clearly uncomfortable. At last he added, "A few weeks ago? I ran into him at a bar. Didn't know who he was, but I didn't like him. I sure as hell don't like him now. If you insist, I'll fire him."

"You don't think you should?"

On a frown, he walked to the window. "I prefer to keep an eye on Buck. If he's working here, we can both watch him. If he's the sort of man who'd kidnap his kids—and I think that's what we're talking about—what happens when Walt and Emma return from camp?"

"What do you mean?"

"What happens after spring break? Rennie, he could snatch the kids from the school playground. Lots of kids, preoccupied teachers—not a hard feat to pull off."

"I hadn't thought of that." The thought chilled her.

"Wouldn't you rather know where he is during the day?"

"Absolutely."

"Then he stays on the job. Agreed?"

"All right."

Troy returned to her side. "Rennie, you're such a hothead. You must steer clear of him. If anything else happens, let me handle it. Promise me."

She took his hand, squeezed. "All right," she agreed.

In the cafeteria of Job & Family Services, Lianna surveyed the empty tables. She spotted Jenalyn at a table in back and started toward her with a sense of misgiving.

The law firm of Oortman & Smith had sent over a letter, an unexpected missive delivered twenty minutes ago.

At Lianna's approach, the social worker waved. "Where's your lunch?" Jenalyn asked. She noticed the letter. "What's that?"

Slipping into a chair, Lianna placed the envelope between them. "I received this from Gleason Smith's office."

"Buck mentioned hiring a lawyer."

"He did? When?"

"He told me a few days ago after a visit with Walt and Emma. At least he's hired Gleason, who's reasonable."

Lianna nodded in agreement. Fresh out of law school, the ebullient young lawyer was in some way related to the firm's senior partner.

"Gleason has requested an emergency hearing." Gingerly Lianna handed off the letter. "He'll ask for the immediate return of the children."

"Can you sway the judge? Explain Buck hasn't finished therapy?"

"We go before Judge Lamby in the morning."

Jenalyn's face fell. "So soon."

"The hearing is merely a ploy. Judge Lamby will refuse to transfer custody immediately. After he makes the ruling, Gleason will ask us to provide a timeline for the children's return. The judge will then direct us to give Buck weekly goals, like proof of attendance at AA meetings. There will be other contingencies, which you and I will discuss. When the timeline runs out, we'll return to court for the true custody hearing. Even then, Buck has no guarantees. I'm not convinced he can adequately parent Walt and Emma."

Jenalyn absorbed the explanation with palpable unease. "I don't like to make waves, but your take on the situation is inaccurate," she said carefully. "This case was never airtight. Going in, we didn't have substantial proof of abuse. Buck's drunk driving conviction . . . it helps. But he's continued with therapy. During his visits with the kids he interacts properly, if not affectionately."

Lianna grunted. "A parent is always on his best behavior with a social worker present."

"The drunk driving citation is the only blemish on his record," Jenalyn stubbornly pointed out. "Gleason might convince the judge that Buck's rage was a result of grief over his wife's death. Fair argument, yes?"

"I'm not sure."

"Better think it through. For all we know, Gleason plans to argue for an immediate transfer of custody."

"Lamby won't agree."

"What are you always telling me? Every case is different. Lots of variables, lots of unexpected outcomes."

True, but Lianna trusted the judge's good sense—and Gleason's. "My opinion holds a great deal of weight," she replied, uncomfortably aware of the defensive notes in her voice. "I'll argue the children are not best served by returning them to their father."

At the outburst, Jenalyn frowned. Quietly she said, "Yes, but your personal involvement in this case has clouded your perceptions. You're incapable of viewing the risks. I'm sorry, but you are."

"Most of my children have provided foster care at one time or another. It doesn't affect my objectivity."

"Sure, and everyone applauds the valiant Perinis. But tell me—did any of those other instances involve a drifter like Buck?

Someone we suspect of significant abuse?"

The question hung perilously between them. *Was* this case different? Lianna recalled her initial interview with Buck, the way he'd wrapped the rosary around his fist like brass knuckles. She'd feared him.

She still did.

"You've asked Rennie to foster two kids whose father may remove them from our jurisdiction the minute custody is returned," Jenalyn was saying. "And why not? Buck only recently moved to Ohio. He doesn't own real estate. Nothing holds him to Liberty. Now he has a smart, young lawyer who understands a drunk driving conviction isn't cause to sever parental rights. You're blind to the facts because of your daughter. Rennie loves the kids."

"She has grown fond of them."

"She called this morning, something about Buck going out to the campground last night. I talked to him. He denies it. But that wasn't the only topic of conversation." Jenalyn sighed heavily. "Rennie asked what she'd need to do to adopt Walt and Emma."

Lianna sat back, stunned. "Adopt them?"

"I told her it was premature to discuss adoption. I didn't know about the letter you'd received from Gleason, of course. Not that it matters now."

Spinning, Lianna asked, "Why doesn't it matter?"

"This morning Buck told Rennie he'd hired an attorney. She didn't take it well."

Alarmed, Lianna asked, "She talked to him?"

"Argued with him," Jenalyn grimly clarified. "A confrontation at Fagan's. Alan Klatka, the mason? His wife is in my prayer group at church. She called me first thing—said her husband was livid about a confrontation between one of his employees and a woman electrician out at the Fagan job. Said they almost came to blows." Pausing, the social worker raked nervous fingers through her ebony hair. "Lianna, I can't tell you how uncomfortable I am with both of them working the same job site. I've never run across this before, a foster parent employed alongside an estranged parent. In a town the size of Liberty it was bound to happen."

Lianna's pulse skittered. An inevitability, sure, but why had it happened in a case involving her daughter?

Clearly distressed, Jenalyn pushed away her uneaten lunch. "I asked Rennie not to confront Buck again." She hesitated before adding, "By the way, he's rented a house on Redding Avenue."

Lianna received the news with a grimace. Buck had been living in a small apartment near Liberty Square. Renting a house was a smart move. It would be easier to regain custody by demonstrating to the court his desire to provide a stable home environment.

Which left her with a nagging worry. *Would* the court transfer custody tomorrow?

Dismissing the thought, she noticed the worry in Jenalyn's eyes. "Good heavens, is there something else?" she demanded.

"Redding Avenue," Jenalyn repeated. "Who lives on Redding that you'd expect to complain about a new neighbor?"

"Don't tell me Buck moved anywhere near Gibby Perkins."

If every small berg in America featured a town crier, Gibby had been Liberty's for half a century. If children played near her pristine brick ranch, Gibby phoned the police. The old woman styled herself as the grand dame of Liberty in her severe plaid skirts and jeweled bifocals. She dominated town meetings and badgered the Liberty superintendent over the increase in property taxes whenever a school levy passed.

Jenalyn said, "Buck is renting near her place. One, two doors down. Yesterday she found him in her backyard. She put in a call to have him arrested. Knowing Gibby, she demanded a sentence without parole because he left footprints on her lawn."

"What did the police department do?"

"Tried to calm her down, of course. Last night, two of the officers went to Buck's place looking for an explanation. He said he was just checking out his new neighborhood. They thought it was harmless. Told him to stick to the sidewalks."

It sounded innocent enough. Even so, Lianna was conscious of the small pebble of fear settling in her stomach.

"So." Jenalyn offered a forlorn smile. "Will you tell Rennie about our court date tomorrow morning or should I?"

Lianna closed her eyes with regret. "I'll go out to the Fagans and tell her," she said.

With disbelief, Rennie leaned against the trunk of the apple tree.

They were alone in an orchard near the mansion. From the new wing, drills whirred and hammers pounded, the sounds muffled and sparse. The breeze fluttered the hem of her mother's conservative blue dress. Shocked by the news, Rennie lowered herself to the grass and clasped her knees to her chest.

"Can I go to the hearing?" she asked, dimly aware of the shock lancing through her.

Her mother's reply was quick and depressing. "I'm sorry, dear. Your participation isn't appropriate. I'm merely telling you in the unlikely event Buck wins."

Rennie clung to her eroding composure. "Meaning he may win?"

"Possibly—but unlikely." Nearing, Lianna patted her shoulder. "The judge will listen to reason. Walt and Emma will stay with you for now."

Something drifted through Rennie, an indefinable emotion, a meshing of fear and defiance that made her doubt the thin assurances. When, precisely, had she stopped believing in her mother? When had she begun trusting her own instincts instead? Lianna was a defining force, an anchor no matter how tumultuous the circumstances. Now Rennie discovered her own powers of navigation.

"Humor me." She rose on unsteady feet. "What's the worst case scenario?"

Her mother muttered beneath her breath, clearly perturbed by the question.

"Mother, I need the truth." She was edgy from this morning's confrontation with Buck. Her interlude with Troy was, by comparison, comforting. More than comforting. But for too many days now, she'd ridden an emotional roller coaster. "Spell it out. What happens if, God forbid, you're wrong for the first time in your life?"

"Rennie, calm down."

"Tell me."

Seeking guidance, Lianna glanced at the sky. "If Buck wins, the children will return to him tomorrow."

"What about camp?"

"Buck won't remove the children from camp," her mother snapped, "for the simple reason that his lawyer will instruct him not to disrupt their schedule. Buck will pick up his children on Sunday like all of the other parents. His lawyer will instruct him to toe the line."

"What happens to me?"

"Having the children at camp complicates things. We usually transfer custody at my office. In this instance, I would ask you to visit the camp on Saturday. Jenalyn would accompany you. Together, you'd prepare Walt and Emma for release back to their father."

A howl of protest barreled up Rennie's throat and nearly broke free. "Then what?"

"None of this will happen! Granted, I'm not promising you'll keep Walt and Emma forever. It would be premature to make such an assessment, but I *can* assure you the court rarely sides with a parent when I bring the full weight of my office to bear."

"To hell with your public standing. I'll have a few minutes with Walt and Emma. That's it. That's all the time we'll have together. They'll be gone from my life, and there isn't a damn thing you can do."

Lianna stood very still. Something darted through her eyes, fast and fleeting. "Honey—"

Rennie covered her mouth with her fist. She battled the irrational desire to scream loud enough to drown out the pneumatic nail gun peppering the air, loud enough to send her mother reeling backward. Instead, she stalked farther into the orchard. She looked up at the sky, a dome of blue. Pink-tipped clouds raced across the horizon. A perfect day.

"I was supposed to go with Troy to Pittsburgh tomorrow." She turned, waited for her mother to catch up. "I'll have to cancel."

Lianna's brows rose. "You were going to St. Justin's? Mae is expecting you?"

"Yes."

"Oh, sweetie—don't cancel. Go to Pittsburgh. It will mean so much to Mae."

"With Buck heading to court? I can't." She couldn't bear to consider Mae's disappointment, but the situation was untenable.

"Unfortunately, Mae was really looking forward to the visit. Not that Troy was. He might thank me for canceling."

"Rennie, listen to me." Lianna clasped her hands in a firm grip. She shook her, once, before adding, "There's no stopping Buck from having his day in court. If he wins—and sweetheart, he won't—you'll return to Liberty immediately. He won't get Walt and Emma before you've had a chance to see them. Think of Mae, what this means to her."

Rennie tried to pull free, to no avail. "Mother, please."

"Think, dear. She never believed she'd have the opportunity to meet Troy. You've begun to love Walt and Emma with a mother's heart. Imagine what the years have been like for Mae. She endured rape but something good came out of it. Something wonderful, *someone* wonderful. She held him close for a few precious days. Then she let him go."

"I can't imagine what Mae went through," Rennie murmured. "Troy is the finest man I've ever known. Oh, he's difficult and maddening." She recalled the heat of his mouth, and his ready desire to protect her. "Beneath his more irritating traits, he's wonderful."

"You love him."

"Mother, stop it. I'm not discussing—"

"Sweet girl, you do. Your passion for Troy is the defining burden of your life."

The bald statement jolted her. How could her mother understand truths that had only recently become apparent? Flustered, she read the sympathy in Lianna's eyes.

"Rennie, I've always known. Doesn't Troy feel the same? Oh, he's terribly noble, sacrificing his own happiness on the altar of his brother's memory. And yours. Lord knows he's sacrificed your happiness too. There's an awful chance you'll both go to your graves single and lonely, although I do hope you'll come to your senses." Letting her go, Lianna looked up soberly. "Sweetheart, please hear me out. Loving Troy as you do, imagine Mae's joy the first time she sets eyes on him. He's such a beautiful man, tortured and sweet, but you really don't understand the essence of the man you adore. He's so much like Mae. So very like her. Can't you find it in your heart to give her the finest gift? Let her meet her son."

Miss Ginnie had a flower petal of yellow paint on her nose and a snake of blue yarn on her wrist. She hauled a purple chair to the head of the picnic table and sat. Girls were seated all the way down the table, eager for the lesson on how to make kites. Emma hurried to the end of the table, glad for room to spread out.

In no time at all, her kite was the best. She wrapped the paper tight around sticks shaped like a cross. The girl with the blubbery cheeks helped tape the paper down. Then Miss Ginnie announced it was time to paint and hurried off to the cabin with one of the big girls. They returned with paintbrushes and crayons and enough paint to make all the kites pretty.

Emma painted fast, swirling flowers and pretty dots in pink and blue and yellow all over the paper until Miss Ginnie told her to slow down, the kite looked weepy.

"My kite won't cry," Emma said. "It's happy."

Laughing, Miss Ginnie reminded her to slow down. But she needed to finish quick.

After awhile Miss Ginnie rolled her eyes. "Go on, child," she said, when Emma looked toward the cabin again and again. "Just for a minute, all right? There's no one spying on us. Peek out of the window. Get back here in a flash."

Emma snatched up her Barbie doll and dashed inside.

The sneakers all over the floor looked like fish thrown on shore. They smelled like wetness. Blades of grass stuck in the laces. She hopped over a pair then tiptoed between the bunk beds. Holding her breath, she went to the window.

Outside, the forest danced with light. There were dark spots, too, near the fat bushes and behind the big trees. Looking at each closely, she prayed to Jesus and Barbie three times.

She wasn't sure if prayers would help. Pa knew how to hide.

One time, in Tennessee, he walked right into the woods behind their house and disappeared. The car with the flashing red lights stayed in the driveway for a long time, the men inside angry. But Pa fooled them like he always did.

There's my girl.

She gripped the windowsill as Pa crept into her thoughts. At the forest edge a black squirrel climbed a tree like lightning, and she tried to keep her mind on its swishing tail. She'd never seen a black squirrel when she lived in Tennessee. They were all over Ohio, black as coal. Not that she missed Tennessee or the house. You had to go to the shack out back to do your business. Not like Rennie's home, where you could go inside and never hear the owls screeching. Even though she still missed Mama, she liked Rennie's place.

Buck, are you here? Walt, give the doll back to your sister! You'll get a toy as soon as I save a few dollars.

Before Mama went to heaven, she spent most of her money keeping up the house and tending the animals. She fed the chickens treats even though they left poop on the grass and pecked at each other. Laughing at their meanness, she'd look back at the house and shout, "Buck, I'm goin' to work now." Emma hung onto Mama until she shook her head, fluttering her lips as fast as the chickens worked their feathers. "Girl, I got to get to work. Go on, now. Pa will feed you dinner."

Pa never got them chow. Right after Mama drove off, he left too. When he'd gone, Walt climbed on a chair in the kitchen and rattled around the cupboard.

Peanut butter, Emma. Use your finger.

Most times Pa came home long before Mama with the smell of firewater on his breath. Standing in the doorway, he swayed like a man caught on a swing. He'd make her and Walt pay if they looked at him the wrong way. It was hard to know the right way to look because your eyes just *looked*. Not that Emma minded the hurting. She didn't mind too much if Pa got tired of giving whoopins' and made them sleep in the barn. They'd crawl onto the hay near the chickens, listening to the birds cluck and settling in for the night. If the moon peeked in through the barn's slats, the air looked like snowflakes. Walt sang to her so she'd forget the air licking ice across her skin.

The barn wasn't bad at all.

On the terrible nights, Pa found them curled together in the bedroom. They knew to run from sleep until Mama came home. Sometimes sleep caught them anyway. Emma would wake, yawning, as Pa rustled Walt from the room. The sight of Walt's feet padding out the door made her heart fall to the dark place.

Girl, hold still.

Inside her head, Emma would cry out. *Pa, don't.* He'd lift her nightgown and tussle with her until she gave up and touched the mean thing. It grew against her fingers, big as death. Pa stripped off her panties.

He'd become a train, huffing and puffing. Emma would slip inside herself, a girl curled up in the corner of a train that carried her down the tracks into a grey place.

Struggling from the memory, Emma pressed her nose to the window's cool glass.

The forest was silent.

Chapter 26

"How are you holding up?" Troy asked.

Rennie pulled away from her inspection of the vineyards streaming past the passenger side of Troy's Mercedes. The traffic on the turnpike had been light all morning. They were nearing the Pennsylvania border.

"I'd feel better if I could talk to Walt and Emma." She juggled her cell phone from palm to palm. "The camp counselors took the kids out on the lake today. There's a cookout afterward. They'll be out of touch for hours."

"Let them enjoy the day."

"Walt promised to catch a fish for me. The biggest one in the lake."

Troy chuckled. "First sign of a boyhood crush. Get ready for other love tokens, like salamanders."

"Works for me."

Irritated by her inability to relax, Rennie tossed her smartphone into the Mercedes' back seat. Her mother and Buck were scheduled in court to hash out the custody arrangements in less than an hour. Would Buck win? It was a worry Rennie wasn't comfortable sharing with Troy any more than she had the fortitude to question the passionate moments they'd spent together yesterday. Given the impending meeting with his birth mother, Troy had enough on his mind.

She said, "What time do you think we'll return to Liberty?"

"Middle of the afternoon at the latest." He threw a glance

rife with amusement. "Third time you've asked."

"Really?" She hadn't kept track.

Presenting a calm exterior took all of her stamina. Of course her mother was correct—Rennie had started Troy on a journey into his past that she was obligated to finish. Besides, worrying herself frantic over Buck's day in court would have no effect on the outcome. Last night she'd called Jenalyn, mostly to discuss the case but also for reassurance. To her relief, the social worker insisted Buck's chances of winning immediate custody weren't good. Still, the worry lingered.

Troy broke into her thoughts. "Should we turn around? I don't know what's going on but you're awfully wound up."

"I'm fine."

"Listen, I'm not happy about leaving the job site either. If Squeak can't manage without you, we'll reschedule with Mae."

"No, he's fine on his own. I left detailed instructions."

"Sure you wouldn't prefer to call Mae and say something came up?"

"Let's not disappoint her. She's excited about meeting you."

"We won't stay long."

"Are you nervous?" The question barely settled between them when the now familiar tension returned to his features. Quickly, she added, "If you prefer not to talk about it—"

"It's all right." Troy sped up, maneuvered past an eighteen-wheeler. "I'm not sure how I feel. I don't like walking into an unknown situation. What are the ground rules? What if she . . ."

His voice trailed off, and Rennie wondered what battlements he glimpsed. Was he frightened Mae expected something from him? His love and devotion?

"I doubt Mae expects anything from you." Reaching across the seat, she patted his thigh. The affection was impulsive and she was relieved by the pleasure seeping into his expression. "Meeting her will be easy. You'll see."

"I'm not a coward."

"I'm not saying you are. This *is* stressful. I'll stay close unless you ask me to leave. Just give the word when you're ready for alone time with Mae. I'll hit the trail."

"Given the choice, I prefer having you around."

The comment, husky and heartfelt, lingered between them.

He reached across the seat and took her hand.

"I'll stay as long as you like," she said, refusing to read too much into the gesture. "Totally your call."

The corner of his mouth lifted wryly. "I'm not talking about today."

She caught her breath. Hadn't she understood as much during their interlude in the mansion's library? She'd yearned for his kiss. She'd yearned for *him.* Her astute mother was correct— she'd always wanted Troy. For years the hope was buried beneath the grief about his brother.

Troy was saying, "If we have a relationship now, it won't be like the last time. One night then goodbye."

She released a nervous laugh. "I hope not."

He let his attention linger on her face. "Rennie, when we made love beneath the Great Oak, we were kids. If we start now, we won't walk away. And it scares the hell out of me." He leveled his eyes on the road. Regret darted through his expression, giving her pause, even as his fingers held hers tight. "I'm a rational man but sometimes . . ."

She squeezed his fingers, needing to understand. "What?"

He glanced at her swiftly. "When we met at the Great Oak for all the wrong reasons, did we bring down a curse? I don't blame you for my brother's death—we're both to blame. There's also your private life to consider. Walt and Emma need all the love you can give them. And what are the odds Buck would come on board with the masons' crew? Crazy, sure, but it feels like another curse. I hired him and you're trying to keep his kids safe."

"Bizarre coincidences happen every day. It doesn't mean we're cursed."

"Whenever we mix, we stir something up. Don't you wonder if we should stay the hell away from each other?"

"Do you honestly believe that?" She prayed he didn't.

"Unfortunately I do, for a lot of reasons I can't easily dismiss. Take Mae's letters. You never should've found them but you did. I never should have hired Buck but I did."

A protest hovered on her lips. The events weren't related. Yet she couldn't deny the fear stealing into her bones. "Like I said, nothing more than bizarre coincidence," she insisted, refusing to see where he was going with this. "The letters don't have anything to do with Buck."

"I'm no mathematician, but the odds are striking. Don't you think it's strange you found the letters? They should've been destroyed during breakthrough. No one should've found a small box in all that debris." His face worked, his eyes darkening. Gruffly, he added, "Long before that, with Jason . . . it's beyond tragic that your confession about sleeping with me sent him on a drinking spree. That should've been the end to it—a hangover and two brothers warring over a girl. Your confession shouldn't have led to his death."

Nausea buffeted her. "He was so angry. Hurt, too."

"Understandable, sure. But what happened between us isn't unusual. We spent all those years throwing insults to hide our attraction—from each other, and everyone else. God, I wanted to believe I hated you." He regarded her with a miserable longing. "You were everything to me."

The comment stamped an exquisite agony on her soul. His honesty unlocked a truth she'd never trusted to anyone, even herself.

Troy was the only man she would ever love. She would have him, or no one else.

Reading the private Braille of her thoughts, he said, "I'll never stop loving you. If things were different and we'd married, had kids . . . Jason would've forgiven us. Not right away. Not easily. But he never could hold a grudge."

Troy's pronouncement gripped her heart. She saw the life they would've led if Jason's death hadn't snuffed out their passion—a home, kids and a marriage that grew stronger by the year.

"When we made love, we made everything rotten," he said, gauging her reaction. His expression was dour. "Jason went out, got drunk, and walked into a store at precisely the wrong moment. The crack-head robbing the place never saw my brother. He just opened fire. If Jason had arrived five minutes earlier, he'd still be alive. Five minutes later? The same. Which doesn't feel like a bizarre coincidence. More like a curse."

"A curse we brought down on ourselves?" *And the people we dare to love.*

Troy's jaw clenched. "It scares me to think we're both responsible for Jason's death. Now, in ways we can't understand, our actions have the power to hurt your foster kids too. Don't ask me how I know—I just do." He paused long enough for an unbidden trill of fear to bolt through her. "Rennie, I didn't explain what happened when I ran into Buck at Bongo's Tavern a few weeks ago."

"Tell me," she said, wishing he wouldn't.

"I watched him do a dart trick no one can do. No one except me. Buck threw the dart with his back to the target. Threw the dart blind from over his shoulder, and hit the mark dead on."

"Another coincidence." She despised the dread coloring her voice. "You're reading too much into it."

"Oh, yeah? A few days ago, I find you in front of the mansion arguing with him. Buck was about to deck you and he's all muscle. You were in danger. Lord, you really were. After, when we went inside, you floored me with your announcement that he's Walt and Emma's father." Troy planted his gaze on the road. "Don't ask me to map any of this out rationally. Doesn't matter. I'm afraid that what happens between us has the power to destroy Walt and Emma, just like we destroyed Jason."

The sorrow in his voice warned of endings. *We brought a curse down upon ourselves.*

He studied her for a long moment. "Beneath the Great Oak, we gave in to the weakest part of our natures," he said grimly. "Here we are years later, starting up again. Now two kids are involved. We must protect them, but the curse we brought down on ourselves brought Buck Korchek with it. If we let ourselves love each other, can we find a way to keep Walt and Emma safe?" He let her hand go. Then he asked, "Did you know my brother intended to marry you?"

Shattered, she stared at him. Was it true? Surely she would've known.

"Jason bought you a ring," Troy said, his voice level, making the turmoil beneath his words all the more poignant. "He didn't call it an engagement ring. But it was a diamond."

Shaken, she pulled her attention to the road. "If I'd known . . ."

If I'd known, I never would've told Jason the truth—

"I don't want any secrets between us," Troy said. "That's why I'm telling you about Jason. If Mae really is my mother—if I am adopted—the lies end there." He paused long enough for the statement to collapse his expression. "I love you, Rennie. I always will."

Heavy with grief, she offered the whisper of a smile. "I love you, too. I always have."

"Good to know." Pain etched his features. "When we were young, we didn't have the right foundation. It was rotten from the start."

"We're older now."

He nodded stiffly. "Yes, we are. If we build a relationship now, we'd damn better make it strong enough to withstand whatever bad luck is coming our way."

The neighborhood surrounding St. Justin Martyr parish was picturesque and serene. Men were out mowing their lawns on this bright morning. Children played hopscotch on the sidewalk. Traffic grew heavy and Troy eased off the accelerator.

Furtively, he regarded the gloomy woman seated beside him. Rennie had pulled herself together, if barely. She was following his cue, burying their troubling conversation behind a thin wall of composure. He frowned. They were both good at shutting down their emotions.

He drove through the wrought iron gates of the parish. Before the rectory he parked with his apprehension rising.

Rennie got out and nodded at the tidy brick building. "Mae promised to meet us inside."

Troy paused to take in his surroundings. On the opposite side of the parking lot, the church was a gorgeous edifice of gold sandstone. To the right, at the far end of the lot, St. Justin's Elementary School nestled amongst fir trees. Behind the rectory, the parish gardens lay within a perimeter of wrought iron that connected to the main railing surrounding the entire parish grounds. Where was Mae's house? Rennie had mentioned a small building somewhere on the property. He couldn't spot it amidst the leafy trees and blooming azaleas.

She came around the hood of his Mercedes. "You'll be fine,"

she said with a bright smile that surely came at a cost. "If you can't think of what to say, I'll do the talking."

She looked so earnest, his heart overturned. This morning when he'd picked her up she'd dashed out of her house in uncharacteristically feminine attire. The bottle green skirt and gauzy cream blouse did for him what two cups of coffee hadn't accomplished—brought him to full attention. Now he was painfully conscious she'd dressed more for him, than Mae.

He brushed against the skirt's soft material. "This is the first time I've seen you out of work clothes."

"An old rag," she joked, plucking at the fabric. "I hate to admit how infrequently I get out of blue jeans."

"You look good."

He was stalling, and she sent another bright smile. "Thanks," she replied.

He stepped toward the rectory. The nerves he'd battled since daybreak increased. "Let's get this show on the road." He flexed his fingers in an unrewarded attempt to diminish the nerves. "I'm as ready as I'll ever be."

The tranquil rectory was pungent with incense. A desk bearing neat stacks of correspondence stood to the left. The receptionist was nowhere in sight. Behind the desk, a photograph of the Pope and a crucifix hung prominently on the wall. Presumably the hallway to the right led to the priest's private quarters.

In a chair tucked in the corner, a woman sat serenely. Mae Sullivan rose to greet them.

Troy went stock-still. He hadn't expected height, and Mae was a tall woman. Her white-streaked blond hair was pulled back from a face strong-boned and striking. Her chin was well defined, her cheekbones high. Her mouth was wide, her nose long and straight. The large ovals of her eyes were a deep Pacific blue.

The nearly perfect reflection shocked him. Mae was his feminine version. Older, but a near carbon copy.

He blinked wildly. *He* was the carbon copy.

Dizzy, he caught Rennie's inquisitive gaze. Her expression revealed she'd made the same, stunning assessment.

Mae was equally dumbfounded. Nervously she smoothed her hands down her canvas shirt. Grass stains peppered her pants. Troy hung his attention on her fingers, long like his own, the cuticles rimmed with faint lines of dirt. A gardener's hands.

She snapped from her stupor. "You didn't need to dress up," she said to Rennie.

"We weren't sure what to wear." Rennie laughed, the sound genuine in the center of an awkward moment. Troy was grateful for her quick response. He'd lost the ability to speak. "I'm sorry."

"Well, don't be." Mae took an awkward step toward the sunlight pooling at the door. Troy realized she was doing everything in her power not to bring him into her sights. "Why don't we stroll through the garden? I finished weeding most of the flowerbeds this week. Everything looks perfect. Would you like a tour?"

Rennie gently looped her arm through his. "That would be lovely. Thank you," she added, allowing Mae to pass before leading him out.

Mae fled through the door. She strode across the parking lot, her thick-soled sneakers smacking on the asphalt. On the other side of the parking lot, she rushed through a gate to the gardens Troy hadn't noticed earlier.

Rennie studied his face. "Are you okay?" she asked.

"No." Woozy, he gulped down air. "She's my spitting image."

"Actually, you're *her* spitting image."

In a humiliating blow to his male pride, he leaned heavily against Rennie's shoulder. She led him forward.

Mae Sullivan *was* his mother. Believing anything less was absurd. He'd expected to meet her with a healthy dose of skepticism. He certainly wasn't prepared for the physical proof of their bond to scatter his doubts like leaves on the wind.

Leaving the gate open, Mae disappeared inside the garden. Nearing with the bulk of his weight on Rennie, Troy took in the trees throwing puddles of shade on the walk. They entered, and she drew him to a stop to admire a curving bed of roses still in bud. The abundant sounds of life greeted his ears—a bird's call, the far-off hum of traffic. The well-tended earth smelled of mulch, the immaculate beds recently layered with wood chips. A large statue of Mary partially hid a fountain, which gurgled and leapt.

Thankfully Rennie's cheer lured Mae back. The women chatted about the abundant variety of plants, the creeping thyme burning magenta beside the path, the azaleas glowing pink. Together the trio walked on. Troy struggled to find his bearings.

"Father Cyprian is our pastor," Mae was saying. "Over the years he's let me expand the gardens. Most of the plants are donated by parishioners, and the steering committee has set aside funds for upkeep."

Rennie cupped a rose with crimson petals. "How long have you worked here?"

"Oh, forever. I started at the age of seventeen, a few months after I arrived."

"My mother mentioned you were quite young when you came here."

"How is she?"

"Busy at Jobs & Family Services. Dad's retired. Actually, he's a gardener like you—he grows vegetables in the back yard. Tomatoes and beans, and ridiculously large zucchini."

"Ah, that sounds like Mario." Mae pivoted, to point into the distance. "Do you see there, past the railing? I've put in an orchard."

She looked expectantly to Troy. For the first time, their gazes meshed. He tried to hear past his thundering pulse.

He cleared his throat. "Your mother worked for my family?" he asked with blundering disregard. *Mae* was his real family.

Apparently he'd spared her feelings. "Oh, yes," she replied, the hopefulness in her eyes increasing. "*Your* mother was very young at the time. She'd only been married to your father for a couple of years. Even so, Jackie ran the mansion with an expert hand. I think my mother was in awe of her. Rennie's grandmother was, too."

Rennie said, "My grandmother worked at Fagan's until a year before she died. At least that's what I've been told. I don't remember her."

"She was a lovely woman. Quite strict with the management of the Fagans' kitchen but very kind." Dropping the subject, Mae examined a rhododendron's yellowish leaf. "I'm not finished amending the soil around this poor plant. Still too alkaline." She straightened, her brows puckering. "You can't stay long, can you?"

"No," Troy replied stiffly. "We have to get back."

"I'm glad you came. We have so much to talk about."

She wavered on the stone path. She was waiting, he knew.

Troy searched for a starting point. A thousand questions churned inside him. How to unearth them? Rennie studied her pumps and Mae regarded him patiently as he raced after the fragments in his mind.

His confusion galvanized her. She began speaking with a calm that belied the potency of her words.

"You were born on a Tuesday at three a.m.," she said, taking him by the hand. She held his fingers lightly, as if they were as fragile as spun glass. "The labor was difficult—you weren't in a hurry to enter the world. Finally you arrived. A large baby. You had that gorgeous hair, even at birth."

The history of his hidden life rained down too quickly. He was caught in rough seas, at risk of going under. "I'm sorry for everything that happened to you," he replied, his voice raw. Now that he'd spoken, the words spilled out. "You lost so much on my account. I didn't know about any of this until recently. I truly am sorry."

She regarded him with bemusement. On a sigh, she rummaged through the pocket of her roomy pants. A plaid gardening glove appeared, frayed and dirty. Next she produced a packet of photographs.

One by one, she held out the photos for his perusal. "This is Susie Blake," she began. "In college now. Dean's list, planning a career in geology. I was godmother at her baptism. Isn't she a doll? This picture—Joshua Piazza on the day of his First Communion. He's an accountant in Pittsburgh, quite wealthy in fact. He's only a few years younger than you, Troy. This photo? Dillon Casper, U.S. Marine. I took Dillon under my wing when he entered kindergarten. He drove the teachers crazy with his antics. This girl here? Judy Thacker. She was horribly shy. The other children tormented her. I'd rescue Judy during recess. She loved planting flowers . . ."

Each photograph gave proof of the children Mae had helped nurture and grow. Troy listened, spellbound. Where was her anger? Raped at the tender age of sixteen. She was beaten and defiled. All her dreams disappeared on one, awful day. With dismay, he realized she was still beautiful. The sun had weathered her skin but her eyes were clear, her mouth a blossomed rose. She hadn't become a nun. Still, she could've gone on to marry and raise a family. Yet she chose a life of isolation on the grounds of a parish that must surely remind her of every dream she'd lost.

Overwrought, he watched her carefully band the photographs back together. When she'd returned them to her pocket, she rested her palm on his cheek. Troy's heart buckled.

"My darling boy. Did you think you were the only one?" she whispered. "God has been very good to me. You were my first, the child of my flesh, but He has put many in my heart. When we love a child, we experience a moment of absolute grace. Wouldn't you agree?"

Instantly, he understood. She'd always loved him—just as she'd loved every child to have the good fortune to pass through her life. Tucked away in a parish garden, Mae Sullivan tended a rich life she'd grown from the debris of her former world.

Had she known he'd arrive one day? He'd appeared cloaked in skepticism, unwilling to believe the fact of their connection.

"Now, don't look upset," she said, drawing him from his thoughts. "This is a day for celebration. Good heavens, this *is* a shock for you, isn't it?" She gestured with concern, adding, "You should sit down. Heavens, where is the folding chair? Oh, dear. Father Cyprian probably moved it from the garden. He worries about rust. Troy, would you like a cup of water?"

Not a glass, a cup—and the child inside him revived from deep slumber. *A cup of water, a cup of milk.* He saw his adoptive mother glowing with the beauty of youth. With a jolt, the memory surrounded him, how he'd scraped his knee in the orchard and had raced to where she stood. Behind her the newly painted sign, *Fagan's Orchard*, captured the noontime sun. Jackie opened her arms to nestle him close but he read the concern in her eyes, the uncertainty—the unarticulated questions she'd driven into him during moments of crisis. He'd never understood what she'd needed to know, why her doubts ran so deep.

By an unintended osmosis, Jackie passed those unspoken doubts to her son. Troy grew up questioning everything, including himself. Now he understood her deepest fear.

You were not born of my body. Can you love me, still?

He assured Mae, "I don't need to sit down. If you don't mind, I'd rather walk."

She matched his pace, the bounce in her step gone. The gathering memories seemed a burden. She said, "Your parents were excited about adopting you. Oh, they felt responsible for what happened to me. Which was nonsense. They couldn't possibly predict that someone working at the orchard . . ." She cut off the thought as she stopped to inspect a young dogwood tree. She walked on, adding, "I loved you desperately, Troy. I was simply too young to mother you."

He glanced back at Rennie, retreating a step to give them space. "I understand," he murmured.

"When I was released from the hospital your mother visited every day at St. Vincent De Paul, a home for girls in my condition. My own mother also came daily, of course. We both relied heavily on Jackie, on her strength."

She'd visited every day? He tried to imagine his elegant mother entering a home for pregnant girls. At the orchard Jackie treated the employees like family. Last winter she'd been overwrought when an elderly receptionist died. She'd never been strong. How had she found the fortitude to care for a teenager so ravaged?

"Jackie never would've broached a discussion of adoption." Mae released a long sigh. "Your parents were such good people. I knew they wanted to start a family—everyone knew—but God hadn't yet brought them a baby."

Troy's knees were loose and wobbly, but he managed to ask, "How long was I with you?"

"Two weeks." She swiped at her eyes. "Fourteen perfect days."

"Not long."

She nodded briskly. "The nuns at St. Vincent's never asked if I'd decided what to do but I sensed their concern. A social worker from Catholic Charities began to visit, a sweet woman. She would've taken you if I'd asked. On the fourteenth day, when your mother arrived as usual, I asked her to keep you. Teenagers don't have much sense of timing—I tossed the question at her head the moment she walked in. She dropped her purse to the floor and a dozen tubes of lipstick spilled out. All those pretty tubes of color. Does she still favor cosmetics? Goodness, I've never learned how to manage the basics of mascara. We were both laughing, crawling across the floor to catch her runaway cosmetics."

Troy stared, his throat raw.

Mae patted his back. "You already *were* her baby in so many ways. I didn't know the first thing about infants but your mother thought I might decide to raise you. She'd taught me how to change your diaper, wash you—the songs she sang to you! She'd fill my room with her heavenly voice and you'd watch her so seriously." Mae chuckled. "All newborns look like sour old men. Don't they? You hung onto every note drifting from her lips."

Rennie caught up with them, the breeze rustling her long hair. Mae grew silent. She'd given him a poignantly full retelling of the events without mentioning his biological father. As she organized her thoughts, Troy nursed an unexpected trill of fear.

He'd done well until now *not* to think about the rest. His life was no longer a familiar map, the boundaries clear. Mae was a cartographer rearranging his world by the minute, delineating regions never before visible.

In the Medieval era, when men believed the world was flat, they drew elaborate maps of Europe and Africa, and what they understood of Asia. At the boundaries of the known world they wrote, *Beware. Dragons live beyond.*

Now Mae was steering him toward new truths. He dreaded what lay beyond. He wasn't prepared to glimpse dragons. For if Mae was his mother, what of his father? She'd been savagely raped. The man capable of such brutality seemed to rise from the garden's tranquil shadows, bringing with him the question Troy dreaded.

If Mae's virtue flowed in his veins, what darker elements lurked beside the good?

Chapter 27

At the opposite end of the grounds a bell clanged. Mae suggested they go in for lunch. A parish, Troy mused, ran on a predictable schedule. They left the garden and Mae surprised them by veering toward the elementary school.

The school corridor roiled with noise. Children stood at attention in each classroom doorway, chattering with their peers. "We'll go through the line first," Mae said, pausing before a freckle-faced girl in a plaid jumper. "Melinda, remind the fourth grade boys not to badger the younger children at recess. They must stay in their own area of the playground."

"I will, Miz Sullivan," the girl promised.

Moving swiftly, Mae gestured at the double doors beyond the last classroom. "This way."

Troy held the door for the women. Posters hung on the walls, some with religious phrases and others urging children to read for fun. In the cafeteria a woman with cropped grey hair loaded Troy's plate with mashed potatoes, cooked carrots and meatloaf. The air churned with expectation. Children began forming a line.

"What is this, dinner?" he asked when they'd seated themselves. The food smelled great. "I don't remember meals like this in the Liberty school district. This looks homemade."

"Made from scratch." Mae cut into her meatloaf. She glanced at him appraisingly. "Jackie put you through the public school system?"

"Jason and Dianne too."

Faint disapproval shuttled through her expression. "I'm surprised," she admitted. "Your parents are so devout. I would've expected them to give you a parochial education."

"I did attend John Carroll for college." He declined to add that his late brother's insistence had steered him away from a public institution. He could've easily chosen Ohio State instead.

She seemed aware of his discomfort. "In an older parish like ours, you find many homemade dishes," she said, steering the conversation back to neutral ground. "The neighborhood is ethnic. Poles, Italians, Hungarians—they always make something special on Fridays."

"Why Fridays?"

Mae pointed to the next table. A pretty Hispanic girl shyly listened to the blond chattering beside her. "Take Delladoria," Mae said. "Her parents are from Bolivia. They work long hours, and barely understand English. Della has four younger brothers. She cooks better than I do and can run a household as well as any adult. Which she does even though she's nine years old."

"The women of the parish ensure children like Della are well fed before they leave for the weekend," he guessed. The explanation touched him deeply. "You have a nice parish, Mae."

"It's a great deal of work made lighter by the help of many hands." She smiled at him then Rennie. "After lunch, let's return to the garden. We'll have privacy to talk."

He wasn't prepared to hear the rest. Like Rennie, toying with her food, he'd lost his appetite.

They returned to the garden. The sun sat directly overhead. Troy shrugged out of his suit coat and loosened his tie. A chickadee swooped down from the trees and circled Mae's head. Looking distracted, she waved it away. Although she walked at a casual pace, the lines in her brow deepened. He went on alert, his thoughts speeding up. She was about to breathe life into her darkest memories.

"I detest the taste of apples," she said. "When I first arrived at St. Justin's, it was simply good luck that no one offered an apple, or cider. I wasn't yet eighteen and had been through quite an ordeal. None of which I remembered."

Silently, Troy willed her to stop. He couldn't stomach a

retelling of the rape, the story of his conception. Yet he heard himself ask, "You had amnesia?"

"I knew my name and that my mother worked for your family. I recalled chatting with Lianna the day before and talking to Mario when he stopped in his bright red car after school. I remembered everything except what happened later."

"I'm glad you couldn't remember."

"Those dark moments were lost until I was about Rennie's age."

Mention of her name brought Rennie's head up. "What happened to make you remember?"

They neared a wrought iron bench. Mae sank down onto it. "After arriving in Pittsburgh, I never understood my aversion to apples. I simply avoided them. I became nauseous if I stood too close when someone bit into one. The tiniest whiff of tart scent made me sick."

"A reaction, like an allergy?" Rennie asked.

"I suppose so." Mae's spine curved beneath the memory's oppressive weight. "One day my luck ran out. We were having an autumn party for the kids in the school—not a Halloween party, mind you. Father wouldn't approve. At the party, the children begged me to show them how to bob for apples. We don't do that anymore—too many Hep B scares these days. I tried to leave the classroom but the children were insistent. One of the girls started crying. You can imagine how I felt. And I thought if I took care, I could demonstrate quickly."

"You bit an apple by accident," Rennie guessed.

Nodding, Mae rubbed her palms across her thighs. "That night, after tasting the apple, I had a nightmare. When I woke, I remembered everything Sweeper had done to me."

A strange light entered Rennie's whisky-hued eyes. "Sweeper?" she whispered.

"He's my father," Troy said, taking possession of the horror.

Mae held his gaze like a fist. "He was young, Troy. Just a year or two older than me."

Rennie sat on the bench beside her. "Mae, you're sure of his name?"

"His nickname, yes."

Rennie's worried gaze found Troy's. "He carved his name on

a wall at the factory," she told him. "The day I met with Dianne to discuss the job quote for the plant? I saw it."

"He swept the floors of the factory," Mae put in.

Troy's patience began to unravel. "So you finally remembered. Did he serve time?"

"He was never caught. So many years had passed by the time I remembered. Too many years."

She grimaced, and Troy asked, "What is it?"

Mae lowered her eyes. "I hardly remember the beating or . . . the rest of it. But I cried for years over the rosary."

"What rosary?" he asked, but he knew. His blood went cold and he knew.

"Your parents gave it to me when they learned I planned to enter the convent." She closed her eyes for a long moment. When she returned her attention to Troy, she added, "Sweeper took it."

"My parents gave you a Fagan Rosary." Evidently they'd love Mae deeply to offer such a rare gift.

"I don't know why he took it. He certainly wasn't religious. Why take something that meant so much to me?"

The answer sickened Troy. The rapist took the rosary as a trophy.

Finding his bearings, he asked, "If he worked at the orchard, did you know his family?"

"Not his mother. I never met her. Sweeper worked at the orchard with his father, Jim. An awful man. Hard-drinking, mean. Whatever Sweeper did to me began much earlier, with every beating he'd endured at his own father's hands."

How could she explain so calmly? Horrified, Troy recalled the police report he'd pulled from the Internet. A brutal rape. An assailant never found.

Sweeper.

During the rape, he broke Mae's jaw and battered her severely. Even now, the evidence of his brutality marred her face. Why hadn't he noticed the scar running along her jaw or the faint, purplish line beside her eye?

Anguished, he searched for a way to comfort her. "Mae, I'll find out who did this to you." He'd ensure Sweeper spent the rest of his life in prison. He'd hire the best detectives in Ohio, track him down—

She struggled to her feet. "No, Troy. I'm not telling you this for revenge."

"Don't ask me to let this go."

"There's nothing you can do."

"Like hell." The oath burst forth before he could recall it. "I have the means to end this, Mae. Connections, resources. Doesn't matter where he's gone. I'll find him."

"Dear boy, you can't," she said, her voice catching. Her sorrow made him want to bellow at the heavens for the injustice. "I visited Liberty ten years ago for my mother's funeral. No one knew I'd returned, but I *did* ask around. I didn't want to risk bumping into him on the street."

"What did you find?"

"He left ages ago. No one in Liberty remembered precisely when. Frankly, I don't care where Buck has gone. It's over."

The mention of Buck tore a strangled cry from Rennie's throat.

Shock lanced through Troy. Instantly, he saw the Great Oak. He saw Rennie at seventeen, the only girl he'd ever loved. He'd taken her on the same patch of ground where his father had defiled Mae.

Self-loathing followed the shock. The sensation blocked out Rennie's sobbing and the confusion on Mae's face. *I'm like Buck. He's a part of me.* The truth rained down in a deluge. As did the ugly truth: the curse wasn't something he shared with Rennie.

The burden was his alone.

He gripped Mae's shoulders. "Buck's full name—what is it?" he demanded, although he knew with terrible certainty.

"Why, it's—" She read the horror on his face then looked wildly at Rennie. "His name is Buck Korchek. Good heavens. You don't know him, do you?"

Chapter 28

Buck Korchek raped Mae.

Shivering on the passenger seat, Rennie wound her arms around herself. They'd only been traveling on the turnpike for twenty minutes when Troy noticed the fuel gauge and pulled into a service stop. He leapt out and filled the Mercedes with gas. They'd hardly spoken since leaving Mae, pale and shaken, before the rectory at St. Justin's.

His face had worn a mask of pain from the instant Mae uttered his father's name.

Buck is Troy's father.

Rennie squeezed her eyes shut. Nausea rolled through her. Lightheaded, she cradled her face in her hands.

Walt and Emma . . . Troy is their brother. He'll help me save them. He will.

The driver side door opened. Troy jumped in.

"We'll take care of this." He brought the engine to life. "Rennie, I swear to God we will."

He peeled out of the gas station. The afternoon traffic leaving Pittsburgh was thick. Accelerating, Troy merged into the traffic.

"How will we handle this?" she whispered. He was driving too fast but she didn't care. She was glad for the minutes he'd shave off the trip. "We can't go to the police with an accusation. The rape is decades old. We don't have proof."

"We'll do a paternity test." Troy's features were grim. "It'll prove Buck is my father."

"How will you make him agree to a paternity test?"

"No idea. I'll call my attorney. There must be a way."

"If we approach Buck with this, he'll leave town. He'll take Walt and Emma and disappear."

Troy cut off a white Volkswagen, sped faster. "We have to calm down, think this through. Buck *will* be arrested."

She thought of the curse he believed in. "This is our fault. We've put Walt and Emma in danger."

"No, Rennie. You've done nothing wrong." He fumbled across the seat for her hand. The affection he offered had her scrambling out of the seatbelt. He slung his free arm across her shoulder, bringing her in tight as he added, "I swear to you I won't let Buck snatch the kids. He's not going anywhere."

They'd already decided to drive to the campground. They'd collect Walt and Emma even though the children were scheduled to stay at camp until Sunday. *Buck was in court with Mom this morning.* Rennie prayed the court hadn't altered the foster care arrangement.

"I'll fill Jenalyn in on the details," she said, of the children's social worker. "She'll contact Mae to corroborate the story. None of which proves Buck is a rapist, but it should be enough for Jenalyn to stop him from reclaiming the kids immediately."

Troy grunted. "We'll do more than that. I'll ask Parker to work on this *asap.*"

"Parker?"

"My attorney. I'm not sure how to prove a crime three decades after its commission. Parker will find a way. He'll also compel Buck to take the paternity test." Troy paused, his expression dour. "It makes me sick, thinking of Buck as my father."

"I can't believe it either." She moved out from under his arm and dug into her purse. "Where did I put my phone?"

The question went right over Troy. "Walt and Emma are my half-brother and sister," he mused. "I never stopped to consider I might have siblings. Certainly not sibs young enough to be my own children."

"I'm glad they'll have you around. You'll protect them." Rennie leaned into the back seat, looked around. "Where *is* my phone?"

Troy stared at the road, hollow-eyed. "And Buck doesn't know I'm his son. He left town right after the rape. He has no idea we're related."

"I'm glad he doesn't know."

"He left Mae for dead. He meant to kill her. Probably thought he had." Troy glanced at her, hanging over the seat. "Found your smartphone?" He pulled out his. "Mine's dead. Forgot to charge it."

She swung back over the seat. "Got it."

"Call your mother. Have her go out to the campground, wait with the kids until we arrive."

"My sister-in-law promised to visit the camp. I'm sure she checked on the kids."

"Make sure someone in your family is out there now."

She powered up her phone. It rang before she'd punched in the number.

"Rennie!"

"Mom?" Her mother's panicky tone sent ice through Rennie's limbs.

"Why haven't you been picking up? I've been calling for hours!"

She threw a frantic glance at Troy. "Mom, what's wrong? What happened in court?"

"Rennie, it's bad. Gleason surprised everyone when he revealed that Buck had entered AA and a grief-counseling workshop. The judge was convinced Buck is simply dealing with his wife's death."

Anger flashed through her. "Didn't the judge care that Buck had beaten Walt and Emma?"

"The judge didn't believe we have incontrovertible proof. His words, not mine." Her mother went silent, and Rennie's vision narrowed to a pinpoint of fear. "Oh, honey, I'm sorry. Jenalyn accompanied Buck to the camp. The children were returned to him."

Chapter 29

Safely hidden behind the curtain, Buck scowled at the police cruiser inching past the house.

It was the fifth cruiser to drive by this afternoon. He'd also seen the Perini bitch from Social Services go by in her tan Camry. What did they want? He'd ditched Jenalyn at the campground after she'd handed over his kids. Somehow he'd even been pleasant until he left her stranded in the parking lot and peeled off. But something was wrong. No one had come to his door but he wasn't stupid enough to think they wouldn't. Later in the day, they'd come knocking. Once they put together whatever it was they had on him.

Get out. Now.

He studied the living room of the house he'd rented. No booze in sight—he knew better than to leave empty bottles in the house. Social Services would send Jenalyn to take the kids back if even a bottle of beer was out. He knew enough to pitch the bottles in the gorge beneath the Great Oak every morning when he drove to the job site at the Fagans.

Afterward he'd kick stones into the hell-driven waters of the Chagrin River. He'd look up the rock-studded escarpment, at the tree.

His life had changed at The Great Oak. He'd no longer been on the receiving end of insults and abuse, the ugly oaths his father once spat at him, the harsh cuffs to his head. *Sweeper.* The other men in the factory had found a sick pleasure in laughing at the cuts on a boy's face, his swollen eyes. At the Great Oak, he'd made sure one person would never laugh at him.

The cruiser disappeared down the street. Buck reached into his pocket.

Hail Mary, full of grace . . .

Whenever he was nervous, he liked remembering Mae' Sullivan's pitiful prayers. He closed his eyes to better recall her slender body writhing beneath him. That was the last time anyone had dared make fun of him. Even now, he wasn't sure what he'd enjoyed more—the blood when he'd battered her face or the sex.

"Pa?"

Walt appeared in the doorway from the kitchen.

"Did I tell you to move?" He shoved the rosary back into his pocket. "Didn't I put you in a chair, boy?"

Walt stood at attention. Buck approached. Every step he took stole something from the boy's eyes.

Grabbing the kid by the collar, he hauled him back into the kitchen. Half-eaten cans of chili and packets of chew littered the countertop. No table—just a few newspapers on the floor and moving boxes nearly packed. Shoving Walt into a chair, he stalked to Emma. She stood with her back pressed to the wall just like he'd left her.

"Don't move," he growled at her. He wheeled on Walt. "Move from that chair again and I'll kill you. Understand? Oh, and I'll beat your sister first. Let you watch. Disobey again, and Emma gets the first whoopin'."

"Yes, sir." Hatred glazed the response.

Buck looked at him, hard. The boy was defiant. If that didn't beat all. Did it matter? Once they crossed into West Virginia he'd take care of him good. Still, he couldn't stop from jerking his fist at Walt's chin. The boy flinched.

Satisfied he'd stay put, Buck strode out the back door. Most of the people on the street weren't yet home from work. He scanned the patchwork of lawns before moving toward the hedge between his property and the place next door. He pushed through the thick branches and sprinted to the Perkins' house.

The Perkins widow was stupid and predictable. Sure enough, he heard her upstairs vacuuming her prim-and-proper house. She moved back and forth behind the lace curtains with the vacuum blasting noise. Buck paused behind the maple tree a few paces from her door. He spotted a kid bicycling past on the sidewalk out front. The kid rode off, and Buck withdrew a pocketknife. In seconds, he'd jimmied the lock.

He slipped inside, cool as a cucumber. *Iceman.* No more Sweeper. All that had changed when he'd raped Mae. He became a man. People stopped pushing him around.

From that moment on, he did the pushing.

Yet he was still coming through the back door like a poor relation. Anger flashed through him. Stuffing it down, he paused by the counter. Where were the old woman's car keys?

Sure enough, the keys to her Cadillac Eldorado dangled on a brass key holder by the back door. Taking them, he sauntered into a kitchen nice enough for royalty. Fancy dishes sat on the sideboard. The oak floor gleamed. The ceiling fan shuddered beneath the power of the vacuum, running upstairs.

On the counter was a fat leather purse. He dug inside.

The search produced three twenties and a fistful of one dollar bills. Pocketing the cash, Buck looked around. He checked the pink cookie jar and several drawers. There wasn't any other cash.

Well, he'd take her car and leave Ohio before the cops came knocking. He'd leave . . . after he got his hands on some real cash.

Recklessly he'd spent last week's pay on gin and a whore in Mentor. He chastised himself for not thinking ahead. Was it safe to pick up his paycheck at the job site?

Stepping out the door, he ran past the truck he'd parked in the driveway. The cops were familiar with his ride. If the truck stayed put, they'd think he was in the house with the kids.

In the kitchen, Walt and Emma hadn't moved.

"C'mon," he barked. "We're leaving."

"That was your mother again," Troy said, tossing over Rennie's smartphone. "Chief Calabrese assured her that Buck hasn't left his house. She's on her way to the police station to make a statement. Next she'll put the chief on the phone with Mae. It'll be enough to arrest Buck."

"What if it isn't?"

"It will be, Rennie."

"You said we're at fault if anything happens to the kids. We'll bring something awful down on them, like we did to Jason—"

Why had he shared his irrational, private demons? "Rennie, you're blameless. Look at me. I deserve to sit beneath ten curses. I'm closed off, short-tempered—most of the time I make everyone around me miserable. I've got too much of Buck's bad instincts in my nature, but I swear I'll change."

"You're nothing like him," she sputtered, comforting him with her ready, if ill-deserved defense. "If you take after either of your parents, it's Mae."

"I hope you're right." Protectively he reached for her hand. She batted him away, her eyes hollow. In a soothing voice, he added, "A cruiser just went by Buck's house. His truck is in the driveway."

"He's home? You're sure?"

"He's been there since he picked up the kids at camp." Troy snapped up his wrist, checked the time. Four o'clock on the dot. "My attorney will be out of court in a few minutes. He'll go to the police station. If the chief isn't positive he has grounds to arrest Buck, Parker will convince him."

Rennie brushed at her forehead, distracted. "Why did the judge make the ruling, Troy? Why did he give the kids back?"

"Just how the system works."

"It's broken." She muffled a sob, and his stomach clenched. "I love them. I was everything they needed. How could the judge be so blind?"

"We'll fix this."

God, please let me fix this. Distractedly Troy glanced at the horizon. Ashy clouds formed above the Ohio State Line. He was already driving eighty mph but he inched it up a notch. Miraculously, he hadn't seen a State Trooper.

Lightning split the sky.

In the passenger seat, Rennie flinched. "Drive faster," she said. "Storm's coming."

Chapter 30

On Route Six, Buck idled the car at the edge of the Fagan estate.

The quiet of a tomb filled the car's backseat. Walt had his arms around Emma, rocking her. The long ruffles on the hem of Emma's dress swayed with his motions. She cradled her doll.

"Where'd you get the dress?" Buck demanded. It was flowery and frilly, something a woman would choose. "Answer me, girl."

Slowly Emma lifted her head. She eyed him blankly. "Rennie bought the dress, sir."

"We're getting rid of it as soon as we reach West Virginia. I've got jeans for you."

"Yes, sir."

"You'll wear them. You'll be happy about it."

"I will."

Muttering a curse, he leaned out the window and peered down the dusty road. The wind picked up, sending an icy blast through the balmy air. Unpredictable Canadian storms. In the springtime they hurtled across Lake Erie with vicious strength. Irritated, he surveyed the road. No cars in sight. They were safe here.

In thirty minutes, the crews at the mansion would break for the night. He'd go in, stay out of sight, and get his paycheck. The lead mason handed out pay at five o'clock sharp. Going in was a risk, but there was no choice.

Settled on his plan, he pulled the pack of cigarettes from his pocket then struck a match. The orchard sloped downward from Route Six. A mile off, workers sprayed the trees with a white mist. Idiots. Soon the rain would wash away all their hard work.

He regarded the summit high above the orchard. From this distance, The Great Oak was a speck on the horizon. He imagined the churning waters in the gorge below, the Chagrin River singing fiercely like his raging heart.

Pulling on his cigarette, he tried to relax. He rolled his shoulders and studied the sky. The brewing storm pulled a curtain of black over the orchard and the road.

Which suited him fine. In thirty minutes, he'd collect his paycheck, take his kids and disappear into the dark.

"Troy, that's the address!"

The house Buck had rented was a bare-bones ranch little bigger than a postage stamp. One of the shutters hung ajar on a picture window hazy with grime. She fisted her hand at her stomach, which was fluttering with panic. The truck *was* in the driveway. Inside the picture window, a lamp burned.

Rennie gripped the Mercedes' dashboard. "Do you see the kids inside?" She waited as Troy's gaze wove across the house. "Are they there?"

"Can't tell. Maybe they're in the kitchen." He slowed the car. "Let's drive down Elm. We'll be able to see the back of the house."

She unbuckled her seatbelt, moved to the edge of the seat. "Pull over."

"You can't go in." He gave a warning look. "Rennie, the police are on it."

"Pull over. I just want a better look."

"Not unless you promise to stay put."

The clammy fear heightened her awareness. He hadn't removed his seatbelt. Guilt nipped at her. She tamped it down.

"I'll stay put," she lied.

He steered the car to the curb.

He'd barely come to a stop when she bolted from the car. She dashed across the lawn, her skirt tearing at her knees.

Troy called out. Ignoring the husky plea, she bounded up

the steps.

On a growl, she rattled the doorknob. Locked. She stopped, noticed the rectangle of glass in the cheap wood. With her fist, she punched through. She reached inside for the lock and burst inside.

The living room rested in a chilly silence. Scattered boxes and filth, and the scent of something rotting that nearly made her retch. Swallowing down the bile, she raced from corner to corner checking for Walt and Emma. The kids knew how to hide.

Bellowing their names, she raced to the kitchen. The bedrooms were also empty.

"Rennie!"

"No one here," she called out. She returned to the living room in time to see Troy's scowl morph into panic.

"You're sure?" He swung around and launched toward the kitchen. He returned, panting. His mouth dropped open. "You're bleeding."

Droplets of blood plopped to the floor. The sight made her dizzy.

She planted her feet. "He's gone. Buck took the kids and he's gone."

Troy wasn't listening. He retraced his steps to the kitchen. Drawers rattled, and he returned with a dishtowel in his fist.

"Not exactly clean, but the best I can do." Taking care not to hurt her, he wrapped the towel around her knuckles. Blood immediately seeped through and he pressed down, causing her to flinch. "You aren't going to faint, are you?"

She stiffened against the black waves crashing into her. "No, I'm not." She gulped in air, froze. "Ouch! That hurts!"

"You need stitches." He knotted the towel then looked up sharply. "What time is it?"

"I'm not sure. Around five o' clock."

His hands shook as he checked his watch. "The lead mason is handing out paychecks. We have to hurry."

"You think Buck is stupid enough to stop for his paycheck? Think again. He's halfway across Ohio by now."

"My instincts say otherwise."

"Forget your intuition. We have to go to the police station." Her voice cracked but she forced herself on. "They'll put out an

APB."

"A guy like Buck lives hand-to-mouth. He needs the paycheck." Troy dragged her toward the door. "For once, Rennie, trust me. We'll alert the police on our way to the mansion."

Chapter 31

The instant Troy parked in the queue of trucks, Rennie was out of the car. She threw off the towel he'd wrapped around her hand and dashed across the lawn. The bleeding had slowed considerably. If she needed stitches, they'd have to wait.

Somewhere in the back of the new wing, a jackhammer split the air. On the addition's first floor, two carpenters were setting in a window. They stopped, brows lifting. She vaulted past with Troy a step behind. Upstairs, she looked out a bedroom window at the man chewing up a cement walkway with the jackhammer. No wonder Alan, the lead mason, hadn't picked up when they'd called from the car. He couldn't hear above the racket.

They'd also called Chief Calabrese. He promised to send a cruiser immediately. Rennie prayed they'd arrive quickly.

The jackhammer cut off. Rain danced across the roof. Lightning followed.

She hurried down the stairwell. Fear pitched through her as she halted before Troy. "Alan's not here," she told him. "Any of the masons outside?"

"A few. They were just paid. One of them said Buck was at the end of the line complaining about the wait. I'll check the backyard to see if he's still there."

"I'll check out front."

She sprinted back outside. Several trucks were pulling out. Icy rain pelted her cheeks and she sent a curse at the clouds swirling above in a growing tempest.

Her muscles sizzled with tension but she fought for composure. There were still a lot of men at the site. Was Buck among them? She walked down the queue checking the driver of each truck roaring to life. At the far end of the mansion, a cream-colored Cadillac Eldorado pulled out. Rennie licked her parched lips. Did any of the Fagans own a Cadillac?

Revving the engine, the driver started toward her and the main road leading out of the estate. In tandem, the sky opened with a howl. Rain fell in sheets. Wiping the dampness from her eyes, she tried desperately to see who was behind wheel.

The brakes screeched.

Buck spotted her, and Rennie's breath stuttered. The squeal of tires, and he jerked the car into reverse. Fishtailing, he changed course. The Cadillac charged down the road leading into the orchard.

She dived into the Mercedes and brought the engine to life. Already the Cadillac was speeding down a dip in the road.

Burning rubber, the Mercedes hurtled forward. The driver side door swung wildly. She slammed the door shut one heart stopping second before smacking the rear fender of a truck pulling out. The blare of a horn barely registered. Eyes riveted on the road, she caught a glimpse of the Cadillac rounding a bend, nearly careening into the apple trees planted dangerously close to the edge.

The road dead-ends at the factory. Buck will be trapped. Hope cut through the fear gripping her. The Mercedes swerved as the clouds unleashed a downpour. A gargled cry barreled from her throat.

Evading the factory, Buck raced down a side road. The road narrowed, rising ever higher. Rennie raced to catch up. Branches tore across the Mercedes' hood as she gunned the engine. Through the curtain of rain she looked higher, at the summit, where the Great Oak stood.

Buck headed straight for it.

Rivulets of mud snaked through the road's loose gravel. Rennie's hands shook on the steering wheel. With her heart in her throat she glimpsed the Cadillac a few seconds ahead of her, bounding off the last inches of road and reaching the summit. The wheels fishtailed.

God, please, no--

Swerving toward the oak, the Cadillac was a bullet aiming for the precipice. A moment too late, Buck slammed on the brakes.

Rennie's heart somersaulted in a dizzying, painful dance. "Walt, Emma—no!"

Careening into the Great Oak, the Cadillac flipped onto its side and skidded *over the precipice.*

Rennie threw the Mercedes into park. The oak's heavy branches stretched toward the roaring thunder like gnarled fingers gripping the sky. She dashed to the edge of the precipice.

"Walt, Emma!"

With numbing trepidation, she peered over the edge. From the gorge far below cool air burst skyward, slapping into her face. Fifteen feet down, the Cadillac teetered on its side. Something hung from the steering wheel, but she couldn't make it out. With sickly relief, she realized the oak's sturdy roots were cradling the car in a precarious embrace. Underneath she spotted a thin ledge, the dirt turning quickly to mud.

Desperate, she slicked the rain from her eyes. *Only Buck is in the car. Please God, don't let them be in the car.* Something moved in the back seat, a ruffle of blue. Emma's arm flailed. She tried to pull herself upright. Terror sank Rennie to her knees.

But only for a moment. She cupped her hands around her mouth. "Emma, stay still! Stay right where you are!"

Walt! He was trying to climb up the back seat. The window was rolled down midway. A twig stuck to the glass, the oak leaves flattened by the rain.

"Don't move!" Rennie bellowed, and Walt froze.

Icy rain nicked her skin but her muscles filled instantly with a surging heat. Miraculously, her thoughts slowed and her vision cleared. She kicked off her pumps.

Seventy feet below, the waters of the Chagrin River churned in protest beneath the assault of the whipping rain. The Cadillac had shaved several feet of earth from the precipice, leaving a mass of the oak's thick roots trailing over the edge. The wind tossed the roots madly. Tearing her gaze from the river's threat, Rennie grabbed hold of the thickest root and began to climb down.

The prospect of plummeting to her death started her teeth chattering. She pressed her face close to the wall, descending with utmost care. The scent of mold assailed her nostrils. She tasted blood in her mouth, felt rock beneath her right foot. Risking a glance at the gorge below, her stomach pitched. The river foamed and swelled, waiting to welcome her and the children to their deaths.

Pricking her ears, she caught Walt's muffled cry. "I'm coming. Don't move."

Her left hand slicked down a root as thick as her wrist. She nearly lost her balance, but held fast to a rock jutting out near her chin. Feeling along with her feet, she almost blacked out with relief when she realized she'd reached solid ground. *The ledge.*

She appraised the Cadillac, listing in the battering rain.

"Kids, I'm here. Stay still!"

Around her left arm she wound a long root. She swung gently to the right. Clumps of earth tumbled into the gorge. Inside the car, Walt lay against the opposite window with the river dancing far below him. Emma curled into his side, sobbing.

With care, Rennie eased her hip against the car. "Walt, climb up the seat," she commanded. "Move slowly. The window is already open. Just roll it down a little more."

She swiped the rain from her eyes. Buck was unconscious in the front seat. His right arm hung from the steering wheel at a gruesome angle. On a tremor, she swallowed the vomit rising in her throat. A shard of bone stuck out above his wrist.

With effort she returned her attention to Walt. His eyes locked on her as he began to move.

"You're my big, brave boy. Climb up to the window, sweetheart. That's right! You can do it."

He reached the window and rolled it down with exquisite care. Rain pummeled his face. He closed his eyes against the torment. The chattering of his teeth wrenched a sob from Rennie's throat.

When he found the courage to open his eyes, she said, "Now, get Emma. Help her climb out."

From above a chunk of earth came loose, thudded painfully into her scalp. Flecks of dirt showered into her eyes. The storm roared, The ashen clouds opened their mouths fully to dislodge sheet after sheet of chilling rain. Beneath them, the river railed at the heavens, the grey waters leaping with fury. Driving rain beat wind into the gorge and a swirl of sound rose up, the sound of a thousand demons chanting against Rennie's attempt to cheat death.

"Emma—come on, sweetie!"

Eyes wide, Emma reached for the window's glass. The bodice of her dress was torn and blood oozed beside her quivering lips. Rennie sent a curse at the gravity the child struggled against. Pushing past her fear, she plunged her arm into the car.

"Grab my hand, baby. Take it!"

Rennie eased her out and swung her to the wall. From behind, Emma latched onto her waist.

"That's right, baby. Don't let go." She looked down to Walt with relief and pride. He was already halfway out the window, moving toward her with admirable calm.

"You're my good boy, my brave boy. Come on, now . . ."

He clasped her hand and gingerly eased his legs from the car. Then he stepped across, reaching the ledge. He ducked beneath the root she'd wound around her arm and pressed flat to the wall. The shuddering of his chest belied the determination in his gaze.

"How will we climb up?" he asked. "It's too far."

The Cadillac listed dangerously over the gorge. One of the roots holding the car snapped. Shrieking, Emma buried her face in Rennie's waist. If they didn't get off the ledge, gravity would soon take them with the car.

Rennie gripped Walt's shoulder. "Do like Emma—wrap yourself around me." Struggling, she hiked her skirt to her thighs and tied the cumbersome fabric in a knot. "Emma, are you holding tight? That's right, baby."

But Walt stared at her with disbelief, his curls glistening in a halo of dampness. Their eyes met, to share the appalling truth. She wasn't strong enough to ascend with two children clinging to her.

Yes, I am.

She breathed fire into her voice. "Walt—grab on!" He obeyed and she looked up, gritting her teeth against the rain hammering her face. She grabbed a root swinging free above her head. "I can only go a few steps at a time. If either of you feel your hands or legs slipping, tell me."

"Emma, you listening?" Walt squeaked, but Rennie had already begun to climb.

The precipice was as slick as glass. Water flowed in growing streams past the chunks of rock embedded in the wall. *It's only a few yards. I can make it.* Heaving against the combined weight of the children, she pulled upward. A rock was too loose in the thickening mud and she grappled for another. She planted her palm on the next rock, which was nearly out of reach. It was firm and she gripped tight.

Something sliced into her foot with lancing pain—she'd forgotten she was barefoot. Walt pressed his face to her breasts and Emma let out a shout. Fire ripped through Rennie's muscles in painful bolts. She heaved a breath, but only for a second. Horror pitched through her. Her toes were losing their purchase. She was slipping—

"Rennie, I've got you!"

Troy threw his upper body over the ledge. His right hand caught her wrist in a numbing grip. The exertion turned his face crimson. He wrenched them higher. Chunks of dirt dislodged and ricocheted into the river. Rennie clawed at the muddy surface, found a rock, heaved up higher. Troy grabbed Walt's arm. Hiccupping sobs tore from Emma's throat but it was all right. Troy had them and he was pulling them, pulling them up to firm ground.

"Oh, God, Rennie! Why didn't you wait—"

Cutting off, he hauled them over the ledge and fell sideways to the ground. The kids rolled across the wet grass, sputtering. The air was knocked from Rennie's lungs as she landed facedown beneath the oak.

Troy scrambled to his knees to help her. She read his gaze quickly—the relief, the agony—and the love. On a groan, he hauled her into his arms.

He kissed her savagely, ate at her mouth with desperate joy. She flung her arms around his shoulders with the pure, perfect sense that she would never again let him go.

His hands tangled in her hair. "I thought I'd lost you," he

said. "I thought I wouldn't get to you in time."

"I'm okay," she said.

Behind them, Walt struggled to his feet. Troy let her go to allow the boy to rush into his arms.

Walt looked to Troy with wonderment. "You saved us!" he cried.

"He did, baby," she sobbed, catching Emma with her free arm. She was still on her knees and nearly frozen to the bone. Yet the storm was no match for the warmth spilling through her. "Everything will be fine. Oh, Emma, don't cry. You're safe."

Troy stood. "Get the kids into my car." Returning to the precipice, he looked over the fearful edge. "Buck's down there," he growled. "We don't have much time."

His haunted gaze swept from the embankment to her. With horror Rennie understood his plan.

"You can't go down!" She rushed to his side. "The ledge will give way."

"I have to try."

"No! You'll die. Troy, you can't help him."

Dragging her back into his arms, he kissed her deeply. He needed to drink in a small portion of the energy that ebbed through her. He needed her courage, she knew, for what lay ahead.

Then he strode to the precipice. He muttered words she couldn't make out.

He went over and down before her first cries lifted into the storm.

Chapter 32

Troy started the treacherous, vertical descent.

Every instinct warned him to turn back. Rain sluiced into a thousand crevasses, turning the dirt to mud and making the rock face impassable. Trying to save Buck was suicide.

Throwing off the notion of climbing back up to stable ground, he pulled Mae into his thoughts. He recalled the bright affection in her eyes and the heroic way she led her life. *I'm made of the same stuff.* Fear crawled across his skin and he went slack for a heart-stopping moment. *I'm not made in Buck's image.* He poured concentration into his muscles, willed them to grow rigid. He'd keep moving.

To his left, deep grooves were visible where Rennie had clawed her way up. But the precipice was more stable in the section he'd chosen even if the slabs of granite jutting out were razor sharp. He weighed more than she did, a lot more, and he didn't trust the Great Oak's roots to hold him. So he descended like a rock climber, gripping fast to chunks of sandstone and slate, feeling a spurt of relief each time his foot settled on the much harder granite.

The Cadillac lay to his left. In the front seat, Buck's head lolled to the side. Flecks of blood spattered his scalp. Troy flinched as he caught sight of Buck's right arm, trapped in the ring of the steering wheel. There was a clean break of bone above his wrist and his fingers were a sickening grey. Suddenly there was movement, the glint of jewelry in Buck's other hand. Troy angled back enough to glimpse the gem-studded chain. Sapphires, rubies, diamonds, emeralds—Buck rubbed the thread of jewels against a cheek grimy with blood.

"I'm coming." Troy barely recognized the harsh baritone of his voice. "Stay where you are until I give you the go-ahead."

Buck gave an unintelligible reply.

"I'm right above the car. Almost there."

Lightning ripped the sky. In the gorge, a tree creaked ominously. An explosion of water ripped from the riverbed, and Troy wondered if a tree had fallen into the Chagrin River. He knew better than to glance down at the roiling waters. He stepped onto the ledge securing the Cadillac in a tentative embrace.

The back windows were intact, but the driver side window was blown out. Rain rushed inside, pooling on Buck's chest. Troy flattened against the wall and shut his eyes against the terror churning his gut. At over six feet in height, it wouldn't take much to send him hurtling to his death.

"Buck, can you move?"

A moan rose from the car. Buck's anguish blended sickly with the thunder rolling with hell's fury. Pulling his eyes open, Troy angled left. Wind and rain whipped his face, making it nearly impossible to see. He managed to crouch low beside the window, reach his hand inside.

"I must free your arm from the steering wheel. This will hurt."

Buck's gaze landed on him, cold and assessing. Troy swallowed down his dread and met his father's eyes with narrowed regard. There wasn't time to explore bitterness or revulsion, or the pity working through his chest. The noxious stranger before him was moments from death's grip. Burying his emotions, Troy focused with pinpoint intensity.

He took hold of Buck's wrist, careful not to touch the protruding bone. Buck's lips curled in a grimace. Fear lit his eyes.

A snarl of fury pierced the air—was it the storm, or his father? Troy worked quickly, his movements awkward as he battled the adrenaline surging through his blood.

The moment he was freed, Buck scrambled forward. "Help me!" His garishly damaged arm hung loosely at his side. But he was a powerful man. With his left hand, he pulled his considerable bulk toward safety.

Troy heard a crack, and the car shifted. "Slow down!" he bellowed, but the warning went unheeded. His father thrust his good arm out of the window, the web of jewels glinting on his fist. Troy flinched as Buck clamped onto his hand.

Fire bolted up Troy's arm. The added weight threatened to send him pitching over the car and into the gorge. On a spasm of pain he was wrenched forward.

Buck squinted through the rain. "Don't let go," he snarled. The remarkable string of jewels around his hand cut into Troy's palm. "You listening, boy? Get me safe."

Grimacing, Troy held on with all his might. *We're going to die.* A metallic scent assailed his nostrils. *We won't make it.* The pump of adrenaline slicking through his veins wasn't powerful enough to save them. His father fought his way up the seat, straining the muscles in Troy's shoulder. A curtain of red fell before Troy's eyesight.

He bellowed another warning, too late. Buck rammed against the rim of the window in furious haste. The Cadillac listed dangerously to the left. Metal ground against rock.

The car broke free.

Troy was jerked violently downward. Death brushed against his lips. Buck clawed for a grip, the jewels pressed between them digging into Troy's flesh. Blood dripped from his fingers making them slick, making it impossible for Buck to hang on. His fingers slipped.

The Cadillac hurtled toward the river with Buck screaming inside.

Freed of the weight, Troy's arm snapped up. His attention shot from the gully to the glittering stones flashing through the air past his face. A crucifix cartwheeled through the air. The chain holding it fast glinted as it wrapped his wrist with a smack of sound.

On the riverbank, the car exploded with deafening noise. Thick plumes of smoke burst skyward. His chest heaving, Troy ignored the taste of ash in his mouth. He caught Rennie's voice punching through the blood roaring in his ears. Then he was climbing, climbing for his life.

"I've got you! Oh, God—I've got you," she cried, grabbing him by the shirt when he came within range.

They fell together onto the grass. Rennie hadn't followed his command to get the kids out of the rain—Walt and Emma scampered forward. They threw themselves against his chest, toppling Troy flat onto his back. He barely heard Emma's wails or felt Rennie's kisses. Walt's hand on his shoulder hardly registered. Dazed, he let the boy help him into a sitting position. Finally the slick moisture of blood on his palm registered in Troy's addled brain. His attention narrowed on the object held in his fist.

With wonderment he regarded the Fagan Rosary. A sob broke loose as he ran his fingers across the matchless jewels that belonged to Mae.

They glowed, liquid color, in the rain.

Chapter 33

In the hospital's emergency bay, Troy sat in the chair with his legs flung out and Emma curled against his chest.

On the gurney, Rennie continued arguing with the doctor. Walt, his forehead wrapped with gauze, rolled his eyes. He slumped to the floor between Troy's legs.

The boy kicked out his legs like a rag doll. He looked spent.

They all did.

Walt asked, "Why is Rennie so mad?"

Troy grinned. "Got me, pal. She's always had a temper. Might be an Italian thing."

"Isn't she tired?" The boy reached to scratch his head, evidently remembered the gauze, and let his hand fall to his lap. "*I'm* tired. She should just listen to the doctor already."

"She doesn't listen to anybody."

"Not ever?"

Not usually."

Walt wrinkled his nose. "What a pain."

Troy chuckled. "Come here." When the boy glanced up at him, he shifted Emma to his left thigh. She was fast asleep. "Jump on up. There's always room."

Walt's brows puckered. "You sure? I'm a lot bigger than Emma."

Troy studied his eyes. He found something of himself in their large oval shape, and the defiance peppered with incredulity. *Brother*. He felt Jason in his heart, Jason whom he'd always love. *Walt is my brother, too.* He thought of Mae with her packet of photographs, the evidence of her encompassing devotion to the children who passed through her life, the outcasts and the shy kids, the mischievous kids and the children who simply needed a hand to hold.

There's always room for more.

Emma made a cooing sound in Troy's ear. *Little sister.* She stuck her thumb in her mouth as she slumbered, the sight irrepressibly dear. Unlike her brother, she'd needed no prodding to find her way to the comfort of Troy's lap.

"Maybe I should sleep over there." Walt waved halfheartedly at the green couch by the next emergency bay.

Troy flicked his chin. "There's room on my lap," he said, thinking, *he doesn't know we're brothers. Not yet.* How to embark on that particular conversation with a child so young? Only time would reveal a way.

Rising, Walt shifted from foot to foot. He appeared dismayed by the possibility of a man displaying affection. His heart swelling, Troy steered him close. Relenting, the boy sat.

He steered Walt's head to his shoulder, pressing firmly to keep him put. "Close your eyes," he said, glad when the boy did. "The doctor will let us go home once Rennie quits arguing about the pain pills."

"Why won't she take one?"

"She's stubborn like a bull."

Considering this, Walt rubbed his cheek against Troy's shoulder, testing his strength. Testing his endurance. *I'm not that strong.* Not if the tears burning his eyes were any evidence.

"Rennie *is* stubborn," Walt said. "How come?"

"When you figure it out, let me in on the secret."

"Okay. I will." Walt hesitated. "Troy?"

"Yeah?"

"Will you stay with us tonight? At Rennie's?"

"I'm staying until she throws me out. But I don't think she will." Considering, he cleared his throat. There *was* the issue of propriety. "I'll sleep on the couch, of course. Guard the home turf and all that."

The explanation satisfied the boy. Taking a cue from Emma, he curled his legs up, pressing his knees against his sister's.

"Troy?"

"Yeah?"

"Where's Pa now?"

"Your father is still in the gorge." Pitying the child, he added, "Don't worry. The police are down there. Firemen, too. They'll get him out."

A long silence and then, "I mean, *where* is my dad? He's dead. Where did he go?"

Uneasy, Troy shifted in the chair. Buck deserved a fiery eternity. He'd nearly destroyed Mae when she was sixteen years old. If not for her indomitable spirit, he would've. And he nearly killed the children when the car he'd stolen went off the precipice. It was a miracle the doctors had found only bruises on the kids. Both had received X-rays shortly after reaching the hospital. Troy had insisted on seeing the film for himself. Not a bone broken despite the ordeal they'd been through.

He turned his thoughts back to Walt's question. The boy was in third grade at Liberty Elementary. The kid loved baseball almost as much as he loved Rennie. He'd wanted to catch a fish for her at camp. He might have, if Buck hadn't appeared on shore with a court order, scaring the counselors and demanding his children.

At last, he asked, "Where do *you* think your father is?"

Head bowed, Walt curled his fist. After a moment he spread his fingers flat against Troy's chest. "Is it okay to think he's in heaven?"

"Sure."

"Angels might help him. They fix all sorts of stuff. Don't they?"

"That's what I've heard."

Walt snuggled close. "The angels will make Pa good," he decided. "I'm sure they will."

Troy took a swipe at his eyes. *You fool—you aren't going to cry, are you?* He couldn't recall the last time he'd submitted to tears. Now the sorrow, not to mention his bone-deep relief, threatened to bring on the waterworks. Which was damn ridiculous.

On the positive side, Walt would learn that men had feelings, too.

From her perch on the gurney, Rennie finally shut up. The doctor, a sloe-eyed saint nearly as tall as Troy, slapped a pill into Rennie's palm then called for a glass of water. Yanking back the bay's curtain, the doctor strode out.

To Walt, Troy said, "I'm sure your dad will like heaven. I hear it's nice."

A nurse waddled in with a Dixie cup. Rennie downed the pill. Relieved, Troy gave Walt a pat, to settle him in. The boy dozed off.

When he did, Troy brought his right arm around Walt's waist and opened his fingers. The rosary sent sparkling color flashing across the room.

Reflecting on his lunch earlier today with Mae, Troy was ashamed to consider he hadn't been entirely truthful. He hadn't told her *why* his parents enrolled him in the public school system. Such devout Catholics would've preferred a parochial school. Guiltily, he wondered why he hadn't taken the honorable route and shared the entire story with Mae.

St. Mary's in Liberty? From childhood onward, Troy fought the duty of accompanying his family to services.

For no sensible reason, he'd mocked the devotion his parents lavished on the Church. He'd despised the nuns who'd tried to chat with him before Mass and the priests who drew him into conversation afterward. Even as a boy he understood that religion spoke of belonging, and he felt like an outsider. Born angry, he grew into a brooding child. Even before he'd begun to catch the doubt in his mother's eyes, before he'd made the doubt his own, he'd kept himself apart. Now he wondered if some facet of Buck's personality had shadowed his life in ways he'd foolishly permitted.

Go with the angels, Buck.

Was there any sense in anger? He wouldn't waste another moment on low emotion. If some aspect of his father's personality once made Troy's blood anemic with doubt, it was over. He'd leave the hate behind.

Life wasn't easy. In fact, it was damn complicated. Now that he'd learned how, he'd fill his days with love.

The conviction barely cleared his brain when he grinned. Truth was, he'd never carried a curse . . . except the one he'd put on himself.

Reverently, he thumbed the crucifix. *I'll return the rosary to Mae in person, a surprise visit.*

Then he reflected on his mother Jackie. Throughout his difficult upbringing, she'd patiently knelt beside him at Mass. She spent precious moments alone with him, allowing him to watch her do up her face. Running behind her in the orchard, he'd delight when she caught him in her arms. The prayers she'd taught him at bedtime wove through his memories, a thousand prayers; a thousand acts of love. The words had never pierced him. She'd bestowed more gifts than he could ever repay.

On his chest, Walt cuddled against Emma. Rennie hopped down from the gurney.

As she approached, Troy understood: his love for her *was* a prayer. His first, ever.

But not his last.

The orchard was chock full of carnival rides, balloons and clowns.

As the five hundred guests at Dianne's unorthodox baby shower celebrated in the orchard, Rennie decided that, in the two weeks since Buck's death, nothing had returned to normal.

Emma and Walt waved to her from the merry-go-round set up on the lawn before the mansion. In the roads wending through the orchard, game booths stood beside more rides. Clowns juggled balls beneath apple trees. A white pony carried children. Dusk approached, and the colorful lights strung through the trees blinked on.

Sighing, she grinned as the merry-go-round spun the children out of view. No, they weren't back to normal. Most nights Emma woke crying from nightmares. Walt rarely ate. They were seeing a good child psychologist now and Jenalyn, ever the optimist, said it was just a matter of time. They *would* heal.

Eventually.

Still, Rennie worried. She needed to get her mind back on preparations for the factory job. Doing so proved difficult. Dropping the kids off at school, having them out of touch during the day—it was an agony. Thank goodness summer vacation was just around the corner.

"Why the long face?"

Startled, she turned and regarded Troy. "Oh. Nothing new." She shrugged. "I was thinking."

With flourish he presented a blue Sno-Cone. "Dianne insists you taste one." He handed it over. "Go on, try it."

"I'm not into blue food."

"Blue is good. It's time to loosen up. Walt and Emma are fine."

When did Troy become a mind reader? Not to mention his male protective instincts were impeccable—he still camped out on her sofa every night. In the morning she'd find him drying off the bathroom sink after he showered and shaved, already in his jeans and work shirt before the kids stumbled down the hallway. All of which was comforting. Given what they'd been through with the kids, Jenalyn wasn't about to make a fuss about the sleepovers. Only recently she'd mentioned that Troy couldn't stay indefinitely.

A boyfriend spending the night—even if he *was* the children's much older half brother—wouldn't look good when Rennie wrapped up the home study and finalized the adoption.

As the children's foster mother, she'd receive the first opportunity to adopt them. Troy had more legal right, given his blood tie to the kids. He'd assured Jenalyn that Rennie should keep Walt and Emma permanently.

His announcement had been delightful yet strangely disappointing. Which was foolish, because Rennie knew he'd remain a part of their lives. They were all beginning to feel like a family even though her personal relationship with Troy was just beginning. Predicting where it would lead was premature.

"You're frowning again," he said.

Startled from her thoughts, she blinked. "Oh. Sorry."

"What's wrong now?"

She toed the grass, stalling. When Troy eyed her impatiently, she said, "Actually, it's Jenalyn. She wants me to talk to you." His attention strayed to the kids, lending her the courage to plunge on. "About the sleepovers."

"I know." He sighed. "My attorney said the same thing. I can't continue to camp out on your sofa. We have to keep your home study in mind." He shoved his hands into his pockets. "I'll stay at my place tonight."

"Good." *Not good.* She'd miss cuddling with him after they'd tucked in the kids. "Thanks for understanding. I go to court at the end of June to finish the adoption. We're only under Jenalyn's microscope until then."

When he remained silent, she sent an impatient glance. Was he listening? Sorrow colored his expression, and worry. *It's the kids.*

How would he find a way to tell Walt and Emma he was their brother? Last week he'd informed his family about his meeting with Mae in Pittsburgh. The Fagan library had been awash with tears. Even Rennie, seated with her fingers entwined with Troy's, needed a box of Kleenex. No anger, no regret—he'd simply informed his parents he knew everything and wanted Mae back in his life.

Then he'd revealed the existence of his young brother and sister. Within days of meeting Walt and Emma, the elder Fagans had set up investments for the children. A trust fund, college fund—the works. Rennie was still in awe at how quickly they'd taken the children into their hearts.

Considering, she brushed her fingers across the frown darkening his lips. "There's no need to rush in telling Walt and Emma that you're related." When his mouth relaxed, she added, "They're young. It'll be hard for them to comprehend how you can possibly be their brother. It's not like you can tell them about Buck and Mae. You'll have to invent something that'll make sense. Something they can grasp."

"That isn't the problem."

"No?"

"I'm ready to sit down with them. Give them the basics. I won't bring up Mae. They're too young for the raw truth." Troy rubbed his chin. "Frankly, I don't want them to grow up hating Buck. They need to forgive, and heal."

"Yes, they do."

Turning from his inspection of the children, he drew Rennie close. He held her gaze as if it were the first rose of summer. "I love you with all my heart," he said.

She sighed. "I love you too. Always."

"Thing is, I don't want to be Walt and Emma's brother." His lips curved wryly. "I want to be their father."

Her heart lifting, she regarded him for a long moment. He wanted to be their father. *Her husband.*

When she finally dared to breathe, she said, "All right. Let's talk to them together."

The Tree of Everlasting Knowledge
Book-Group Discussion Questions

1. Early in the novel Rennie thinks, "Sociopaths weren't born into the world; they were beaten into existence." Is her belief valid? Does the depiction of Buck's teenage years, portrayed in dialogue and narration, support this claim?

2. Each of the novel's point of view characters delivers key aspects of the plot:

—Why is Emma's point of view incorporated but not Walt's?

—Why does the novel begin in Troy's point of view? In the opening scene, does he have more to lose than Rennie? How is his viewpoint used to initially characterize her?

—Much of Mae's backstory is given in snippets of memory in Chapter 15 as she strolls through the parish garden with Father Cyprian. Do her recollections dovetail with facts regarding her life delivered earlier by Lianna? By Rennie? Does Mae's depiction of Buck serve to humanize him for the reader or make him more repellant?

—Buck's point of view arrives late in the novel. How does this serve to accelerate the pace of the chapters to follow?

3. At different points in the story both Rennie and Mae pause to appreciate Cardinals. Mae especially admires how the birds, "dared to burn crimson in a world rendered monochrome by the threat of predators." How are Cardinals used to tie Rennie and Mae together? How does each woman "dare to burn crimson" despite the threat portrayed by Buck?

4. In Chapter Five, Buck Korchek is introduced with a rosary he "wound around the fleshy portion of his hand like a weapon meant to add power to the damage caused by his fist." Later, in

Chapter 11, we see Jackie Fagan clutching her rosary as she enters her late son's bedroom. Compare the symbolic use of the rosary in these two scenes. Who relies more heavily on the rosary, Buck or Jackie? Why?

5. How does the Fagan Rosary come to symbolize Mae's character as the novel progresses? In Chapter 32, how does the rosary foreshadow Troy's character growth as he attempts to save Buck?

6. In Chapter 6, Troy reveals he enjoys Bongo's Tavern because it "represented the antithesis of a life of privilege, the cultivated world where he towered over his family like an awkward relation. *Different.* He was an aberration in the Fagan gene pool." Soon after this scene, the reader learns that the Fagans intentionally kept his adoption secret. Do you think some adoptions should remain sealed? If not, when should the Fagans have told Troy about the rape of his biological mother?

7. How did you react to Emma's depiction of sexual abuse in Chapter 25? Were you prepared for this revelation? Did this scene color your perception of other characters? If Jobs & Family Services had known of the abuse, should they have severed Buck's parental rights?

8. The Tree of Knowledge is a potent biblical symbol, central to the Eden Story. In the novel, is the Great Oak used in a similar way? How does the Great Oak serve to move the story forward?

9. The book's structure revolves around the Perinis and the Fagans. Both Rennie and Troy are portrayed through interactions with their respective families. How are those interactions similar? Different? What purpose do the secondary characters of Liza Perini and Dianne Fagan serve in the plot?

10. The late Jason Fagan is a character in absence. How does his younger sister, Dianne, bring him to life for the reader? Have you ever "met someone" in absentia?

11. The sense of taste is a critical plot device in the story. Did it strike you as plausible that Mae recalled the most horrific events of her life after drinking apple cider? Have you ever experienced the recollection of a faded memory through one of the five senses? Which one? Was the experience pleasurable or frightening?

12. Christine Nolfi is an adoptive parent of four children. Does she provide any take-away lessons for the reader regarding adoption? Regarding foster-adopt laws in the United States?

Dear Reader: If you enjoyed The Tree of Everlasting Knowledge and posted a review, please contact me at christinenolfi@gmail.com for a special gift. I truly appreciate the kindness. Please write "Review Posted" in the subject line of your email.

You'll also find me at www.christinenolfi.com or please visit my Facebook Author Page. On Twitter: @christinenolfi

About the Author

Award-winning author **Christine Nolfi** provides readers with heartwarming and inspiring fiction. Her debut *Treasure Me* is a Next Generation Indie Awards finalist. The Midwest Book Review lists many of her novels as "highly recommended" and her books have enjoyed bestseller status. Visit her at www.christinenolfi.com.

Also by Christine Nolfi

Second Chance Grill

Treasure Me

The Impossible Wish

Four Wishes

The Dream You Make

The Heavenscribe series

Reviews Sell Books

57199037R00175

Made in the USA
Lexington, KY
08 November 2016